Also by Kim Redford

Cowboy FIRE

KIM REDFORD

sourcebooks
casablanca

Published by Sourcebooks Casablanca, an imprint of Sourcebooks
P.O. Box 4410, Naperville, Illinois 60567-4410
(630) 961-3900
sourcebooks.com

Printed and bound in Canada.
MBP 10 9 8 7 6 5 4 3 2 1

Chapter 1

VIOLET ASHWOOD NEEDED A COWBOY. SHE NEEDED SINGLE. She needed spicy. She needed stunning, like the hotties in the *Wet & Wild Cowboy Firefighters* calendar sold to benefit the all-volunteer Wildcat Bluff Fire-Rescue. Her copy of the popular calendar lay open to the photo of Mr. July on the seat beside her. He was enough to inspire someone—like her—to come all the way from San Antonio to Wildcat Bluff County way up by the Red River.

As she drove her bright-white SUV, feeling a little on the sassy side, she glanced at the full-color, glossy image of Mr. July again. Grrrr...what a hunk. He'd been caught with the hint of a smile—she'd swear naughty—on his too-full, too-sensual lips that went perfectly with a whipcord body that suggested great strength. All muscle. He had a strong face—high cheekbones, wide jaw, straight nose—with dark hair and five-o'clock shadow. Slightly slanted eyes the color of luminous jade wouldn't miss much. He appeared to be about thirty years old with six feet of broad shoulders, narrow waist, and long legs.

In the photo taken at the firefighters' dunking booth during Wildcat Bluff's Wild West Days, his body was revealed right down to his six-pack abs as he emerged soaking wet, water dripping down his open denim shirt and jeans. A line of eager cowgirls were caught in the picture's background, waiting for their turn to dunk him again. The cowboy firefighter calendar alone would probably ensure a stampede to this year's annual Labor Day weekend event, so women could get a chance to dunk their favorite firefighter and watch him emerge...wet and wild.

Oh yeah, she wanted Mr. July. She wanted every little bit of him. And she intended to have him.

Once she reached him—her very own personal cowboy firefighter—she planned to persuade him to be the handsome face and hot body of her new online matchmaking website plus dating app. She wanted the real deal, not city gloss, and she'd come to the country to find it. She hoped it'd be the turbo boost she needed to make her site stand out from established dating services when she launched in the next few months.

Of course, she really shouldn't call Mr. July *her* cowboy firefighter, even though she thought of him that way. Love didn't come easy...at least not to her. She accepted that as a given fact. Somehow or other, she never found the right guy, or he never found her. She wasn't the only woman who felt that way. Maybe it was the day and age they lived in. Maybe it was too many choices but too little commitment. Maybe it was too much work and not enough time for relationship development.

She planned to create a place where people could strike up friendships around mutual interests and develop a meeting of the minds before they ever met in person. Maybe her idea was old-fashioned, but she was a romantic at heart and she believed in long-lived love for everyone. Mr. July ought to get attention for her website, and then love could take its course.

And so she'd come to Wildcat Bluff County on the recommendation of a friend who'd told her that Wildcat Bluff County had an unusually high percentage of love, commitment, engagements, and marriage.

She had taken that information and run with it. She was deeply bonded to the idea of happily ever after for men as well as women, and she'd put her whole life on the line to make it happen for others. No failsafe for her. She'd walked away from her job. She'd pulled out her life savings. She'd enlisted support from a tech friend. Now she'd make or break her world for love...right here and right now.

As she tooled down Wildcat Road, she glanced left and right, the plains rolling out around her. It was late March, and spring had just sprung in North Texas. Birds and bees. Bluebonnets, Indian paintbrush, and crimson clover were beginning to turn the landscape beautiful shades of blue, orange, and red mingled with the bright spring green of freshly growing grass.

She'd timed it right to be out in the country to enjoy the season of new growth just as she was beginning her own exciting new venture that was all about the springtime of life…and love.

She didn't figure too many people knew about the Cross Timbers anymore, but she'd researched the area before coming here. Sandwiched between East Texas and West Texas, the area was a unique bit of land that had once stretched from the Kansas border to the Hill Country in Central Texas just north of San Antonio. Each side of the plains was densely bordered by sturdy post oak, flowering cedar elm, hard-as-nails bois d'arc, blossoming dogwood, Virginia creeper, and thorny blackberry.

In the old days, the Cross Timbers had been part of the Comanche nation. There had been a brushfire every year, so the thicket line that made up the border grew back too dense to penetrate. Comanche warriors had used the prairie between the two lines as a secret passage, so enemies couldn't see or attack them.

Not much of the Cross Timbers was left anymore except in Wildcat Bluff County, where local folks, many descendants of the Comanche, still protected thousands of acres, although they kept the wild fires under control, so the thicket line didn't grow back as dense.

Thinking about fires, or lack of them, brought her full circle to the cowboy firefighter calendar and her current mission.

She'd rented a furnished house on a ranch. She'd been lucky to catch the listing online the first day it'd been posted, because most everything she'd been finding requested either a year's lease or was short-term, like B&Bs or hotels or cabins. She only had three months to get all she needed in Wildcat Bluff County and get her dating site up and running. If not, she'd have to go back to San Antonio and pick up hourly work to keep her lonely hearts club afloat until it, hopefully, took off on its own.

In the name of a good cause, she'd fudged a little on the requirements for the rental. Okay, if truth be told, she'd fudged more than a little bit…but how hard could it be to pose as a cowgirl? She already had the clothes. She'd bought them for boot scooting. She hailed from near the Hill Country, big ranch territory. She'd been on the back of a horse a time or two without falling off. And she was willing to do some work, like throwing out hay or feed for animals.

She'd brokered a deal with the owner for cowgirl work in exchange for dropping the lease from a year to three months, negotiable if she decided to stay longer, which wasn't even on her list of possibilities because she couldn't afford it. As far as she was concerned, her rental agreement was totally win-win for everyone involved in it. Anyhow, a little fudge—particularly rich, dark chocolate—never hurt anybody.

She was anxious to get to her new home and unpack what she'd stuffed into her SUV, but first things first. She had Mr. July on her mind, and he came foremost. When she hit town, she'd called the Wildcat Bluff fire station. Somebody named Hedy had answered the phone and burst out laughing when she'd explained how she was looking for Mr. July. She didn't know what was funny about it, but she'd gotten his whereabouts, so that was all to the good.

And she was going to see him in action, since he was currently fighting a fire. Glory be but she was one lucky lady. And it just went to prove she was in the right place at the right time, fudge and all.

She'd dressed to impress. She wore a little violet-flower-print flirty skirt that swirled just above her knees, paired with a violet-tinted long-sleeve blouse and her favorite lavender heels. She'd make a lovely feminine contrast to the macho firefighters in their big jackets and heavy boots.

Yes, life was good. And love for lots of lonely hearts was on the wing.

By the time her GPS directed her down a gravel road, she had to wonder if it'd gone haywire, but at least it wasn't sending her off to some toll road in the far distance. She might have turned back, but she saw black smoke billowing up into the sky, so she knew she must be approaching the blaze. And Mr. July…her soon-to-be very own cowboy firefighter.

Hedy had told her to look for something called a booster because it'd be a bright-red truck with a water tank and coiled hose on its flatbed. She was to find the scale house first, then she would see the booster and the firefighters.

She followed the smoke, heading down the gravel lane that meandered away from Wildcat Road, the local main highway. She arrived at what must be the scale house because a section of the lane veered off, so dump trucks could drive between two low fences in front of a small, beige metal building with a white roof. Information and caution signs sprouted on either end of the fences. It had to be the scale for weighing trash to figure the cost of the service. A large yellow bulldozer was parked to one side, ready to push objects deep into the landfill.

She saw the red booster up ahead, but she figured she shouldn't get too close to the fire with her vehicle, so she parked beside the bulldozer. When she opened her door, acrid smoke stung her nose. Something toxic must have been burning down in the dump.

She grabbed a purple cardigan in case it was a little cool outside. She stepped out of her car, slipped on the sweater, and quietly closed the door behind her. As she started across the hard-packed bare ground, she wished she'd worn something else. Cowgirl clothes, particularly boots, would have been just the thing for the dump. Hindsight was a wonderful thing, but it didn't help her much now.

Three people were clustered near the booster on the edge of the dump. A cowboy firefighter wore a yellow fire jacket, green fire pants, black leather boots, and a bright-red helmet. He held the nozzle of a long hose stretched out from the rear of the truck. Mr. July!

He looked as good in person, maybe even better, than in his photograph. She felt her heart pick up speed at the sight.

A tall, strawberry-blond cowgirl stood near him dressed in similar firefighter gear. She'd slung a large fire extinguisher by its strap over one shoulder. On the other side of her, a cowboy stood in a relaxed position as he surveyed what was below. He wore a blue plaid shirt, big rodeo belt buckle, Wranglers, and boots.

As she neared the booster, she accidentally kicked a rock and sent it careening toward them. At the sound, all three swiveled to look at her with the same expression of surprise in their eyes...followed by suspicion. She couldn't blame them for not immediately trusting her, because she obviously wasn't dressed for a dump, and they didn't know her.

"Hello." She gave a little wave. "Hope I'm not disturbing your work, but I'm looking for Mr. July."

The cowgirl laughed so hard she almost dropped her fire extinguisher.

The cowboy grinned with humor alight in his eyes.

Violet couldn't imagine what was so funny. First, laughter at the station. Now, laughter at the dump.

"How'd you find me?" Mr. July gave her a cautious once-over with his jade-green eyes.

She hesitated at his response because he didn't appear too friendly...at least, not in the usual Texas way.

"Hedy, I bet." The cowgirl laughed again.

"Yeah," the cowboy said.

"Am I interrupting your firefighting?" They didn't actually look all that busy...nothing like in videos and movies. They sure weren't rolling out the welcome wagon either. But she couldn't let that deter her. She was on a mission of love. She walked right over to Mr. July, where he stood near the edge of the dump.

"Don't fall over," he said. "You're not dressed to be sashaying around a dump or a fire."

She didn't respond because he was right and she had no comeback except she hadn't planned to meet him at a dump. She glanced down. Piles of black tires in all shapes and sizes burned like crazy with red flames leaping up and down and around as black smoke billowed upward before being caught by a breeze and tossed higher into the air.

"We're not fighting a fire," Mr. July said.

She looked up into his eyes and felt the ground shift a little under her feet, most likely from loose dirt and high heels. Still, if she'd thought he was hot before, now he rivaled the blaze.

"As you can see, we're burning old tires," the cowboy said. "I'm in charge of the dump today, so if you haven't got business here—"

"Now, Cole, you're still just a little touchy ever since that vanload of ladies tried to kidnap you from the station and take you back to Dallas."

"You know good and well they didn't try to kidnap me. You've always got to dramatize every last thing." Cole narrowed his brown eyes. "Although…I have to admit, they were pretty persistent about taking me home."

"It's those crazy calendars you spearhead every year." Mr. July shook his head. "We've had more women running loose in Wildcat Bluff hunting cowboy firefighters than the law ought to allow."

The cowgirl laughed even harder. "I'm doing every one of you single guys a favor…if you'd just admit it."

Violet felt her heart sink. This was not the reaction she'd expected when she'd come up with her plan in San Antonio.

"Who are you anyway?" The cowgirl held out her hand. "I'm Sydney Steele."

Violet appreciated the gesture and shook Sydney's hand. "Good to meet you. I'm Violet Ashwood."

"We're mostly a friendly bunch around here, but our cowboy firefighters have turned out to be a little more popular than anybody expected," Sydney said.

Violet reassessed her situation. She'd never dreamed the calendars had inspired lots and lots of women to come here looking for cowboy firefighters. For these folks, she was just one more in a long line of hungry females.

Sydney winked at Violet. "They won't let me put their real names in the calendars, but I'm happy to introduce you to Kemp Lander...Mr. July."

"Thanks," Kemp said. "I won't forget that when it's time for the next calendar."

Sydney simply chuckled. "That other big lug is Cole Murphy. He's our current dump manager."

"He's doing a good job of getting things cleaned up around here," Kemp said. "That's why he's burning all those old tires."

"And we're making sure the fire doesn't get out of hand." Sydney gestured toward Violet. "Now you know who we are and why we're here. What's your story...if there is one beyond Mr. July?"

"I'm from San Antone." She gave them a bright, positive smile, determined to turn the situation in her favor. "I'm here because I have a proposition for Mr. July—I mean, Kemp Lander."

Sydney gave a big sigh.

"You'd better get in line. He has more offers from out-of-town ladies than he can shake a stick at. Don't you, Kemp?"

"Cole's right. Drama is your middle name," Kemp said.

"You've got to admit those calendars help keep our fire station afloat," Sydney said.

"Yeah." Kemp just shook his head as he looked at Violet. "So what do you want with me?"

Sydney laughed at his words.

"I mean, why are you here?" Kemp asked in his deep, melodic Texas drawl as he gauged Violet's mettle with his sharp eyes.

"It's just that..." Now that she was in Mr. July's presence, she felt a little starstruck. It'd been easier to talk to his photo.

"Just spit it out," Sydney said. "I doubt it's anything we haven't heard before this very day."

"And most likely about two dozen or more times." Cole gave Violet an encouraging smile. "Still, it's always good to hear again."

"Lonely hearts." Violet focused on Kemp. "How do you feel about them?"

Kemp narrowed his eyes, causing a few fine lines to fan outward from the corners. "I don't feel anyway about them."

"What about a lonely hearts club?"

"What in tarnation is that?" Kemp leaned toward her. "Is this a joke? I can guarantee you I get enough of that from my cousin. Did Hedy put you up to it?"

Violet straightened her back, getting all five feet five inches to work to her advantage. She hadn't expected him to be so...well, defensive. "This is no joke. I'm asking you—"

"You got to admit, this is a new angle," Cole said.

"I like it." Sydney stepped up beside Kemp. "Like an online blog or something?"

"Sort of." Even as she answered Sydney, she kept her gaze on Kemp. "Have you ever used a dating service?"

"No. Do I look desperate?"

"You've come to the wrong county if you think guys around here need a dating service," Cole said. "We're knee deep in honeys."

Violet ignored the other two and maintained eye contact with Kemp. He was the one she had to persuade. She'd invested too much hope in his image for too long. "You don't need to be desperate to want to find your perfect mate...and that means love."

"Mate? Love?" He looked away from her and toward the burning tires.

"Yes, love. And whatever you want to call a solid relationship. Husband. Wife. Partner."

"What makes you think there is such a perfect thing?" He glanced back at her with hooded eyes that seemed to help him keep his secrets buried deep.

Maybe she'd made a huge mistake. Maybe Mr. July was a lost cause. Maybe…but no, she wouldn't give up so easily. She'd come too far to back down at the first challenge. Anyway, what was that old saying? Love conquers all.

"They're popular," Sydney said. "I hear dating sites have helped a lot of lonely people find love, although you have to be careful about posers. But why do you think Kemp needs to register with a dating service?"

"And why would you come all the way from San Antone to tell him?" Cole asked.

Violet took a deep breath…now or never.

Chapter 2

"Cowboy Heart-to-Heart Corral." Violet spoke in a determined contralto voice as she looked straight into Kemp Lander's eyes.

Kemp just stared at her, trying to figure out what she was talking about. Maybe he was slow today, but more likely her hot looks distracted him. He'd had his mind on the burning tires and putting together enough money to buy a prize bull to strengthen his herd of cattle. Most ranchers stocked Angus nowadays, but he was partial to the white-faced, red-bodied Hereford. He planned to make his mark with that breed.

"It's my new online dating service." Violet smiled, a happy gleam in her eyes.

"Dating service?" He figured she expected some type of response, since she was looking at him, but he was clueless about how to handle it.

"And I want you—Mr. July—to be the face and body of it."

He just stood there stock-still, like you did when you'd had a shock or didn't want to give away your position. In this case, she was so out of the blue that she might as well have been in a different universe.

"Clever name." Sydney filled the silence, giving Kemp a bright smile.

"Yeah." Cole gave him an even bigger grin.

Kemp ignored what amounted to his friends' smirks as he looked at Violet a little closer. She was a beauty, all right...in the same league with the bull he wanted on his ranch. She was flashy like a Fourth of July explosion of color and sound in a midnight sky. She had an hourglass figure that was a little old-fashioned, particularly since she'd encased all those delectable curves in tantalizing clothes, and the high heels she wore deserved to be outlawed in the state of Texas for the mental health and physical well-being of its male citizens. And then she had to go and top it all off with short, curly, blond hair about the shade of ripe wheat and eyes the color of bluebonnets. Plump lips painted a pale shade of pink matched her nails.

"I take it you're surprised," Violet said, "but I'm quite sincere about wanting you."

If he wanted to shell down the corn, being totally honest, he wanted her, too, but he preferred hands-on to pictures...and he'd like to be living in the same universe when he got hands-on.

"Please give me a chance to make you an offer I doubt you'll refuse."

He glanced at his friends, recognizing the twitch of their lips for held-back laughter because they knew, as well as he did, that the last thing he wanted in his life was more embarrassment, and getting his mug plastered all over a dating site would surely do it.

"I'm willing to pay you." Violet didn't sound quite so upbeat or happy anymore.

Finally, he just kind of lost it. "If it weren't for bad luck, I'd have no luck at all."

"If you're talking about Daisy Sue, that business is over and done with." Sydney gave him a sympathetic smile, as if to cheer him up.

"Anybody could lose a cow," Cole said with more sympathy.

"I didn't lose that cow." Kemp took a deep breath, wanting to disappear onto his ranch but needing to defend himself more. "Cousin Les...let's just say he's still got his mangy hide intact after botching the simple task of moving a cow from one ranch to another."

"Everybody's got *that* cousin in their family." Sydney gave him another sympathetic smile.

"Anyway, it was simply a case of mistaken transport or identity or some such, wasn't it?" Cole said helpfully.

Kemp didn't even try to sort out the truth that had become gossip-garbled by local ranchers. Besides, he'd come to hate sympathy. It made you feel lower than a snake's belly. "Trouble with Les is that he's got enough charm for a dozen men. Life's trials and tribulations—particularly women—come too easy for him."

"Forget him," Sydney said. "Daisy Sue is home. You made that happen."

"Yeah. Still, I got caught up in that Fernando the Wonder Bull circus at Steele Trap Ranch when I brought her home."

Sydney chuckled. "You've got to hand it to Storm. She knows how to please Fernando's and Daisy Sue's fans."

Kemp finally laughed, thinking back to the ridiculous line of fans along the road that led to the barn. "Your daughter is about like my cousin. They've both got more charm than ought to be allowed."

Sydney and Cole joined his laughter, nodding in agreement.

"Excuse me," Violet said. "I've come a long way to see Mr. July and make him an important offer. I'd really like a moment more of his time."

"Pardon us," Sydney said. "We are being rude, aren't we? It's just that there's always something going on in Wildcat Bluff County, and this time Kemp was at the center of it."

Kemp decided to man up. "You couldn't know it, coming from San Antone and all, but I'm trying to keep a low profile. I'd prefer not to be the laughingstock of the county ever again."

"It wasn't that bad." Sydney gave him a bright, fake smile.

"Not one bit," Cole said with a straight face, although his lips twitched at the corners.

"I doubt I'll ever hear the end of it." Kemp just shook his head, figuring he might as well enjoy the joke on himself—as Texans were wont to do—and embellish the truth into a humorous tall tale, no matter how his pride as a rancher had been stung.

"Something else will come along soon, and then Daisy Sue's disappearance and reappearance will be old news," Sydney said.

Kemp eyed Violet a little more closely, hoping against hope she wasn't that something to come along.

"In fact, here's your perfect opportunity," Sydney said, teasing him.

That was just what he didn't want on Violet's mind, or anybody else's. He needed to head this off at the pass. "I regret you've come all this way for nothing, but I've got a ranch to run and it takes priority."

"I understand you're a busy and important man." Violet smiled sweetly at him.

If he wasn't careful, she was a woman who could get under his skin…and leave him wanting what only she could give him. She might be into hookups, but he wasn't. He was a cowboy who'd want it all when he found the right cowgirl. He wanted love and commitment and family. He didn't figure Violet came even close to fitting those needs. She was a city gal with business on her mind, no matter how she might present her lonely hearts club. She'd go back to the city when she was done getting what she wanted from the country.

"He's busy anyway," Cole said, "and everybody is important in helping out our community."

"Firefighters?" Violet asked.

"And EMTs, as well." Sydney glanced down at the fire in the dump, then back. "Violet, I appreciate you coming all this way because of our calendar, but we are all really busy running our ranches, fighting fires, or responding to emergency medical calls…not to mention taking care of our families and friends."

"I understand," Violet said.

"I'm not sure you do." Sydney adjusted the strap of her fire extinguisher. "I produce our cowboy firefighter calendar to fund Wildcat Bluff Fire-Rescue. It's one of several benefits that our county promotes during the year to support our all-volunteer fire station. Just because our county has its share of hunky men doesn't mean they're for sale." Sydney cocked her head to one side, giving both cowboys a thoughtful look. "Although…maybe we ought to consider a new fire-rescue benefit. Something like *Buy a date with the cowboy firefighter of your dreams*. Now that'd be a fun fund-raiser."

"And popular," Violet said.

"No," Cole said.

"Absolutely not." Kemp knew danger when he saw it. When two smart women got together in their county, somehow or other they ended up plotting ways to get the menfolk involved in their shenanigans. Yeah, it always benefited their community, but it still seemed like a high price to pay.

"Cowboy firefighter auction." Violet grinned. "That could only spur interest in Cowboy Heart-to-Heart Corral."

"Never going to happen." Kemp glanced down at the burning tires, wishing the fire were completely out so he could leave. "Let's table this idea before it gets legs."

"Right," Cole said.

Sydney gave them a sweet smile, which Kemp knew from experience was really dangerous. Once she got up a head of steam, there was no stopping her or any of her cowgirl cohorts.

"I'm certainly not pushing anyone to do anything, but would you please just consider my offer?" Violet gave a hopeful little smile.

Kemp felt her smile go straight to his gut, but he couldn't let a smile sideline his plans.

"You haven't really had a chance to make him an official offer," Sydney said. "Kemp doesn't know what he's getting into or not getting into. He needs more information. Don't you, Kemp?"

"Sydney, you know my situation. I can't take time out of running my ranch. I'm at a critical stage."

"What if I donated a small percentage from Cowboy Heart-to-Heart Corral, providing there's actually a profit, to Wildcat Bluff Fire-Rescue?" Violet asked.

Kemp groaned, knowing how that offer was going to affect Sydney, who, along with Hedy Murray, ramrodded the fire station.

Sydney's blue eyes lit with inner fire. "Now that'd put a different spin on the entire matter."

"This is getting way out of hand," Cole said. "We don't know anything about this woman or her business or her real intentions. Let's take a step back and get our ducks in a row."

"True." Sydney adjusted her can on her shoulder again. "It just all sounds like fun…and good for our community. But like I said, Kemp should know more about your intentions."

"I absolutely agree," Violet said. "I'd like to talk with Kemp in more detail, so he might be more inclined to help me."

"That sounds reasonable to me." Sydney glanced at Kemp. "Are you willing to at least give her a chance and hear her out?"

He looked out over the horizon. If he didn't do it, he'd never hear the end of it from Sydney. Even worse, he didn't want to see hurt in Violet's pretty eyes by rejecting her out of hand.

"Are you up for a meeting with Violet?" Sydney asked.

"Chuckwagon Café. Six tonight. She can buy me dinner and present her plan." Maybe he was being persuaded by a pretty face and Sydney's strong arm, but he didn't see any reason to be a grump and not enjoy supper with Violet before he sent her on her way home.

Violet grinned and spun around in happiness, sending her skirt swirling around her legs.

He tried not to groan at the sight. Maybe supper with her was a bad idea. He didn't have time for her or any woman right now.

"You won't regret it. I promise." Violet turned serious. "And truly, if I can't persuade you about the value of my lonely hearts club, then you aren't right for my website. Love. I need you committed to love, or it'll never work."

"That's a good point," Sydney said. "Love really does make the world go 'round."

Violet glanced down, shook her head, and then looked back up. "I'm afraid I've never been lucky in love. It's one of the reasons I'm so determined for my dating site to work for others."

"It's never too late," Sydney said. "Maybe your new venture is just the push you need to turn your luck around."

Violet shook her head again. "I want to help people. That's my main goal."

"It's a good one," Sydney said.

Kemp felt his concern about Violet's dating site ratchet down a notch. How could a woman with her looks and energy and concern for others be unlucky in love? He guessed it was possible, although he didn't see how. Maybe his bad luck and her unlucky love could cancel each other out, so that they both got their luck back. At least it was an upside to the situation.

"Anyway, thank you all for being so patient with me." Violet smiled at the group as she stepped back. "Kemp, I look forward to seeing you tonight at the restaurant."

"It's just a café in Old Town. Can you find it?"

"Sure. GPS, you know."

He nodded as he watched her turn and walk in her too-high heels away from them. He watched her get into her car, showing more of her toned legs, and he kept watching until she drove away and he couldn't see her anymore.

"She's pretty, all right," Cole said. "But don't let her get to you, or you'll be just what she wants you to be."

"Would that be so bad?" Sydney asked.

Kemp glanced at them, shaking off the mesmerizing effect of Violet. "You know I just bought the ranch. It may be small compared to the big ranches around here, but I put my life savings in it. You know good and well I quit my job as Lulabelle & You Ranch foreman to make a go of it. A place of my own is all I've ever wanted, and this is it."

"Good acreage," Cole said.

"Make-or-break time for me. I could lose it all if I don't stay on the ball right now."

"If you need help, you know you can call on me," Cole said.

"Me, too." Sydney reached out and squeezed Kemp's arm. "Our whole community is nothing if not supportive, but we're all independent cusses doing everything our own way, too, so we understand it's your ranch."

"Thanks. Independent cuss is right. It's my dream, and it'll take all I've got to make it work." He glanced down at the tires, burning low now but still red-hot...like Violet.

"She's fancy, you know," he said thoughtfully. "Fancy clothes. Fancy ideas. Fancy love. I'm just a hardworking cowboy. I don't know a thing about fancy."

Chapter 3

HALLELUJAH RANCH.

Violet read the faded red letters on the gray, splintered oak sign overhead as she rumbled across a cattle guard made of rusted metal pipes. She hit a rough washboard gravel lane that led upward. If not for the shiny new fence made of barbed wire with metal posts that surrounded the place as far as the eye could see, she might have thought she'd arrived at a derelict ranch...not her idea of home sweet home. But whatever she found up ahead, she'd make the most of it, because this was where she was going to hang her cowgirl hat for the next three months.

Everything was turning pretty here, with the bright-green growth of spring in trees, grass, and wildflowers. Of course, down in San Antonio country, she was accustomed to year-round natural beauty fueled by winding rivers and the warm climate. She particularly liked the cactus when it bloomed once a year. Up here the temperature was still a little chilly, so she was glad she'd brought a few cardigans to wear with her shirts and jeans, blouses and skirts.

As she glanced from left to right, taking it slow and easy on the rutted road, she saw white-faced, red-bodied cattle clustered under a stand of oak trees around a deep blue pond. While some cows drank water, others munched on the tender shoots of new grass. It was quite the bucolic scene, lovely and lonely at the same time.

She glanced down at the calendar to see the face of Mr. July.

"You brought me here." She spoke to his photo like she had so many times before arriving in Wildcat Bluff County. "Why? Will I ever know?"

She thought about it a moment. What was it about a single picture that could cause a woman to give up everything in a bustling city and make the long trek across Texas to a ranch in the country? Of course, she had lots of reasons, but would she have done it if not for Mr. July?

She'd met him now. Kemp Lander. She liked his name. It was perfect for him. But reality had crashed into fantasy on their first encounter. He didn't want her or her ideas. She didn't expect him to fall instantly in love with her. She'd never thought that. It was more that she'd felt compelled to come here. She'd known deep down in her gut, where all her best decisions were made, that she must come here, because this county was where she'd find the answer to her own lonely heart, as well as help for all the lonely hearts out there.

She understood only too well the deep longing for a mate to share life and love. It was a constant ache. She was used to it now, so she accepted the feeling like she did a craving for sugar. You went on with life, still wanting to share the burdens, wanting a shoulder to cry on, wanting to be held close…and that didn't even begin to address the need for physical closeness in its most intimate terms. She was hungry for a loving partner, but she was funneling that energy into creating a platform to help others.

Unfortunately, she had arrived at Hallelujah Ranch with a big problem. It was one she hadn't foreseen. Mr. July was more than a little skittish.

A house rose up on top of the hill ahead. Soon she'd have her stuff out of her car, into her new abode, and be totally committed to her vision. She glanced at Mr. July's photograph again.

She reached over and closed the calendar. She didn't need his picture now that she'd found him. He was strong and tough, but there had been kindness in his green eyes, as if he'd known heartbreak or hard life or both.

She patted the closed calendar. "I think I sold you short in my mind. I think there's more depth to you than you let others see. I think you're more important to me than I ever could've imagined before meeting you."

She straightened her shoulders in determination. "You've given me one chance to persuade you. I owe it to lonely hearts everywhere to make it count."

She also accepted the fact that if he truly wasn't interested, then he wasn't right anyway. She would simply look further afield. One good thing, though…if he turned her down and wanted her gone, he couldn't throw her out of her new home.

She wasn't staying in the main house on Hallelujah Ranch because the owner lived there. She didn't know whom she'd be meeting later, since a rental company had handled her contract with the ranch, but she'd be happy to work with the person that showed up. She'd live in the nearby log cabin, and a key should be waiting for her under the front-door mat.

As she drove up to the big house, she was surprised that it looked unusual for a ranch. Town, yes, but country, not so much. She got a better view as she drew closer. The structure had the appearance of a peaked-roof farmhouse with three narrow windows near the top that, inside, would mostly likely be a long loft. On the ground floor below were another three windows, one a picture window between two narrow ones. Windows in sets of three appeared to be a major theme of the house, because in front, three narrow windows appeared on one side of the entry, while on the other side jutted a three-sided bay window. She liked the pale-yellow wood with burgundy trim accent.

What made the house really unique and set the time period was the peaked, Gothic arch set on two large, square columns over the portico entry with a fan design above the door. She knew enough about architecture that this Gothic touch would have only been popular during the Roaring Twenties, revisiting the Tudor period from the 1500s. But still…on a Texas ranch?

She wouldn't be living in that house, but she'd certainly like to see inside the eclectic building. Hopefully, she'd receive an invitation to visit at some point in her stay on the ranch.

As she turned left on the road toward her cabin, she was surprised to see a dovecote designed as a miniature replica of the main house. She hadn't seen one in real life before, only in old photographs of European houses. The pigeon home was surrounded by classic flowers that evoked nostalgia for a bygone era. Pink azalea bushes formed a border around the foundation, while orange daylilies and lavender irises rose, vibrant in the sunlight, in flower beds near neatly trimmed rosebushes.

Between the vision of the house, the dovecote, and the gardens, she felt as if she'd stepped back in time to the decadent era of the twenties. Bootleggers were heralded as lifesavers because of Prohibition, which had outlawed liquor sales, leading to illegal bathtub gin and country liquor stills. Folks weren't about to give up their alcohol, no matter the new law, so for thirteen wild years, lots of folks made fortunes running whiskey to illegal places to drink.

And here she was on Hallelujah Ranch, conjuring up a time so often depicted as romantic, and she'd done it simply by seeing a Gothic entry from that era. She figured her only excuse for her flight of fancy was that she was on a romantic mission of her own…not where love was born in face-to-face speakeasies, but in online chat rooms where words took on the power of love.

She drove on up to the small log cabin that was surely no more than seven hundred square feet. It was absolutely adorable, with a red metal roof that rose to a sharp peak over what must be a loft upstairs. A gray and brown river-rock chimney rose high on one side of the building, while a deep, covered front porch with a railing graced the front. A crimson front door in between two screened windows beckoned her to step right up and enjoy one of the two rocking chairs. She liked the bright-red color that accented the all-wood structure. It added snap and pizzazz that reminded her of the Gothic entry next door. Green sage bushes shielded the open area under the cabin, and three wooden steps led up to the open porch. She could easily see being comfortable and at home here.

She parked on the gravel area beside the cabin, turned off her car's engine, and sighed in relief. It'd been a long drive before she'd had the extra venture to the county dump, so she was more than ready to relax.

She had a couple of hours until dinner at six, so she wanted a shower and time to get her thoughts straight before she met Mr. July, or Kemp, again. This time she'd wear a sweater and jeans. She didn't think fashionable would cut it with him, because he appeared to be a practical, bottom-line kind of guy. Fine. She could be the exact same way when she was on a mission.

She opened her car door and stepped outside. Quiet, too, so unlike the city. She might get to like it, at least in the short term. She glanced around as she took in her surroundings. Cattle switched their long tails across their backs as they cropped grass in the pastures. A mockingbird with blue, gray, and white feathers serenaded her from a nearby leafy elm tree. And a white-tailed rabbit burst out of a clump of grass and tore across the pasture. Yes, she might like it here, but how could it ever compare to the city?

She opened her back door, grabbed her laptop case, and put the strap over a shoulder. She picked up her cosmetic bag and looped its strap over her other shoulder. Finally, she grabbed the insulated bag that contained food and her soft-sided, expandable carpetbag. After she shut the door, she took the few steps up to the front porch and set down her bags. She found the key under the red doormat and unlocked the front door. She glanced around again, but nothing moved except the mockingbird, who completed its song and flew to a different tree.

Now or never. Once she stepped across that threshold, she was ready to begin her new life.

She picked up her bags, set them down just inside, and shut the door behind her. She walked into the living room that stretched the length of the house to another porch that extended across the back that she could see through the windows. The wood walls and high ceiling were a mellow shade of pine. She was wowed by a bright-red leather sofa positioned against the wall across from the fireplace, along with a matching easy chair. A cedar coffee table held an arrangement of dried flowers. Yes, she could easily get comfortable here.

The open floor plan suited her perfectly. She turned to the right, walked past the staircase, and entered the kitchen. Compact and efficient. Stove, sink, and cabinets against one wall with a river-rock-fronted bar that had a granite countertop at a right angle with two wood stools snuggled up to it. She slid her laptop strap off her shoulder and set her computer on the bar top.

From there, she moved into the small bathroom and was wowed again. Someone had gone to a lot of trouble and thought to decorate it. They'd chosen rustic wood cabinets with galvanized insets and a trough, galvanized light over the framed mirror above the porcelain, oval sink. A glass door enclosed a red-tiled shower that made the room charmingly complete. She opened the linen cabinet and found a set of red towels. In a basket on top of the sink's cabinet she found a variety of bottles and soaps filled with wonderful scents. She read the attached note, "Fresh and Homemade from Morning's Glory." She could easily enjoy this type of luxury.

She walked back to the entry and picked up her bags. She set one on the kitchen counter, the cosmetic bag in the bathroom, and carried the other upstairs. Another surprise. Right in the center of the room that ran the length of the house and under the peaked ceiling of lemony-yellow pine rose a large, round bed covered in a scarlet silk bedspread with purple, lavender, and green throw pillows in its center. No other furniture. It was definitely impressive. She looked around and found built-in cabinetry for her clothes.

Who had decorated this cabin and the house? She'd like to meet the man or woman. At the very least, she'd enjoy getting to know the ranch owner.

She quickly put her clothes and shoes away, stored her bag in the concealed closet, and went back downstairs. She opened the door to the back porch and was pleased to see a white metal glider sofa with red cushions. Perfect. She took a deep breath of the sweet country air and shut the door. She felt really happy with her choice of where to live for three months.

She went into the kitchen and put away her food. She hadn't brought much, because she'd known she could buy more in town. She set orange juice in the stainless steel fridge, along with her favorite Tex-Mex takeout and two bottles of Hill Country wine. She found red glasses in a cabinet and poured OJ into one, then sat down on the leather sofa to relax. As she sipped, enjoying the cool sweetness, she looked at the fireplace where a wicker basket held several logs. She bet it was still chilly enough here at night to enjoy a good roaring fire with a glass of wine.

When she'd finished her orange juice, she set the glass on a sandstone coaster with a Wildcat Bluff Fire-Rescue design on its surface. She leaned her head back against the sofa. Life was good. And she intended to make it even better.

A little later, she heard a pickup pull up outside the ranch house, a door slam, and then footsteps head her way. She figured that person had to be the ranch owner. She was glad they were going to meet so soon.

She stood up, smoothing down her skirt, although by now it was sadly wrinkled, before she walked over to the door. She heard someone step onto the porch. She opened the door with a smile… and saw Mr. July.

"You!" She could hardly believe her eyes.

"You!"

Chapter 4

"WHAT ARE YOU DOING HERE?" KEMP TRIED TO ALIGN THE reality of Violet Ashwood standing in the open doorway of his cabin with his expectations. He'd rented to a cowgirl. What was Violet doing here?

"Better question," she said, "what are you doing here?"

He hooked a thumb toward his ranch house. "I live here."

She glanced past him, then looked back with a puzzled frown on her face. "What do you mean?"

How could she not understand? Maybe she felt as confused as he did. No doubt she was hot as a jalapeño, but she represented trouble with a capital *T*. Lonely hearts club? He didn't even want to think about it.

"Is there another cabin? Do you rent, too?"

"No." He held out hope this was all a bad-luck mistake. "I'm the owner of Hallelujah Ranch."

She put a hand over her mouth as her eyes grew wide.

He felt a sinking sensation in the pit of his stomach. "You're my new renter? My cowgirl?"

She nodded with a slight smile.

"Please tell me you're not what you appear to be...straight from the city with no notion about how to work a ranch."

"Well, how hard can it be?"

He actually felt a little woozy at her statement. This appeared worse and worse. He needed the help. He'd negotiated for the help. He'd signed on the dotted line for the help. Worst of all, he needed the help to hang on to his ranch. Why had he let a rental agency handle the contract? He should've talked with her directly, then he'd have known she didn't have a clue about ranch work.

"I mean, I'm ready, willing, and able to do whatever you need me to do around the place."

"Ever use a posthole digger?"

"A what?"

"You use it to dig a hole for the bottom of a fence post. It requires quite a bit of upper-body strength. A ranch needs a lot of fence line to contain cattle and horses."

"I noticed your new fence on my way up here. It looks good... and not like it needs any more posts to be dug by me or anybody else."

"Do you know how to string barbwire?"

"No."

"Use a tractor to transport hay?"

"No."

"How about preg a cow?"

"What's that?"

"Check to see if a cow is pregnant."

"I'm not sure I want to know how you go about that, but I suggest your cows see a vet."

"No, then?"

"Definitely no."

"Rope a cow?"

"Not this week."

He almost enjoyed teasing her and seeing her blue eyes flash fire. If his situation had been different, he'd have a different take on her. As it stood, he needed the help. He couldn't afford to hire. Everybody he knew was already worked to the limit, so she'd been his best bet to help keep his ranch afloat while he got it up and running.

"I'm sure I can meet my commitments, other than that preg bit, if you'll just tell me what to do and how to do it."

He sighed, looking every which way except at her. If he stared at her too long, he'd forget why she was supposed to be here and focus on how he'd like her to be here. She'd look real good... wearing nothing at all...in the middle of that big, round, red bed upstairs. But he squashed that idea before it had a chance to bloom full bore, like a rose opening its petals to the sun.

"I realize you might be a little disappointed..."

"A little?" He stared at her. "Look, this is a trimmed-to-the-bone operation. I just got the ranch. I have zero funds for operation. I need you to be a cowgirl."

She straightened her shoulders and raised her chin. "I *am* your cowgirl."

Heaven help him, he wanted her to be *his* cowgirl in every sense of the word. If he stood there much longer, he wouldn't care what she could do or not do just so long as she was *his* cowgirl in *his* bed on *his* ranch. He glanced up at the window that would allow sunlight to streak across the big, red bed, then shook his head. He had to get a grip on the situation.

"Truly, I'm willing to work hard for you...if you'll work hard for me."

"Are we back to your lonely hearts club?"

"Yes."

"I already told you—"

"That we could discuss it in more detail."

"This changes matters," he said.

"No, it doesn't." She stepped back into the cabin. "In fact, we don't need to wait for dinner. Why don't you come inside now?"

Maybe he ought to just get it over with. She was bound to be able to find another cowboy—somebody like his cousin Les—to do the job.

"Okay?" She gave him a tentative little smile.

He had to admit he liked her can-do attitude and hopeful smile. If he wasn't careful, he might forget her limitations as a cowgirl.

"Okay?"

He nodded because he'd agreed to hear her story.

She stepped back into the living room. He followed her, leaving the front door open behind him. He glanced around. The place looked like it had when he'd made sure it was ready for her. He wondered how it would appear when she made it her own. Maybe she'd toss black undies across the crimson cover on the bed upstairs. That thought gave him a rush.

"Would you care to sit down?"

He quickly took the chair, not about to share the sofa with her because that way led to thoughts that could only get him into trouble.

"Would you care for something to drink? I brought Hill Country wine. It's a nice, dry merlot."

"Thanks." He could use it about now. Cool down. Warm up. It didn't much matter. It'd be something to do with his hands and mouth that didn't involve Violet Ashwood's delectable body.

When she handed him a stemless wineglass about halfway filled with a deep red liquid that went with the bed upstairs, their fingers briefly touched and sent a spark zinging through him. Chemistry. It was the last thing he needed at the moment, with so much on his mind, but he acknowledged the feeling as one of life's special, rare treats.

She set a similar glass down on the coffee table, then sat on the end of the sofa near the chair, crossed her legs, uncrossed them, tugged down the hem of her skirt, and finally looked at him.

He took a sip of wine, appreciating it, appreciating her.

"Is it okay?"

"Real fine."

"Good. I like it." She picked up her glass, eased it up to her mouth, and swallowed wine.

He watched her throat move, noting the smooth, pale skin that fairly begged to be stroked and kissed. He jerked his gaze away. No need—no need at all—to go there.

"I suppose I should apologize for misrepresenting myself when we agreed on the contract."

"You think?" He tightened his grip on the glass, then relaxed before he broke it and sent shards of sharp crystals flying across the room.

"I didn't know I'd be renting from you."

"Would it have made a difference?"

"Yes, of course."

"How?"

"I don't want you to throw me off the ranch."

He felt his gut tighten. He ought to do that very thing. "We have a contract."

"You might try to break it."

"Maybe." For some damn reason, he didn't want to do that. He'd already grown to like her here in his cabin…just a few steps from where he knew he'd be having midnight fantasies about her. "Why wouldn't you have come here if you'd known it was me?"

"Conflict of interest or something like that." She sipped her wine, then snared his gaze with her blue eyes. "I want you to want to be—"

"Mr. July?"

"Yes."

"I never was, you know. It was just a picture snapped at Wild West Days."

"I know, but still…"

He realized she wanted him to be *her* fantasy as much as he wanted her to be *his* fantasy. What a crazy, mixed-up situation. Wasn't reality enough for anybody anymore? Maybe it never had been. Maybe now everybody thought they had a chance to play out their fantasies, so they took it.

"Anyway, I plan to be in Wildcat Bluff County for three months. I'm willing to do whatever you need me to do on the ranch. I'm a quick learner." She took a deep breath, set down her glass, and leaned toward him. "If I don't perform to your satisfaction, you can let me go."

"Perform to my satisfaction?" He felt another rush that sent him glancing upstairs. Red bed. Black underwear. Pale skin. He could see it so clearly, he almost felt like they were already up there.

She grabbed her glass—as if picking up his thoughts—and downed a swallow. "I mean, perform as a cowgirl."

"I know what you mean." He didn't look at her. He didn't want to give himself away. He didn't want her to know the effect she was having on him. But he did have to consider that she'd come a long, long way for Mr. July. That was him. It wasn't an intellectual adventure. It wasn't mental, no matter how she couched her desire. It was physical, pure and simple. He understood that. He could work with it.

"I really do want to help people find love."

He glanced over at her. She was sincere. At least that's what her big, blue eyes conveyed to him. "Why?"

"It's important. Isn't it important to you?"

"No. My ranch is important. It's all I've got on my agenda right now."

"You might decide to help me." She set her glass down again. "You haven't heard me out yet."

He finished off his wine and carefully put his glass on the table. He'd like to state his proposal…and it'd have nothing to do with a lonely hearts club. It'd have nothing to do with hearts at all.

"Would you like to hear now?"

"That's why I'm here."

She leaped up, hurried over to the bar, grabbed her laptop, and came back. She set it on her lap and turned it on.

"How far along are you with the website and app?"

"A friend is handling that for me, although I have lots of input."

"You haven't used my photo yet, have you?"

She glanced to the side, then back again. "A little bit?"

"How much is a little bit?"

"Well…I only have the one picture."

"Right."

"I put it on the opening page." She swiveled her laptop around so he could see the screen. "Mind you, I'll pay you and donate to the fire station."

He felt his gut clench at the sight, then he just shook his head and chuckled at the whole wild idea. From one photograph in a calendar, he'd potentially go global, if she had her way.

"You look good, don't you?"

"I look like a guy all wet from a dunking booth." He leaned back in his chair. "There are twelve firefighters in that particular calendar. And we aren't the only cowboys in calendars. Why me?"

"I don't know." She turned her laptop around so she could see his picture again.

He couldn't help but recognize the tender look that transformed her from budding entrepreneur to a woman on the cusp of…he didn't have a name for it…or he didn't dare name it… Worst of all, that tenderness might be something he'd want to bottle and keep on a shelf for him alone, much like the old moonshine bottles he'd picked up from all over the ranch and set on his mantelpiece.

"In the photo, you just seemed right to give lonely hearts hope that there was a sensitive but strong man out there who would do all in his power to keep their love safe."

Kemp sat there for a long moment. He felt speechless. How in the world had she ever come up with that idea from his photo? Not only that, but she believed in her idea enough to come here and find him. It was flattering as all get-out, but it also came with responsibility. He'd hate to see her blue eyes turn sad with him to blame. And still, he didn't have time for fantasy. He had to stay focused on reality. He'd worked his entire life to get a ranch of his own, and he had no intention of losing it by getting all moony-eyed over a hot non-cowgirl. Love, marriage, and family came much later—much, much later, after he'd secured the future of his ranch.

"Anyway," she said, glancing at him wistfully, "I thought we could take more photographs of you on your ranch and with other firefighters and even include little things you say to encourage folks to use the site. Not that you'd have to write those words. I'd do it for you. Really, I wouldn't require much of you beyond a few photographs."

"Violet, you seem to be a nice, well-intentioned person." He took a deep breath before he forged ahead. "But like I said, I've got a ranch to run and it's taking everything I've got to do it."

"I understand." She closed her laptop and patted it. "Maybe if you get to know me better as I help you on the ranch, you'll come to see the importance of my lonely hearts club."

He watched her tamp down that tenderness. He immediately missed it. He even felt as if he'd lost a lot with it. Didn't make one lick of sense, but nothing much had since she'd arrived in Wildcat Bluff. He stood up, needing to get back to work.

She set her laptop down and rose to her feet.

He walked over to the front door.

She followed him. "I'm here for three months unless you kick me off the ranch."

He stepped out onto the deck, thinking about her words.

She joined him, then gestured around the area. "It's beautiful here. I really want to stay."

"Okay." Maybe he was a fool, but he couldn't turn her away because, well, it wasn't the cowboy way. Besides, there was just something about her. No matter, he was staying miles away from her lonely hearts club. "You're my cowgirl for three months. But no other agreements."

"Thanks." She looked up at him with a smile...and that tenderness came back into her sky-blue eyes.

In that moment, he knew without a shadow of a doubt that he could turn into a sucker for that look alone.

Chapter 5

VIOLET THOUGHT SHE'D GOTTEN HER WAY WITH KEMP, BUT she didn't feel like it. Mind versus heart. He needed cowgirl help. She'd never considered that fact when she'd negotiated the contract. She'd only considered her own needs...and desires. Did that make her insensitive? Maybe. Practical? For sure. Caught between a rock and a hard place? No doubt. She'd just have to become, in short order, the best cowgirl ever. Maybe there was an online class for it. If not, maybe she could get that Sydney Steele, who looked like she could rope a cow and ride a horse in her sleep, to give some pointers. But that preg business was definitely a nonstarter. Beyond that, she was Kemp's to command.

"Guess I'd better get back to work," he said.

"I'm stronger than I look."

He glanced down at her with a smile curling his lips. "You work out?"

"Yes."

His smile turned into a full chuckle. "Around here, we don't work out. We work outdoors."

"Oh, I like that. Can I use it on the site?" She felt exhilarated by his words. They were fun. They were sexy. They were clever. And absolutely the right tone for what she wanted to get across to lonely hearts.

"Sure. That's an easy one."

"But it's profound."

He laughed harder. "If you say so, but it's simply the truth."

She looked deep into his green eyes that had gone kind of dark with an indefinable emotion. She felt a little mesmerized by him. It was a good feeling. She wished she could capture this moment and share it. She realized now he was unconsciously sexy. That was what made his photograph work so well. It must have been the very quality that had reached out, grabbed her, and never let go.

"Like I said, guess I'd better get back to work."

"What can I do? I mean, I'll change clothes first."

He glanced down the length of her and took a deep breath. "You bring any jeans? Boots?"

"Yes." She felt proud that she'd had the foresight to pack the right threads. "I'm not a complete novice. I've been boot-scooting."

"Fancy stuff?"

She looked at him from head to toe. He wore faded, frayed Wranglers and a soft, often-washed denim shirt with scuffed, blunt-toed brown boots. He'd tied a red bandanna around his neck that appeared just as work-worn as his clothes. She didn't have anything that was in the same comfortable league or right for a working cowgirl.

"Yeah…about what I thought." He pointed south. "If you'll go to Gene's Boot Hospital in Old Town, they'll fix you up with the right clothes."

"You don't mind if my work is delayed a bit?"

"Tomorrow is soon enough to start."

"Thanks."

They grew silent as they looked at each other, and time stretched out as if it no longer existed while a crow cawed overhead and the scent of wildflowers swirled around them.

Kemp cleared his throat, breaking the moment. "Work awaits."

"Mine, too. I mean, work on the website."

"Right." Still he didn't move, as if he didn't know the way home or was already home at her cabin.

And into that silence came the flutter of wings overhead that were faint at first, then louder and louder.

Violet glanced up in astonishment as she watched a bird descend toward them. It was a pretty pigeon with bright feathers gleaming in the sunlight. She liked birds, particularly pretty birds in town, like sparrows, pigeons, and grackles. But she hadn't expected to see a pigeon flying alone on the ranch.

Finally, the bird gracefully floated down, made a perfect landing on the horizontal bar of the railing that surrounded the porch, and folded its long wings back until the feathers made a smooth finish from the dark-gray head to iridescent green neck to plump gray breast.

"Don't move," she said. "We might scare that bird away."

"Clyde, I'm thinking." Kemp chuckled softly as he held out his left arm, fingers closed in a fist.

"Clyde? You know this bird? You keep pigeons?"

"Sort of."

"What do you mean, sort of? I saw the dovecote."

"Yeah, well, it's a long story and not one I'm completely privy to."

"Really?" Things kept getting curiouser and curiouser.

Clyde spread his wings, lifted off the railing, and gracefully landed on Kemp's arm. He turned his head and examined Violet with one eye, then turned his head and eyed her with the other one. Seemingly satisfied, he turned back toward Kemp.

"He's got something on his ankle." Violet looked on in amazement, feeling as if she'd stepped completely out of her element now. "Is he a homing pigeon? I mean, did he bring you a message in that capsule?"

"Most likely."

"What? Who sends messages by pigeon instead of just sending a text? I thought that was some sort of lost art and not necessary anymore."

"Doves and pigeons have a long history of living alongside country folk. It's not a lost art. Racing pigeons are still a popular sport. They're faster than you can imagine."

"I'm sure, since I haven't imagined it at all. Still, Clyde is a very pretty bird."

"And smart."

"I'd guess so since he just flew here with no GPS or map or anything." She laughed at her own joke.

Kemp chuckled and gently stroked the top of Clyde's head. "He's a homing pigeon. He could never get lost. I'm sure you know birds and animals have that instinct because it keeps their species alive."

"But who sent him?"

"Buick Brigade." He pulled a small, rolled piece of paper from the tube on Clyde's leg.

"I know I'm getting in deep here and sound like I know nothing, but I don't care. I'm fascinated by everything I've seen since I arrived in Wildcat Bluff County."

"You're just in the country now. That's all."

"Who or what is the Buick Brigade?"

"There's really no complete answer to that question."

"No?"

He gave her an enigmatic look before he raised his arm and let Clyde hop over to his shoulder, where the bird nestled down and cooed in contentment.

"That's so sweet."

"Buick Brigade." He ignored her reaction in favor of her previous question. "They're four ladies who drive those big tanks of Buicks. They're from Destiny, a small town north of here above the Red River. And each one lives in a Victorian mansion, side by side."

"That's interesting, as well as unusual." Wildcat Bluff County became more fascinating all the time.

"They're like a lot of matriarchs in small towns. They know everything that's going on and take an avid interest in it. They're powerful, so never doubt that for a moment."

"Oh, I wouldn't. Experience and knowledge is a potent combination in men and women."

"True." He stroked Clyde's throat, up and down. "I think maybe the ladies of Destiny have taken an interest in you."

"Me? How would they even know I'm here?"

"Far as anybody in the county can tell, they pretty much know everything in real time."

"Are they single? Maybe they want to join my lonely hearts club."

He chuckled. "You may be close to the truth. They're all about love for others. They might interfere or intervene in anyone's life at a moment's notice."

She joined his laughter. "They sound like wonderful characters."

"On the outside looking in, you might say that." He held up the message. "But if you're the one they've targeted to help, then it's a different story."

"Fortunately, I don't need help…except for you." She gave him a sassy smile, hoping he would soon decide to help with her project.

He returned her smile with a shake of his head.

"I wonder, could I get a photo of Clyde snuggled up to your neck? The old adage is true because a picture is worth a thousand words." Kemp appeared more masculine than ever to her because of his gentleness with the delicate bird.

"Let's find out what the Buick Brigade has to say." He unrolled the small piece of paper. "I'll read it to you."

"I'm sure it has nothing to do with me, but I'm all ears."

"It says here, 'Pigeon-gram. Lonely hearts unite. White lightning sears all. Destiny requires a visit.'" He held the note up for her to see. "That's all it says."

"I guess they heard about my lonely hearts club…probably from Sydney Steele." She looked at Clyde and he looked back. "What do you suppose they mean by 'white lightning'? A thunderstorm?"

"Maybe. But more likely they mean moonshine."

"Really?"

"This place wasn't named Hallelujah Ranch for nothing. We're talking the Roaring Twenties here. Somehow or other, this ranch and Destiny were tied together in the past."

"You don't know how?"

"Nobody does anymore…except maybe the Buick Brigade or Jake the Farmer."

"Why don't you ask them?"

"No point. They know lots of stuff, but they only tell when it suits their purpose."

"They are powerful."

"Yep." He ran a fingertip across the top of Clyde's head and was rewarded with a coo of pleasure.

Clyde gave her a look with one eye, then the other, before he abruptly spread his wings and took flight. He circled overhead, then took off at a blurring speed toward the north.

"Homing pigeons are usually trained to only one place, their original birth home, but they can also be trained to two homes. That's the case with Clyde and Bonnie for Hallelujah Ranch and the Buick Brigade."

"Bonnie and Clyde!" Violet couldn't keep from being startled by the names. "Weren't they the notorious Texans killed by the law?"

"Yeah. After the 1929 stock market crash, outlaws became popular during the Depression. They were romantic figures. Many were bootleggers until 1933, when liquor became legal again. Maybe the Buick Brigade heard stories of Bonnie and Clyde from their folks. Anyway, the ladies of Destiny picked those names for a reason." He looked north, as if following Clyde's flight home.

"It'd be interesting to know why."

Kemp appeared thoughtful. "Bonnie left behind poetry. She wanted more in life than being a waitress in a Dallas café."

"I guess being part of an outlaw gang gave her a pathway to stardom."

"Once she hooked up with Clyde, there was no turning back."

"Maybe they were lonely hearts until they found love with each other."

"Live fast. Die hard."

"It's kind of sad." She looked north, too. "I wish love had been enough for them."

"Maybe it was until they got on the wrong side of the law." He held out the note to her on the palm of his hand. "If I'm not mistaken, this message is for you."

She picked up the note, feeling an electrical zing between them as she touched his bare flesh. She felt an involuntary shiver run through her. If she'd thought his handsome photograph had a powerful effect, if she'd thought his sheer presence had a powerful effect, if she'd thought his deep voice had a powerful effect, she'd known nothing about powerful effects until they touched skin to skin. *Incandescent* was the only word she had for what he did to her. He simply set her aglow.

If that happened to Bonnie when she met Clyde Barrow, and the same thing happened to him, then Violet could understand their wild ride into infamy and immortality. They were driven by a force so powerful it could not be denied.

Love. What if it were one-sided and there had been no Clyde for Bonnie? What if she fell in love with Kemp Lander and he never felt the same?

Lonely hearts. At least she could find love for others, even if she never had it herself.

"We need to go see the ladies," Kemp said, still looking north.

"Why both of us?"

He glanced down at her, green eyes dark with something unreadable. "You're on my ranch and that means under my protection."

"Protection? That sounds so medieval."

He leaned toward her. "Make no mistake. While you're with me, I'll keep you safe."

"Safe?" She glanced around the ranch. "Surely it's perfectly safe here."

He gave a deep sigh. "I'm having a little trouble with trespassers."

"Trespassers?" She wanted to stop repeating his words, but he kept surprising her.

"They're cutting barbwire to get onto the ranch and digging deep holes."

"Whatever for? Aren't cattle rustlers supposed to be the problem on ranches?"

"Yes. And they are an issue."

"Do you know why the trespassers are digging holes?"

"Maybe." He sighed again. "There's an old rumor. No way to prove if there's any truth to it. But it persists as a local legend."

"And?"

"Bootlegger gold."

"Excuse me?" She felt her eyes widen in astonishment. "Do you mean like from a bank robbery? Maybe even a Bonnie and Clyde heist?"

"Nobody knows. It's just a legend. It'd make more sense if it was a bootleggers' cache of coins from selling illegal moonshine."

"Wildcat Bluff County gets more interesting all the time. That's sort of romantic, too," she said.

"Not really. It's a problem. I'm trying to catch them, but no luck so far."

"When did it start?"

"About the time the property changed hands. That'd be when I bought it."

"They probably think you're too busy establishing the ranch to pay any mind to a few holes here and there."

"If so, they think wrong. Trespassing can escalate. That's my concern, particularly since you're here now."

"I'm okay."

"I installed a motion-sensor light and camera. And I'm nearby. Call me if you see or hear anything unusual."

"I'm not sure I'll know what's unusual on a ranch."

He smiled. "Good point."

"If it helps, I'll be careful about going out at night. I don't have any place to go anyway."

"Reminds me—let's get up to Destiny pretty soon. The ladies will be expecting you."

"I'd like to meet them. Is Destiny very far away?"

"Not as the crow—or pigeon—flies." He grinned at her. "Not to worry. You're safe with me."

She didn't say it, but she didn't believe her heart was safe anywhere near him. And still, she'd never tell him no.

Chapter 6

"ANYWAY, I'D BETTER GET BACK TO WORK." KEMP REALIZED he'd talked too much, spilled his guts about this and that. It was all important to him, but not necessary to share in detail, except he'd wanted to keep Violet's attention on him. Well, that and alert her to possible issues, now that she was living in Wildcat Bluff County. Still, those blue eyes of hers were just so expressive, lighting up with wonder, excitement, happiness, that he couldn't resist watching them show the play of her emotions. If he wasn't careful...

"Thanks for stopping by. I look forward to working with you." Violet smiled as if not quite sure of the work ahead but determined to do the job. "And I'll get the right clothes."

He gave her a quick nod. He had to get out of there before he succumbed to any little thing she might propose. As his foot hit the first step down, his phone alerted him to an incoming call from the fire station.

He jerked his cell out of his pocket. "Hey, what's up?"

"Worrisome news," Hedy Murray said.

"How bad is the fire? What and where?"

"No fire. Grab your EMT bag."

"Who's hurt?"

"Nobody. Storm says Daisy Sue is not acting right."

"Hate to hear it, but I'm no vet."

"Ann Bridges is out on a call and I can't get ahold of her."

"What about Sydney or Slade or somebody on Steele Trap Ranch? They're on-site and trained the same as me."

"They're all out of pocket except for Storm…and she's having a conniption fit. Besides, she asked for you."

"Why?"

"You know why. Daisy Sue trusts you, so your presence will reassure her. Also, you know cattle, and you're an EMT."

"I'll do my best."

"That's all we ever ask of our firefighters."

"I'm on my way." He clicked off and glanced at Violet.

"Whatever is it? Please let me help. It'll be my first job as a cowgirl."

"You're not dressed for a barn."

She kicked off her high heels. "You may need an extra pair of hands. Let me be your assistant."

"Are you sure?" He didn't know what to expect. She might come in handy to soothe a little girl.

"I'm not squeamish—at least not too much."

"Go grab your boots while I get my EMT kit. Meet you at my truck. And please don't dawdle."

"I don't dawdle." She turned and hurried inside.

Her response surprised him, but he liked it. He took the steps two at a time and hit the ground running. He didn't want Storm to worry any longer than necessary. He had firefighting gear in his pickup, but he'd just restocked his EMT kit and hadn't transferred it back to his truck. He knew better, but he'd gotten busy with other things and hadn't done it. Big mistake. Lives depended on volunteer firefighters always being prepared to drop everything and rush to the rescue. Now he'd lose precious minutes, but he vowed he would never get in that position again.

He opened the front door of his house, rushed to the kitchen, and grabbed his kit off the counter. He glanced around for anything else he might need to take with him, jerked the roll of paper towels out of its holder, and called it good.

He ran to his pickup. Violet was waiting for him. She held a pair of fancy purple boots in one hand. She'd also changed from her skirt into skinny jeans. She looked good…almost like a cowgirl. He felt a blast of hope that she'd work out all right.

He tossed the paper towel roll at her. She caught it easily with one hand. His hope ratcheted up another notch.

"Truck's unlocked. Take shotgun."

He belatedly realized she might not know what he meant, so he hesitated in case she needed further instructions, but she was on it. She opened the passenger door, climbed into the truck, sat down, and closed the door.

He jerked open the back door, set his EMT bag on the floorboard, slammed the door shut, and rushed to the driver's side. He slid behind the steering wheel, started the engine. The wheels spun, then grabbed hold and the truck shot forward.

He hit the ruts in the road fast and hard. The jarring sent Violet bouncing up and down on her seat. No help for it. Speed was vital, time always critical in an emergency and never to be wasted on niceties. But he noticed that she held on and did not complain. That was another mark in her favor.

"Where are we going?" She glanced over at him as she kept a grip on the sides of her seat.

"Steele Trap Ranch." He skidded onto Wildcat Road and headed south.

"Is it nearby?"

"Pretty close."

She leaned down and pulled on one boot. "Is Daisy Sue a cow or horse or pig?" She pulled on the other boot.

"She's a prize cow. Pregnant. Have you heard of Fernando the Wonder Bull?"

Violet turned and looked at him. "She's *that* Daisy Sue?"

"Right. And the love of Fernando's life."

"I haven't followed the story too closely, but I know there are lots of fans."

"Storm Steele is only nine years old, but she's the brains behind that entire media surge."

"Folks love the Fernando and Daisy Sue story. Right?"

"Right. Now they're following Daisy Sue's pregnancy."

"And she's in trouble?"

"Sounds like she might be."

"What can you do?"

"Not much, probably, but I—we—can try to reassure Storm until Ann gets there."

"Ann's the local vet?"

"Yes. Ann Bridges." He glanced at Violet, caught her serious look, and then focused on the road again. "The ranch is coming up soon. Best thing we can do is be calm and positive no matter what we see or hear or—"

"I can do it."

"Good. Here we are."

He slowed, turned off the rutted road, and drove under a black metal sign with a cutout that read "Steele Trap Ranch." A clear blue sky with a few fluffy, white clouds shone through the open letters. He rattled over the cattle guard and accelerated up a winding lane to the crest of a hill.

Atop the hill, the road split. He stopped his truck. The muddy Red River stretched out in both directions below. On their side of the river, to the left, a big metal barn rose up beside a barn made of wood. Several corrals could also be seen, as well as an open-sided shop with a flat, silver metal roof, and a multivehicle garage. To their right, several houses extended down the road with generous spans of acreage between them.

"We're going to the new barn, the metal one. That's where Daisy Sue will be."

"Okay."

He drove fast toward the two barns, slowed at the last second, dug in his brakes, and slid to a stop in front of the new one. Its metal sides were a traditional barn red. Its shiny silver roof gleamed in the sunlight.

A cowboy in denim and scuffed, high-heeled cowboy boots leaned an elbow on the top slat of a corral attached to the new barn. He appeared a little frayed around the edges, especially his battered straw cowboy hat, but his stance spoke of a weathered, bred-in-the-bone toughness. An Aussie cow dog prowled back and forth in front of the cowboy. He wore a bright red bandanna around his neck over a leather collar.

"You ready?" Kemp glanced at Violet. "If you want, you can stay in the truck."

"I'm with you all the way." She gave him a cocky smile. "Got to earn my cowgirl spurs."

"Good point."

He threw open his door and jumped down to the ground, rushed to the back door, opened it, and grabbed his EMT kit. He hurried to the front of his pickup. Violet was there, ready to go. He noticed she had remembered the paper towels.

The cowboy stepped away from the corral and came toward them. The dog trotted beside him.

"Violet, this is Oscar Leathers," Kemp said. "He's the ranch foreman. And that's Tater, his right-hand cow dog. Oscar, meet Violet Ashwood. She's the new tenant in my cabin. She's in the county on business."

"Pleased to meet you." Oscar tipped his hat, revealing a shiny, bald head, then he glanced at the dog. "Tater, mind your manners."

Tater sat down, held up his right paw, and grinned up at Violet, pink tongue lolling to one side.

"You're very handsome." She leaned down and shook Tater's paw.

"Got to say, Tater's got an eye for the ladies." Oscar grinned a lot like Tater.

"We're here to see about Daisy Sue," Kemp said. "You don't seem too worried, and you know cows."

"You know a bit about cattle your own self." Oscar adjusted his battered Stetson more firmly on his head. "Daisy Sue, she's resting easy, far as I can tell. She's big. Could be she'll calve early, but let's wait for Ann's opinion."

"Right."

Oscar hooked a thumb over his shoulder. "Better pay your respects to Fernando. He's down in the dumps. He doesn't like being separated from his ladylove."

Kemp looked at the watching bull. "Hey, Fernando."

The massive bull had a sleek, black coat. He stood just inside the corral, his sharp, dark eyes missing nothing.

"Is that really him?" Violet asked. "He's even bigger in real life than in his photos."

"He's big, all right. Thousand pounds, easy," Oscar said. "Hottest Angus sperm on the market."

Kemp smiled at how Violet's eyes widened. "They sell it," he said.

"Oh." She gave a little wave to the bull.

Fernando stared at her and snorted as if in reply.

"What are y'all doing out here?" A little girl with a wild mane of tangled ginger hair and big hazel eyes rushed out of the new barn and hurtled toward them. She wore well-scuffed cowgirl boots, faded denim jeans, and a T-shirt. "Fernando the Wonder Bull" was emblazoned on the tee in sparkling rhinestones. She skidded to a stop in front of Kemp and put her hands on her hips. "Well?"

"You're right. We should be in there," Kemp said.

"Who's that?" The young girl pointed at Violet.

"Violet Ashwood. She's my new tenant. Violet, this is Storm Steele."

Storm turned her sharp, hazel-eyed gaze on Violet. "So you're the one. Mom told me about meeting you at the dump. Guess you're okay. Come on!" She whirled around and ran back toward the new barn.

Kemp glanced at Oscar. "You coming?"

"Tater and me are staying put to keep Fernando company till Ann gets here. Sydney said Storm thought Daisy Sue should be inside, so she's inside. Heads-up, Storm's worried sick, and she's a little more on the growly side than usual."

"Yeah. I noticed." Kemp couldn't help but smile. He knew only too well what everyone knew—that the nine-year-old ball of energy had a will of iron when she set her mind to something. She was definitely a chip off the old block.

"Come on!" Storm glared at them over her shoulder at the barn's entrance, then rushed out of sight inside.

Kemp glanced at Violet. "Ready?"

She nodded. "Nice to meet all of you." She threw a smile at Oscar, Tater, and Fernando. "Let's go."

They set out after Storm.

Kemp walked by Violet's side. He noticed with mild but pleased surprise that they moved easily together, stride for stride, as if they were partners who had walked together often. He glanced down at her. She wasn't that tall, not compared with his six feet two inches, but she had long legs that easily ate up the ground as fast as his legs. He liked her can-do attitude. He liked her.

He stepped back to let her enter the barn before him out of courtesy. She stopped right inside and glanced up at him with a question in her eyes. He nodded as he glanced around.

Inside, the new barn was shadowy and cool. It smelled of oats, hay, and manure. Those were comforting scents to a cowboy because they probably meant all was well. He glanced down the length of the center aisle. Stalls lined each side. Most of the stalls had closed doors. He searched for the pint-size ramrod.

Storm popped her head out of an open stall halfway down the aisle and beckoned with both hands. "Kemp, come on. She knows you're near. She trusts you like nobody else."

"I'm on my way."

Storm looked at Violet. "Daisy Sue was missing for months. Nobody could find her. Fernando was beside himself with worry."

"Kemp, were you in charge of the ranch where she went missing?" Violet asked.

"Right." No way, no how did he want to go there, but he bucked up. "I involved my cousin Lester. I know better. He's *that* cousin. I guess everybody's got one. Anyway, he was supposed to pick her up and move her, but it turned out he didn't. You'd have to know Les. He's got an eye for the ladies, and when he meets a new one… well, he forgets anything else, except maybe rodeo."

"Nobody's ever met him." Storm grinned with a mischievous glint in her hazel eyes. "Folks around here wonder if Kemp made up his cousin Les, just to make himself look better after losing Daisy Sue."

"You know good and well she wasn't ever lost," Kemp said. "She just got caught up in a herd when cowboys moved a load of cattle from Lulabelle & You to East Texas on the Tarleton family's other ranch."

"But you figured it out and tracked her down." Storm turned serious. "Everybody knows it wasn't your fault. You're a good rancher."

"I saw a clip online of Daisy Sue arriving here," Violet said. "Kemp, were you driving that big truck with the trailer?"

"Yeah." He was trying to forget the whole incident, but it was just too entertaining for people to let it go. "Better let me see Daisy Sue."

Storm smiled, reached up, and patted his forearm. "You'll be a big comfort to her."

"Hope so."

He walked into the stall, glad to see they'd chosen a double one. The floor was strewn with fresh, clean hay. Daisy Sue lay in the center. She turned big, dark eyes on Kemp and raised her head slightly in greeting. He saw she had a huge belly. How far along was she? He didn't figure even the vet knew exactly, because Fernando had been visiting Daisy Sue on the sly at night. The famous bull was a master at opening gates. Crossing from his Steele Trap pasture to Lulabelle & You pasture to visit Daisy Sue was no problem for Fernando the Wonder Bull.

Kemp set down his EMT bag beside the open stall door, then went to the center and knelt beside Daisy Sue's head. He gently stroked down her face with the fingertips of his right hand as he examined her by sight alone.

She was a beautiful Black Angus, prime quality for the breed, but she appeared lethargic. Fortunately, she didn't appear to be in pain.

He glanced up at Storm. "Is she eating?"

"She's been in the pasture with spring grass."

"Any unusual discharge?"

"No. She seems weak, so Mom had us bring her in here."

"Good idea. Maybe you need to change her feed."

"That's what Oscar thinks, too."

"Ann will know what's best." He looked back at Daisy Sue as he continued to stroke down her long nose. She licked his hand with her pink tongue. He smiled at her and rubbed the top of her head.

"She's a beautiful cow," Violet said. "Do you need me to do anything? I mean, anything a cowgirl would do?"

Kemp gave her a quick smile, realizing she was actually trying to fit in and do her job. "Just stay calm."

"Okay."

He looked back at Daisy Sue. He hoped she wouldn't have a troubled pregnancy, but this was her first calf and... He stopped his worrisome thoughts in their tracks when he heard a truck pull up outside.

"That ought to be Ann," Storm said.

"Just in the nick of time." He stood up. "I want a vet's opinion because, as much as I hate to admit it, I'm a little worried about Daisy Sue."

"Fernando's most worried of all," Storm said.

He gave Violet an encouraging smile as they waited for the veterinarian. He hoped for everyone's sake, especially Daisy Sue's, that Ann would reassure them all was well.

Chapter 7

VIOLET HUNG BACK, STAYING JUST OUTSIDE THE OPEN entrance to the stall. She didn't want to get in anyone's way, because she saw she wouldn't be much help. She squeezed the paper towels in her hands, but a roll of paper towels seemed inconsequential in the face of a really big pregnant cow.

How had she ever thought she could pretend to be a cowgirl? Maybe she should've stayed in the truck. Maybe she should've stayed in San Antonio. Maybe she should've thought through this entire cowgirl idea. But her thoughts froze when Kemp turned and caught her gaze. Some emotion swam up from the depths of his eyes, hung there, quivering with intent, and then he flung it outward straight as an arrow—so very, very straight—into her heart. She caught her breath as the truth hit her. No maybes in the world could have kept her away from him.

She'd fallen hard and fast. Love had come to her finally—not with a photograph, but with a real, live cowboy firefighter. She drank him in, so greedily, so hungrily, so needily—from the dark stubble on his face to the straw sticking to the knees of his jeans where he'd knelt beside Daisy Sue. Happiness surged through her, turning her hot...so very hot.

And then she fell from the heights of heaven to the depths of earth. Nothing could be worse. She couldn't tell a soul or she'd lose all credibility with her lonely hearts club. And most of all, she could never let Kemp Lander know, because not only did he not love her, but he didn't want her on his ranch or to be part of her dating site.

What a mess. And yet, it felt so good. Love. No wonder nothing else could assuage lonely hearts. Love. No wonder lonely people searched long and hard for it. Love. No wonder she felt a calling to make it possible for everyone.

And in that instant of total clarity, she heard the rapid pace of boots striking the center aisle, coming toward them. Kemp tore his gaze from hers and looked in the direction of the footsteps. Storm brushed past her as she hurried out of the stall.

Violet simply stood there, feeling so stunned by her revelation that she couldn't move an inch...except in her mind, where she was struck by one hard truth—she didn't want to share Kemp, not even one little inch of him. And yet, here she was all set to share him with the world.

"What's the trouble?"

Violet jerked around at the sound of the authoritative alto voice. A tall woman with short silver hair, a long lean body, and sharp blue eyes barreled down the aisle. She wore denim—jacket, shirt, jeans—with scuffed, black cowgirl boots. She carried a battered black nylon, multipocket, multizipper equipment bag in her left hand.

"Ann!" Storm pointed toward the stall. "Daisy Sue. She's just not acting right."

"Last I checked, she was okay," Ann said.

"Fernando's worried about her." Storm wrapped her arms around her middle. "And she's so big."

"Hey, Kemp," Ann said. "Did Storm call you out?"

"I'm always glad to visit Daisy Sue, even if an EMT isn't much help for her."

"Glad to see you on the job, but I'll take over now." Ann pushed past Violet, stopped, and looked at her. "Who are you?"

"Violet Ashwood."

"She's my new tenant," Kemp said. "This is Ann Bridges, our county veterinarian."

"Good to meet you," Violet said.

Ann looked Violet up and down, as if checking her out like she would a cow or horse for health and well-being. "Wait a minute. You're lonely hearts club, aren't you?"

"Yes." Violet could see nothing remained a secret in Wildcat Bluff County for long. She'd need to remember that, particularly in regard to her feelings for Kemp. She had a big secret and she intended to keep it.

Ann looked down at Daisy Sue, then back at Violet. "Good idea. You get that site up and running, let me know."

"You're interested in a dating site?" Kemp sounded astonished at the idea.

Ann gave him an annoyed glance before she knelt beside Daisy Sue. "Look at me. I spend all my time around animals, either in my clinic or on ranches. When do I have time to find a guy?"

"I didn't know you were looking for somebody," Storm said.

"I'm not." Ann put her hand on Daisy Sue's distended stomach. "Like I said, when would I have time? Truth of the matter, I'm staring down the barrel of fifty. It's about time I had some fun in life, did something besides work till I'm bone tired and not worth anything to anybody."

"You're the best in the business," Kemp said. "Everybody depends on you to take care of their animals."

"Don't I know it? Still, my assistants are getting better all the time." Ann spread her hand over Daisy Sue's stomach and then glanced up at Storm. "I'd like to get an ultrasound."

"No," Storm said. "I told you before. Fernando wants to be surprised. He doesn't care if it's a boy or a girl."

Ann opened her bag and pulled out a stethoscope. She leaned over and used it to listen to Daisy Sue's heart and lungs before she moved farther down her distended stomach. She sat back, smiled a little bit, and then put her stethoscope away.

"What?" Storm asked.

"She's been out in the pasture, hasn't she?" Ann stood up.

"Yes," Storm said.

"She's heavily pregnant, and she may be weak due to mineral deficiencies that interfere with proper metabolism and muscle function. It sometimes happens in early spring when pregnant cows are put on growing forage, like wheat pastures."

"What do we do?" Storm sounded worried as she looked from Ann to Daisy Sue and back again.

"If we give her calcium or magnesium, she should be fine."

"That's a relief," Storm said.

"I'll do a blood draw for a lab test, then I can more exactly pinpoint the problem."

"Okay."

"If that doesn't do the trick, we'll go from there."

"Whatever Daisy Sue needs, she gets," Storm said.

"Except an ultrasound?"

"Right."

Ann shook her head. "Keep her in the barn for now."

"Fernando misses her."

"He can visit her, but I don't want her stressed, so keep his visits and visitors in general to a minimum."

"Okay." Storm nodded.

"Let me draw the blood now." Ann opened her bag and removed a syringe. "When I get the lab results, I'll talk with you and Sydney."

"Thanks…but is that it?" Storm asked. "Can't you do something else?"

"Not now." Ann finished filling the syringe with Daisy Sue's blood. She put her equipment back in her black bag. "Stay with Daisy Sue until your mom returns."

"I hope she gets back soon." Storm glanced around the group with a determined look, then sat down beside Daisy Sue. She placed a comforting hand on the cow's back.

Ann looked at Kemp and Violet. "I'll walk y'all out."

"Storm, if you or Daisy Sue need me, just call," Kemp said.

"Thanks." She looked up, gave him a warm smile and a thumbs-up.

"Daisy Sue is a beautiful cow." Violet wished she knew how to do more or even understood better what was going on.

"Yes, she is," Storm said. "If you want help with your website, let me know. I'm pretty good with social media."

"Thank you. Someone is working on it for me, but I'll remember your offer." Violet liked everybody she had met in Wildcat Bluff County. Storm was worried sick about her cow, but in the midst of the crisis, she'd just offered to help a stranger.

"Storm, I'll see you and Daisy Sue later." Ann walked out of the stall and into the aisle.

Violet followed and matched the vet's fast pace, Kemp right behind her. They emerged from the shadowy interior of the barn into the bright sunlight outside.

Ann stopped and motioned Oscar to join them.

"What is it?" he asked as he stroked Tater's head.

"I don't want Storm to hear this, but I'm concerned about Daisy Sue," Ann said. "I hope I'm right about the minerals. That's an easy fix."

"Don't let Fernando hear you," Oscar said. "He'll be out of that corral so fast, it'll make your head spin."

"He's smart," Ann said, "but he's not *that* smart."

"He's intuitive like all animals." Oscar leaned toward her. "And you know it."

"Don't make no never mind," Ann said. "Daisy Sue is my concern, not Fernando."

"You're right." Oscar glanced over his shoulder.

Violet noticed that Fernando was watching them with his intense, dark eyes.

"I'll keep a close eye on both of them," Oscar promised.

"Good," Ann said. "I'll run that test. And I'll talk with Sydney. Don't let Daisy Sue out of the barn."

"Okay." Oscar gave a sharp nod. "You got it."

"Is there anything we can do?" Violet felt invested in Fernando and Daisy Sue now that she had met them. And in Storm, too.

Ann gave her a quick smile. "Best you can do is get that dating site up and running. I'm not getting any younger."

"If the cowboys in this county find out you're looking, they'll be parked outside your house." Kemp chuckled as he teased her.

"Don't even think it." Ann smiled. "I know them all too well. What I need is a guy from somewhere else…maybe even Oklahoma."

"I'll keep you in mind as I develop the dating site," Violet said.

"Good." Ann took a step toward her truck.

"And let us know if we can help," Kemp said.

Ann gave them a wave, then got into her pickup and drove away.

Oscar took off his hat and ran a hand over his bald head. "Maybe I'd better throw my hat in the ring."

"Tater, too?" Violet couldn't resist teasing him.

Oscar laughed and nodded. He reached down and patted Tater's head. Tater responded with a bark.

Kemp laughed. "Maybe I misjudged this entire dating-site thing." He shook his head at the two of them.

"You're just behind the times." Oscar winked at Violet. "Got to go where the action is."

"I don't want any action," Kemp said. "I've got a ranch to get up to speed. That's plenty on my plate."

"Suit yourself." Oscar turned to Violet. "Let me know when you want my photo, but any gal who likes me has got to like Tater, too. We're a team."

"Right." Violet didn't know if he were serious or not, but she wasn't about to turn down anybody looking for love, human or dog.

"Let's get out of here before you sign up every cowboy on the ranch." Kemp gestured toward his truck.

Violet walked over to Kemp.

"Don't forget!" Oscar called after her.

Kemp opened his pickup's passenger door for her. She stepped up and sat down. He shut the door, then walked around to the driver's side, opened that door, and sat down beside her. He glanced over and shook his head.

She wasn't about to say *I told you so*, but she could tell he had it on his mind.

"Who in tarnation would've ever guessed Oscar Leathers, a confirmed bachelor if I ever saw one, was looking for love?" He started the truck's engine, then headed down the hill.

"Well—"

"And Ann Bridges. She's a smart, good-looking woman, but I doubt any cowboy in the country ever dreamed she was looking for love."

"Well…"

"Is it something in the water?" He glanced over at her. "Or is it you?"

"Well—"

"Nobody, and I mean nobody, talked about dating sites or advice to the lovelorn or lonely hearts till you came to the county."

"Maybe I just make it seem possible."

"You make what seem possible?"

"Love."

"Love?"

"Some folks…not you, of course…get lonely, even when they have friends and jobs, and even when they're busy, and—"

"Love takes time. Did you ever consider that fact?" He drove under the Steele Trap Ranch arch and hit Wildcat Road.

"Did you ever consider that it might be worth a little time and effort?" She felt irritation overcome her good sense. She shouldn't antagonize the man who could kick her out of her current home or at the very least make things unpleasant.

He glanced over at her, jaw working as he ground his teeth. "I don't have the time or the energy. I already told you I'm up against a wall."

"I wasn't talking about you. I get it. You don't have time for love. You aren't lonely. You don't need anybody."

"I didn't say that. I didn't say any of that."

"You came close." She'd had enough. With a surge of sudden emotion, she didn't care if he never appeared on her dating site or if he kicked her off his ranch.

He slowed down, took a deep breath, and glanced at her again. "What if I did want somebody in my life?"

"Well, you don't, so there's no point in going there."

"I can go there if I want."

"No, you can't. We've already established that fact."

"We did not."

"Did so."

He abruptly pulled off, parked on the shoulder of the road, and turned toward her. "Are we having our first fight?"

She rolled her eyes, feeling ridiculous. Why was she antagonizing him? And then she realized it must have to do with being in love. Her hormones were all out of kilter. She had to get a grip.

"Does it mean that much to you?" he asked in a gentle tone.

"What? My lonely hearts club?"

"No...well, yes...but more than that."

"What then?"

"Love."

She shut her eyes, drawing from a deep reserve to remain calm. The last thing in the world she needed to discuss with Kemp Lander was love. She didn't know if she could control her emotions well enough to not give herself away to him.

"Really...I want to know."

"Yes. It's important for people."

"What about you?"

She gripped the edges of her seat. "I...me...no, I want to help others."

"Why not love for you?"

She didn't dare look at him, or who knew what he'd see in her eyes? "Let's just say it's never worked out for me in the past."

"Why not?"

He'd finally pushed her too far. She glanced at him...and got hooked by that look in his eyes again. She focused back on the road. "What about you?"

"Me?"

"Girlfriend? Wife? Somebody?"

"No time."

"Never?"

"Let's just say it's never worked out for me in the past."

She heard him throw her words back at her, but she just let them fall into pieces at her feet. They were getting nowhere except heading to a place where they would hurt each other. She didn't understand how or why it had happened, but something between them had just exploded into life. It wouldn't do. No time or place for love or emotions, not in her life. They were too messy and way too dangerous...particularly to her heart.

"Let's leave it." He pulled back onto the road, handling the steering wheel as if careful not to break it.

"Suits me."

But whatever had come alive didn't go away, of course. Somehow or other, he'd left her wanting more of the connection she'd just experienced with him. She felt vulnerable and totally unprofessional. Cowboy Heart-to-Heart Corral was supposed to heal hearts, not break them. But no way around it, her heart was well on the way to being broken.

To make sure everything went as planned for her lonely hearts club, she must never ever let Kemp—or anybody else—find out she'd fallen head-over-heels in love with Mr. July.

Chapter 8

KEMP CROSSED THE CATTLE GUARD TO HIS RANCH AT A SLOW pace, mostly because he didn't want to rattle teeth, but also because he realized he felt reluctant to let Violet leave him. Once at the house, she'd go her way and he'd go his way.

He didn't know what had happened since he'd met her, but she made him think in ways he hadn't in a long time because he'd been totally focused on getting his ranch up and running. Love? Now she had Oscar and Ann thinking and talking about it. Was it really that important in the scheme of life? They had perfectly good, satisfying lives. What made them want to reach out for more?

He had a perfectly good, satisfying life, too. He glanced at Violet. She sat quietly with her hands in her lap, appearing withdrawn. No wonder. She didn't want to get into it with him again. He'd pushed her. Why? He had no idea, but it'd brought out the fighter in her. He liked that about her because it revealed her inner core of strength. What he didn't want to admit was that he'd wanted to strike an emotion in her, even if it was only irritation.

He focused on the road leading up to his house, thinking furiously. He bet she wouldn't last three months. She'd just get everybody stirred up, then she'd ride off into the sunset, back to San Antonio. Now that was a city steeped in romance, what with the outdoor River Walk enticing folks to linger with slow walks, tasty food, and plenty of hand-holding. Now why'd he go and think of that?

Violet had pretty, almost delicate hands, with long fingers that looked like they could hold hands really well or stroke gently across bare skin. Okay, that did it. She was hot. Anybody would agree with his assessment in that regard. Still, that fact didn't, by any stretch of the imagination, translate into love.

He'd just been too long without a woman. Maybe that was the basic motivation propelling her lonely hearts club—men and women too long alone. He could believe that more easily than a sudden wild stampede to true love. Oscar, for example. Kemp just shook his head at the thought of the dyed-in-the-wool cowboy bachelor leading the cowgirl of his dreams down the aisle, Tater at their side. Who could have ever imagined that Oscar had secret dreams of his own personal ladylove?

No way to stop the stampede to love now, particularly since he was a part of it. But Violet was stirring up a kind of trouble in Wildcat Bluff County that wouldn't be easy to stamp out. From what Kemp had witnessed so far, it could turn into a raging fire that consumed all in its path.

Love! He'd just have to be careful he wasn't caught up in the conflagration, or all his firefighter skills wouldn't be enough to put it out.

He drove up to the front of his house, then turned and headed the short distance to her cabin.

"No need to drive me over there," she said. "I can walk. It's not far."

"I want to see you safely home." He ignored her protest and stopped his truck near the cabin's stairs. "I'll walk you up."

"Thanks…but it's not necessary."

"I think you're looking for another argument."

"I'm just trying to be considerate." She opened her door and held it there.

"So am I." He realized he was goading a reaction from her again and decided he'd better stop it. "Anyway, thanks for coming along."

She turned blue eyes on him. "Do you think Daisy Sue will be all right?"

"She's getting the best care, so I'd think so. Ann is probably just being wisely cautious."

"I hope that's all."

"You aren't the only one."

"Do you need me to do anything around the ranch right now?"

"Not today. You need clothes…and maybe even to acclimate here."

She chuckled. "Do you think that's possible?"

He grinned, liking her more all the time. "Once they get a taste for it, city folks have been known to turn country fast."

"Does fast mean in a few years?"

He chuckled, liking her humor, too. "People change faster than cats. Now cats, they can take years to accept a new situation."

She laughed, looking right at him with bright eyes.

He felt his breath catch because they were laughing together, looking at each other, sharing a moment that stretched out and out…way beyond the humor of the moment into quite simply the sheer pleasure of each other's company.

How long they would have held that moment together, he didn't know, because about that time he heard an engine turn over—big, maybe a one-ton truck—in a back pasture. He glanced past her and out the door.

"What is it?"

"There's no reason for a truck to be on my ranch."

"Trespassers?"

"Maybe. I'll go check it out. You hurry upstairs."

"No way," she said.

"What?"

"I'm going. You might need backup."

"What could you do if I did need help?"

"Hand me your phone. I could take your picture as they drag you away and send it to the law." She grinned mischievously. "And I'd drive away to save your pickup."

"You're all heart."

"You know it."

"I hoped you'd say you had a Sig stashed on your body some-where and you knew how to use it."

"Dream on."

"Self-defense is an important tool out here. 911 is more myth than reality."

"Surely there's a sheriff or…"

"Sure. Sheriff Calhoun. I'll get hold of him right now. At the least, I want this trespass recorded on the dispatch log."

"I get your point. If I lived here long enough, I'd take up target practice."

"Good." He called the sheriff.

"Wildcat Bluff County Sheriff's Office. How may I direct your call?" the dispatcher said.

"Kemp Lander here. Trespasser alert. Sounds like a one-ton near the back road. I'm headed there now. Maybe I can catch them in the act. Doubt a deputy can get here in time, but I'd like somebody to check out the back road into the ranch. We might get lucky."

"Will do," the dispatcher said. "A deputy is on the way right now. Please preserve any evidence."

"Thanks." Kemp clicked off and glanced at Violet. "Are you sure you want to go?"

"Yes." She shut her door.

He turned around, drove back down the lane, and cut across beside the house to a gate that led into a pasture. He stopped, let-ting the engine idle as he glanced over at her. "Get the gate, will you? It'll save time."

"You bet. That's cowgirl work." She popped open her door.

"Wait. Do you know how?"

"I'll figure it out." She hopped out, ran up to the gate, fiddled with the latch, then swung the gate back to make room for him.

He drove through the open gate and was pleased to see her shut the gate behind his pickup. She obviously understood enough about pastures that she knew he wouldn't want cattle running loose through a gate that had been left open. A rancher could get fined by the sheriff for loose cattle on main roads and annoy neighbors who had to deal with them.

"All done." She stepped back into the pickup.

"Good job."

"Thanks."

As she shut the door, he heard the one-ton truck start up again in the distance. He hoped he could get there in time, but he had to pinpoint the location and cross rough acreage. Fortunately, he had a four-wheel drive that could take cross-country without tearing out the pickup's guts.

He lowered the windows, doing his best to listen to the other engine as he drove east, correcting as he went, but he kept losing the sound under the noise of his own engine. Finally, he stopped, listened, and corrected his course.

He glanced over at Violet. She rode with both hands clutching the sides of her seat, swaying with the pickup as it bumped and jumped over rough ground. He smiled, despite the situation. She had the makings of a real cowgirl...too bad she'd probably soon head back to the city.

Dust filled the cab, along with the scent of fresh spring grass and wildflowers as he plowed forward. Cattle had scattered away from the direction he was headed, so that told him he was pinpointing the trouble area. Last thing he wanted was spooked cows or cut fence that let them loose. Even if the trespassers got away, at least he'd be there early enough to repair the fence and keep the cattle from roaming the countryside. He couldn't afford the time and effort to chase down a single cow. That's why he had bought the best fence he could afford and expended a monumental effort installing it himself, to avoid an even larger outlay of cash.

Up ahead, he finally saw dust in the air near a small copse of trees, just as the sound of the big engine revved up. Then he saw it—a one-ton making for a wide space of cut fence and downed posts.

A tall, lanky guy with a baseball cap pulled low over his eyes, wearing torn jeans and a sweatshirt with the neck and arms cut out, held on to the metal headache rack that stretched horizontally across the back window of the big truck. They obviously meant serious business because they were towing a flatbed trailer with a backhoe digging machine chained onto it. They could do a lot of fast digging with equipment like that, and it wasn't cheap. They were investing plenty of time, energy, and money into their search of his property.

Kemp hit the gas and shot into the meadow, hoping against hope to catch them. They'd removed their license plates, so he couldn't get a read on them that way. If he could get ahead of their truck, he could angle in front and maybe bring them to a stop, if they didn't plow into him. He knew where they were headed, and he had to stop them before they reached the paved blacktop county road on the far side of his property.

He gunned his engine and began to catch up, unhindered because he wasn't hauling a backhoe on a flatbed with a man hanging on in back. But then, to add insult to injury, the trespasser holding on to the headache rack gave him the finger.

Kemp just shook his head. He couldn't wait to bring these guys to justice.

But it wouldn't be this day. A family of deer consisting of several does and fawns leaped across his path, then spread out in a line, one after another, as they headed toward the safety of nearby woods.

He threw on his brakes to avoid hitting them and watched the truck hit the blacktop and power away.

From there, they could turn down a number of dirt roads or make it to Wildcat Road and be gone.

He hit the steering wheel with his fist, frustrated at the situation, feeling his emotions ratchet up, threatening to spiral out of control. He grabbed his phone and called the sheriff.

"Wildcat Bluff Sheriff's Office," a calm, steady voice said.

"It's Kemp again."

"Status?"

"Saw them but lost them. Two guys in a one-ton hauling a backhoe on a flatbed trailer."

"Serious business."

"Yes."

"I'll alert the deputy. He might catch them on the road."

"Good. I'll sign a detailed report later."

"Okay."

"Thanks."

Kemp clicked off again and set down his phone with a sigh.

"Sorry." Violet leaned over and placed a warm hand on his bicep. "You almost had them."

With that touch of her hand, he felt his emotions change, and for a moment he almost forgot the intruders.

Heat swamped him. He glanced over to see her expression, but she had quickly removed her hand, placed it back in her lap, and now looked out the window.

Maybe she was just being kind, but it had seemed an intimate touch, like one you'd give a friend or more than a friend. Maybe he ought to join her lonely hearts club after all. If he didn't watch it, he'd be right there with Ann and Oscar. Maybe even half the county.

He cleared his throat. "Thanks. At least we got a look at them."

"They aren't just trespassers. They've got a bad attitude, too."

"Yeah." He thought about that single-digit salute. It didn't bode well for them backing off anytime soon. He had an escalating problem.

"Do you think they found something?"

"Don't know. Let's go see." He watched the deer till they were out of sight to make sure they had escaped to safety in the woods.

"Okay."

He turned his pickup around to head back. "There's not much for the sheriff to go on since it's just another cut fence, but at least I'll get it on record. Now I'll need to rent a backhoe again to fill in another deep hole. I won't risk a horse, cow, deer, or other animal breaking a leg or falling in and being unable to get out."

"I never thought of that problem."

"It's extra work for me."

"They're putting a lot into their search, aren't they?"

"Yeah. I'd guess they've got metal detectors, too, so they'll know where to dig."

"Bootlegger gold." She glanced over at him. "Do you think it really exists?"

"If there were any, it probably got spent by bootleggers long ago."

"I suppose so."

He drove back to the meadow, stopped beside a deep hole, and got out of his pickup. He walked over and shook his head at the destruction.

She joined him. "Guess they didn't find what they were looking for, did they?"

"No way to know. If they found it, they took it with them."

"If they have metal detectors, they must have found something, or they'd never have dug here."

"Good point." He saw something glint in the sunlight and knelt to pick it up.

"What'd you find?"

"Rusty metal bottle cap."

"Look. Here's broken glass." She nudged an object with the toe of her boot. "And what's this?"

He looked at what she'd uncovered. "Fancy spoon. Big, too." He picked it up, then turned it over and over in his hand.

"Looks like a serving spoon. It's tarnished so black that it might be solid silver and worth something."

He held it out to her. "If you like it, you can have it."

"Really?" She shook her head. "No, it's yours and it might be valuable."

"You saw it first and I want you to have it." He grinned at her. "It's pretty, so it suits you." He belatedly realized what he'd implied when she turned pale pink, as if embarrassed at his compliment.

"Thank you." She took the spoon without touching him and gently rubbed the dirt from it. "It's a violet pattern!" She held it out for him to see.

"In that case, the spoon definitely belongs to someone named Violet."

She gave him a quick smile and nodded in agreement. "It's engraved, so I bet it belonged to an entire silverware set." She turned it over and checked the back. "Oh yes, it's sterling."

"I wish you had the entire set." He smiled at her as she looked wistfully at the pretty piece. "Who knows, maybe we'll find all the forks and knives and teaspoons that go with it."

She looked down into the ditch, shaking her head. "I doubt it. I bet this was accidentally thrown away. Some woman long ago probably received the silver set for her wedding. She'd never have intentionally parted with it."

He glanced around the area. "I'd guess this was an old trash-dump site."

"That's what they're digging up?"

"I bet. No trash pickup back then, so they'd probably have had several trash sites."

"Yeah." She stroked the spoon thoughtfully. "It's kind of fun. I wish we could find something ourselves."

"Better be satisfied with the spoon. It's probably the most valuable thing left from the bootleggers."

"Still, it's romantic that it's from that era and all. It's lain here so long, just waiting to be found. I wish I knew its story. I wonder if we'll ever know about the woman who once used it to serve food she'd prepared for her loved ones."

He watched as she stroked the silver spoon, appearing wistful for a bygone era or as if for someone she'd once known and lost. He felt a little chill and glanced up...nothing but blue clouds and green grass.

"If this spoon could talk, I bet it'd have quite a tale to tell."

"As far as tall tales, there's another legend about Hallelujah Ranch. You'll hear it one way or another, so I better tell you now."

"What?"

"The place is supposed to be haunted."

"Ghosts?" She looked at him in surprise.

"Not true, of course. I figure the people that came here searching for bootlegger gold over the generations fueled the rumor to keep other searchers away."

"I kind of like it."

"You've got a romantic streak."

"Hallelujah Ranch is definitely a romantic place."

"It's just a ranch like any other."

She smiled at him, pink lips turning upward as her blue eyes lit with an inner fire. "I think it's special. And it's the perfect place to start my lonely hearts club."

He smiled back at her, holding their connection, drawing it out, wanting it to last as the world around them slowly disappeared until there was nothing and no one but the two of them standing together on the edge of the pit.

Chapter 9

Violet rode shotgun again as Kemp headed back to the house. She hoped she hadn't given herself away, but the romantic spoon had triggered something in her…something that no longer wanted to be hidden…something that wanted to shout *love* from the rooftops. She kept her lips pressed together, afraid she'd open her mouth and simply tell him the truth of her feelings.

She glanced down at the spoon she clutched in both hands. Of course, it was her imagination that it had anything to do with her change in perspective. And yet the silver spoon that had lain cold so long in the ground was now warm in her hands, as if she'd brought it back to life.

She knew she was being fanciful, but there was something about Hallelujah Ranch that defied rational thought. She'd felt it from the first. And for that very reason she knew her lonely hearts club would be an inspired creation that would surely help others find the love in life that could be so elusive. She'd stepped into a romantic world fueled by Roaring Twenties legends…and it seemed only right because cowboys were legendary heroes.

"I'm going to drop you off at the cabin, then go back, meet the deputy, and fix the fence." Kemp glanced over at her.

"Can I help?"

"You've done enough."

"If I were a real cowgirl—"

"No need to go there. I can handle this myself." He stopped in front of the gate.

"I'll get it." She started to set down the spoon, but she didn't want to be parted from it, so she tucked it in the pocket of her jeans and stepped down to the ground.

She quickly unlatched and pulled open the metal gate, and then waited for him to drive through. When he was on the other side, she shut the gate and joined him in the cab.

"Thanks. You're a quick study."

"I do my best."

He drove up to her cabin, stopped, and turned to her. "Listen, it's been kind of a rough day for you."

"It's surely been unusual…and interesting."

"What about I take you to supper later?"

"I thought I was supposed to take you."

"You already gave me your dating site spiel."

"And you turned me down, but I haven't given up."

He grinned, shaking his head. "I can see you've got a stubborn streak."

"Could be." She smiled back.

"Look. I've wrangled you around enough today that I owe you a meal at the least."

"I admit I'd like to try some local food."

"Good. When I get back, I'll take a quick shower and come over here. Okay?"

"Okay." She felt a warm, happy rush at the prospect of spending time with him without anything else to distract them. And she might yet persuade him to get on board with her plans.

"Good. It won't take long, if I don't run into problems. If I do, I'll call."

"I'll keep my phone handy."

She couldn't seem to tear her gaze away from his green eyes, so she felt behind her and opened the door. Still he looked at her and she looked at him as time stretched out and silence built around them, until a crow cawed loudly overhead and broke the moment. She blinked, coming back to earth, and quickly got out of the truck. She could feel his gaze on her when she shut the cab door, turned, walked up the stairs, and opened the door.

When she didn't hear him drive away, she glanced back. He still sat there, watching her as if there were nothing else in his world except her. She smiled and waved, hoping to break the spell. He nodded, then turned and drove away.

She walked inside and shut the door behind her. He hadn't wanted to go. He hadn't wanted to leave her. She pulled the spoon out of her pocket. It wasn't just warm now. It was hot.

Hallelujah Ranch. Was it Kemp's lonely heart that had brought him to a place that needed a hero, a man strong enough to heal a past cast in shadows of truths or untruths? And had her own lonely heart brought her here, too? She stroked the violets that climbed up the long handle of the shell-shaped spoon, feeling fanciful and romantic and hopeful that there was love enough for everyone.

She walked over to the bar and set the spoon on the countertop. The contrast between old and new was strong, but they also appeared to complement each other. She glanced around the area. Diffused sunlight filtered through the back windows to bathe everything in a rosy glow.

She felt a little shiver of anticipation. Had Kemp asked her out on a date, or was he simply fulfilling an obligation to his tenant? She wanted date. She didn't want obligation. One implied a flirty skirt while the other insisted on practical denim. She sighed as she stroked down the length of the spoon with one fingertip.

How would the former lady of Hallelujah Ranch have dressed for an important occasion? It'd have depended on whether she was a modern flapper or Victorian lady. Violet thoughtfully picked up the spoon and examined the design. Hallelujah's lady would most definitely not have been modern, like Bonnie with her wild ride to fame alongside Clyde. Hallelujah's lady would have chosen skirt over pants, so Violet would, too, if for no other reason than to fit in with Hallelujah Ranch's rich history.

How long did she have before Kemp came back? She had no idea, but she'd take a moment to check her email. She sat down on a stool at the bar and opened her laptop. Everything she was experiencing and seeing in Wildcat Bluff County would translate into wonderful copy, visuals, and point of view for her lonely hearts club.

She answered several emails, checked other dating sites, and finally leaned back in satisfaction. Even with everything going on here, she was staying on top of business. And then she thought back to Mr. July and how his photo had brought her here. Only now she knew him as Kemp Lander, and he was so much more than she could ever have imagined in San Antonio.

Did she go forward with her original plan or pull out now? What if he never agreed to her idea? What if she couldn't tolerate even the thought of sharing him? But how would she replace him? What would make her site special? She needed a hook to entice folks to come to Cowboy Heart-to-Heart Corral and stay awhile. Mr. July had been that hook. If she abandoned her idea now, she'd lose precious launch time…even if she could figure out something just as special.

She closed the lid on her laptop with a snap. She was getting ahead of herself. She hadn't even been in the county a complete day. She needed to catch her breath before she made any big decisions.

Right now, she should have one thing and one thing only on her mind—Kemp Lander. She wanted to at least make friends with him, even if he never agreed to her idea. She was living on his ranch and working for him, so she should make the absolute best of the opportunity to learn new things, meet new people, and expand her horizons. As far as love, she just needed to keep it on a back burner.

She picked up the spoon and headed up the stairs. At the top, she stopped and gazed at the big, round bed with its crimson cover. She tossed the spoon onto the center among the brightly colored pillows. It landed faceup. Crimson bed and silver spoon went together. Decadent. And luxurious. She wasn't used to that type of life because she was normally a practical person. Maybe *romantic* was a better word…and in that case, the bed and spoon absolutely fit with her current life.

But thoughts of romance were for later, when Kemp picked her up for their first date. And that was how she was going to think of their dinner together. Date. Now what had she brought to wear that would fit the occasion?

One by one, she pulled most everything out of her closet from hangers and drawers, then tossed each piece on her bed. Nothing suited. She felt really dissatisfied. She wanted to wear something special for him, but she didn't seem to have it. She suspected that nothing in the world would have been perfect enough for him. And that told her way more than she wanted to acknowledge. She was trying to keep this love thing on a back burner, but it kept blazing to the front.

Finally she extracted her guilty pleasure. It was an impractical purchase she'd selected on a whim right before she'd left San Antonio. She pulled the hanger out of the closet to reveal a violet-tinted dress with a long-sleeve, fitted bodice and full skirt with a ruffle around the hem that ended just above her knees.

Would he like it? Maybe if she paired it with white, lacy underwear and strappy sandals. She stopped her thoughts in their tracks. He wasn't seeing her bra or panties or anything else. It was a simple dinner to unwind after a long day. She put the dress back and slammed the door shut on it, along with any romantic thoughts that went with it.

She grabbed jeans and a lightweight lavender sweater off the bed. They'd do perfectly well with her boots. She'd still wear the white underwear, but only she'd know about the lace.

She opened her jewelry roll, selected a simple gold heart on a short chain, and closed the clasp around her neck. Fortunately, she'd brought a small jewelry polishing cloth with her. She walked over to the bed, picked up the spoon, and polished until the metal turned from black to silver and gleamed in the light. Satisfied with the result, she carefully placed the spoon on a lavender pillow.

She put her rejected clothes back in the closet, stripped off what she was wearing, grabbed a purple cotton robe, and headed downstairs. She'd be clean, well groomed, and professional when he came to get her.

She liked the bathroom. Shower only, but such a shower. It was all travertine tiles with sleek, stainless fixtures and a rain shower-head. Amazingly enough, she found violet-scented goat milk soap, almost as if it'd been placed in a basket particularly for her because of her name—or if she really wanted to be romantic, it'd been selected in anticipation of her finding the violet-design spoon.

She dropped her robe and stepped into the shower. And it felt so good after such a wild and wooly day. She lathered up her crimson washcloth, loving the soap scent, loving the water, loving the sense of standing on the edge of a new and wonderful world of happy surprises. She chuckled at the turn of her thoughts, because she was really getting into the legendary land of Hallelujah Ranch.

She didn't stay too long, although she could have spent forever under the gentle spray of water, but life awaited her in the form of Kemp Lander. She was ready to meet that life head-on and take a stand for her lonely hearts club. And lovers everywhere.

She brushed out her long hair, lightly applied makeup, and then slipped into her robe and hurried back upstairs. She stopped at the crimson bed that dominated the room, practically begging to be used by lovers. Had Kemp pulled back those covers for a sassy, flashy cowgirl? That thought definitely gave her pause. She didn't want to think it, so she tossed the idea away. He had his own house and his own bed, so why would he bring someone here? A traitorous thought wound its way out of the depths of her mind and burst full bloom. Why would he pass up a beautiful, round, red bed when it belonged to him, and him alone, to share as it pleased him?

She grabbed her underwear off the bed and jerked it on, trying desperately to get him off her mind, get love off her mind, get sex off her mind. She pulled on her top, pants, and boots. She hurried as fast as she could to cover up her traitorous flesh that wanted nothing more than to fall onto the bed with Kemp's arms around her, whispering that he loved her and would always love her.

She put a hand over her mouth, as if that would stop the thoughts. She couldn't go on this way. Somehow she had to control her reaction to him. She leaned over the bed and picked up the silver spoon. She gently rubbed her thumb across the embossed trail of violets. Hallelujah's first lady would have understood about love. She would counsel caution...not a fast dance, but a slow waltz.

With that in mind, Violet gently placed the tarnished silver spoon on the purple velvet pillow, nestling it there—after the cold, hard ground—in warmth and softness.

And she walked downstairs, ready to begin her slow dance.

Chapter 10

Violet had hardly made it downstairs before she heard a knock on her front door. Kemp. She felt her heart pick up speed because only a door separated them. Was all in order? She glanced around the room. Laptop was closed. Purse was beside it, as was her phone. She was as ready as she was ever going to be, so she walked over and opened the door.

He stood there with his beige straw cowboy hat in hand. He'd cleaned up really well. Dark hair was still damp from his shower. Tanned face was freshly shaved. He wore pressed Wranglers with dark-green, pearl-snap shirt and shiny, pointy-toe, black cowboy boots.

She almost felt underdressed. Perhaps a skirt had been the best idea. And yet he didn't appear to mind her clothes one bit. In fact, he'd done a quick up-and-down glance that had taken in her appearance with one big gulp and finished with a hungry gaze focused on her lips.

She felt hungry, too, but not for dinner. He looked good enough to lick and nibble all over and over and over until he begged her to satisfy his insatiable desire. And it'd have nothing to do with food.

"Hungry?" he asked.

"Chocolate." She said the word before she thought about it because, somehow or other, rich, dark, sweet candy went with him and the big, red bed upstairs. If she wasn't careful, she might just drag him up there and be done with it. Oh yes, it'd be heaven in a small cowboy cabin.

He chuckled, a deep, rich sound. "You want dessert first?"

"First. Last. And always." Oh yes, he was her dessert, and only he could satisfy her.

"They might have chocolate cream pie at the Chuckwagon Café today. Great barbeque there, too."

"Pie." She tried to turn her mind from Kemp's body to pie or barbeque, but it wasn't easy.

"Are you okay?" He cocked his head to one side as he considered her. "Do you still want to go out?"

"Yes, of course." She had to get her mind in the game or risk losing all. "Guess I got distracted with work."

"Yeah. It can happen."

She noticed that a little dark chest hair peeked out above the top snap of his shirt. It'd go all the way down his chest, lower and lower and lower still. When she realized she'd let her eyes travel downward with her thoughts, she snapped her gaze back to his face.

"Uh, you really are distracted, aren't you?"

She rubbed her neck, feeling hot and uncomfortable. How was she going to endure an entire evening with him?

"Would tomorrow be better?"

"No." She could hardly talk at all, so she walked over to the bar, picked up her phone, put it in her purse, slipped the strap over her shoulder, and turned back to him. She wished he'd worn looser jeans. How was she going to keep her mind on business or anything except how he filled out his Wranglers?

"If you don't like the Chuckwagon, we could go someplace else."

"It's fine." She took a few steps closer to him, but now she caught his scent that registered somewhere between musk and citrus. How could she think straight when she was inhaling him with every breath?

"Are you ready to go?"

"Yes." She walked around him and straight out the door. She took a big breath of fresh air to try and clear her mind.

"You got your key?" He followed her outside.

"Key?"

"Cabin key."

"I guess it's in my purse."

"Maybe you better check before I lock the door."

"Yes, of course." She fumbled around in her purse until she found it on a horseshoe keyring. She held it up in triumph, swinging it in front of him.

"Good." He gave her a questioning look before he locked and shut the door. "Ready?"

She gave him a bright smile, dropped the keys back in her purse, and rushed down the stairs, almost tripping on the last one.

"Careful." He stopped beside her. "Maybe you decided to finish that bottle of wine."

"No." She smiled brightly again, hoping it'd distract him from her odd behavior. Honestly, how hard could it be to pretend you didn't love somebody? Well, obviously harder than she'd ever imagined before this very moment.

"Okay. Let's go then." He walked over to his pickup, opened the passenger door, and waited for her.

She took a deep breath as she thought about the ramifications of sitting with him in an enclosed truck cab. It hadn't been so bad before when she'd ridden with him, but that was before she'd conjured up so many images of him in her big, red, round bed with its little pillows that could be used to prop up... No, she absolutely wasn't going there, particularly with him so close to her.

Once inside the cab, she sat perfectly still, feeling almost fragile, as if a move in any direction would unbalance her precariously balanced emotions. When he sat down beside her, buckled his seat belt, and started the engine, he filled the cab with such a strong masculine force that she caught her breath.

"Have you been to Old Town?"

She gave a rueful smile. He sounded so normal, while she was teetering on the brink of total surrender. Love. Maybe it wasn't such a good idea if it caused this type of disruption.

"Old Town?" He glanced at her, then back at the lane as he headed away from the house.

She took a deep breath. "I've only been to the dump. Fernando's ranch. And your ranch."

"In that case, you're in for a treat. I'm glad I'm the one to introduce you to Wildcat Bluff's heritage."

"I'll be happy to see it." She was thankful she sounded almost normal.

He turned onto Wildcat Road, pointing out the bluebonnets and swaths of Indian paintbrush blooming in brilliant colors along the highway.

"It's lovely here," she said.

"Spring is a good time to visit." He drummed fingertips on the steering wheel. "Could be you'll stay through to autumn. I think you'd like it."

"I'm sure it's lovely." When had they become so stilted with each other that they were discussing the seasons? She supposed it was better than the weather, but still…

"Did you say you're hungry?"

"I haven't eaten since Waco."

"That's a long time."

"Yes."

"You'll like Chuckwagon food."

"I'm sure it's delicious." She squeezed the sides of her seat with both hands, trying to relieve some of the tension that was zinging between them. How had they reached this uncomfortable point? And then it hit her. They must both think this was a date—their first date—and they weren't sure how to act since they didn't want to make a misstep.

"Great pie."

"Yes." She looked out the window for anything that'd be a

distraction from their stilted conversation. "Look, there's a man hoeing a garden just on the other side of that fence."

Kemp hit the brakes and jerked his pickup onto the shoulder of the road. He cut the engine.

"What is it?"

"That's Jake the Farmer."

"And?"

"He's a centenarian."

"Wow. And he still farms?" she asked.

"He's one hundred fifteen hearty years old...and he plans to hit one thirty."

"Impressive."

"He's lived on that farm his entire life, so he knows most everything about everything in the county."

"Does he have help?"

"No family. Folks bring him supplies and check in on him. Otherwise, he's pretty independent."

"I'd like to meet him."

"That's why we stopped here. I thought you'd enjoy meeting him. Plus, he might know something about the spoon."

When Kemp opened her door, she stepped down to the ground ready to talk with another interesting person who resided in a county that was getting more fascinating by the second.

He held out his hand. She clasped his work-rough palm, and he threaded their fingers together. It was an intimate gesture that surprised her. She walked with him to the barbwire fence between the road and the pasture.

"Nice weather," Kemp said.

Jake the Farmer stopped his work, but he didn't look up as he held his hoe straight—from ground to sky—with one strong hand, as if the lowly hoe were a jeweled scepter. He was all deeply tanned skin stretched taut over a strong bone structure with cheekbones so prominent they would've made any fashion model drool with envy. Long, silver hair had been pulled back into a single plait. He gave the impression of reaching to the sky with his slender body that appeared supple as a teenager's.

"Sir, this is Violet Ashwood. She's from San Antone."

Jake turned slightly toward Violet and lifted his head, as if sniffing the air, and turned milk-white eyes on her.

She froze, surprised by the realization that he was blind. And yet, he was out here hoeing his garden.

"Good to meet you," Jake said. "What brings you to our fair county?"

"I'm starting a lonely hearts club," Violet said.

"Lonely hearts." Jake nodded. "That's not an unknown condition for most folks."

"I agree." Violet returned his nod, even though she knew he couldn't see it. "I want to ease lonely hearts."

"She plans to start her online dating site right here in Wildcat Bluff County," Kemp said.

"I heard this was a very romantic county," she said.

"You've got that right." Jake smiled warmly. "It's romantic from way back."

"We found a silver serving spoon in an old dump site on Hallelujah Ranch," Kemp said. "It might be from the old bootlegger days."

"It's a violet design. And it's expensive, particularly for that time period," she said.

"We're just wondering if you remember anybody around here having a silver set like that." Kemp grasped the top of a fence post, as if to emphasize his point.

"Violet design, you say?" Jake turned his head toward Hallelujah with a painful expression on his face. "That'd be Lady Mauve all over again. Beautiful woman with beautiful taste."

"Bootlegger?" Kemp asked.

"That…and so much more," Jake said. "There's a lot on

Hallelujah that has never reached the light of day, at least these days."

"What do you mean?" Kemp asked.

"It's Lady Mauve's story. I'm not sure if it's my place to shine light on her remarkable past."

"It's a long time ago," Violet said.

"Not for me." Jake gave her a sad smile. "For me, it's like yesterday. I will say, folks came to Hallelujah from all around to party."

"Do you mean there was a speakeasy?" Kemp sounded interested in that news.

"Lady Mauve never did anything by half. She never entered a room she didn't own. She never started a business she didn't expand. From bootleg to speakeasy was an easy step for her." Jake turned away from Hallelujah Ranch. "When she went, she left a cold trail. But if I know her—and I did—she'd have preserved her legacy for the right person to find at the right time."

"If there was a speakeasy, it's long gone now," Kemp said. "There's nothing like that on the ranch or I'd have seen it."

"You found the spoon, didn't you?" Jake asked.

"I found it," Violet said.

Jake turned his head toward Violet, studying her as if he could clearly see her. "Love. Romance. Hearts. Maybe you're the one to resurrect the past. I'd say the silver spoon has put you on the right path."

"Could you be more specific?" Kemp asked. "We'd like to find the whole silver set."

"Can't help you there. My sight's not what it used to be." Jake grinned, making a joke of his lack of vision. "But I'll give some thought as to how I can still be of service to Lady Mauve...and you."

"Thank you," Kemp said.

"Violet, good luck with your lonely hearts club," Jake said. "I hope you heal many a lonely heart."

"That's my plan. It was a pleasure to meet you." She smiled at Jake, then grasped Kemp's hand.

He led her back to the truck and opened the door.

She sat down inside, wishing Jake had told them more, if he'd known more, but still glad that she'd met such an interesting man.

Kemp said nothing as he joined her, started the pickup, and headed toward Wildcat Bluff.

Chapter 11

KEMP COULDN'T BELIEVE IT. OF ALL THE PEOPLE IN THE world, it'd have to be Violet Ashwood. She didn't fit on a ranch. She planned to use him. And when she was done with him and anybody else in the county that helped her lonely hearts club, she stood a good chance of dumping them and going back to the city.

And somehow it'd all be his fault. No, it'd be Sydney Steele's fault because she'd insisted on the cowboy firefighter benefit calendar that had lured Violet to Wildcat Bluff County. In the end, it wouldn't matter whose fault it was because there'd be plenty of broken hearts to go around for everyone. On the other hand, maybe Violet wasn't that coldhearted. Maybe she really believed in love and was putting her heart and life behind her idea.

He held back a sigh as he glanced over at her. Couldn't she wear anything that didn't set him off? At least she wasn't in that short skirt and high heels. He ought to burn the whole mess, so he didn't ever have to lay eyes on her wearing it again. And yet, her not wearing it would hurt almost as much as her wearing it.

And why the hell did she have to find the spoon? He could only blame himself for that, because he'd taken her to that old trash pit. And Jake had raised even more questions about Hallelujah Ranch. It must have been something back in the day. Kemp was under no illusions. Cattle and hard work were his world. At least, that's the way he'd viewed the world until Violet turned those big blue eyes on him.

He'd fought his reaction to her, but he was fast losing ground.

It'd only been one day since he'd met her. How would he feel after a week or a month or the three months when her lease was up? She might think she was creating a lonely hearts club, but it could just as easily turn out to be a broken hearts club.

And still he wasn't willing to pull out. Was a broken heart worth a special time in the sun? He glanced at her again. She was quiet, watching the countryside as he drove toward Wildcat Bluff. Maybe she was contemplating Jake's words. Maybe she was making plans for her dating site. Maybe she was thinking about him…about how they'd held hands like teenagers just beginning to explore what they might mean to each other.

He slowed down. He didn't want to share her. He didn't want to take her to the Chuckwagon, where he'd need to introduce her all around and they'd fawn on her till she wouldn't even remember he was there. She might choose another cowboy firefighter instead of him. How would he react if he saw her being lured away by a guy who'd bend over backward to please her and be with her and help her?

No, he didn't want to share her. He slowed down even more on the edge of Wildcat Bluff. Was he willing to risk a broken heart for her? He wasn't Cousin Les, who could love 'em and leave 'em. When he loved, he'd love forever.

"Chocolate." He said the word knowing there'd never been a choice. She was it. "Isn't that what you wanted to eat?"

She looked at him with wide eyes. "You said barbeque and pie."

"I know, but now I think I was being selfish."

"Selfish?"

"Yeah, I wanted barbeque," he said.

"Barbeque is good."

"There's a chocolate shop in Destiny."

"You're kidding me. Can it possibly do enough business?"

"Mail order, too."

"Wow. Wildcat Bluff County is full of endless surprises."

"Rich history, I guess." He pulled to the side of the road and stopped his truck.

"Isn't the Buick Brigade in Destiny?"

"Yes."

"Would we need to see them?"

"No."

"You're sure? Maybe they won't know we're in town…if that's where we go."

"They'll know, but if we go to Destiny Chocolatier, they'll understand."

"Will it be open? It's getting kind of late."

"It's already closed."

She frowned. "Then why did you suggest it?"

"I've got a key."

"A key to the shop?"

He sighed, realizing he was going to have to explain. "Bertha Waldron gave it to me."

"Bertha? Oh, I didn't realize you were involved with somebody."

"Not me." He shook his head at his blunder. "She's one of Cousin Lester's loves. Truth of the matter, women never get over him."

Violet chuckled. "I'm beginning to want to meet this cousin of yours."

He groaned. The last thing he wanted was for Les to turn his many charms on Violet.

"That bad?"

"That good, if cowgirls are any judge."

Violet laughed harder. "Oh, well, in that case I'm sure he's taken."

"Forget it. He's never taken. He's the one who takes and everyone is happy about it."

"Well, if he's how we got a key to a chocolatier, then I'm happy about him."

"And here's the funny thing. He hates chocolate."

"Then what are you doing with the key?"

"Bertha thought that if she wasn't around and Les had a sudden chocolate attack, as in craving for it, he should be able to get into her shop and pig out."

"But you said he hated chocolate."

"He does, but for her, he *did* pig out on it. Made him sick, too. Still, he'd do anything for his current love."

"Why give you the key?"

"He was long gone by then."

"And never to return?"

"Never say never about Les. He's nothing if not the most unpredictable cowboy on the rodeo circuit. That's how he wins. He's more unpredictable than the animals."

"He sounds like he'd fit right in to Wildcat Bluff County."

"Don't even think it." Kemp shuddered at the thought of the havoc and mayhem from *that* cousin. It'd be worse than dealing with an out-of-control wildfire.

"Okay. Let's talk chocolate." She held out her hand, palm up.

He reached over and squeezed it even as he wanted to do so much more. She was under his skin, despite everything he'd told himself. No way around it. He wanted what he wanted. He was even willing to put a broken heart on the line for her lonely hearts club, because she'd come to town, and in few hours, she'd made him realize that he really did have a lonely heart.

Come hell or high water, he was making a play for her, but he couldn't let her know how deep his emotions were running, or she'd try even harder to rope him into her dating site. If he could pretend to be like Les, she'd think he just wanted to have fun and all would be well.

He made a U-turn on Wildcat Road and headed for Destiny.

"Is it far away?"

"Not too far." He decided to fill the time—and keep his mind off what he really wanted them to be doing—with a bit of county history, since she'd seen so little so far. "We're proud of our heritage around here. People come to see Old Town in Wildcat Bluff or go to Sure-Shot for a touch of the Old West."

"Is Destiny like those towns?"

"Not too much. They're Western, while Destiny has Victorian touches."

"That's interesting."

After a time, he drove up a rise and crested the top of a cliff overlooking the muddy Red River as it made its way east toward Louisiana before eventually joining the Mississippi River, heading south to the Gulf of Mexico. To the west, buildings rose above the flat-topped mesa.

"There wasn't ever a ferry at Destiny like there was at Wildcat Bluff," he said.

"Why not?"

"It's too high above the river. You'll notice there aren't many trees…at least not since the first settlers arrived and created the town."

"They didn't like trees?"

"They used the lumber to build their homes."

"And they wanted a pretty vista." She pointed across the river at the tree-lined, red-tinted earth of Oklahoma.

"Right. And it looks as if they didn't want anybody to sneak up on them, so they created a clear field to return fire, if necessary."

"Defensive, then?"

"By now, it's anybody's guess, but that's an accepted reason."

"And the Buick Brigade?"

"Story is that four businessmen—their ancestors—came with plenty of money and a need to watch each other from their front porches. Maybe they were foes in the beginning, but their descendants are friends now."

He turned his truck west and followed the two-lane highway.

"You'll notice the road up here doesn't end in the town. That's probably defensive, too."

"Guess they were protective of their privacy and…"

"Safety."

"Did they have outlaw shootouts here like in Wildcat Bluff?"

"And Sure-Shot." He pointed toward the town. "Far as we know, it's always been quiet, genteel even, in Destiny."

"But it's like they were expecting trouble."

"Yeah."

"But it never came."

"Far as we know."

"That's good."

"Right." He rolled into town and eased his truck to the side of the street so she could see it all. "Here's Destiny."

Four three-story Victorian homes stood side by side on large lots on the south side of Main Street. A small dovecote built as a replica of each house had been set on a tall pole at the front corner of the homes. A single-story carriage house and former stable had been built behind each house.

The painted ladies came in four colors with accent trim. The first on the block was pale yellow with gold. The second was fuchsia with purple. The third was white with navy. The third was aqua with green. They all had wraparound porches, octagonal turret rooms, multipeaked roofs, distinctive ornamental trims, and wide entry staircases with elaborately carved handrails. Each home had a unique whimsical design, from a steamboat with keyhole windows to gingerbread fantasyland to multicolored stained glass to jewel-cut fascia.

On the other side of the street, single-story buildings with Western false fronts painted white promoted businesses on hand-carved, hand-painted signs that hung above the continuous boardwalk under a connecting portico—Destiny Books and Coffee Parlor, Destiny Sweetheart Café, Destiny Mercantile, Destiny

Feed and Fashion Emporium, Destiny Junk and Antiques, and Destiny Chocolatier.

On either side of the businesses, twelve small, single-story farmhouses with peaked roofs spread out, six to each side. Each house had been painted a different pastel color and gleamed like a long rainbow in the late-afternoon sunlight. All had matching gray slate roofs. And the front lawns were enclosed with white picket fences. Not a single vehicle was in sight, although there appeared to be horizontal parking spaces in front of the business buildings.

"It's almost as if time forgot this town," Violet said. "And it's so beautiful, like an oil painting from the late 1890s. Those mansions are definitely Queen Victoria era. And it's so perfectly maintained, you'd never know the buildings were well over a hundred years old."

"I'm glad you like it. Each lady of the Buick Brigade lives in one of the painted ladies."

He slowly drove down Main Street. Nobody was out and about. It'd be dark soon. Destiny Chocolatier was last in the row of businesses, so he turned down the alley beside it and parked in back. He cut the engine and turned to face Violet.

She smiled. "This is an unanticipated treat."

"Maybe a little like your River Walk in San Antone?"

"Yeah. Destiny is a romantic sort of town, too."

"Let's go inside and see what we can rustle up in the way of food."

"I'm about starved, so anything and everything will taste wonderful."

"We can do better than wonderful. You'll see."

He got out of his truck, walked around, opened the door, and helped her down to the asphalt. He held on to her hand as he shut the door and locked his truck. He kept holding her hand as they walked to a door. He only let her go to fish the key ring out of his pocket and open the back door of the chocolate shop.

He stepped inside, glanced around to make sure all was okay, then gestured her into the shop. After she joined him, he locked the door behind them.

"Oh my, it smells wonderful in here…totally decadent."

"Good. That's what Bertha is going for. Look around while I text her that I'm here and will leave cash for what we eat."

He pulled his phone out of his pocket, sent a quick text, and received a single word reply, LES? He hated to disappoint her, but he did with the next text. Nothing more to say after that. He put his cell away, then flipped on wall sconces for soft light as he followed Violet into the main room, trying to see it with her fresh eyes.

Bertha hadn't gone Victorian or Western with her decor. She'd gone Roaring Twenties all the way. Sleek and modern. Glamorous ladies in Erté prints accented the white walls, along with sepia-tone posters of Douglas Fairbanks, Gloria Swanson, and Josephine Baker.

Small, round white tables with matching chairs were scattered across the room on a black-and-white square-tile floor. The focal point of the room was a long counter with a glass front that held chocolate confections of all types and sizes. Violet stood in front of it shaking her head in wonderment.

"Looks good, huh?" He walked up to her, feeling proud that he could have given her something that surprised and delighted her so much.

"Where do I start?" She glanced at him, then back again. "I could easily gorge myself till I was sick."

"No need." He chuckled. "We'll take some home."

"That'd be wonderful." She took a deep breath. "But really, I need food, no matter how much I want to indulge in these delicacies."

"I'll take care of that, too."

"How?" She stepped back, taking time to look around the room. "This is delightful."

"There's a connection between Destiny and Hallelujah, but I don't know what it is."

"Does anybody?"

"I'd guess so." He pushed through the low swinging door that separated the candy counter from the dining area. "Like you, I'm not from around here."

"You aren't?"

"I'm from East Texas. I came here as foreman of Lulabelle & You Ranch, then decided to stay when I got the opportunity to buy my ranch."

"I take it you must really like it here."

"It turned out to be more home than I could've imagined in the beginning. Now I'm here to stay, and I'm slowly being accepted by locals. Everyone who comes here needs to prove themselves."

"What do you mean?"

"I'd guess there are lots of different ways to do it, but you either fit, or you don't."

"I still don't understand."

"Folks who fit in here care about the community and help whenever needed, like our volunteer firefighters."

"That makes sense."

"Wildcat Bluff County is tight-knit, but it's also warm and welcoming to those who love it."

"It's definitely got a charm all its own."

"That it does." He grinned, ready to give her another surprise. "For now, I want you to have another treat. Why don't you take a seat at the table of your choice? There's plenty. I'll serve you supper."

"Really?" She looked surprised and impressed. "Where will you get it?"

"In the kitchen. Bertha usually keeps a couple of lunches from the Sweetheart Café in her fridge just in case she or someone else gets hungry when everything else is closed for the night. No choice, but it's always good."

"Sounds perfect. Need help?"

"Not a bit." He gestured toward the chocolate. "While I grab the to-go containers, why don't you fill a couple of boxes with candy?"

He grinned when her blue eyes turned dark. Who knew— other than Les—that the way to a woman's heart was through chocolate?

Chapter 12

Violet opened a white box. Destiny Chocolatier's logo was stamped on the box in gold foil. She set the open box on the glass countertop, grabbed a sheer pop-up sheet, slid open the glass door behind the counter, and was hit with the overwhelming scent of sweet chocolate confections.

Happiness rushed through her at the anticipation of the first melt-in-her-mouth taste. Such beauty. Such temptation. So many choices. How could she ever make a decision? Choose her favorites?

Of course, any and all would be delicious. White chocolate. Oh yes. Blackberry chocolate. Oh yum. Cherry-centered chocolate. Oh heaven. Rum-flavored chocolate. Oh, oh, oh...

"Can't make up your mind?" Kemp asked with a smile as he walked back into the room.

She laughed at the absurdity of his question. "Never. Not in a million years. Maybe I should just close my eyes and grab any and all."

"Bertha would be glad to hear you're so appreciative of her creations. Some of those candy molds go way back in time. They've belonged to her family since they emigrated from Germany generations ago."

She looked at the designs more closely. "Look, here's one in the shape of a cuckoo clock."

"Pretty."

"There are a lot of German descendants in the Hill Country, so I'm used to fine food, but this is still remarkable. The oldest bakery in Texas is in New Braunfels, and I love it."

"If you're here in the fall, we could go to Oktoberfest just down the road in Muenster."

"There's a big one in New Braunfels. Food, beer, music, and folks are always great there."

"Ours is smaller but still fun."

"I bet it is." She felt wistful at the idea of going to an Oktoberfest with Kemp. They'd share it all. It'd be so special. Still, that was in the fall. Where would she be by then? Right now, she wasn't at all sure she wanted to be back in San Antonio, but she set aside the future for now.

"Maybe if you ate real food first, chocolate choices would be easier."

"This is as real as it gets." She glanced up and saw that he held a tray with glasses, two white Styrofoam containers, and cloth napkins. "Smells good. What did you find for us?"

"Come and see."

He walked over to the nearest table, set down the tray, and then quickly positioned everything on the tabletop before putting the tray on a nearby table. He gestured toward the food, pulled out a chair, and grinned at her.

She set down the box of chocolates and felt her stomach rumble. She hurried over and sat down.

He joined her on the other side of the small table and pointed at the food. "We're lucky. That's sweet tea to drink and chicken salad on croissants to eat."

"This is lovely. Thank you." She picked up a napkin and spread it across her lap.

"Let's chow down." He took a big bite of his sandwich.

She picked up the soft croissant and bit into chicken salad with walnuts and green grapes and what could only be homemade mayonnaise. She moaned in satisfaction.

"It's good, but I didn't think it was that good."

She smiled at him over the edge of her sandwich. "You're obviously no connoisseur of chicken salad."

"Can't say I am or that it's on my to-do list. Steak. Barbeque. Those I can get excited about."

"Sounds like a guy." She smiled as she took another bite. She really was hungry. She sipped tea, enjoying the company and the setting.

"Right."

She got down to the serious business of filling her stomach… until she realized they were watching each other eat, and she felt her breath catch in her throat, because it was sensual and exciting and fascinating to watch him bite into his sandwich, mayonnaise smearing across his upper lip…and then he licked it off with the tip of his pink tongue, watching her watch him…and then she knew he'd done it on purpose. Was he flirting with her over a croissant sandwich, or was she imagining it? She picked up her tea and took a quick gulp of the icy liquid to cool down. It didn't help. She was fixated on the possibility of seeing the tip of his tongue again and imagining how those lips, that tongue, would feel against her hot—so impossibly hot—skin.

"Do you want dessert?"

"Yes." And she knew exactly what came to mind and it had only one name—Kemp Lander.

"Chocolate?"

She just sort of moaned at the idea, although she was really still thinking about him.

"Rich, decadent brownie?"

"Oh my…"

"They're from the Sweetheart Café, too. With vanilla ice cream."

"You're just trying to bring me to a point where I'll never be satisfied with anything else again."

He grinned, his green eyes sparkling. "I bet we could figure out something that'd satisfy you even more."

She froze, feeling her heart ratchet up. He *was* flirting with her. Maybe he was like his Cousin Les, a love 'em and leave 'em kind of guy. But would that be so bad? At the moment, it didn't seem bad at all. It seemed really good…at least the love 'em part.

"We can take the chocolate candy home, where we can continue satisfying you."

She smiled, or she thought she smiled, although she wasn't too sure at the moment because his words were lifting her into another reality. Chocolate *and* Kemp, together. She wasn't sure, but it could very well be illegal.

"You'd like that, wouldn't you?" He hesitated, cocking his head to one side as he contemplated her.

"Yes."

"Great. Let me pick up this stuff, and I'll come back with the brownies." He stood up and filled the tray with discards.

"I'll help."

"No. This is my treat. Well, technically it's Bertha's treat, but she'll be happy to know we enjoyed being here."

"But—"

He was quick. She had to give him that. He was away and through the swinging doors before she could even stand up. She was almost relieved to have a little space to herself, so she could get her emotions under control. She could handle this and never let him know how she really felt about him.

"Here you go." He set a plate with a large brownie and a big scoop of ice cream in front of her, then he added a fork and a spoon. He put the same items on his side of the table and sat down.

"Looks wonderful."

"It is."

She picked up her fork, cut into the brownie with a dollop of ice cream, then placed it all in her mouth, closing her eyes. "You're right." She took another bite. "It's absolutely wonderful."

He nodded, quickly ate the rest of his brownie, set down his fork, and leaned back, eyes shuttered, as if he'd never been watching her as if she were dessert.

"Thank you so much for bringing me here."

"Glad it worked out."

She leaned toward him. "Maybe this isn't a good time to bring it up, but I'm hoping all this food has put you in a mellow mood."

"Are you back to your dating site?"

"I never left it. You really are perfect for it."

"Thanks for the compliment, but—"

"I'd really like you to represent Cowboy Heart-to-Heart Corral when my site goes live. I wouldn't require much more from you than a few stills and videos. Maybe we could get you riding a horse or roping a cow or something else that is evocative. I'd be happy to pay you, whatever it takes to get your consent."

"For one thing, I'm too busy."

"Love. Friendship. Happiness."

"All those things are better found face-to-face instead of face-to-screen."

"You make a good point, but not everyone has that opportunity. My dating site will simply up the odds and reduce the time."

He nodded but said nothing.

She added, "I don't give up easy."

"No cowgirl worth her salt does."

"Maybe I need to prove my worth to you as a cowgirl first."

"That'd be a good start." He stood up, obviously ending their talk, gathered everything from the table, and placed it on the tray. He headed toward the back, stopped, and looked back. "Why don't you select some candy, then I'll run you home?"

She watched him walk away, appreciating his backside but already missing their comradery, even if she hadn't gotten him to agree to her plan…yet. She straightened her shoulders and stood up. Now or never. She wasn't about to miss a chance to enjoy what surely was the best chocolate, or near enough, in the world. She went back and began her selections, quickly filling the white box with one piece of chocolate after another. She finally, reluctantly, closed the lid on a full box, wishing she could add just one more piece.

He walked back into the room, saw what she was doing, and joined her. He picked up another box and began to fill it with a wide assortment of candy, picking here and there at random.

"You're taking a box home, too?"

He glanced over with a grin. "Do you really think one box is enough for you?"

"But it's so much."

"Not *too* much. And remember, there's always more here. I think you and Bertha are going to get along just fine. Your businesses seem to go together."

"Oh. That's a great idea." She gave him a quick hug, then realized what she'd done and stepped back. "Excuse me. It's just—"

"No need to apologize. You can hug me anytime you want. I'll always be up for that."

"It's just that including decadent chocolate as part of my lonely hearts club is such a good idea."

"That's *your* idea, not mine."

"Without you, I'd never have had it."

"How would it work?"

"I don't know, but maybe Bertha could promote Destiny Chocolatier on my site. Short blogs about how she makes her candy creations along with photographs and maybe even recipes. It might benefit us both, since chocolate is so romantic."

"I bet Bertha would like it. She already does a large mail-order business." He completed his box, then closed the lid and set it on top of the one she'd already filled to the brim. "There's something else…"

"What?"

"Did you like the soap and lotion and scent in your bathroom?"

"It's wonderful. And it's violet. Did you do that on purpose because of my name?"

He shook his head. "That was Morning Glory. Once she heard your name, she was determined you should have no other scent. She makes it all herself or works with local artisans to create it."

"You're thinking that might work well with my lonely hearts club, too?"

"Yeah. It's romantic, isn't it?"

"Would guys buy those types of things for their loved ones?"

"Absolutely." He gave her a rueful smile. "I hate to say it, but it'd be quick for one thing. For another, they'd be sure of selecting the right present. Gifts aren't as easy for men as they are for women."

"I don't know. If you get into the right mindset, like saddles, bridles, boots, hats, or maybe fishing equipment or even a new electric tool for their workshop collection. I have to admit all of that can work for women, too."

He laughed with her.

She realized they were sharing another of those moments when everything around them simply disappeared in a haze. She inhaled, catching his musk-and-citrus scent again. The scent was as intimate as the moment.

"Anyway, I'm glad we came up with some ideas for you to play around with that don't include me." He pointed toward the back door. "Are you ready to go home?"

"Yes." She reached out and touched his bicep, feeling the muscle harden under her light touch. "Thanks. You've been so kind and such a big help, even after my cowgirl deception. I'll do my best to repay you."

"Your smile goes a long way in that direction." He covered her fingers with his warm, rough hand.

And her smile grew even bigger.

Chapter 13

KEMP DROVE TOWARD HALLELUJAH RANCH AT THE SLOWEST pace he could possibly maintain without causing traffic problems. Had he just met Violet earlier that day? It seemed like he'd known her forever, or as if he should've known her forever.

She sat beside him with the white boxes balanced on her lap. She appeared a little stiff, as if not sure what surprise came next in Wildcat Bluff County. Had he come on too strong? He hoped not, or maybe he was ready for her to know he was interested in her.

Still, she must be reeling after meeting so many new folks in one day. Each one was a little wilder than the last one. She probably felt a little tired and disoriented, although she seemed to adapt well to whatever was thrown at her. Good thing, too.

As he neared the ranch, he still didn't want to let her go. He wanted to solidify where they were, so they didn't slide back the next day or the day after that. She'd met enough people now, so she might reach out to them instead of him. He wanted to be her go-to person in the county. And he ought to be. She was staying on his ranch, and she was working as his cowgirl. He just needed to make sure she came to him first, if and when she needed something…as long as it wasn't posing for Cowboy Heart-to-Heart Corral.

He rattled across the cattle guard and hit the rutted road. He needed to fix the drive up to his ranch house, but it hadn't been a priority till now. He wanted it smooth for Violet, since she'd be coming and going across it. He didn't know when he'd get time, but he'd try to get to it soon. First, he had to fill in that big hole the trespassers had left. He'd try to get on that tomorrow.

He glanced over at her. Tonight, she was on his mind. He figured that most likely she'd be on his mind all the time now. A woman like her didn't just disappear when she was out of sight. She stayed put. And the way he was feeling, he didn't want her far from him, not in mind or body.

He slowed even more as he neared his house. Soft yellow light glowed from his porch light, same as the light on her front deck. On impulse, he stopped and looked at her.

"Do you want to come to my place? We could share a few pieces of candy."

"Now?" She glanced over at him, quiet and contained in the shadows of the truck's cab.

"Yes. It's still pretty early and…" He sighed, knowing he wasn't going about this right, but not about to give up either.

"I'd like to see the inside of your house, although now probably isn't the right time. I'm pretty tired, and I'm sure it's been a long day for you, too."

"I thought we could kind of unwind for a bit. Maybe wine instead of chocolate."

"Did you really think I'd share my chocolate?"

He smiled at her response because she hadn't outright rejected his suggestion. "Tell you what. There's a rose arbor on the patio at the side of the house. It's nice this time of night. Smells sweet. You might like it."

"Roses and wine?"

"Absolutely."

"Okay. I'll stop by for a little while, then I really need to get some sleep before I hit the ground running tomorrow as a cowgirl for a rancher."

He chuckled at her words. "Maybe he's more understanding than you think."

"We'll just have to wait and see."

He turned off the truck's engine. "I'll give you a tour of the house another time."

"That'd be great." She patted her white boxes. "Will my candy be safe if I leave it here?"

He smiled, nodding. "It's not bootlegger gold, so it should be safe."

"Good." She set her boxes on the floorboard before she opened her door.

When he got out, she met him in front of his pickup. He could already smell the roses because their scent grew stronger at night in the humidity.

He clasped her hand and was rewarded when she let him twine their fingers together. He walked with her to the side of the house, opened the small gate in the white picket fence, and led her under the white arbor that was heavy with crimson roses winding down and along the fence. He flipped on a lamp that cast light on the roses and left the patio in soft shadow.

Romantic. At least that's what he'd thought when he'd first seen it. He hadn't created it, but the area definitely had a woman's touch. Women were different. It's like they came fully formed, while men came as unformed clay that had to be worked and reworked into a viable form—or at least a form that women would accept. He hadn't cared much until now, but his life had changed since he met Violet. Now, he very much wanted her to like the roses. And him.

He led her over to an outdoor metal glider painted bright white that must have been from the twenties, since it had that look. It was big and comfy with plush, rose-tinted cushions that fairly begged to be shared on a night like tonight. He'd positioned a hand-carved cedar table there. It didn't match, but it worked when he wanted to sit outside with a drink.

"This is lovely." Violet held out her arms to either side to encompass the entire patio. "And it smells divine."

"Thanks. I can't take credit for creating it, but I like it." He gestured toward the glider. "Why don't you have a seat? I'll get us a couple glasses of wine. Muscadine okay?"

"Sounds good. Do you want help?"

"Just relax out here."

"I will." She sat down and moved the glider back and forth with one foot touching the terra cotta tile, smiling to herself in pleasure.

He watched her a moment, thinking she made the patio come alive, then he went inside and made his way to the kitchen. He liked Slade Steele's muscadine wine, so he always kept several bottles on hand. He opened one and poured a generous amount into two stemless wineglasses. He left the bottle on the countertop and made his way back outside.

She sat where he'd left her, moving back and forth with her head leaning against the high back of the glider, her eyes closed, obviously taking in the quiet of the night and the sweet scent of the roses. She was picture perfect. He really didn't want to disturb her, but she must have sensed him, because she raised her head, focused on him, and smiled with a soft look in her blue eyes.

As if she'd released him, he walked forward, sat down beside her, and handed her a glass.

She held up her wine. "Cheers."

He clinked his glass with hers.

"Oh yes." She tilted up the glass and took a sip.

He leaned back and drank his own wine, feeling relaxed, contented, and at peace. He could almost imagine the arbor had been created especially for her and had just been waiting for her arrival. He wasn't being his usual practical self, but there was just something about her.

"It's wonderful here." She spoke softly, voice husky with emotion. "I never dreamed it could be like this. I just felt compelled to come here."

"Mr. July?" He chuckled at the idea that his photo had brought her here, but he felt complimented now in a way he hadn't before this moment.

"Yes. You know that. But there was something else."

"What?"

"In Wildcat Bluff's cowboy firefighter calendar, there was such a wonderful sense of community, of comradery, of one-for-all and all-for-one."

"Now that you mention it, I can see that's true."

"It's exactly what I want to create in my lonely hearts club."

"You mean you didn't see any lonely hearts in the calendar?"

"Not a one."

"You're wrong."

"I am?"

He set his glass on the table and turned to her. "What about Mr. July?"

She set her glass down, too. "He appeared not to need a single other person in the whole wide world."

"You're wrong."

"I am?"

"What if Mr. July had a lonely heart?" He heard a sound out on the road, but he ignored it because he was so intent on Violet.

"Would he want to do something about it?"

Kemp smiled as he leaned toward her, reached up, and cupped her jaw with his long fingers, feeling her soft skin, seeing her eyes widen in surprise. He hesitated, giving her a chance to pull away, but she didn't. Instead, she leaned toward him, a smile matching his smile as their lips came close...so very close to their first kiss.

"Hey, Cuz!" a deep voice called from outside the patio. "You here all alone in the moonlight?"

Violet jerked back, looking toward the arbor in shock.

"Oh hell," Kemp muttered under his breath as he realized that sound he shouldn't have ignored was Lester's clunker of a pickup.

A tall, lithe form erupted from the arbor, all kinetic energy and muscular agility encased in tight Wranglers, blue snap shirt with white piping, and red alligator cowboy boots. He came to an abrupt stop at the sight of Violet and swept his white, high-crown cowboy hat off his head in a wide gesture that ended with the hat over his heart.

"As I live and breathe, the fair sex has come to save Hallelujah Ranch." He cast a hard look at Kemp. "Cuz, you didn't tell me you were courting the most beautiful woman in the whole of Texas."

"Violet, this is Cousin Lester Lander."

Les walked forward and dropped to one knee in front of her. "My dear, your beauty rivals the sun, moon, and stars. I'm forever in your debt for this moment to bask in your glow."

Violet put a hand to her mouth and gave a little giggle.

Kemp ground his teeth. He'd never gotten a girlish giggle from her. Trust Les to know how to do it. His cousin should look ridiculous on his knee, but somehow he could pull it off when no other man could—or even wanted to. Except now that he thought about it, he knew that the DJ named Wildcat Jack on the local radio station had about the same reputation as Les and the same effect on women. They both ought to be outlawed, but it'd never happen because women would never allow it.

"And you might be?" Les asked, leaning closer to Violet.

"I'm Violet Ashwood. I'm staying in Kemp's cabin for a few months."

"Lordy, you don't say." Les stood up, towering over them. "I'm in luck, since I'll be around a few months, too."

"What do you mean?" Kemp had an uneasy feeling about his cousin's sudden arrival. He doubted it could bode well.

"Truth of the matter, Mom kicked me out." Les appeared perfectly unconcerned about it.

"That's not the first time."

"She sent me here. She said I owed you after that Daisy Sue business."

"You don't owe me. Go home."

"Nope." Les gave Violet a big, white-toothed grin. "Scenery is a lot better here than at home."

"Don't let Aunt Dotty hear you say that."

"She said you needed help on your new ranch, and I was the one to do it." Les walked away, circled the patio as if he had too much energy to stand still, and turned back. "And so here I am." He flung his arms out to his sides.

"Where are you planning to stay? Not on my ranch." Kemp didn't figure his cousin would be around long, not if there was any work involved with it. He had a way of making money on the rodeo circuit and squirreling it away, so he had no real need to work at a steady job.

"Bertha, bless her heart, insists I stay with her."

Kemp chuckled at that idea.

"For the sake of love, or romance, one must sometimes ride the wild bronc, no matter the consequences." Les winked at Violet.

She smiled back, cocking her head to one side as she looked at him from head to toe.

Kemp knew what she was seeing in his cousin. Les had it all. Charm. Looks. Talent. And he got by on it. Maybe life was just so easy for him that he'd never settled down, even though he was pushing thirty-five. He was six two or so, with the broad shoulders that a cowboy developed from a lifetime of wrangling horses and the long, muscular legs for hanging on to the orneriest mounts. If that wasn't enough, he had thick, blond hair that he wore long and pale-blue eyes that were always dancing with some inner humor. Yeah, Les Lander was nothing but trouble for every male in his vicinity...and the last man Kemp wanted around Violet.

"I'm working on the ranch while I'm here," Violet said.

"Cowgirl work." Kemp sounded grumpy and knew it. "Les, that means I don't need you."

"Oh, Violet, loveliest of flowers," Les said. "That means we could work together."

"Right." Kemp glanced from one to the other. "Mucking out stalls and such…"

"Nothing sweeter than the scent of violets," Les said.

"We're having a little trouble on the ranch," Violet said as she glanced at Kemp.

He shook his head, trying to warn her off. Les was a trouble magnet. If trouble didn't exist, it'd appear as if by magic. In this case, they already had enough trouble without his cousin's special touch.

"Do tell." Les perked up, a gleam in his blue eyes.

"Trespassers," Violet said. "They're looking for bootlegger gold."

Les jerked his head toward Kemp. "There's lost gold on your ranch and you didn't tell me?"

"There's not any gold. It's just an old legend."

"I'll get a metal detector," Les said.

"No." Kemp stood up. "Les, I don't need any more trouble. You know how you are."

"I admit to nothing."

"What about that business with Daisy Sue?"

"Not my fault."

Violet stood up, too. "She's pregnant."

"Daisy Sue?" Les grinned and slapped his hat back on his head. "I'll pay my respects to the expectant mother."

"You don't know the Steele family," Kemp said.

"I'll meet them. And the beautiful Daisy Sue."

"She may have a troubled pregnancy, so I doubt they'll want any visitors," Kemp said.

"But I wouldn't be a visitor." Les smiled at Violet. "I'm practically family."

"You never even saw her," Kemp said. "I found her and brought her home."

"Still, I'm part of the legend, since you asked me to escort her to safety."

"But you didn't," Kemp said.

"Small matter."

Finally, Kemp gave it up and chuckled at his cousin's reasoning. No point in getting upset. Les was *that* cousin...and he always would be. Everybody loved him, and they always would, no matter what.

"I'd better go." Les grinned. "Bertha's waiting for me, and let me tell you, can she get impatient. Might stop by tomorrow to sort out work."

"Better call first," Kemp said. "I may be out in a back pasture."

"If I can't find you, I'm sure the lovely Violet will be around and can bring me up to speed."

"She'll be with me." Kemp dropped whatever good thoughts he'd had about his cousin. When it came to Violet, he obviously could be easily riled by another guy.

Les just grinned, then walked over and plucked a red rose from the arbor, brought it back, and handed it to Violet. "Good night, fair maiden. I'll see you soon." And then he was gone, letting the gate swing shut behind him.

Kemp watched Les jump in his truck and head down the lane with a trail of dark smoke snaking from the pickup's tailpipes in the moonlight. Kemp breathed a sigh of relief that Les was gone, although he knew it'd be short-lived, now that his cousin was in the county.

"So that's Cousin Lester," Violet said thoughtfully.

"Yeah."

"Do you suppose he might be interested in my lonely hearts club?"

Chapter 14

VIOLET DECIDED THE NEXT DAY THAT SHE HAD HER WORK cut out for her. Life couldn't be all about her dating site. She had obligations as a cowgirl. She might be a little confused about what that meant exactly, but she needed to get up to speed as quickly as possible. Kemp needed her to help him. She needed him to help her. Maybe they could meet in the middle and help each other.

First things first. She needed new clothes. Everything she'd brought would be messed up, if not outright torn up, working on a ranch. She realized that she'd been living in a fantasy world before she'd arrived at Hallelujah Ranch. Cowboys and cowgirls were a lot more than hats, boots, and Wranglers or horses, cattle, and range. They were all about grit, fortitude, and determination. And they knew how to work together to get a job done, no matter if it was taking care of cattle or fighting a fire. She didn't want to be a weak link in a community that pulled together to make life better for everyone.

She'd heard Kemp out and about by six in the morning. She figured most folks in the country were out of bed by five to take care of chores as they started their long days. He hadn't come to see her or ask for help. He was probably giving her time to acclimate, but she didn't want to be a burden. He needed help now. She'd been up for hours, too, working on her dating site as she pulled together ideas and copy from the single day she'd spent in Wildcat Bluff County. She'd met enough people and experienced enough events that she'd had to revamp a number of her ideas. She wanted real.

She intended to give it to those who were looking to move past fantasy images and find down-home folks who wanted to connect.

Now that it was time for local stores to open, she was ready to rock and roll. She needed everything to outfit herself as a hard-working cowgirl. She glanced down at her clothes. Skinny jeans and sparkly sweater with upscale cowgirl boots didn't cut it, but they were the best she could do on this particular mission. She'd return a whole new person, at least on the outside, and that was a good place to start her transformation to cowgirl.

She glanced around the cozy cabin and smiled. She liked it here, more than she could've imagined back in San Antonio. She'd thought her sleek, modern apartment there was just the ticket. Now she was getting different ideas about what made a lifestyle suitable to a person. She'd go back in three months, but she'd never see the city the same way again. And that suited her just fine. She wasn't just expanding the world of others with her lonely hearts club. She was expanding her own world as well.

She grabbed her purse and keys off the bar top, hesitated, and glanced around again. She felt as if she'd been waiting forever for life to take hold and transport her into a bigger world. No longer. She'd taken the reins of her own life and she was the driver now... not the passenger.

Outside, she sniffed the clean, fragrant air. Cows grazed on new green grass in the pasture. Birds trilled in treetops overhead. Real life. She gloried in it in a way she couldn't have imagined before arriving here. Heart to heart. That's what she felt, as if her heart were reaching out to the hearts around her...and all of life was responding in kind.

She hurried down the stairs and got into her SUV, anxious to get started with her day. She felt filled with energy, purpose, and expectation. Happiness lured her onward. She could hardly wait to discover what was around the next corner of country life.

She drove past Kemp's house, down the lane, and rattled across the cattle guard to the road that would lead her into the small town of Wildcat Bluff. Beauty everywhere, she soaked it up, as if she'd been waiting forever for it. She didn't play music. She didn't listen to news. She didn't think about the future. She simply reveled in the moment.

How different from the day before. She glanced at the seat where Mr. July's photo had kept her company on the long drive from San Antonio. She didn't need that photograph anymore. She had the real deal. He was so much more, so much better than her fantasy. And her life had taken on the vibrant hues of a rainbow instead of the muted shades of a computer screen.

When she hit Main Street, she smiled at the sight of the row of one- and two-story buildings built of pale stone and red brick nestled behind a white portico that covered a long, wooden boardwalk. Sunlight glinted off store windows. She felt as if she'd stepped back in time, into an Old West town like the ones she'd seen in tintype photographs. Yet everything appeared as fresh as if it'd been constructed yesterday. Folks here loved their town—it showed in the care they'd taken to preserve every little bit of it.

Wildcat Bluff Hotel anchored one end of the street. It was an impressive, two-story structure of red brick, with a grand entrance of cream keystones and brass planters filled with rosemary bushes. She slowly drove past it, looking for the store that would help her turn into a cowgirl. She saw Morning's Glory, Adelia's Delights, Lone Star Saloon, Thingamajigs, the Chuckwagon Café, and Gene's Boot Hospital. Pickups were nosed in all along the front of the café, but she pulled into an empty spot in front of the western wear store.

She stepped out of the car and headed for Gene's Boot Hospital. As she opened the store's door, she chuckled at the idea that she might someday actually need to bring in a pair of cowgirl boots for repair. Stranger things had happened, so she shouldn't laugh at the idea.

A bell on the door tinkled overhead as she stepped across the threshold. The colorful sight of clothes, boots, saddles, and bridles mingled with the scents of leather, fabric, and perfume. Heady stuff.

"What can I get you?" A tall, rangy, weathered cowgirl in plaid shirt, jeans, and boots drilled her with blue eyes crinkled at the corners from many a day on horseback in the sun.

Violet glanced down at her clothes, then back up. "I need some practical cowgirl clothes."

"For what?"

"Work."

"Ranch? Riding and roping? Rodeo?"

"I'm...well, I'm working at Hallelujah Ranch."

"Oh, Lord have mercy." She walked out from behind the counter and stopped in front of Violet. "Kemp Lander's lonely-hearts-club lady. Right?"

"I guess you could say that."

"Just did, didn't I?"

"It's that I wouldn't describe myself that way."

"No?" The salesperson grinned as she tossed a long strand of dark hair over one shoulder. "Not good enough for you?"

"I'm his cowgirl."

"Lordy, you got to just love life." She stuck out her hand. "I'm Birdy."

"Violet."

"Every single gal in town has had their eye on him since he came to town, but he's had no time for anything but work."

"I'm work oriented myself."

"They'd have cowgirled for free." Birdy narrowed her eyes. "He's paying you?"

"In a way."

Birdy looked her up and down. "If you've earned your cowgirl spurs, I'll eat mine."

"On-the-job training."

"This is too rich."

"I need work clothes."

"You do know that clothes don't make the woman?"

"I just need durable stuff."

"You need more than that, but I don't sell experience."

"Kemp's going to provide it."

Birdy hooted. "What kind?"

"Cowgirl stuff, of course."

"Of course." Birdy just shook her head. "I can outfit you. I'm happy to take your money. Beyond that, you're on your own."

"That's fine." Violet glanced around the store, wishing the encounter were going easier. Skepticism was one thing, but this was more than that. She just wasn't sure what.

"You're the talk of the town, you know."

"What?"

"Lonely hearts club." Birdy tossed her hair back again, as if she picked up the habit from interacting with horses all her life.

"I hope local folks are interested in the Cowboy Heart-to-Heart Corral."

"Interested? They're downright giddy."

"Really?"

"The ladies would be a lot happier if you hadn't corralled Kemp, but I figure you must know your business if right off the bat you got the guy nobody could get."

"I didn't get him."

"Hah. You're living on his ranch. You're working as his cowgirl. If you can't make hay with that, then you're in the wrong business."

"It's a professional relationship."

"Nothing is professional between men and women." Birdy looked Violet up and down again. "Besides, you've got good lines. Folks that deal with animals can't help but notice if you'd make a good mate or not."

Violet took a step back. All she wanted were some serviceable clothes, not an education in bloodlines as marriage material.

"He's in the market for a fine Hereford bull. Damn fool went for that breed instead of Angus."

"They're pretty."

Birdy grinned, revealing white teeth. "He's got his work cut out for him, doesn't he?"

"Guess so. Could you help me with clothes?"

"Happy to take your money. What's your size? Better let me pick out what you need. If you get into colors and style, we'll be here till Sunday and you still won't have what you need to work a ranch."

"Okay." Violet gave her sizes. She felt uneasy about the whole idea, but she couldn't disagree since she had no clue what to buy.

"Basically, I'll get you started with two sets of everything. Wranglers, Western shirts, leather belts, cowgirl boots. A jean jacket. When you see how they work out, you can come back and get more or something different. How does that sound?"

"Okay."

"Glad you've got the sense to listen to somebody with experience."

Violet watched as Birdy swiveled away and started picking up stuff from every part of the store. She looked to know her business, so that was a comforting thought in the midst of so much unknown.

Birdy returned and set the jeans, shirts, socks, and belts on the countertop. "If you hate the colors, tell me now."

"Blue is fine."

"You'd better try on the boots. No pointy toes for hard work."

"Thanks." Violet sat down on a nearby bench, opened the boot boxes, and quickly tried on both pairs.

"What do you think?"

"They're fine."

"Am I good or am I good?"

Violet glanced up with a grin. "You're good."

"Experience."

"Ring me up, please." She set the boots back in their boxes and set the boxes on the countertop.

Birdy set two red bandannas on top of the other merchandise, then quickly entered amounts in her cash register.

"Thanks." Violet paid for it all with her credit card and then picked up her packages.

"Anytime." Birdy leaned forward. "When you get ready, be sure and bring fliers here. I'll be happy to hand them out to folks...after I take my own first."

Violet smiled happily. "I'll do it. And thanks for the support."

"Don't you know? We cowgirls gotta stick together."

"You bet." She turned to leave, then stopped and looked back. "About Gene. Does he still repair boots?"

"Maybe in heaven. He was that good. But you're about a hundred years too late."

"Regret I missed him."

"Don't be. From all I heard, he was a miserable ole cuss but the best in the business." Birdy grinned. "Could've been dealing with all those Texas cowboys for years on end turned him sour."

Violet returned her grin. "I'll try not to turn sour."

Birdy chuckled. "Sweet thing like you with a hot thing like Kemp? Not a chance."

Violet laughed as she walked to the front door. She waved goodbye, then stepped outside. She really appreciated all the support for her lonely hearts club that she was getting from local folks. She'd been absolutely right in coming to Wildcat Bluff County.

And now all she needed to do was wow Kemp Lander with her new cowgirl duds.

Chapter 15

A WEEK LATER, KEMP WATCHED VIOLET MUCK OUT A STALL IN the horse barn. True to her word, she'd tackled becoming a cowgirl with gusto. She'd do the dirtiest jobs without complaint. She'd cleaned and oiled all his leather saddles and bridles. She kept oil and gas in his ATV, mowers, weed-eaters, and other equipment. She'd quickly figured out there was nothing glamorous about running a ranch, but it hadn't stopped her from doing her job as a cowgirl.

He was proud of her. Even more, he liked having her about the place. He liked seeing her quick grin when she learned a new skill. He liked sharing supper with her after a hard day's work. He just flat-out liked her. For that reason, he'd kept his distance, but he didn't think he could do that much longer. He was coming to know her body too well, seeing, dreaming, wanting. Right now, he saw a little skin through a rip in the right leg of her jeans. She hadn't bothered to iron her shirt, and she'd gotten a big, black stain on the blue fabric. She didn't clean her work boots anymore, so they had built-up cow and horse manure on the soles. Like other working ranchers, she just left them outside her front door at night.

All in all, she was fitting in like he'd never have dreamed possible when she'd first arrived at Hallelujah. She still had a long way to go before she was a real cowgirl, but that was a small matter when she was willing to learn and he was willing to teach. If she didn't have that lonely hearts club on her mind and taking up a good part of her life, he'd be completely content with the situation.

He hadn't seen Cousin Les after he'd stopped by to say Bertha had put him to work in her shop and they were overwhelmed with business. No wonder. Cowgirls from several counties were probably staking out the place for an encounter with Lester, and he'd enjoy it like crazy.

For the moment, all was okay in his life, so there was no need to go looking for trouble. It'd probably find him soon enough anyway. He left Violet with the rake and walked outside to see what needed to be done next.

As he stood there looking out across his land with satisfaction, he thought he smelled smoke. He glanced up at the clear blue sky, then turned in a circle, checking every direction and seeing nothing suspicious until he faced north, toward Destiny. A wisp of white smoke curled into the air. Fortunately, at the moment, there wasn't much of a breeze, so the fire wouldn't be driven toward his ranch or Destiny, but that could change at any moment.

He jerked his phone out of his pocket and called the fire station.

"Wildcat Bluff Fire-Rescue," Hedy Murray answered. "Kemp, what's up?"

"Smoke up toward Destiny. Did anybody alert you they were burning brush, tree stumps, anything?"

"No. And no one else has called it in. You'd better check it out."

"Will do. Smoke's a little too close to my ranch for comfort."

"What's over there?"

"Pasture...and an old, abandoned farmhouse. Decrepit. Dried up. Could be that."

"Can you get to it if it's on fire?"

"Seem to recall an old wood-and-wire gate. If fire doesn't block my path, I'll go in that way."

"Okay. I'll alert firefighters and send two rigs to get whatever it is under control."

"I'm on it."

He called Violet.

"Kemp, what is it?" she asked when she answered her cell phone.

"I'm going to check out a possible fire nearby."

"Oh no! What do you want me to do? I'll help."

"You're not trained for it. Right now, let the horses into the pasture close to the barn."

"Okay."

"Once they're safe, go to your cabin and wait for me there. Keep your car keys handy. If you need to get out of there, I'll call, or if I can't do it, somebody else will alert you."

"Okay." She inhaled sharply. "Kemp, stay safe."

"I will. Same to you." He cut the connection, stuffed his phone into his pocket, and focused on the matter at hand. He had cans, gear, and old towels in his truck he could use to start trying to contain fire the moment he got there.

He jogged over to his truck, jerked open the door, grabbed his keys from the floorboard, jumped in, started the engine, and made for Wildcat Road.

He didn't drive far before he turned onto a road that was as much grass as gravel. He bounced down the abandoned road going as fast as was safe till he reached the old gate. He leaped out and fast-walked to the fence. The smell of smoke was stronger now and the fire was picking up its pace judging by the layers of smoke he saw spiraling into the sky. House or pasture? He'd prefer the house because containment would be easier.

He raised the wire loop off the top of the gatepost, then jerked the bottom out of the lower loop, pulled the gate to one side, and anchored it against the barbwire fence so it wouldn't be in the way of rigs and firefighters.

He ran back to his pickup and drove toward the smoke. He was cautious, watching for danger in case the blaze was spreading across the pasture. When he reached the structure, he breathed a sigh of relief.

House fire, not grass. If firefighters arrived soon, they could contain it. He parked his truck in the pasture far enough away from the burning building so it wouldn't be in the way of the boosters or get caught up in the blaze itself.

He got out, looked around, didn't see any more flames anywhere, and breathed another sigh of relief. If he hadn't been outside and smelled the smoke…

But he had been and the house wasn't fully engulfed yet, although heat radiated outward. The structure was a dried-out husk of gray, weathered wood, more firetrap than anything. It probably hadn't been used, even to store hay or equipment, for ages. And then he had a thought. Had somebody been squatting there, maybe building a campfire? Was someone still inside?

He jerked open the back door of his pickup, reached in, and pulled out a high-visibility orange-and-yellow parka. Fortunately, he was wearing tough boots and jeans. He exchanged his cowboy hat for a hard hat. He slipped on the jacket, tucked leather gloves into his pocket, and slung a fire extinguisher by its strap over each shoulder.

He cautiously approached the house, evaluating as he checked around the perimeter. No glass left in the windows, so the dry wood was fully exposed to oxygen, allowing it to burn fast. The blaze was expanding in size, pumping smoke from a window at one corner.

Every fire had a personality of its own. This one felt almost surprised, as if it hadn't been prepared to eat up a house.

Heat lapped at him, along with smoke, as he moved closer, trying to get a better look at what was going on.

He caught a glimpse through the smoke that grass near the corner was starting to burn. He wasn't a moment too soon.

He pulled a can off one shoulder, went closer, and aimed the nozzle. He sprayed down the bare ground and tall grass at the burning corner, knocking back the flames as he edged closer to the open window to get a better look.

He bumped something with the toe of his boot and glanced down. The long handle of a metal detector protruded from the charred grass.

It hit him. He bet the gold hunters had been staying right here near his land, using the abandoned house as a base. It was a good idea, from their viewpoint. He'd never have thought to look for them here. He also bet they'd used a camp stove inside, and the fire had gotten out of control.

He sprayed around the window, but it was too hot to get closer. He looked around for the gold hunters, but he figured they had run away, leaving a dangerous fire in their wake. But he'd seen the smoke in time, before it spread across pastures and hurt not only land and buildings, but animals and people as well. Now he had more reason than ever to make sure the trespassers had a real close encounter with Sheriff Calhoun.

He continued his walk around the perimeter, moving farther and farther back as the fire consumed more of the structure. He didn't see anyone, but he found trash in the form of fast-food wrappers, a grungy towel, and one dirty sock left behind by the squatters.

He stepped away, spraying as he went, while flames and smoke surged higher and higher into the blue sky.

He checked the wind. They had a slight breeze from the south now that was pushing the fire north. There wouldn't be any saving the structure. Containment was what mattered now.

When he heard the wailing of sirens out on Wildcat Road, he felt a surge of energy and relief. Firefighters were on the job. The fire wouldn't spread, no lives would be lost.

He looped the can's strap back over his shoulder and jogged out to meet his friends.

The first booster came barreling through the open gate with lights blazing and sirens shrieking. A second one followed right behind it. They stopped side by side at a safe distance from the house.

At times like these, Kemp knew all the fire department benefit events were worth the effort—and that included the calendars—because they had good equipment that serviced an entire county.

Hedy hadn't sent the red engine with a two-thousand-GPM pump capacity and one thousand gallons of water with thirty gallons of class A foam, but it was available for big jobs. She'd sent two of the smaller booster trucks that had three-hundred-GPM pump capacity and 250-gallon water tanks. The two rigs should be enough. They wouldn't need to call in the engine or pump extra water from a pond or stock tank due to the absence of fire hydrants in the countryside.

Sydney Steele stepped down from the driver's side of the first rig. She wore full turnout gear in bright yellow, including a protective helmet and thick gloves. Cole Murphy leaped from the other side of the booster and hurried to the back of the rig. Two other firefighters jumped down from the other booster and hurried to the back of it.

"Glad to see you," Kemp said as he reached them.

"Anything we ought to know?" Sydney started disbursing the roll of hose from the reel on the back of the booster.

"Far as I can tell, nobody's here," Kemp said. "I think it may have been squatters with a campfire or camp stove that got out of hand."

"It happens." Cole grasped the nozzle while the line continued to unspool. "Instead of kicking dirt or pouring water over the flames, they just run off and leave it."

"Folks don't understand how quickly fire can spread, particularly if there's even a slight breeze," Sydney said.

"We try to educate the public," Cole called as he headed toward the house with the nozzle of his line from the other rig.

"We need more outreach. Maybe in the schools," Kemp said as he stepped away from the rigs, so he could move around the house and control stray sparks that might escape and start a brush fire. He slipped his extinguisher off his shoulder and prepared to spray if necessary.

Sydney expertly waved the nozzle of her hose and expelled

high-velocity water on the house. She braced with both feet, because the hose had to be held stable or it could twist, turn, and buck like a wild rodeo bull. The other firefighters kept up a steady flow with the line from the booster's water tank. Smoke and steam rose upward from the house as the streams of water fought back the flames.

While the others kept up their water barrage, Kemp sprayed foam on stray sparks here and there in the tall weeds. He glanced up at the house to check the status. Good news—they were beating back the fire, despite the orange and yellow flames spitting and licking and clawing to take back what they gave up.

He emptied one can, tossed it aside, and aimed the nozzle of the other one he carried, well aware of the heat, steam, crackling fire, and firefighters hollering to each other as they brought the fire under control.

Finally, they all backed away from the house while they watched the dwindling blaze. Water hissed as it hit the smoldering remains of what had once been a family's home. Pops and cracks and groans and crashes filled the area as the house slowly collapsed in a blackened heap of debris, leaving one corner starkly upright.

"Good stop." Sydney glanced around the group.

"Thanks," Kemp said. "That fire was getting out of hand. If y'all hadn't gotten here so fast, I might've lost structures on my ranch."

"Not to mention the blaze could've roared up to Destiny," Cole said.

"You deserve credit for alerting us so quick." Sydney looked in the direction of the small town. "That would've been a major loss to the county. Don't even want to think about it," Sydney said. "All's well that ends well."

"Yeah." Kemp sighed in relief and then gave a chuckle to ease the tension. "Do any of you really think that fire would've dared give the Buick Brigade trouble?"

Sydney laughed. "Good point. Guess the town was never in danger."

"Right." Cole smiled as he looked in the direction of Destiny, too.

"Meant to ask," Kemp said. "How is Daisy Sue coming along?"

Sydney's humor drained away. "We're keeping her in the barn, so she doesn't exert herself. Ann prescribed extra vitamins and special feed. We're all hoping Daisy Sue doesn't lose her baby."

"How's Storm taking it?" Kemp asked.

"In stride," Sydney said. "You know my determined offspring."

"Sure do," Kemp said.

"She says all will be well." Sydney moved back toward the booster, bringing the hose with her. "We ought to believe her. She's the one who never lost faith when most of us thought Fernando was gone for good."

"Sure enough," Cole said. "He arrived home on Christmas, just like she said he would."

"She never lost hope that Daisy Sue would get safely home, too." Kemp walked with the group back to the boosters.

"Thanks again," Sydney said. "You made that possible."

"Regret it took so long."

"All's well that ends well…just like this fire," Cole said.

Kemp watched as the hose wound back up on the boosters, feeling glad he had such good friends.

"Why don't you get on back to your ranch?" Sydney said. "Cole can stay here to catch any stray sparks or hot spots. I want to check on Storm and Daisy Sue."

"If you want, I can contact Sheriff Calhoun." Kemp glanced around the group for confirmation.

"Don't bother," Cole said. "We'll be here, so I'll call him."

"Make sure y'all bag that as evidence." Kemp pointed toward the long handle in the blackened grass.

"What is it?" Sydney asked.

"Metal detector," Kemp said. "I wonder if the trespassers on my ranch haven't been staying here."

"Gold hunters?" Sydney asked. "You'd think by now they'd get the message there's no buried treasure on Hallelujah."

"Yeah," Kemp replied, agreeing. "But I've been plagued with those guys leaving big holes on my ranch lately."

"Does the sheriff know?" Cole asked.

"He knows, but so far there's not much he can do." Kemp shrugged, wishing he could catch them in the act. "Anyway, they've lost their happy home now."

"Maybe they'll give up," Sydney said.

"Either way." Cole walked closer to the metal detector. "We'll make sure we bag it and check inside the structure for whatever might be left after the fire."

"Thanks." Kemp glanced around the group again. "Do you need me for anything else?"

"Not us." Sydney grinned, a teasing glint in her blue eyes. "You might want to relieve your cousin Lester since he's bound to be getting a little frayed around the edges with all that female attention."

"Les?" Kemp laughed. "Not likely. At least Bertha doesn't have to worry about him eating all the candy."

"Why not?" Sydney asked.

"Just between us, he *hates* chocolate."

And with laughter ringing in his ears, Kemp headed for his truck, wanting to get back to Violet and let her know that all was well.

Chapter 16

VIOLET CLAPPED HER HANDS, RUNNING THE LAST OF THE SIX horses that had been in the barn into the nearby pasture. She glanced up at the smoke spiraling into the sky. It was too close for comfort, but she'd heard the sirens, so she knew firefighters were on the job. Kemp hadn't called her, but he'd said he wouldn't unless there was danger to her and the animals. She could only assume they were getting the blaze under control.

She closed the gate, but she lingered outside the fence near the horses because they were uneasy with the scent of smoke in the air. Suddenly, they all threw up their heads and thundered away from the direction of the fire toward the back corner of the pasture. She nodded in approval. Instinct told them to get as far away as possible, and they'd heeded the message. Now she could go to her cabin, which was her safe place.

She closed the barn door before she walked past Kemp's house and up the stairs of her cabin. No birdsong greeted her in the trees above. They'd all flown to safety, much like animals on the ground must have run away. She opened the front door, snagged her car keys from on top of the bar, and stepped back outside. She sat down in the rocker. She didn't want to be confined inside the house. She set her phone on the small table so she didn't chance missing a call.

She wondered if Lady Mauve had ever sat outside watching for revenuers or bootleggers making their runs or maybe she'd held her silver serving spoon ready to dish up enticing food. No way to know after so long a time. It didn't even matter anymore, except that it made her realize how she worried about Kemp's safety as Lady Mauve must have worried here, too.

When had Kemp come to mean so much to her? Had it been from the first moment she'd seen his photograph, or from the first moment he'd looked into her eyes in real life? Or that electrifying moment in the rose arbor when he'd almost kissed her? She wished Lester hadn't interrupted them. If he hadn't, maybe she'd know now if her emotions were based in reality or fantasy. A kiss would tell her. Surely a single kiss, his lips to her lips, would reveal the absolute truth.

She sighed, wanting his kiss, wanting reality not fantasy. She wanted him safely home with her. And then, he was. He drove under the Hallelujah Ranch sign, up the lane, and pulled to a stop in front of her cabin.

She jumped to her feet and hurried down the stairs, feeling her heart beat faster as he stepped out of his truck. He looked tired and dirty, but safe and sound. She took long strides toward him.

When he heard her footsteps, he glanced up. A slow, hot smile curved his lips. He jerked off his cowboy hat, hitting the crown against his thigh to knock off debris, put it back on, and shut the door of his truck with the heel of one boot.

"If you aren't a sight for sore eyes, I don't know what is." He looked her over from head to toe.

She glanced down at her torn and stained shirt and jeans. She chuckled. "If you like a dirty cowgirl, then I'm all set."

He grinned. "You look perfect."

"I won't hold you up. I just wanted to make sure you and the other firefighters are okay."

"We're fine. Fire's under control." He held out a hand. "Come on up to the house and I'll tell you about it."

"I don't want to get in your way. I'm sure you'd like to get cleaned up and eat and whatever."

He cocked his head to one side, still smiling. "I'd like nothing better than to talk with you, although I do need a shower."

She could just see a wet and wild cowboy firefighter, totally naked as he stood under a spray of water. The image was even better than the one in her calendar. She smiled in return, hoping he couldn't read her mind.

"You can rustle up some food while I clean up."

"I could run over to the Chuckwagon and pick up ribs or hamburgers or something."

"No need. Chuckwagon leftovers are waiting for us in my fridge."

"How can I say no to leftovers?"

"Chuckwagon grub is even tastier after it sits a bit." He gestured toward the house.

"I *would* like to hear about the fire."

"Good. I've got some news I want to share."

"Really?"

"Shower first."

"Right." She was anxious to hear what he had to say, but she was hungry, too...well, for food *and* the sight of him in his shower. At least she could take care of one of her hungers.

She walked with him to his front door. He opened it and gestured for her to precede him.

She took several steps up to the small portico, then walked inside onto an oak-slat floor that had to be original. The living room had three tall, narrow windows on the front. Three wide windows on the east wall had deep window sashes painted bright white, a striking contrast to the warm ochre of the walls.

He had drawn the blinds up to the top. Muted evening light softened the contours of the room. The high ceiling was covered with floral-patterned tin tiles painted white. All in all, it was a warm and cozy room. A large area rug in a brown-and-rust leaf pattern spread out under a dark-brown leather sofa and a matching love seat. But her eyes were drawn to an antique Tiffany lamp set on a small Art Deco table beside a leather recliner.

As she walked over to the colorful lamp, she heard Kemp step inside and shut the door behind them.

"That's not a real Tiffany." He pulled off his boots and held them in one hand as he moved over to her. He turned on the lamp. "But it's vintage from the 1920s. Several companies mimicked the Tiffany lamp style in cheaper, lesser quality models."

"It's still beautiful." She admired the poinsettia globe's vibrant colors and the flower-accented brass base.

"I wish it were the real deal." He shook his head as he stroked fingertips across the glass globe. "I'd be in the money to the tune of maybe a million bucks."

"Really?"

"The real deal is pretty rare."

"How do you know so much about Tiffany lamps?"

He gestured around the room. "I've added a few pieces to the house, but I bought the place furnished and I've left it mostly like I got it."

"Someone really loved this place, didn't they?"

"Looks like it." He stepped through an open doorway. "In here is the kitchen. It's updated, so it's easy to use."

She followed him and glanced around the long area that utilized the same colors as the living room. White cabinets, white appliances, and a white with brown-vein pattern marble countertop dominated the kitchen that led to floor-to-ceiling triple bay windows. In front of the windows nestled a small handmade cedar table with matching chairs that had red-and-white-checked cushions.

"This is wonderful. I love the windows. It's such a beautiful, cozy breakfast nook." She walked over, glanced to the right, and saw an oak staircase that led upward.

"My bedroom and bath are up there," he said. "There's a big closet that I think used to be a small bedroom."

"Makes sense. Some people do that in older homes with small rooms."

"Why don't you get Chuckwagon out of the fridge while I get a shower? We can eat in here. There's a formal dining room, but I don't use it much."

"Go ahead." She turned and looked at him. "This place is just as great as the cabin."

"Glad you like it. I'll add furniture as I go along and probably make some changes later, but for now, it'll do."

"Mind if I take a look around?"

"Go right ahead," he said as he bounded up the stairs.

She stood very still as she looked out the window over a green pasture, realizing that she was in Mr. July's space. It was his very own home with all the personal and private things that made his life complete. She couldn't have imagined such a thing in San Antonio. Actually, she couldn't have imagined it before this moment. Kemp was so much more than his photo, so much more than Mr. July, so much more than a hot body. He was a first responder, and that made him kind, considerate, and willing to put his life on the line for others. She realized now that the cowboy firefighter calendars were a tribute to the cowboys who made life so much better for everyone.

She turned around and walked back through the kitchen, noting the countertops were clean of clutter, as if he didn't use the area much or mostly brought home takeout. She'd be happy to put something together for them. But again, it didn't seem real, didn't seem possible that she was here with the man of her dreams, the man she'd planned for so long to be the face and body that would make her lonely hearts club appeal to women everywhere.

And yet…how could she contemplate sharing him now that she knew him?

She walked into the living room, her footsteps on the oak floor sounding loud in the stillness of the house.

Night was falling fast outside, purple shadows closing in. Birds were singing their last songs of the day before they went to perch until dawn.

She moved through open folding doors and realized she'd been in the sitting room, or parlor as it had been called in the old days. Now she was in the living room at the front of the house with another set of deep bay windows, but otherwise, it was absolutely empty.

She could only imagine that it might once have contained beautiful Art Deco furniture. She supposed the former owners had probably taken the furniture for their own homes or sold it to others. She wished she'd seen those pieces, but she did appreciate the spacious area. She thought about going to Dallas and finding special pieces to fill the room, not only with furniture, but with love and laughter as well.

And yet…this was Kemp's home that he didn't share.

She walked into the dining room. A simple oak table with six matching chairs had been centered under a bronze geometrically shaped chandelier with six candle bulbs inside it.

She opened the door to a small room that he obviously used as an office, with contemporary furniture and a large computer screen on a desk to hook up to his laptop. And next she found an updated bathroom that had white bead board halfway up the walls, a white marble cabinet top, and an enclosed shower.

From there, she discovered a sunroom with a row of back windows and a door that led onto the patio. She opened the patio door and caught the sweet scent of roses in colors ranging from yellow to coral to peach to crimson still visible in the last rays of the setting sun. A white wicker set of sofa, chair, recliner, and table with indoor plants made the room a perfect place to read or sit with a loved one. It was a very romantic room.

Tour over, she went back to the kitchen. If she was smart, she'd stay professional, put her feelings and desires aside, and find a way to persuade Kemp to help her with Cowboy Heart-to-Heart Corral.

She looked in the refrigerator and saw several white containers that she figured were Chuckwagon takeout, so she pulled them out and set them on the countertop. She quickly sliced sausage and brisket to reheat along with baked beans to serve with potato salad and fried okra. A whole pecan pie completed the meal.

She found cotton placemats and napkins that matched the cushions on the chairs and set them on the table. She added red stoneware plates, silverware, and red glasses with water to the placemats. By now she knew the decorator of the cabin had left her mark on this house, too, because she'd obviously loved the color crimson.

She scooped veggies into separate bowls and set them on the table. She placed the meat on a platter and put it in the microwave. She'd wait to heat it until Kemp came back downstairs, so it wouldn't get cold. She cut two big pieces of pie and slid them onto dessert plates. Last but not least, she opened a bottle of wine and poured the liquid into two stemless wineglasses.

She stepped back and eyed her handiwork. The meal looked pretty and delicious at the same time. She stopped and glanced around as reality struck her. She'd just prepared a meal for Kemp—Mr. July—and it'd seemed like the most natural thing in the world.

As if that very thought conjured him, she heard the wooden stairs creak and glanced up.

Kemp descended on bare feet. He appeared as delicious as the food, his dark hair damp and curling slightly above his shoulders. He'd slipped on a Wildcat Bluff Fire-Rescue T-shirt that fit snugly across his muscled chest along with a pair of gray sweatpants. How could dinner compare?

"Looks good." He stopped beside the table. "You hungry, too?"

"Oh yes. Looks really good." She inhaled the scent of sage-and-citrus soap. "And I'm starved...absolutely starved."

Chapter 17

"Let me heat the barbeque." She whirled away to get him out of sight and collect her senses from his powerful effect.

"Thanks."

She hit a button on the microwave and watched the plate inside turn around and around.

"What you did with the table—it doesn't just look like good food," he said. "It's pretty, too."

"I found pretty things in the cabinets. I hope you don't mind me getting them out to use."

"Mind? No way. I won't usually go to the trouble, but I do like to see a nice table like the women in my family set."

"It wasn't much trouble." She picked up a red potholder, slid the platter out of the microwave, carried it to the table, and set it on a red-and-white-checked tile trivet.

"Good. I wouldn't want to work you." He grinned with a mischievous glint in his eyes. "At least, not work you in here. The ranch is a different matter." He pulled a chair out from the table for her.

She smiled back as she sat down, realizing he'd been trained like most cowboys in polite manners.

He eased into the chair on the other side of the table, picked up his napkin, and placed it in his lap.

As they loaded up their plates, silence descended on the kitchen and night fell outside the bay windows, turning the landscape into mysterious shades of darkness highlighted here and there by moonlight.

"Delicious." Violet forked another bite of potato salad into her mouth. "Chuckwagon really is good food."

He nodded as he speared a piece of sausage. "They do a big business in the county. Folks even come from Dallas and Fort Worth, and those people know their barbeque."

"San Antone and the Hill Country aren't exactly slouches when it comes to barbeque either. This is excellent."

"Guess it all depends on the cooks, the meat, the sauce. That's what draws folks back time and again."

"I'm glad. I like the Steele family. Ranch. Café. Fernando the Wonder Bull."

Kemp chuckled, shaking his head. "Storm may be just nine years old, but she doesn't let any grass grow under her feet when it comes to promoting that famous bull."

"Is there any news on Daisy Sue's condition?"

"Watch and wait, far as I know. Everybody's concerned she's not having an easy time of it. Fernando's fans are getting more concerned by the day."

"How did Storm create such a big fan base for Fernando?"

"He did it himself. He was rustled and, against all odds, escaped captivity and walked across North Texas to get home by Christmas."

"I remember that story on the news."

"His bravery and determination caught everyone's attention."

"And now Daisy Sue is doing the same thing."

"Yeah." Kemp set his fork down on his empty plate. "And just wait till their kid comes along."

"I hope I'm still here for the big event." She stood and picked up their empty plates.

"You better be. You're committed to Hallelujah Ranch for three months."

She glanced back at him. He looked serious, no teasing in his voice or his expression. "I need to get my project off the ground."

He sighed and leaned back in his chair. "You haven't given up on me, have you?"

She set the plates on the countertop, then walked back and sat down across from him. "That's why I'm in Wildcat Bluff County."

He pulled the plate with his piece of pie close to him and dug in with a fresh fork.

She followed his action, but she didn't feel so hungry now.

He ate a couple of bites before he set down his fork. He looked out the windows, then back at her. "Maybe we can compromise."

"What do you mean?" She felt her taste come back with the advent of sudden hope. She cut a piece of pie, tucked the wedge into her mouth, and sighed at the wonderful taste.

"You've come a long way. You've made a strong commitment. You've invested a lot of time and effort in something you're obviously passionate about."

"I am. Everyone deserves true love."

He raised an eyebrow. "What about you?"

"Me?"

"True love."

"I'm looking for others…not myself."

"Why not?"

"It's just that I've never been lucky in love."

"I can't imagine why not."

"Let's let it go at that." She forked another bite of pie into her mouth, but she'd lost her taste for it again.

"I don't see how you can promote something you don't believe in."

"I *do* believe in it."

"Prove it." He leaned toward her with a challenging gleam in his green eyes.

"Prove it?" She leaned back, wanting to get away from that gleam because it looked like nothing but trouble. "How?"

"Kiss me."

She took a deep breath, wanting that very thing and not wanting it at the same time. Mr. July was getting more dangerous to her heart every moment she was in his company.

"Chicken?"

"No. Of course not. It's just—"

"You're not willing to put yourself on the line."

"I didn't think you were interested in—"

"I'm not interested in posing for your website, but I *am* interested in you."

"Oh." She felt her face flush at his words as heat rushed through her entire body.

"I thought you might be interested in an experiment, seeing as how you've come all this way."

"Experiment?"

He tossed his napkin on the table, stood up, and held out his hand to her. "Join me in the moonlight?"

"Have you been taking lessons from Cousin Lester?"

He chuckled, eyes lighting up with inner fire. "If I were, he'd think me a poor pupil. He's a sixty-second wonder."

She smiled, feeling glad he'd taken her joke in stride.

"Let's go out on the patio and discuss our options." He stepped closer to her with his hand still held out.

She gestured toward the dirty plates and table full of dishes. "Shouldn't we clean up?"

"It can wait. I can't."

That sold her. She grasped his hand, palm to palm, as she stood up. She could feel the roughness of his skin, see the stubble of his beard, and smell the soap he'd used in his shower. It was all heady stuff.

He led her into the sunroom, turned on a lamp for soft illumination, and opened the back door so that pale light spilled outside. The scent of roses in bloom filled the night air and moonlight cast a silvery glow over the patio.

"Why don't you sit on the glider while I go back and get our wine?"

"Okay." She really couldn't say more as she watched him go inside because she felt as if her heart were in her throat.

When he returned, he handed her a glass, clinked hers with his, and nodded as if he'd made a decision.

She took a sip and returned his smile. She felt good, happy, contented. It was a mild, sweet-scented spring night with a handsome man by her side. If she could convey this setting, this feeling, to her lonely hearts club, she felt sure people would positively respond in droves.

"I ought to get this out of the way." He sat down beside her, set his glass on the table, and turned to look at her with a question in his gaze.

"What?"

"I'm not sure how much to tell you about the fire."

"Is it a secret?"

"No...but I don't want to worry you. On the other hand, I want you to stay safe."

"Now you *are* worrying me."

"Okay. Here's the deal." He spread his hands wide. "We found a metal detector beside the burning house."

"Oh no." She set her glass beside his on the table, going serious in an instant. "Do you think the intruders..."

"No way to know for sure, but it seems likely they were using that old abandoned farmhouse to hide out in. It'd put them pretty near my ranch, so they could come and go whenever they wanted to search for metal and dig with the backhoe."

"Makes sense. Did you see anything else that'd give you a clue to their identities?"

"No. Structure was a total loss, but the sheriff and firefighters will check the ruins when it cools down. I figure the trespassers had a camp stove or built a campfire and the blaze got away from them."

"They might have been smoking, too, and dropped a cigarette or didn't snuff out a burning butt."

"That, too." He picked up his glass and sipped wine. "Doubt we'll ever know for sure."

"I'm glad you told me."

"I want you to stay safe. Be aware outside."

"I will."

"We just don't know how far they'll go or how much they'll escalate."

"You need to be careful, too."

"I will." He leaned toward her. "Now, about your lonely hearts club…"

She leaned toward him. "Yes?"

"Do you really need me?"

"I want you." She immediately wished she'd chosen different words.

"I want you, too." He set down his glass. "What are we going to do about it?"

"I meant—"

"I know what you meant, but can't you mean something more, something personal, something just between us?"

She felt her heart pick up speed. She caught his gaze…and felt as if she'd always belonged here in this moment with this man.

"Something special?"

She had to respond, but she couldn't find the words. If he looked at her with any more heat in his eyes, she might spontaneously combust. "I…" And then she threw caution to the wind, leaned forward, and kissed him. It was just a soft, fleeting, tender touch before she moved back.

"I hope that was only an appetizer." He grasped her shoulders with both hands and gently tugged her toward him.

She leaned into him, feeling his heat, his strength, his power. She wanted it all. She didn't want to compromise. She raised her face, waiting for his kiss…waiting…waiting…

"I want you to know that I don't do this lightly. I know you really only want me for your lonely hearts club. I know you'll go back to San Antonio when you get what you want here. I know all that, and I still want to kiss you. I need to kiss you. I plan to kiss you. It's just that I'm a serious kind of guy. I want you to know I'm not like Cousin Lester. And—"

"Kemp, I swear if you say one more word, I'm taking the pie and going home."

He grinned, chuckling. "You'd take the pie? That's serious."

"Yes, it is. And I'm serious, too." She put her palms, one on each side, on his face. "Please, just kiss me."

And he did…tender at first, then with growing passion until he lifted her up, set her on his lap, leaned her head back against his arm, and held her tightly.

She felt his heat and strength and desire build as one kiss followed another and he delved deeply into her mouth, hugged her closer and closer as if desperate to meld their bodies so they could never be separate again.

Finally, he raised his head, kissed the tip of her nose, gave her a slight smile. "And I thought the fire was hot."

Chapter 18

Kemp gazed at Violet. He'd come a long way in a week, from a cowboy who wanted nothing more than to secure his ranch to a cowboy with a not-ready-for-primetime-cowgirl dominating his thoughts. She wasn't just hotter than the fire he'd fought—she was sweeter than the roses scenting the air around them. Hot and sweet. Sexy and sassy. Smart and tender. Was he a goner and hadn't known it until now?

He didn't have time for love. A little slipup one way or another and he could lose his ranch. He had gold hunters trespassing, digging holes, and now setting a fire, whether intentional or not. He didn't want to deal with danger or legends or lonely hearts clubs. He just wanted to run his ranch, make enough money to secure it, and maybe, now and again, head down to Wildcat Hall, his favorite honky-tonk, to enjoy a bit of fun. But now?

"Did you know your bottom lip fairly begs to be nibbled on?" she asked.

"No." He barely got the single word out when his entire body went rigid while the blood in his brain rushed south. If he'd thought hot before, now he knew he'd been wrong. Inferno…nothing less.

"No one has ever told you that before?"

"Never."

"Well, it's true. I've thought so since I first saw that picture of you."

"You noticed my lower lip?"

"Well, not at first." She traced his lip with her fingertip while she cocked her head to one side as if considering her next move.

He was waiting for it and thought it was kind of like not knowing what a wild critter would do next but watching in fascination for it to happen.

"Your lip came later." She changed from her fingertip to the pad of her thumb, rubbing back and forth, back and forth, as she created heat and friction and excitement. "I'm glad I'm the first woman who truly understands your lower lip. And its needs."

"It's not the only part of me with needs."

"Really?"

"Oh yeah, really."

"Do you want your lip nibbled on?" She glanced from his mouth to his eyes as she gave him a mischievous smile.

"Yes." And he gave her the hottest look that he figured he'd ever had in his eyes.

"Do you want *me* to do it?"

"Yes."

"Now?"

"Yes."

She cocked her head again, as if considering whether or not to actually do it.

He grew completely still, waiting, wondering, wanting. She had him on tenterhooks and looked to be enjoying the power. Little minx. Truth be told, he enjoyed being teased by her.

She leaned toward him—oh so slowly—as she slid her hand to his jaw and cupped it with long, warm fingers to hold him in place.

When he felt her stroke his bottom lip with the tip of her tongue, he didn't believe he'd ever known anything more erotic...until she lightly set her teeth to his sensitive flesh and gently nibbled from one corner of his mouth to the other, then plied his swollen lip with her wet tongue, upping the sensuality as she licked and nibbled to her heart's content before she finally sucked his lower lip into her hot mouth.

He wasn't made of iron. He was all red-blooded male. And

she'd set him on fire with her wild ways. He'd had enough of teasing and tormenting. He kissed her, thrusting into her mouth to give her a taste of her own desire. When he felt her respond, arms snaking around his shoulders, he lifted her up, slipping down the glider until he was prone on his back and she was above him. And then he gently let her down the length of him, body to body, and cupped her rounded bottom to pull her into his hardness…needing her in a way he'd never needed anyone before.

She cradled his face with both hands, exploring it with her lips, her tongue, until she turned and nibbled his earlobe, teasing the contours with the tip of her tongue before she pressed hot kisses down his neck to the hollow there.

He moved his hands upward, learning her body by touch alone…all the soft curves that beckoned to be followed by his mouth. He craved her like she craved chocolate.

"Upstairs," he finally said on a groan.

She lifted her head to look him in the eyes. "What's upstairs?"

"Bed." He realized he'd been reduced to single words because his mind was functioning on about two brain cells.

"Is the cover crimson?" She gave a little quirk of her lips.

"Red."

"Perfect. I find I've grown attached to that color since living in your cabin."

"Attached, yes…" He'd become real attached to the woman living in that cabin, but he didn't say those words because he heard an all-too-familiar sound outside.

"What's that awful racket?" She cocked her head as she glanced at the rose arbor.

"I can't believe it. I absolutely cannot believe it." Every cell in his brain abruptly came online.

"What?"

He gently lifted her so they could sit side by side on the glider.

"What?"

"Les. That's his old clunker of a pickup. He won't buy anything better because he says he likes to know that a cowgirl loves him for himself, not a fancy truck."

"Well, I can't believe he's here either." She crossed her arms over her chest, as if in defense. "He's got the worst timing in the universe."

"Tell me about it."

Lester picked that moment to burst through the open arbor, all tall, long-legged strength and powerful shoulders. He came to an abrupt stop in front of Violet with his hands behind his back. He wore form-fitting, creased Wranglers, with a green-and-white-checked Western shirt with white pearl snaps, along with his trademark red alligator boots and a white cowboy hat. He'd tied his long, blond hair at the nape of his neck with a leather thong.

"What are you doing here?" Kemp asked, sounding testy and not caring about it.

"I come bearing a gift." Like a magician, Lester held out a big white box with the Destiny Chocolatier logo embossed in gold on it. "Violet, I bring this present to you straight from the chocolate shop. I picked out every single piece myself, so they're all the best of the best."

"Oh my," she said, smiling.

"Give that here." Kemp stood up and held out a hand.

"It's not for you." Lester took a step back.

"I'll take it." Kemp took a step forward, not sure why, but he was suddenly furious that Les had the nerve to buy candy for *his* cowgirl.

"No." Lester turned toward Violet, still holding the box.

Kemp clamped a hand on one edge of the box of chocolates.

"Let go." Lester jerked the box toward him.

Kemp jerked it back. Soon they were in a tug-of-war.

"Will you two stop it?" Violet got to her feet. "Just give the candy to me."

Kemp and Lester stood toe-to-toe, glaring at each other as one pulled the box one way, then the other pulled the box the opposite direction, back and forth, neither giving an inch.

Violet reached for the box, but her movement distracted them and they tugged at the same time, knocking the box high into the air. When it started to descend, the top fell open and the candy came down—piece by piece—to splat in dark-brown splotches all over the patio.

Kemp's anger instantly vanished because he felt not only that he had overreacted but also that he had deprived Violet of something special.

"Cuz, what came over you?" Lester pointed at the smashed candies. "I'm not cleaning it up."

"Me either." Violet abruptly sat down.

"I'll get a broom later," Kemp said. "It's my mess."

"It sure is." Lester sat down beside Violet.

"I'll buy Violet more tomorrow." Kemp sat on the other side of her, noticing that they were all quiet now as they stared at the spilled candy.

"I don't want it." She pointed at the floor. "That's my chocolate."

"I'm sorry." Kemp wished he could undo the last few minutes, but he was stuck with his actions.

"I didn't know you hated chocolate, too," Lester said.

"It's not that." Kemp didn't want to go into his sudden possessive feelings for Violet.

"I suppose you guessed I brought candy for a reason," Lester said.

"Reason?" Kemp glanced at his cousin.

"Yeah." Lester shook his head. "You know how guys buy flowers and candy to give when they've been bad…or even thought about being bad."

"You've been bad?" Violet asked, sounding interested in that news.

"No," Lester said. "I guess in this case you'd consider chocolate a bribe. That usually works, too. Only now the whole thing is a mess."

"What whole thing?" Kemp felt more uneasy all the time, because he never knew what his cousin would be up to next.

"You wanted to bribe me?" Violet asked.

Lester abruptly stood up, paced across the patio, careful to avoid stepping on brown splotches, and turned back. He flung his arms wide. "Violet, use me. Please."

She giggled, pointing from him to the chocolates and back again.

"I know," Lester said. "It's not the best presentation in the world, but it would've been a lot more effective if not for somebody's cousin. But what can I do? He's *that* cousin."

"I apologize, if that helps," Kemp said.

Lester tossed a narrow-eyed glance at his cousin before he focused on Violet again. "Look at Kemp. Now look at me."

"Okay," she said with a straight face.

"He's a cowboy."

"Okay."

"I wear Wranglers, too."

"Okay," she said with a big grin.

"That means I'm as much a cowboy as Kemp."

"Les, what are you getting at?" Kemp was unable to follow his cousin's logic, but that wasn't so unusual.

"Sydney Steele came into the shop this morning," Lester said.

"Before the fire, I'd guess," Kemp said.

"Heard about it. Cowboy firefighters saved the day." Lester looked Kemp over before he focused on Violet again. "I'm not a firefighter, but I'm a tried-and-true cowboy. And I'm going to volunteer as a firefighter." Lester put his hands on his hips and thrust out his chest. "Then I *will* be a cowboy firefighter."

"Les, it takes training and staying in one place long enough to support a community. When did you ever let any grass grow under your feet?" Kemp asked, hardly able to believe his ears.

"That's not the point," Lester said. "I'm ready, willing, and able to do whatever it might take to help out."

"Did you find an old cache of moonshine someplace?" Kemp asked.

Lester smiled at Violet with a twinkle in his eyes. "I found out from Sydney today that a lovely lady who came all the way from San Antone needs a cowboy to help her promote her lonely hearts club."

"Oh no!" Kemp knew where this was headed and needed to stop it fast, because it was just like his cousin to take advantage of a situation that involved a woman.

"I also heard that Kemp here isn't interested in performing his cowboy firefighter duties by appearing on such a dating site," Lester said.

"Don't go putting words in my mouth." Kemp was getting hot under the collar.

"When I get to be a firefighter, I'll be happy to pose for any calendar or participate in any dunking booth or any other fund-raiser that you and the lovely ladies of Wildcat Bluff County deem beneficial for our community." Lester gave Violet a big grin.

"If I were you, I wouldn't say anything close to those words around this county," Kemp said.

"Fighting words?" Lester asked.

"Could be," Kemp said. "Sydney is always trying to rope cowboy firefighters into doing stuff we'd like to avoid."

"If it'll help folks around here—and I'm coming to appreciate this community more every day I spend in Bertha's shop—I'll do whatever is asked of me." Lester moved closer to Violet.

"Maybe it's time you went home," Kemp said. "Haven't you caused enough trouble already?"

"I'm sincere." Lester ignored Kemp. "Violet, I'd be honored

if you'd feature me in your lonely hearts club. I'd be happy to be interviewed, photographed, quoted, anything you think might get your project blazing away."

Kemp jumped to his feet. "That's it." He pointed toward the exit. "Out of here. Violet's not going to use you."

"I don't know about that." Violet stood up and looked Lester over from head to toe. "Lester is a good-looking guy. And he's willing, so that counts for a lot."

"Thank you. I do my best." Lester glanced down modestly, then back up at Violet. "And I do seem to have a way with the women."

"Out!" Kemp pointed at the rose arbor's exit again.

"I wouldn't charge you a dime," Lester said. "I'll bring my own wardrobe to photo shoots. You tell me what you want, and I'll get it. There's this great store I discovered in Old Town called Gene's Boot Hospital."

"I've been there," Violet said. "It is great."

"You're not buying new clothes because you're not going to represent Cowboy Heart-to-Heart Corral." If Kemp had been mad before, now he could hardly think straight. If he let Violet spend any time alone with Les, dressing and undressing and posing and who knew what all, his cousin would try to charm his way into her big, crimson, round bed. And that thought made him see red like a challenged bull.

"It's not a bad idea," Violet said. "I need somebody. Lester is here and volunteered to help. Kemp, you don't want to do it so—"

"*I'll do it.*" Kemp gritted the words out between clenched teeth. He was going to regret this tomorrow, but tonight, no way in hell was he going to let his cousin spend any time alone with *his* very own cowgirl-in-training.

"What?" Violet jerked her head around to look at him.

"What?" Lester asked, sounding shocked with that one word.

"I said I'd do it. I'll be Violet's model, whatever she wants for her lonely hearts club." Kemp glared at Lester. "*I'm* the reason she came all the way from San Antone. *I'm* the one she saw in the Wildcat Bluff Fire-Rescue calendar. *I'm* the one she wants to represent her dating service."

"Oh, Kemp, really?" Violet's blue eyes grew wide with excitement.

"Yes. I said I'd do it and I will, but I still have the ranch to run."

"And I'll help. I promise."

"Oh yeah," Lester said. "I was supposed to help out here, too. I prefer the chocolate shop. Bertha needs me more than you do. Besides, Kemp, you always get all the fun. And accolades."

"Me?"

"Right. You. Think about it. You're still the hero for finding Daisy Sue and bringing her home. Me? I got zilch. And now you're going to be the face and body of Cowboy Heart-to-Heart Corral. Me? Zilch."

"But that's all just trouble," Kemp said.

"Far as I'm concerned, trouble is highly underrated." Lester stalked over to the exit and then turned back to look at them. "Violet, if you'll make me Kemp's understudy, I'll take the job."

"You've got it." She gave him a big smile.

"Thanks." He frowned at Kemp. "Guess the only thing left for me to do is help Sydney and Bertha and Hedy plan the biggest blowout cowboy firefighter fund-raiser Wildcat Bluff County has ever seen."

"That sounds like trouble," Kemp said.

"Cuz, you know how it is. Trouble is my middle name." Lester gave Violet a wink, and then he sauntered through the rose arbor's exit and out of sight.

"It's true." Kemp turned back to Violet. "Trouble really is his middle name even if it isn't on his birth certificate."

"In that case, it's a good thing you're my new star."

Chapter 19

"On horseback, I feel like a real cowgirl," Violet said the next afternoon as she rode down a trail with Kemp.

"You look like one and you been working like one." He turned slightly, saddle leather creaking, to smile at her.

"However, I do believe horses should come with an on-and-off switch and stop-and-go pedals." She gazed between Blaze's sorrel ears at Kemp's broad, muscular back where he rode ahead of her on his buckskin.

"Not satisfied with the basic design?"

"Suggested upgrades."

He laughed. "Horses come perfect. You saddled and bridled your own mount today. You're coming along just fine without upgrades."

"Thanks." She tightened her grip on the reins, enjoying the feel of the leather in her hands. "I put out feed and water, too."

"Fishing for compliments?" he asked.

"A good boss knows when to encourage a cowgirl as she learns new skills."

"Are you saying I'm a good boss?"

"Are you fishing for a compliment?"

"Always."

"Okay. You're doing good, too."

She wasn't sure if it was such a great idea to follow Kemp on a trail ride, but he knew the way and she didn't. Even more to the point, she kept getting distracted by the sight of him, as if his horse were an extension of his body, much like a centaur in old tales.

Truth be told, it wasn't the way he rode his horse. It wasn't the way he sat his saddle. It was the way his broad, muscular shoulders moved under his shirt as he guided his mount with the single-loop reins.

He was hot and he was making her hot, so she looked away from him at the lush, green growth of hardwoods, cedars, and pines with understory trees nestled beneath the huge old growth. Wildflowers poked up their colorful heads among the tall, green grass. A blue jay burst out of a tree, fussed at them, and flew into a bright-blue sky accentuated by a few lazily drifting, fluffy, white clouds.

And yet she couldn't be distracted from Kemp for long. A bucolic countryside vista was nice, but it couldn't compare to a cowboy firefighter. She watched him ride a little longer, sighing at the sight. She wondered if she'd ever be that comfortable on the back of a horse. At the moment, her knees were starting to ache from keeping the soles of her boots clamped down in the stirrups, so she didn't chance falling off. Not only would it be embarrassing, but it'd probably hurt, too. She might even break a bone. With that last thought, she pressed down on the inside of the stirrups even harder.

She enjoyed riding a horse. She felt tall and strong with the massive animal moving so smoothly beneath her. Once she developed the right muscles, she'd be able to ride for hours at a stretch just like other cowgirls. It was an exciting goal.

After a bit, they rode out of the tree line into a green-tinted, grass-filled pasture. Golden sunlight streaked across the blue-green water of a large pond nestled in the center. A long line of silver fence stretched across the far side of the pasture until it disappeared into the trees. Hereford cattle grazed in the grass and drank from the pond.

She had to admit it was a beautiful sight, with or without a good-looking cowboy leading her. He just made the scene complete. In fact, she might use such a romantic setting on her website. She stopped Blaze, who tugged on the reins as he lowered his head to chomp grass. She hooked the reins over the saddle horn. She pulled her cell phone out of her pocket and took one photo after another. She felt more excited by the moment. Yes, she could definitely make this work. She hardly felt the ache in her knees anymore. Besides, it was a small price to pay for her lonely hearts club.

When she was done, she slipped her phone back in her pocket and looked around for Kemp. He'd stopped his horse near the fence, where he waited for her to join him. She clicked to Blaze and lifted her reins to urge him to go. He tore off a last bite of grass before he ambled forward.

"Let's follow the fence," he said. "I want to make sure those trespassers haven't been out this way."

"Okay." She rode up beside him.

"I haven't seen or heard anything from them since the old house fire, but I've been busy closer to home, so I'm concerned they might be slipping in and out without me knowing it." He headed down the fence line.

"Maybe they gave up after losing their hideout." She stayed up with him, checking the fence, too, since she figured she could at least recognize a broken or loose wire.

"There's no way to know for sure they were staying in that house. Sheriff Calhoun didn't find any evidence to incriminate anybody. He found a burned-up camp stove and the metal detector. Still, that's enough to be suspicious."

"At least they've left us alone for a bit."

"Yeah." Kemp gestured at the fence. "So far so good."

"If you find a problem, you can teach me to fix fence."

"Okay." He gestured toward his saddlebags. "Just in case, I brought tools with me."

"I can see it'd be a good idea to always be prepared when you're this far from the barn and on horseback."

He chuckled. "You may not have heard it, but cowboys are well aware of an old saying."

"What is it?"

"There's tough, then there's cowgirl tough."

"Oh, I like it. I want to be cowgirl tough."

"You're on your way."

She shook her head at the incongruous idea but still liked it. "How did that notion come about?"

"Nobody wants to fall off or get bucked off their mount in the back pasture of a ranch. That means your horse hightails it to the barn while you're left to hoof it in on foot and that's a long way, any which way you look at it. With that in mind, cowgirls are going to stay on that horse no matter what."

She glanced down Blaze's long mane as she reconsidered her situation high in the air. "And what if you had a broken bone and couldn't walk? At least you could call for help with a cell phone."

"Maybe not."

"Not on ranches?" She glanced around in alarm.

"There're some hotspots nearer the house or road, but you can't count on help if you're riding the range. You're on your own, and that's the way it has always been for cowboys and cowgirls."

"I'm definitely all in for cowgirl tough."

"Good. I thought you might be." He smiled at her.

She returned his smile, planning to ride as often as she could get the time, so she could become cowgirl tough.

As they rode together, she realized that she was enjoying the lifestyle. She hadn't given that aspect much thought before leaving San Antonio. She'd simply gone with her instinct to follow the calendar, which had led her to Mr. July in Wildcat Bluff County. And now? Nothing about the city would ever feel the same again.

Cowgirl tough. She'd keep the term in mind as she forged ahead with her lonely hearts club. It didn't have to mean riding a horse. It could just as easily represent every obstacle confronted and overcome in life. It might also be the exact way she needed to think of herself, or at least aspire to be, while she tackled her current goals.

As they rode the fence line, she felt as if they had done this many times before because it seemed so natural to be together on horseback, under a blue sky, with the future stretching out before them. And now they would be working together, not only on the ranch, but also on her dating site.

She lagged behind him, letting the reins loosen in her hand as she inhaled the flower-scented air and enjoyed the sights around her. It was so lovely, so quiet, so peaceful…until Kemp groaned and pulled his horse to a stop up ahead.

On alert, she urged Blaze forward to catch up. When she stopped beside him, she groaned, too. The trespassers had come and gone through the back fence, leaving a gaping hole. They'd also left a deep, wide hole and churned-up soil in their quest for bootlegger gold.

"Guess I'll be learning to repair fence today." She tried to make light of the matter, but nothing she could do would ease the problem for him.

"Here we go again."

"Do you think they found what they were after?"

"No way to know." He stepped down and walked over to the hole.

"Is it bigger than the last one?" She followed his action and stopped beside him on the rim of the deep hole.

"It's about the same." He knelt down, picked up a handful of dirt, and let it sift through his fingers.

She knelt beside him as she looked over the area. She saw a small object glint in the sunlight, so she leaned over and grabbed it. She rubbed dirt off a rusted metal container that turned out to have once held chewing tobacco.

He pulled out a small object, rubbed off the dirt, and showed her a blue glass medicinal bottle with a rusted lid.

"I wish we'd find another piece of silverware."

"If there was anything of value here, they took it."

"It's a wonder they missed that spoon the first time."

"They probably heard us coming, so rushed to get away ahead of us," he said.

"If they found the gold, would we ever know?"

"I doubt there's ever been any here. It's just a legend."

"I kind of wish it were true." She tossed the tin back into the hole.

"As legends go, it's a good one."

"Yes, it is."

"Do you want to keep the bottle? It's pretty."

"Please."

"I'll put it in my saddlebag for you."

"Thanks."

He shook his head as he rose to his feet. "If this keeps up, I may have to buy a backhoe. It'd be cheaper than rentals in the long run."

"Sorry you have all this extra work and expense. Is there anything I can do to help?"

"You're already a big help on the ranch." He tossed the small bottle back and forth between his hands.

"Thanks. I'm learning fast."

He opened his saddlebag, placed the bottle inside, and pulled out a roll of baling wire, wire cutters, pliers, and leather gloves.

She walked over and looked at where the wire had been cut, pulled back, and twisted around the metal poles on either side. Whoever had done it had known what they were doing because it was a neat job. They'd exerted the least amount of effort to achieve the maximum amount of result.

"I'll just untwist the barbwire and twine a short piece between the cut ends so that it's strong again," he said.

"Seems to me those guys are experienced with fence, or they learned on the job from cutting fence and digging holes."

Kemp paused with wire cutter in hand. "Good point. I hadn't thought of it. Not everybody knows how to handle barbwire, do they?"

"It's strong, dangerous stuff. I'd think you'd need to know how to work with it."

"Cowboys?" He cut a short length of wire.

"It must be somebody that knows something about fences or—"

"They watched an online video about how to build a fence."

"Do those exist?"

"Everything else how-to does, so why not fences?"

"Good point. We saw those guys, even if it was from a distance. They know how to drive a truck, work a backhoe, and cut fence. They have to be strong, too. That tells us a lot, doesn't it?"

He twisted strands of wire together using his pliers and then glanced at her with a nod.

"What do you think?"

"Plenty of cowboys or just good ole boys in Texas and Oklahoma have all those skills."

"And a few might have heard the bootlegger gold legend."

"They wouldn't think cutting a little fence and digging a few holes was a big deal…except for the trespassing part."

"And if they found gold, nobody would know."

"Right." He finished the job and stepped back.

"It'd be worth the chance of getting caught on trespassing charges, wouldn't it?"

"Yes. They might even like the sense of danger, since it isn't too dangerous."

"An enraged bull is probably the most trouble they figure they'll encounter on this ranch."

"Right. If they don't get caught by an irate rancher with the business end of a shotgun pointed at them."

She had another thought. "What if they're sure they won't be caught by that irate rancher?"

"What do you mean?"

"Somebody might be keeping an eye on the place for them."

"Lookout?"

"Somebody local?"

"That's definitely something to think about." He walked over to his horse and put away his gloves, wire, pliers, and wire cutters.

"We need to be more watchful."

"Right." He looked down the fence line. "Let's get out of here."

Chapter 20

"I don't know about Blaze, but I do believe I deserve an apple and a rubdown." Violet rode beside Kemp into the shadow of his big barn cast by the setting sun.

"Sore?" Kemp glanced at her in concern. "I'll be happy to give you a little tender loving care."

"Thanks." She gave him a warm smile, mind lingering on the thought of a rubdown from him. "I'm not sore yet, but my knees may not hold me up when I step down."

"My fault. I shouldn't have taken you so far until you build up more riding muscles."

"I wanted to go. I just didn't anticipate that it'd be so much more strenuous than my usual mode of transportation, like driving a car."

"You'll get used to horseback."

"You bet I will." She patted Blaze's neck. "But be gentle with me when I get down."

"Wait for me to help you." He slipped off his horse and walked over to her. "Now take it easy."

She swung her right leg over the back of the saddle, put that foot on the ground, and then her left foot. She felt her knees buckle, but he caught her and quickly turned her around so that she was pressed to his chest with his strong arms around her. She trembled…maybe more from his nearness than her tired muscles. She started to move away, but he held her closer.

"Don't rush it."

She felt his breath warm against her ear and felt his tenderness toward her, so she leaned into him, fully relying on him. In that moment, she realized that she was coming to trust him to be there for her in so many different ways. She hadn't thought she needed support. She'd even thought it might be a weakness. She'd thought she'd been smart by avoiding entanglements. Now she realized that in protecting her emotions, she'd created her own path to a lonely heart. And she found that she didn't want to live in that world any longer.

She reached up and slipped her arms around Kemp's neck, cradling him so they were as tightly meshed as she could make them.

He pressed a kiss to her ear. "How are you?"

"Better...now." She eased back slightly so she could look up into his green eyes.

"Good." He loosened his arms but still held her close. "Can you stand on your own now?"

"I'm okay." She stepped back from him, feeling proud of all her new skills.

"Bet you're going to be sore tomorrow."

"I suspect so, but that's fine."

"What you need tonight is a hot bath and a glass of wine."

"I'll get a shower. That'll feel almost as good."

"No. I'm serious. We'll put salt and lavender oil in the water and let you soak."

"You forget, I don't have a bathtub in the cabin."

"I didn't forget. You can use my tub."

"Yours?" She felt a little thrill at that idea. *Intimate* didn't even begin to describe it. And yet, what had she just thought about her lonely heart? Maybe she was ready to chance her heart. Maybe that was why she'd made the long trip from San Antonio. Maybe she'd had an ulterior motive from the moment she'd seen Mr. July in the cowboy firefighter calendar. One thing for sure, between the two of them, they'd turned her life upside down since she'd arrived on his ranch. And she liked it.

"Yes. Mine." He glanced at the house, then back at her. "I need to call Sheriff Calhoun and update him on the trespassers. After that, I'll take care of the horses. You don't need to be involved in either, so why don't you go ahead while I finish up here? Tub's in the bathroom upstairs."

"I can help."

"No need. Sooner you soak those muscles, the better."

"You're pampering me. Tough cowgirls don't need it."

"Let me do this for you. It's little enough for all your help."

She hesitated, torn between wanting to be independent and wanting to soak her sore muscles.

"House is unlocked." He hesitated, as if just remembering something. "You know where the wine is in the kitchen. And there's a terry robe hanging behind the bathroom door. It'll be too big for you, but it's better than you going all the way to your cabin to get your stuff."

"Thanks. I'm not going to pass up such a good offer."

"Great." He looked her over. "Do you need me to carry you to the house?"

"Oh, no…but thanks anyway."

He grinned, eyes lighting up. "I wouldn't mind carrying you over there one bit."

She chuckled, shaking her head at his obvious excuse to get her in his arms again. "Why don't you take care of business while I take care of me?"

"Sounds like a plan."

"Thanks for the trail ride."

"Anytime."

She gave him a smile before she turned and headed for the house. She was surprised that she felt pretty normal, no soreness yet. Most likely tomorrow would be a different matter, but maybe she wouldn't get stove-up from her long ride. Maybe she was well on her way to being cowgirl tough.

She entered the patio, walked through the garden room, and made her way into the kitchen. A light over the range softly illuminated the area. She poured a glass of merlot before she moved over to the breakfast nook and glanced out the windows as darkness fell over the ranch. It was just as beautiful here at night as it was during the day.

She started up the staircase. A light on the landing beckoned her upward. She abruptly stopped and glanced back. When had she become so comfortable in this house? She hadn't been here often, and yet somehow, it felt like home. She could only imagine that it was because Kemp lived here and he was beginning to feel more like home every moment she spent with him. She wasn't sure how to explain that fact, so she simply let it be, grasped the white handrail, and quickly climbed the creaky wood stairs to the upper floor.

One spacious room extended the length of the house. Triple windows surrounded with white casings were on one end and two white doors on the other. On the east wall, a brown leather recliner and cedar table with a beaten-copper lamp topped by a beige shade nestled in front of a built-in bookcase painted bright white. A king-size bed with a sturdy cedar headboard and matching nightstands that held small porcelain lamps dominated the west wall.

She turned on the lamp beside the bookcase before she opened one of the two doors and peeked inside. A huge, walk-in closet with double windows on the outside wall had double racks on each side with a contemporary chest of drawers, table, and chair in the center. No doubt the large space had once been a small bedroom converted into much-needed storage space.

Kemp hadn't nearly filled the large closet. Hatboxes. Boot boxes. Miscellaneous boxes. He'd hung up clothes, but he'd also just tossed some on top of the chest and table to be dealt with later. She coveted that fine closet even as she shut the door on it.

Next to the closet was the bathroom. It'd been upgraded to keep the time period intact while still adding luxurious perks. The room consisted of another large window with a wide, white casing, wood paneling painted white, and the original oak floor. A white claw-foot tub looked perfect with matching toilet and pedestal sink. A metal basket beside the tub held more of Morning's Glory products of lavender soap, salts, oil, and bubble bath. A nightlight cast the room in a soft lavender glow.

She set her glass of wine on the floor beside the tub, then she shut the door behind her, looked for a lock, but didn't see one, so she simply shrugged and pulled the big, white robe off the hook. She set it beside a small table that held fluffy, white bath towels, hand towels, and washcloths. She turned on the water. As it gushed into the tub, she poured in every lavender choice from the basket before she tossed in a washcloth.

On a contented sigh, she jerked off her boots, stripped off her clothes, dropped them to the floor, and stepped into the just-on-the-edge-of-too-hot water. It felt wonderful. She picked up her glass of wine, took several sips, and set it back on the floor. She slipped down the tub until she could rest the back of her head on the rounded edge and let the bubbles rise up to her chin. She smiled in delight when she realized she could turn the water on and off with her toes, because she didn't have to move another muscle of her body.

She felt the dry wine, warm water, and lavender scent slowly relax every muscle in her body. If this luxury was at the end of every trail ride, Kemp would never be able to keep her off a horse.

As the water cooled, she reheated it by turning the knob with her toes over and over again until—finally—the tub wouldn't hold any more liquid. She sighed, knowing she'd soon have no excuse to prolong her bath. She loaded up the washcloth with sweet-smelling lavender soap, washed all over, and soon felt clean, refreshed, and relaxed, as if she hadn't been on a trail ride earlier.

As she contemplated getting out of the tub, she heard footsteps on the staircase, causing it to creak as someone came upstairs. She immediately went rigid. Kemp? Trespassers? Friends? Enemies? If she stayed in the country much longer, she was definitely going to get a pistol and learn to use it.

She sat up, looked around for an exit, but there was only the unlocked door and the too-high window. She glanced down at the water. Fortunately she was mostly covered by white bubbles, but she still felt vulnerable. She swiveled her gaze to the big robe. That was her ticket to a modicum of safety…at least she'd feel more prepared for whatever on her feet.

She stepped out of the tub, leaving wet footprints on the white mat, and grabbed the robe. She slipped her arms into sleeves that extended to her fingertips, pulled the front together even though it overlapped so much that it hung loose, and quickly pulled the belt around her waist and secured it loosely with a single tie…just as a knock came on the door.

"Violet?" Kemp called from the other side. "Don't mean to disturb you. I just want to make sure you're okay and let you know I'm inside."

She felt a huge sense of relief wash over her. She walked over to the door and opened it.

He did a quick up and down glance before he focused on her face. "I ought to give you that robe. It never looked so good on me."

"Thanks." She smiled at the compliment.

"I got you out of the bath, didn't I?" He shook his head. "I knew better. I tried to stay away, but then I got worried about you."

"I'm okay." She held out her arms to either side to show him the truth of her words…and felt the robe gap open and cool air hit her heated flesh. She'd accidentally exposed her breasts. Shocked, she jerked the front of the robe together, but it was too late. His eyes had already turned to green fire.

"You're a lot more than okay," he said in a voice gone rough.

She looked him over, too. It looked like he'd had a shower because his hair was damp. He'd put on clean clothes, so he now wore the T-shirt and sweatpants—dark green this time—that she knew he liked to relax in at home. Plus, he was barefoot again. All in all, he appeared perfectly delicious.

"I, uh…" He took a step backward. "I guess I should rustle up some supper."

"Are you hungry?"

He dropped his gaze down, then up again. "Yes."

"Me, too."

"What do you want to eat?"

She focused on his feet. He had long, straight toes, high arches, tan skin. She wondered if he was tan all over. Maybe he sometimes fixed fences wearing nothing but his birthday suit. Maybe he skinny-dipped in the pond. Maybe he stretched out, arms folded behind his head, flat on his back in a field of clover with only his cowboy hat over his face to shield him from the hot rays of the sun.

"Are you trying to make up your mind about what you want to eat?" he asked.

She licked her lower lip, imagining what his skin would taste like when kissed by the sun.

"You're thinking about chocolate, aren't you?"

She felt her nostrils flare as she caught his scent, somewhere between musk and citrus. Would he taste like oranges or tangerines or lemons?

"You're definitely thinking about chocolate. I can tell by the look in your eyes."

"Chocolate is good, but you're—"

"As a matter of fact, I bought you a big box yesterday."

"Really?" She focused on his broad chest under the T-shirt stretched taut across his thick muscles.

"Don't you believe me?"

"I…uh…"

"If you don't, it's because I spilled that other box, isn't it?"

"Chocolate is good, but I'd like—"

"Cuz Les is…well, he's *that* cousin, and he got under my skin the other night. I'm still sorry about the mess. It's why I bought you a new box."

"Where is it?"

"Kitchen." He stepped back. "I'm going to run downstairs and bring it back up here, so you'll know that's what you get after supper."

"I want dessert."

He smiled, reached out, and tucked a lock of her blond hair behind one ear. "I know. You always do."

"First."

He cupped her cheek, leaned down, pressed a soft kiss to her lips, and then turned, walked quickly away, and hit the stairs.

With him gone, she thought she might come to her senses, but she didn't. She didn't even want them anymore. In fact, she'd just tossed them away. What good were they anyway?

She turned back, picked up her glass of wine, opened the bathtub drain, and stepped into his bedroom. She eyed his big bed with its dark-brown suede cover for a moment before she moved over to it and set her glass on a nightstand. She went over to his bookcase, but she didn't bother to even glimpse his book collection. She simply slipped out of the white robe and tossed it on the chair. She returned to his bed and threw back the covers to reveal crimson sheets. Why was she even surprised? Rich brown and richer red. She could definitely go with it.

With a little, satisfied smile, she slipped under the covers and picked up her glass of wine to wait for his return.

Chapter 21

As Kemp reached the top of the stairs with the box of candy, he wondered if he could persuade Violet to spend the night. She could stay in the downstairs bedroom. She could sleep late the next morning. He was concerned that she'd wake up too sore to get out of bed, need his help, and he wouldn't be there. Even more, he didn't want to walk her back to the cabin and leave her alone. Maybe he was being too protective or maybe he just didn't want to admit that he wanted her in his house and he'd use any excuse to keep her with him.

He stopped on the next-to-the-top step and realized he'd clutched the box so tightly that he'd smashed one corner. He eased his grip. If he wasn't careful, he was going to make a mess of these chocolates, too. But it told him something. He'd come to care for her. He worried about her. He wanted to be with her. How it had happened so fast, he didn't know, but love was like that. Wait. Love? He wasn't willing to go that far, but he might be well on his way.

He glanced back at the box. Now he'd smashed another corner. No telling what shape the chocolates would be in by the time he finally gave them to her. He just hoped he hadn't melted them with the heat of his hand.

He was hot and bothered by the revelations that had been pinging around in his mind, particularly since he'd seen her breasts. He should have left her alone. He should have waited for her to come downstairs. He should have fixed supper with nothing more on his mind than feeding her.

Instead, he'd had to come upstairs. He'd had to disturb her. He'd had to surprise her. And because of all that, he'd had to see the beauty that he would never in a million years be able to forget... even if he never got to cup those full mounds with both hands. And on the tail end of that thought, he crushed the cardboard box and smashed the candy inside.

He just stood there looking at it. How could he present her with another mess? He'd planned it so well. He'd thought about how pleased she'd be with a fresh box of chocolates. He'd known she'd be happy and forget all about the patio incident. Now she'd remember it all and how he was the one who couldn't keep from ruining her candy.

So be it. He wasn't getting her into his bed anytime soon. She was probably hiding out in the bathroom. She'd probably put her dirty clothes back on and covered them with his big robe just to be on the safe side from his prying eyes. She'd probably insist on going to the cabin with no supper, no him. He felt the box give a little more in his fist. He sighed. If he didn't get rid of it soon, there'd be nothing left but a few smears and him with a regretful expression on his face.

He took the final step to the top floor. He saw the empty robe first. It'd been casually tossed on his chair so that the belt hung down to the floor. He walked farther into the bedroom. Nothing could have surprised him more than to see Violet sitting up in *his* bed under *his* covers—shoulders bare—and holding *his* wineglass.

"For me?" She held out her hand.

He looked from her to the box as he tried to get his mind to click back into gear because she'd knocked him for a loop.

"Chocolate?"

"It had a little mishap on the way up here."

"Surely Lester didn't try to take it from you."

"No." He wished Bertha had never opened that shop. If she hadn't, he wouldn't be in this mess now with a befuddled brain.

"Is it not for me?"

"It's for you. I'm just not sure if you'll want it now."

"Did you drop it down the stairs or something?"

"Something." He walked to her side of the bed and held out the crushed box. "I wanted to do something nice for you."

She set down her glass and accepted the big box with both hands. She glanced up at him with a question in her eyes, then back at the box. Dark goo oozed from one corner.

"I know. Maybe the chocolates are still good."

She pried up the lid and set it on the nightstand beside her glass. Misshapen dark objects—flat, elongated, liquefied—filled the bottom of the box along with crushed little paper cups that had originally held the molded pieces.

"I'll take it back." He reached for the box, intending to hide it out of sight somewhere, but she wouldn't let him have it.

Instead, she stuck her fingertip into one of the cups of goo, swirled it around until it was covered in chocolate, and looked up at him.

He guessed she was making a point about the mess, but she didn't need to. He was well aware of it.

"Come closer." She gave him a mischievous smile.

"What?"

"Taste test for me."

"You're kidding."

"Please…with sugar on it?"

He sighed, knowing this was his penance for candy mayhem and leaned toward her.

She painted his lips with chocolate. "Now your lower lip *really* looks like it needs to be nibbled on."

He couldn't keep from smiling as she turned his disaster into her pleasure. He licked his lower lip. "Tastes good."

"That's chocolate for you. It never lets you down."

And that was when it *really* dawned on him that she was in his bed. She was naked in his bed. She was waiting for him in his bed. And all he'd been able to think about was a crushed box of candy. He must have truly lost his mind somewhere between the bottom of the staircase and the top of it. He had his mind back now. He might not know what to do with melted chocolate, but he knew exactly what to do with two lonely hearts.

"Closer."

He'd never argue with a woman high on chocolate, even just the scent of it, because the bedroom now smelled of cocoa, sugar, and excitement. He leaned toward her.

"You're still not close enough." She swirled her fingertip in the goo, then reached up and painted his lips again.

He didn't lick this time. Instead, he bent down so she could do it for him. She didn't make him wait long. He felt a featherlight kiss against his mouth, then the stroke of her tongue across his lower lip, the nibble of her teeth, and finally the press of her lips in a longer kiss before she leaned back and looked at him with blue eyes gone dark.

"You taste good." She patted the bed beside her. "I want to taste you all over. Do you mind?"

"No." One word was all he could get out or needed to say. He wanted romantic for her and no distractions for him, so he snapped off the lamp and left the room bathed in the soft, silvery light of the moon pouring through the windows.

"Strip for me."

He glanced back at her in surprise. She had a little smile on her lips, now smeared with chocolate, and a teasing glint in her eyes. He shouldn't let her near a lonely hearts club because she wouldn't be lonely for long. Good thing he'd cut Lester off at the pass, because if his cousin ever experienced anything like this, he'd never leave Wildcat Bluff County.

"Now would be good," she said on a more urgent note.

"Will it make up for my candy disasters?"

"That depends on how we put the chocolate to use."

"Do you mean there's a way to salvage the situation?" If she meant what he thought she meant, he'd be happy to smash every box of chocolates in Destiny. If Lester wasn't eating candy in Bertha's shop, he was a fool because he was missing out on the added value of it. But then again, who knew?

"With chocolate, where there's a will, there's a way."

"I've definitely got the will." He jerked his T-shirt up and over his head, then tossed it down on top of his discarded robe.

"And I've got the way." She stuck her fingertip back into the box, came out with it covered in chocolate, then slipped her finger into her mouth and sucked while she watched him watch her.

She might as well have roped, tied, and branded him with chocolate because he belonged nowhere except in that bed with her. He stalked over and jerked the covers down so he could see her…every last little bit of her soft, scented flesh. And he groaned because she was everything and more than he'd imagined since the first moment he'd met her. Soft, pale skin stretched over lithe muscles with rosy-tipped breasts and a blond triangle between her thighs.

He took a deep breath to steady himself and smelled chocolate, lavender, and the scent that was hers alone. She was in his head now, and there was no getting her out, even if he wanted to. Love. She knew a thing about healing lonely hearts. Maybe that was her great gift to the world, or at least to this county. And to him.

If he'd been hard before, now he was on fire because every sense in his body had come alive in response to her. He untied the cord of his pants and let them drop to the floor.

She smiled, letting her gaze travel up and down his body.

He felt that look, that smile, clear to his gut.

"Come closer." She scooted over, still holding the box of candy.

He sat down on the edge of the bed, kicked off his sweatpants, and turned to her. He wasn't sure what to expect next, but whatever it was, he wanted every little bit of it. And he'd give just as good as he got.

"Lay back."

He looked from her dark-blue eyes to the dark-brown candy and back again. She expected him to trust her enough to let her take the bit between her teeth and lead them where she wanted them to go. He wasn't used to letting go of the reins. He was used to being in control. He was normally a man on a mission with no room for sidesteps. But if his cowgirl wanted to turn tough, he was all in.

He licked his lower lip and tasted chocolate. Maybe he'd been too serious too long. Maybe he needed a woman who'd tease him, cajole him, and lure him into a whole new level of happiness. Maybe it was time to cut the traces and head out for the unknown...led by a newborn cowgirl named Violet.

He plumped his pillow, lay back, and folded his arms under his head, exposing his entire body to her. He was more than willing to let her play with him, because later he'd get to play with her.

"You're so beautiful," she said with a smile.

"So are you."

She leaned over him, dipped her fingertip into the chocolate, and slowly finger-painted down the front of him. Lips to nipples to navel to hard tip. She even included his big toes. She made him so hot that he felt the chocolate run in rivulets across his skin.

"You're melting like ice cream in the sun."

"I'm Fourth of July hot."

"I'd better do something about it before you make a mess."

"I'm innocent of messes this time."

"I doubt you're ever innocent."

"I'd be happy to prove you right."

"Lie still." She chuckled as she set the box aside on the bed, then she leaned over him again.

He took a deep breath, steeling himself for what was to come.

He wasn't sure he could stay still, but he was going to do his best to let her have her way with him for as long as possible. With the first stroke of her tongue across his nipple, he groaned and clutched the covers in both fists. He felt on fire.

"Good?" She turned her attention to his other nipple, licking, stroking, nibbling as she lapped up the chocolate.

He shuddered and clung to the covers, or he'd have picked her up, tossed her on her back, and gone deep.

"I do so like the taste." She drank from his navel next, toying with the tip of her tongue while her hands followed, teasing the muscles of his chest and shoulders with light touches from her fingers.

He clenched his teeth, holding still by sheer willpower alone against her onslaught of his senses. He wanted her more than life itself.

When she touched the tip of her tongue to the tip of his arousal, he almost lost control. He never wanted the sensation to stop and yet he desperately needed it to stop. She gave him no relief…not even when he groaned and dug his fingers into her hair to restrain her or encourage her, he wasn't sure which one.

Finally, she raised her head and looked at him, blue fire in her eyes and chocolate smeared across her face.

That did it. He picked her up by her waist, swiveled on the bed, and gently laid her on her back, spreading her legs so she was completely exposed to him. He feasted with his eyes for a long moment before he smiled in anticipation.

"Chocolate?" she asked.

He pulled the box toward him, found an almost intact piece of solid candy, and put it in his mouth.

"What about me?"

He smiled again, then leaned forward and kissed her, pushing the chocolate from his mouth into hers, so they shared the sweet cocoa as it melted and melded them together during their long, long kiss.

When he came up for air, she had chocolate smeared across her face, so he slowly licked her clean, moving downward…painting her with his tongue as she had painted him…growing hotter with every taste…feeling her heat up at his touch…until he reached that triangular core of her. He stopped and glanced up at her face.

She smiled, blue eyes shining with desire and something much more, something that evoked the same feeling in him. Tenderness. She cared for him just as he cared for her. He felt his emotions turn gentle. No longer playful, urgent, or needy. Now he wanted to be connected with her in the most intimate way, so they were no longer separate people, but joined together as one. Nothing else would satisfy him.

She held out her arms, still smiling.

He reached over and opened his nightstand. Fortunately, he'd bought condoms soon after he'd met her. He'd hoped but hadn't actually believed until now. He tore open the wrapper and slipped on the condom.

He knelt between her legs, slid his palms up and down her satiny inner thighs, felt her grasp his shoulders, and gently pushed inside her. She moaned softly and pulled him tightly to her. But it wasn't nearly enough. And so he thrust harder, deeper, quicker, spiraling ever higher, taking her with him every step of the way.

"Kemp!" She clutched his shoulders as if her life depended on him and his life on her.

That did it. The sound of his name on her lips pushed him completely over the edge. He groaned as he hit the peak of passion and felt her join him on that high plateau of ecstasy. They hung there together for a long moment and then fell back to earth together…no longer lonely hearts.

Chapter 22

A WEEK LATER, VIOLET SAT ON HER FRONT PORCH AS SHE looked out over the pasture where Hereford cattle grazed, some with spring calves by their sides. At that sight, she thought about Daisy Sue and her problem pregnancy. She'd heard Storm was getting more frantic by the day that she might lose the calf or the cow or even both, although Ann, their excellent veterinarian, did her best to reassure everyone that all would be well.

And so Violet focused on the beauty and new life around her. Wildflowers sprouted more colorful by the day. Trees held more green leaves. And grass grew taller and thicker. Her own life mimicked this advent of spring. She had changed in ways that she wouldn't have thought possible in San Antonio. Oh yes, she'd hoped for change, but she'd planned to bring it to others. Now she could give testimony to the power of sharing life with another through love.

Love. She hadn't spoken that word to Kemp yet. And he hadn't said it to her. Maybe it was too soon. Maybe she was concerned that he didn't feel the same intense emotion for her that she felt for him. Maybe she didn't want to upset their fragile relationship. In any case, they were both so busy creating their dream worlds as they helped others, him as a firefighter and she with her lonely hearts club, that neither was taking a chance on disturbing the precarious balance. And for now, that was all right. Later…well, later was for later.

She wondered about the bootlegger gold. She wondered about Lady Mauve, the former lady of Hallelujah Ranch, and her silver spoon. She wondered about the trespassers. It took her mind off the approaching deadline to launch Cowboy Heart-to-Heart Corral. She wasn't nearly ready for it, although marketing had already started. She needed to plan a photo shoot with Kemp as the star. She'd been putting it off, because she no longer wanted to share him, particularly with women everywhere. She had to get over her reluctance, since she'd come here for that very reason. She couldn't back out now, not with his agreement in place.

She'd also agreed to meet with Sydney and other Wildcat Bluff Fire-Rescue folks to plan the fund-raiser that would auction off dates with cowboy firefighters. Could they pull it off? Would cowboys actually participate? Would the local radio station livestream the event, so it could be picked up on her dating site? So many questions. So little time. How was she going to get it all done in the next couple of weeks? Somehow she had to do it or lose momentum for her dating site.

She glanced down at the list she'd created and shook her head. She needed help. Maybe she could enlist the folks who'd expressed interest in her lonely hearts club, like Ann, Oscar, Birdy, and the Buick Brigade.

As if she'd conjured a pigeon with her thoughts, she heard the flutter of wings and Bonnie—maybe, instead of Clyde this time— landed on the railing and cocked her head to look at Violet with one eye and then the other.

She could see a band around one leg, so Bonnie must have been carrying a message. She hadn't removed one before herself, so she hoped the pigeon would let her. She stood up, took a few steps to the railing, and slowly held out her hand. Bonnie waited patiently.

Violet felt soft feathers against her hand as she gently slipped the small piece of paper free. She unrolled it, then read out loud. "Pigeon-gram. Time is of the essence. Destiny awaits your presence."

She looked back at Bonnie. "I wish I could send a message with you, but maybe your return will let the Buick Brigade know I'll be there soon."

Bonnie cocked her head again, eyes bright and shiny, then once more took to the air and zipped away north.

She needed to visit Destiny. She rolled the message between her fingertips as she thought about her situation. She'd put off the visit too long. They'd probably expect her to arrive with Kemp. Maybe she could make the trip count double. Bertha and Lester were at the Destiny Chocolatier. Maybe Sydney and Hedy would meet her after hours there, so they could make plans for the fire-fighter benefit together.

She set the pigeon-gram on the small table beside her chair, picked up her phone, and placed a call.

"Hey, Violet," Sydney said. "What's up?"

"I wondered how the plans for the benefit were coming along."

"At the moment, slow. It's a good idea, but I've got my hands full here at the ranch with Storm."

"How is Daisy Sue?"

"We're keeping her in the barn. She's stable for now, but we're not taking any chances. Anyhow, when Storm worries, everybody worries...and that includes Fernando's fans, so that's a whole lot of worry."

"I hear you. Listen, I'm going to be in Destiny later. I thought maybe we could meet at the shop, since Lester and Bertha will be there. We could make plans for the benefit auction or just compare notes."

"Good idea. I can do it. We need to get this show on the road and publicize it. I'll let Hedy know. She'll want to join us."

"I think Kemp will be there, too."

"Great. Let me know a time later."

"Okay. See you then."

Violet clicked off and just sat there, thinking about how quickly she'd been accepted into the community. She was grateful for their warmth and willingness to help her.

Kemp was out in a back pasture, so she couldn't make plans with him until he returned to the house, because he was out of cell phone range. Maybe he'd be back early, but he was fixing fence, so she couldn't count on it.

She stood up, walked over to the railing, and looked out over the pasture. She felt uneasy, as if she'd forgotten something important. That'd be easy to do with so much on her mind, but it wasn't the dating site. It was something else. And then she remembered the silver spoon. She needed to take it with her because she wanted the Buick Brigade to see it. Maybe they'd know something about its history. She could also tell them about meeting Jake the Farmer.

She picked up the pigeon-gram and went inside, glanced around at the living space that had quickly become so comfortable and familiar to her. She set the rolled piece of paper on the bar before she walked into the kitchen. She'd set the silver spoon on the countertop, where she could see it. She hadn't yet used it because it seemed more decorative than utilitarian.

She picked up the spoon, stroked the cool silver violets engraved along the handle, and set it on the bar beside the pigeon-gram, so she wouldn't forget it when she went to Destiny. For now, she'd just go ahead and change out of her yoga pants and be ready to go when Kemp got back. At least, she hoped he could go with her. As far as she knew, he didn't have anything else planned for the evening…and she figured she'd know since they'd been spending those hours together.

She climbed the stairs and opened the closet door. She selected faded Wranglers and a dark-blue sweater that would be comfortable when the temperature dropped that evening.

She stripped down to her undies, pulled on a terrycloth robe, tied the belt around her waist, and went back downstairs. As she was refreshing her makeup in the bathroom, she heard the doorbell ring. She froze, wondering if it could be Kemp already. She hoped so. She retied the belt around her waist, walked to the front door, and opened it a crack.

Kemp grinned at her, standing there with one hand hidden behind his back.

She smiled, so happy to see him. "You're home early."

"Couldn't stay away." He grinned bigger. "Brought you something." He whipped out a large wildflower bouquet and held it toward her.

"Oh, they're beautiful. Thank you." She went up on tiptoes and kissed his cheek.

"I'll bring you flowers more often if that's the thanks I get."

"You might get even more thanks later." She accepted the bouquet, sniffed the sweet fragrance, and stepped back. "Come on inside while I put these in water."

"I saw them in the pasture and thought of you." He shut the door and followed her.

"I'll enjoy them." She walked into the kitchen, trying to think what she could use to hold the flowers. "Did you finish the fence?"

"Pretty much."

"Good. I've made plans and I hope you'll like them." She found a clear glass pitcher in the upper cabinet, filled it with water from the faucet, and arranged the flowers in it.

"I hope your plans have something to do with you getting out of that robe and getting into your bed upstairs."

She chuckled as she set the vase of flowers on the bar near the silver spoon and pigeon-gram.

"No?"

"Maybe later." She pointed at the small piece of paper. "Bonnie or Clyde brought a message from the Buick Brigade earlier."

"We never did visit them, did we?" He picked up the pigeon-gram.

"Maybe they understand that we've been distracted with everything going on at the ranch."

"Maybe." He unrolled the paper and read the message. "We'd best get to Destiny. Is that your plan for us?"

"Yes. And I called Sydney. I asked her to meet us at the chocolate shop, since Lester and Bertha will already be there. I thought we could discuss the benefit auction."

He groaned as he tossed down the pigeon-gram. "Sydney's not really planning to go through with that it, is she?"

"I think so."

"Are you really going to get involved with it?"

"It's for a good cause."

He walked across the room, then turned back. "And I thought the calendars and the dunking booth were bad."

"It'll also draw a lot of attention to Cowboy Heart-to-Heart Corral when KWCB livestreams it."

"Can you even corral that many single cowboys in the county? I bet they hightail it to the next county before they're auctioned off for a date."

"Lester won't."

"Yeah…but that's Les. He'd probably sign up for a date every night for a month, if I know him."

"That's not a bad idea. Lots of cowboys and lots of dates."

Kemp groaned again. "I'm not doing it. I already agreed to your dating site, but this is right over the top."

She walked over to him and loosened the belt on her robe. "Pretty please?"

He looked at her robe. "No."

"Pretty please with sugar on it?" She let the belt fall to the sides of her robe, and the fabric gaped open to reveal her crimson bra and panties.

"You're not playing fair." He swallowed hard.

"It's for a really good cause." She ran her fingers up the front of his green snap shirt. "Wildcat Bluff Fire-Rescue needs our help to help other people in the county."

"I already volunteer as a firefighter and EMT." He slipped the robe over her shoulders so it hung in the crook of her arms.

"You're so generous." She lowered her arms and the robe slid all the way to the floor.

He looked her up and down, then sighed out loud.

"What if I bought the date with you?"

"You'd do that?" He glanced back at her face, appearing suspicious. "You know women from Dallas with big bucks might come and start bidding wars."

"Well, you're worth a lot." She moved in close so that she could feel his heat without touching him.

"Damn straight," he said with a smile.

She tucked her fingertips under the top of his shirt and snapped open several of the pearl snaps to reveal chest hair.

"It might set you back a pretty penny to protect me."

"You'd be worth it."

"Where would you take me on a date?"

She cocked her head to one side as she toyed with his chest hair. "Let's see, we could go to Old Town in Wildcat Bluff or Sure-Shot or Destiny or—"

"Too public."

"You want intimate?"

"Yes."

"Picnic by the pond?"

"You're getting warmer."

"Picnic on your patio?"

"You're colder."

"Picnic in the pasture?"

"Now you're cold."

She stroked across the bare flesh under his shirt and felt his skin pebble in response. "How about…picnic on the big, round, red bed upstairs?"

"Now that's sincerely hot." He covered her hands with his own and squeezed them.

She smiled up at him. "We have a deal then?"

He chuckled and shook his head. "I forgot we were talking about the auction."

"I didn't."

"I suppose you're going to rope me into this thing like you do everything else."

"It's for a good cause."

"You'll buy me?"

"I'll buy you."

"You'll take me upstairs to our red bed?"

"I'll take you up there."

"You'll feed me?"

"I'll feed you whatever you want to eat."

He grinned again. "You're all I want."

Chapter 23

KEMP HOPED THIS WAS A GOOD IDEA, BUT THAT WAS A forlorn hope. Nothing had been a good idea since Violet had turned up. No, take that back. Everything *with* Violet had been good. What wasn't so good was everything around them, but he was determined to set it right.

He glanced over at her as she sat in the passenger seat of his pickup with her purse in her lap and the silver spoon in her hand. He focused on Wildcat Road as they headed up a hill on their way to visit the Buick Brigade. Nobody ever knew how an encounter with the four ladies of Destiny would turn out because it never went like anybody figured it would go, so they didn't bother trying to guess ahead of time. It set a certain tension, because those ladies were formidable. They loved and protected Wildcat Bluff County in their own way, which, time and again, turned out to be the right way. He just hoped that proved to be the case again, particularly now that Violet would have her very own encounter with them. He was glad he'd be there for her, because…well, you just never knew.

After a time, he drove up a rise and crested the top of the cliff overlooking the Red River. He turned west on a two-lane road toward the buildings that rose above the flat-topped mesa.

When he reached Destiny, he slowed as he drove down Main Street. Most of the businesses had already closed up shop, but Destiny Chocolatier was still open. Warm, yellow light beckoned customers to come inside.

He made a U-turn, drove back down the street, and parked in

front of a Victorian house painted fuchsia. Purple trim accented its wraparound porch, octagonal turret room, ornamental trim, and multipeaked roof. A wide entry staircase with an elaborately carved handrail led up to where four women stood on the portico under a purple, gingerbread-laced edge of roof.

"This is Doris's house," Kemp said. "I've been here once before, because they were interested to meet me when I bought Hallelujah Ranch."

"I wonder why."

"I'd guess to make sure my intention for the ranch and the county was the best."

"How do you suppose they knew we would be here right now?"

"No point in wondering anything about them. They just know. Somehow, they always know."

"Okay. I can live with that."

"Good."

"What is that little building?" She gestured toward a small structure that echoed in color and design Doris's house, except it had been built on wooden pillars.

"Dovecote."

"Is that where Bonnie and Clyde live?"

"Yes."

"It's pretty."

"I agree." He nodded toward the mansion's portico. "We'd better join them, or they'll think we're rude to keep them waiting."

"You're right."

"In case you wonder, and no one has ever asked because that would really be considered rude, they're close to ninety if they're a day. They know everything—absolutely everything—that goes on in Wildcat Bluff County. They've been friends all their lives, and they've outlived one or more husbands."

"They're so interesting," she said.

"They're also tough. Meet you at the door with a shotgun

cradled in their arms kind of tough. But fair. Kind. Smart. And they love Wildcat Bluff County with the kind of devotion and protection that a mother gives her children."

"I like their attitude."

"Then let's go introduce you."

"I'll just leave my purse in the truck and take the spoon." She gave him a quick smile before she slipped her purse under the seat.

"Good idea. Best to travel light here." He got out, walked around the front of his truck, and opened the passenger door.

When she stepped out, he held out his arm in the formal way that he knew the Buick Brigade appreciated, like the old days of ladies and gentlemen.

Violet hesitated just a moment, obviously surprised by his action, and then grasped his arm with one hand while holding the silver spoon with the other.

He led her up the sidewalk, mounted the staircase with her, and stopped in front of the four ladies. They stood erect, as if they'd practiced walking with a book on their heads at a young age and never lost the knack.

"We're so happy you could make it. I'm Doris." She smiled with a toss of her silver, shoulder-length hair as if out of habit when it had once been much longer.

"We appreciate the invitation," Kemp said. "May I introduce Violet Ashwood?"

"Certainly." Doris beamed at Violet, her brown eyes lively. "You're lovely, my dear. Thank you so much for joining us today. These are my dear friends, Louise, Blondel, and Ada." She indicated each one with a graceful gesture of her hand. They ranged from short to tall, slim to plump, hair dark to platinum, with clothing that ranged from trim pants to full skirt.

"I'm so happy to meet all of you," Violet said. "I particularly enjoyed meeting your beautiful pigeons."

"Thank you," Doris said. "They are lovely birds."

"I take it they got home okay?" Kemp asked.

"Of course," Doris said. "Please join us in the parlor for tea."

"Thank you." Kemp waited for the ladies to precede him into the house.

He wished he didn't have to go back into that parlor because it was a dangerous place for a man of almost any size, but particularly one with his height and breadth. Still, there was no choice. He'd just have to be extra careful where he put his feet and what he sat on, and remember to keep his arms and hands close to his body so he didn't accidentally knock something over and break it, because almost everything in that room was easily breakable.

He followed the group into a cool, shadowy hallway of dark-wood wall panels. A worn, faded Aubusson runner covered an oak floor.

They turned through an open doorway and emerged into a brighter room. Delicate lace curtains over floor-to-ceiling windows had tied-back maroon velvet drapes.

He stood still as he waited for the ladies to sort themselves, because there was hardly any space to move for the crowded delicate furniture, gewgaws on every available surface, and colorful scarves and tablecloths covering almost everything. Violet wisely stayed right beside him.

Soon Doris and Ada sat across from Blondel and Louise on matching Queen Anne love seats made of gilded wood with maroon velvet upholstery. A small table between the two settees held a tray with a delicate china teapot in a violet flower pattern and six matching teacups with saucers, plus a plate stacked high with misshapen cookies.

Kemp knew the two delicate chairs that were left empty on either end of the table were for Violet and him, because he'd sat in one before. He had worried the entire time about it breaking under his weight. He hadn't broken it, so he hoped he would be lucky again today.

"How kind of you to join us," Doris said.

"We're happy to be here." Violet smiled around the group.

"Please sit." Blondel indicated the chairs with a wave of a long-fingered hand that displayed several sparkling diamond-and-gold rings.

"Yes, please," Doris said.

He caught Violet's gaze and indicated with a nod of his head for her to take the chair that looked the least stable. When she sat down without incident, placing the spoon on her lap, he eased into the other chair, barely fitting into it.

Doris picked up the teapot, poured liquid into all the cups, and handed them around the group.

He balanced the cup and saucer in one hand, hardly daring to move for concern about spilling tea or breaking china.

Ada raised the plate of cookies and held it out to Violet, who selected one first, and then it was Kemp's turn. He carefully balanced the cup and saucer on one knee and gently took a sugar cookie. He couldn't tell what its shape was supposed to represent, but that wasn't unusual with Ada's cookies. She was renowned for her delicious cookies in unrecognizable shapes.

He tried to keep a smile on his face or at least a pleasant look as the group munched cookies and drank tea. He quickly ate the cookie, knowing he was dropping crumbs on the antique rug beneath his feet, but there was nothing for it except to push on through.

The tea was weak, kind of sweet, and maybe it was something called jasmine. Sweet tea was one thing. This stuff was to be avoided at all costs in the future, but the ladies appeared perfectly happy with it, so that was all that mattered today.

Finally, Doris set her cup and saucer down on the table. She looked at Violet with a smile on her pink-tinted lips. "I see you brought the silver spoon. We heard from Jake that you'd found it."

"Would you like to see it?" Violet set her cup and saucer on the table, then picked up the spoon from her lap.

"If you don't mind, I would indeed," Doris said.

"We all would." Louise set down her cup and saucer and then patted her platinum helmet of teased and sprayed hair.

Violet held out the spoon, silver shining in the last rays of the sun coming in through the windows, with the handle extended toward Doris.

"Thank you, my dear." Doris grasped the spoon and pulled it close so she could examine it. "It's absolutely beautiful, isn't it?"

"Yes, it is."

"Violet pattern. Yes, beautiful." Louise accepted the spoon and ran a fingertip down the embossed hand to the seashell-shaped scoop, and then she leaned forward and handed the spoon to Ada.

"I wonder." Ada put a fingertip to her plump chin as she stroked down the length of the spoon. "I might be able to use one of my decorative spoons as a cookie cutter. I bet I could press in a design like this violet pattern."

"Good idea," Doris said.

Kemp didn't say a word, figuring any tinkering Ada did with her cookie designs would still have them looking like a melted Texas or a smashed cowboy boot. Good thing the shapes didn't affect the taste.

When Blondel received the spoon, she handled it with great care, turning it over and over as she examined it. "Violet is a lovely name for a lovely lady." She pointed at the delicate teapot. "Violet-pattern silverware. Violet-pattern china set. And now our very own Violet arrives at Hallelujah Ranch."

Kemp took a deep breath. Now they were getting to the thrust of the visit. He carefully set his cup and saucer on the table.

"Love is a great gift." Doris handed the spoon back to Violet.

"We wondered if you might know anything about this spoon that we found in an old dump on Hallelujah Ranch," Kemp said.

"We were just kids back then," Blondel said.

"Still, we listened outside closed doors, didn't we?" Doris grinned at her friends, blue eyes dancing with humor.

Ada nodded in agreement.

"There was traffic—fast cars, fast men, fast women—on the roads between Destiny and Hallelujah during Prohibition from the Roaring Twenties into the thirties Depression era," Doris said. "They also used Red River barges."

"Moonshine?" Kemp leaned forward, eager to hear this tale.

"Of course," Ada said. "People were not to be denied their pleasures."

"And there was great profit to be made, if not caught by the revenuers." Louise glanced around the group, patting her hair again.

"Why Destiny? And Hallelujah?" Kemp asked.

"Location," Blondel said. "Neither place can be caught by surprise."

"As to the spoon's history, I don't know for sure." Louise pointed at it in Violet's hand. "Still...a woman called Lady Mauve ruled the roost at Hallelujah. She kept schedules. She granted jobs. She maintained quality control. She hired muscle. And she retained the best lawyer money could buy to keep everyone as safe as possible."

"She never left Hallelujah," Ada said. "All came to her."

"She loved beauty." Louise gestured toward the spoon again. "She most likely had a beautiful silver set."

"Yes, indeed," Doris said.

Kemp leaned forward, more interested all the time. He'd had no idea his ranch had such a fascinating history.

"Wasn't beauty Lady Mauve's downfall?" Blondel asked.

"No, dear." Ada shook her head. "Love was her downfall."

"True," Louise said. "He was a charming, handsome scoundrel, that lawyer of hers."

"And jealous," Ada said.

"Well, she was a legendary beauty. Irish. Porcelain skin. Violet eyes. Black hair," Blondel said.

"And everyone loved her because she was powerful, provocative, and protective." Ada smiled pensively, as if remembering someone she'd known well.

"Well, not everyone loved her," Blondel said.

"He did love her," Louise said. "He loved her too well. Jealousy and moonshine didn't sit well with him."

"The lawyer?" Violet asked.

"None other," Ada said. "At least that's the story as we pieced it together."

"But nobody knows for sure." Doris appeared pensive. "One day Prohibition was over. Bootleggers were over. Revenuers were over. Lady Mauve was gone."

"And they took all the excitement with them," Blondel said.

Ada looked straight at Violet. "Only now you're here, and excitement is in the air again."

"We heard about your lonely hearts club." Doris gave Violet a big smile.

"We think it is a wonderful idea," Blondel said.

"We give you our total support," Louise said.

"Thank you. That makes me very happy." Violet clutched the spoon to her heart. "I'm doing my best to get my dating site up and running. Kemp is a big help."

"We're getting there." He didn't know what else to say, except something about the ranch. "I suppose y'all heard about the gold hunters trespassing on Hallelujah. Any words of advice?"

"Everyone thinks big money is the end-all," Blondel said.

"But it's not," Louise said.

"Not that it isn't helpful," Ada said.

"True," Doris said. "But in the end, there is only one thing that matters."

"What is it?" Violet asked.

"Love." Doris stood up, indicating that the visit was at an end. "That's why we love your lonely hearts club."

"Thank you." Violet rose to her feet.

"Thanks for the tea and cookies." Kemp joined Violet. "Ready to go?"

"Yes, of course." She gave a little wave to the ladies, then tucked her hand into the crook of his arm.

He maneuvered them out of the house as quickly as possible, down the staircase, and into his truck. He revved the engine, and then he eased back onto Main Street.

Fortunately, it had all gone well…and he hadn't broken anything.

Chapter 24

"That was an amazing experience." Violet tucked the spoon into her purse for safekeeping, then looked at Doris's painted lady one last time.

"Those Victorian houses are something, aren't they?" Kemp said as he drove away.

"Wonderful. And that story about Lady Mauve and Hallelujah Ranch hardly seems real."

"Sounds more like a movie script."

"Except it had no real ending," Violet said.

"It's been close to a hundred years since all that bootlegging was a big deal across America. Facts are probably long gone. Speculation is most likely all we'll ever have to go on."

"Now that we're thinking about it, maybe we'll run across something at the ranch that'll give us more clues."

"Hope so," Kemp said. "Guess we'd better focus on what's next on our list for today."

She chuckled at his comment, because it sounded like something longtime couples would share. She felt warmly content at the idea.

"Chocolate shop?" he asked.

"Yes."

He made a U-turn and headed down the other side of Main Street. He passed single-story, white buildings with Western false fronts. He slowed down in front of the sixth store, Destiny Chocolatier.

Violet looked at him. She suddenly felt selfish. She'd talked him into all of this for her sake. "You don't have to get involved in my plans, you know."

"What?" He glanced over at her with a puzzled expression on his face, then returned his attention to the street.

"You've been reluctant from the start. Lester could do the photo shoot, and he's already involved in the fund-raiser. Besides, I'm the one who is reluctant now. It's just come home to me that I'll be taking you away from your work at the ranch at a vital time."

Kemp abruptly pulled into a parking spot in front of Destiny Chocolatier and hit the brakes. "Are you saying you prefer Lester to me? I'd understand it, because plenty of women do."

"What?" She felt terrible that he'd even think she meant that. "Of course not. I want *you*...not your cousin."

"Are you sure?"

"Yes." How could she fix what she'd just broken? "I was trying to be sensitive to your needs, instead of ramming through what's important to me, even if it's at your expense. I'm sorry if it didn't come out right."

He turned off the engine. "It turned out fine. I appreciate you thinking about me that way."

"Lester can't hold a candle to you." She held out her hand, and he grasped it with warm, strong fingers.

"He's left a trail of broken hearts in his wake, but every single one of them would welcome him back in an instant."

"I admit he's got charm, looks, and quick wit, but I suspect it is all surface. You, on the other hand, are deep, sincere, and there for me every step of the way since I arrived knowing practically nothing about Wildcat Bluff County."

"Thanks." He squeezed her hand. "Let's don't talk anymore about Lester taking my place. It's not going to happen."

"Okay." She grinned, suddenly feeling lighthearted and mischievous. "But don't complain when you're under the hot, bright lights at our photo shoot."

He frowned. "What hot lights?"

She chuckled, leaned over, and kissed his freshly shaven cheek. "Sunlight."

"I don't want it to be a big deal."

"It won't be. And I'll take it easy on you."

"Not too easy." He lifted her hand and kissed her palm, tracing her long lifeline with the tip of his tongue.

"Do you suppose I could persuade you to buy me another box of chocolates tonight?"

"I already had it on our to-do list."

"Perfect."

"Let's go. They're starting to watch us through the windows. Somebody will be out pretty quick to herd us inside."

"The store is closed, isn't it?"

"Yeah…except for our group."

She gripped his hand, then let go. "I feel a little apprehensive. These are your friends. I've only met a few of them. I'm the outsider."

"You may have started as an outsider, but you're quickly becoming an insider with all your fancy ideas."

"Am I too fancy?"

"I'm right partial to fancy." He smiled at her with softness in his green eyes.

She returned his smile, knowing the expression in her eyes had gone soft, too. In fact, she felt kind of gooey inside.

"You know what?" He grinned.

"What?"

"If they hadn't already seen us, I'd turn this truck around and go straight to your cabin."

"You're thinking about our big, red, round bed, aren't you?"

"Fancy, isn't it?"

"Real fancy."

"We could get round chocolates to go with it," he suggested.

"Raspberry ones."

"That'd do it."

"Oh yeah."

As they smiled at each other, she saw a shadow loom over Kemp's truck window, followed by a loud knock. He lowered the window and there was Lester, grinning at them with a knowing look in his eyes.

"Get a room," Lester said, grinning even bigger, "or put it on hold and come join us."

"Les, you've got the worst timing in the world." Kemp sighed.

"Hah! I've been told I've got great timing by better folks than you."

"Women?" Kemp asked.

"I'll never tell." Lester smiled at Violet as he raised an eyebrow. "Can't you keep this guy in line?"

She smiled back. "Can't you?"

"How? He's *that* cousin. Come on inside. Folks are waiting." And Lester sauntered back into Destiny Chocolatier.

Violet laughed. "If he got any cockier, you could sell tickets to his show."

"Don't even think it. You know good and well it'd be right up his alley."

She laughed again. "I think they broke the Texan mold with him."

"They broke something." Kemp glanced at her. "Ready to brave the good folks of Wildcat Bluff?"

"I'm as ready as I'll ever be."

"Just don't sit close to Lester."

"Oh my, no." And she couldn't keep from laughing harder.

Kemp joined her laughter as he opened his door and stepped into an early evening with a touch of coolness in the air. He walked around the front of his truck and opened her door.

She stepped down, feeling like a seasoned cowgirl who was

used to the height of a pickup. She joined Kemp on the boardwalk and caught the delicious scent of chocolate. Bertha had created beautiful displays of tiers of candy in a variety of shapes and sizes that could be seen through the sparkling display windows.

"If I'm not mistaken," he whispered as he pointed at a display, "those are round raspberry chocolates."

She chuckled as she looked closer. "I do believe you're right."

"Let's get some before we leave."

"Absolutely."

He opened the door and a brass bell jingled to announce their presence. She walked in ahead of him and glanced around the shop.

A few folks sat in chairs at the round, white tables that dotted the black-and-white square-tile floor. Violet admired again the glamorous Roaring Twenties art prints that accented the white walls, along with the sepia-tone posters of famous people of that era. And yet, everything paled in comparison to the long counter with its glass front that held sugary confections of all types and sizes.

A hush descended over the group. They turned as one and looked at Violet and Kemp.

"For those of you who haven't met her," Kemp said, "this is Violet Ashford." He put a warm hand on her back.

She smiled around the room. Folks here were mostly dressed in shirts, jeans, and boots. Even if they didn't know it, they had the perfect look for her Cowboy Heart-to-Heart Corral.

"I'm so pleased to meet you. Welcome to the Chocolatier." A tall, blond, blue-eyed, plump cowgirl held out her hand. She wore a full apron in a horse-riding-cowgirl pattern over her western shirt and jeans.

"Violet, this is Bertha Waldron," Kemp said.

"I'm glad to meet you, too. Thanks for hosting us here this evening." Violet shook Bertha's hand.

"Happy to do it anytime."

Lester hurried up to them. "And it wasn't even as a favor to me."

Bertha chuckled. "Les, you get plenty of favors from me, so there's no need for more."

"Bertie baby," Lester said, "there's always a need for more favors."

Everyone in the room laughed at his words, then silence descended again before Oscar and Tater sidled in close to Violet.

"Tater figures you need some eye candy for your dating site, and I'm the perfect guy for it." Oscar looked like a born-and-bred cowboy in his faded, ripped Wranglers and denim shirt.

"I already told you, Kemp scored that big win," Lester said. "And I'm his understudy."

Oscar scratched his bald head, rubbed his silver stubble, and squinted brown eyes at Violet. "How about I take the second understudy spot?"

Violet liked the idea of expanding the range for her dating site. Everyone needed love, no matter their age. Anyway, Oscar looked so hopeful, she couldn't turn him down.

As he waited for her reply, Oscar adjusted the blue bandanna around Tater's neck.

"I think that's a fine idea."

"No kidding?" Oscar appeared surprised, dark eyebrows rising upward. He patted Tater's head. "Hear that, old boy? She's gonna make me a star."

"Understudy means there's not much chance for us." Lester gave Kemp a narrow-eyed look. "My cousin's got all the luck."

Oscar cocked his head at Kemp. "Nothing says he won't hit a spell of bad luck before it's all said and done."

"True enough." Lester gave Kemp a contemplative look, as if considering options.

"And another thing," Oscar said. "I want to be auctioned off like a prize bull. After all my years as a cowboy firefighter, I deserve to be wined and dined by some comely lass from hereabouts or from as far away as Dallas. Tater here agrees with me that I'm bound to bring a big price." He patted the dog's head.

Sydney Steele gave Violet a smile as she walked up. "Oscar, that's fine and dandy, but don't get any ideas about running off with your comely lass. You're the best ranch foreman in the county, and I won't lose you."

Oscar chuckled, winking at her. "You never know what a man in the throes of love is gonna do."

"That's right," Lester said.

"Violet, you're the mover and shaker here," Sydney said.

"Oh no, I—"

"We'd never have come up with the idea of Buy a Date with the Cowboy Firefighter of Your Dreams fund-raiser if you hadn't come out of nowhere and turned up at the dump that day."

"Les and I have been making plans for the big event," Bertha said. "It's almost all he'll talk about, so we've got lots to share."

"Great," Violet said. "I'm not sure how much I can contribute, since I know so few people here. But I do want to make sure we cross-promote with Cowboy Heart-to-Heart Corral."

Sydney nodded. "Storm couldn't be here, since she spends all her free time with Daisy Sue and Fernando, but she wanted me to remind everyone that she'll also cross-promote on Fernando's website."

"That's wonderful," Violet said. "How is Daisy Sue?"

"Ann added minerals to her diet, and she's been stronger since then. Still, it's just not an easy pregnancy."

"I'm staying close to the barn," Oscar said. "Tater, too."

"You know we appreciate it." Sydney smiled at him. "You're the most experienced cowboy on the ranch."

"I do my best."

"Violet, lots of folks are involved in our benefit, but they couldn't be here," Sydney said. "I'll share a bit of their input."

"Thanks," Violet said.

"KWCB, our local radio station, will livestream the event and will cross-promote with your dating site."

"That's wonderful news," Violet said. "I'll be happy to meet with the station and coordinate."

"You'll get a chance to meet lots of folks before this is all said and done," Sydney said. "For now, we just wanted to touch base and get the ball rolling with you."

"We already got it rolling," Lester said. "Like Oscar, I can't wait to be auctioned off."

"That's why we're putting you in charge of rounding up enough cowboy firefighters to make this fund-raiser a success," Sydney said.

"Happy to do it." Lester grinned. "Easy as pie. I mean, what guy wouldn't want to be bought by a woman and then wined and dined by her? Load me up with date nights."

"Not every guy will be quite so enthused," Kemp said.

"Can't imagine why not." Oscar patted Tater's head. "Load me up, too."

"Oscar, why don't you help Lester with that job?" Sydney asked.

"My pleasure. Tater's too."

"If you need it, I've got a list of possible candidates," Sydney said. "And I'm not above twisting a few arms for a good cause."

"We know how persuasive you can be," Kemp said. "Nobody'll forget the dunking booth for a long time."

"Great." Sydney laughed. "Wild West Days is coming up over Labor Day Weekend again, and guess what."

Kemp groaned. "Another dunking booth."

"Absolutely." Sydney smiled mischievously. "It was a huge hit last year."

"It's a terrific fund-raiser," Bertha said. "If there's anything we can do to help with the launch of your dating site, just let us know. Otherwise, we'll focus on Buy a Date with the Cowboy Firefighter of Your Dreams."

"Thanks. I'll let you know." Violet glanced at Kemp. "Right now, Kemp has agreed to be the face of Cowboy Heart-to-Heart Corral."

"Lucky dog. He gets all the breaks." Lester gave Bertha a sideways glance of appreciation. "But I get the lovely lady of Destiny Chocolatier, so I've definitely one-upped him."

"Cuz, you always one-up me and everybody knows it." Kemp chuckled.

"Not always." Lester nodded toward Violet.

"Folks, why don't we sit down and make more plans?" Sydney gestured toward the tables.

"First, Violet wants to fill a candy box to take with her. And she's partial to raspberry," Kemp said.

"Go ahead and do it while we settle in," Bertha said.

Kemp walked with Violet behind the long candy counter, then popped open a white box and set it on the countertop. He slipped on plastic gloves, then handed her a pair to use for picking up candy.

"All this looks wonderful. I don't know how to make up my mind which is best." She pulled on the gloves.

"Remember, red and round."

She selected pieces and tucked them in the box. As she tried to make up her mind, somebody's cell phone trilled in the shop. She glanced up and saw Sydney answer her phone.

"I've got to go. Y'all carry on without me." Sydney tucked her phone back in her pocket.

"What is it?" Bertha asked.

"Daisy Sue." Sydney looked worried. "Ann is on her way to check on her condition."

"Sorry," Lester said. "You'll let us know the results, won't you?"

"Yes." Sydney glanced at Kemp. "Would you come to the ranch? Daisy Sue, Storm, and Fernando will be comforted by your presence."

"You bet. I'll do whatever I can to help, even if it's nothing more than being there for them."

"We're on our way, too." Oscar and Tater headed out.

"It's okay if you want to leave me here while you check on Daisy Sue." Violet closed the candy box and sealed it with a gold sticker.

"I'll be happy to take Violet home," Lester said.

"No. Y'all can catch up on plans later." Kemp put an arm around her waist and leaned down so his lips were close to her ear. "I want you with me," he whispered. "Good times or bad times, I want us together."

Chapter 25

KEMP TURNED OFF WILDCAT ROAD AND DROVE UNDER THE black metal sign with a cutout that read "Steele Trap Ranch." The last red-orange rays of the setting sun shone through the open letters. They appeared to be on fire. He didn't like that portent one bit. Pregnancy problems in cattle always concerned him, but if caught early, they could usually be solved so that the cow delivered her calf safely. He also didn't like the fact that Daisy Sue kept having problems.

Violet sat stiffly beside him, clutching her purse and box of candy as if they could ward off trouble.

He gripped the steering wheel tighter as he followed the winding lane up the hill toward the group of barns, corrals, workshops, and garages. He parked in front of the new, metal red barn where Daisy Sue had been kept the last time he'd seen her. He wasn't the only one who had parked in that area. He noticed pickups that belonged to Sydney, Oscar, and Ann. A couple of other trucks he didn't recognize were there, too.

He glanced at Violet. "Do you want to come inside or stay out here? Are you squeamish? It could be messy, or—"

"If it won't bother anyone, I'd like to come inside to offer moral support if nothing else."

"Thanks. I'll be glad to have you there."

"Okay." She set her purse and box on the floorboard.

When he opened her door, she stepped down, and he gave her a quick, reassuring hug. He glanced around the area. A massive, black bull with a forlorn look in his dark eyes stood just inside the corral.

"Let's go pay our respects to Fernando."

"Okay."

He walked with her, hand in hand, over to the corral.

Fernando watched them until they were close, then he raised his head, sniffed the air, and lowered his face over the side of the railing.

"How are you doing?" Kemp asked.

Fernando tossed his head to convey his displeasure with the entire situation.

"We're going to see Daisy Sue now," Kemp said. "Ann's with her, so she's getting the best care."

"She's a beautiful cow," Violet said.

Fernando turned his big, dark, expressive eyes on her, and he snorted gently toward her.

"We'll see you later." Kemp squeezed Violet's fingers and then started for the barn, walking with her. "I hated to leave Fernando alone."

"Me, too."

He kept hold of her hand as they entered the dim, cool building. The barn smelled of oats, hay, and manure, familiar scents to a cowboy. He looked down the length of the center aisle. Stalls lined both sides. Most had closed doors. He heard voices and saw lights in the stall about halfway down the aisle, where Daisy Sue had been when he'd last visited her.

Sydney, Oscar, and Tater stood outside the stall. They glanced up at the new arrivals. Sydney put a fingertip to her lips to signal for them to be as quiet as possible.

Kemp shrugged. What was going on? Maybe Ann was examining Daisy Sue and didn't want anyone else in the stall, which was understandable. But when he peeked in the open doorway, he could hardly believe his eyes. Only Storm would have pulled off such an event.

DJ Wildcat Jack of KWCB's Wildcat Den, wearing his long,

silver hair in two plaits and a fringed leather jacket, held out a mic while the radio station's tech guys livestreamed an interview.

Storm and Ann stood on either side of Daisy Sue with a yellow sunflower positioned between her black ears. Storm looked just as sharp as the cow on the front of her trademark hot-pink "Fernando the Wonder Bull" T-shirt. The shirt was emblazoned with rhinestones. Ann had a stethoscope draped around her neck.

"Dr. Bridges," Wildcat Jack said in a serious tone. "Fans across the globe are concerned about Daisy Sue's health. How is she today? And how is Fernando handling her difficult pregnancy?"

"Let me answer first about Fernando," Storm said. "He is his usual stoic self, even though he is worried about the possibility of losing the love of his life and their child…as are we all."

"Thank you for sharing that insight into Fernando the Wonder Bull's current temperament." Wildcat Jack turned toward Ann. "Dr. Bridges, will you please share your assessment of Daisy Sue's current condition?"

"She responded well when we changed her feed and added minerals to her diet."

"We're all glad to hear that news," Wildcat Jack said. "And now?"

"She has swelling under her belly as she approaches term. That is not so unusual, but it is uncomfortable for her." She gestured toward Daisy Sue. "Fortunately, it should be resolved after she calves."

"I'm sure all of Fernando and Daisy Sue's fans are thrilled to hear this news."

"Yes, that is the good news. However—"

"I don't like the sound of that," Wildcat Jack interrupted.

"My concern now is that she might develop an abdominal hernia."

"What does that mean?"

"In late pregnancy, a cow might suffer rupture in the lower portion of the abdominal wall, perhaps due to abdomen muscle weakness. This condition would allow the uterus to drop with nothing between it and the skin."

"I've heard of hernias in humans. They're not life-threatening, are they?"

"Not normally. In the case of a pregnant cow, we might see swelling about the size of a football that is mostly fluid until it becomes larger and moves down to hock level. That would mean that the heavy uterus and fetus within it have dropped out of the abdomen."

"I know our viewers are more concerned than ever for Daisy Sue at this news. Please reassure us that a hernia will not negatively impact Daisy Sue or her calf." Wildcat Jack looked and sounded hopeful.

"If she develops a hernia, she should be able to give birth to a live calf. At that point, I would examine her to make a hernia determination."

"That means you would repair the damage."

"Yes, I would certainly do my best."

"At this point, we're talking what-ifs, aren't we?"

"Yes. Sometimes swelling under the belly is mistaken for an abdominal hernia. I'm not making that mistake, although it could still happen. However, I am concerned about the size and swelling under her belly."

"We all are," Wildcat Jack said. "What are your plans for her now?"

"She will be kept here in the barn where it is safe and she will not be jostled or disturbed until she gives birth."

"I'm glad to hear it." Wildcat Jack gave the camera a relieved look.

"I want to reassure everyone that Daisy Sue is receiving the best care and her prognosis is good…at this point."

"Thank you, Dr. Bridges," Wildcat Jack said. "Naturally, everyone is wondering about Fernando. We know this is difficult for him. Do you have him on tranquilizers or relaxants?"

"I'm very cautious with all medications. In this case, Fernando is a calm, steady bull who is handling the stress quite well."

"I'm glad to hear it." Wildcat Jack glanced toward Storm. "Are you allowing him to visit Daisy Sue?"

"Yes." Storm gestured toward the veterinarian. "Dr. Bridges advised us that it would be in their best interest to spend time together each day."

"I'm sure viewers will be happy to hear that news about the loving couple," Wildcat Jack said.

"Fernando and Daisy Sue want me to express their appreciation for all the support during this momentous occasion of their lives," Storm said. "We're unable to hold a calf shower, but people have been generous in sending gifts. I show Fernando and Daisy Sue every single baby blanket that arrives in the mail. They particularly like cow motifs. And I'm storing the calf feed in a separate stall in the barn. Their little one will surely enjoy all of it soon."

"And that just goes to show the love folks have for their favorite couple," Wildcat Jack said.

"I'll be sharing photos of the calf gifts online soon," Storm said. "Right now, all my time and attention is focused on keeping Daisy Sue safe and Fernando happy."

"That's a tall order for a little girl, but if anybody can do it... it's our very own Storm Steele of Steele Trap Ranch. Dr. Bridges, Storm, thank you so much for sharing part of your day with us." Wildcat Jack smiled at the camera. "And that's it for our special Fernando and Daisy Sue update. Stay tuned for more classic country music coming your way from KWCB, the Wildcat Den, on the beautiful Hogtrot Ranch in Wildcat Bluff County, Texas."

"That's a wrap." Nathan Halford of Thingamajigs turned off the bright lights.

"Thanks." Storm nodded to the group, then wrapped her arms around Daisy Sue's neck and hugged her.

"Anytime, sweetie," Wildcat Jack said. "We're not doing you a favor. You're doing us one. Fernando and Daisy Sue's ratings are always sky-high."

"People do love them." She adjusted the sunflower on Daisy Sue's head before she turned back.

"I appreciate it, too," Ann said. "It's always good to share information about animals. You never know when just one person who heard that report will be aware of the difference between belly swelling and abdominal hernia, so that a cow's life is helped."

"I'm with you," Wildcat Jack said. "I'm a cowboy from way back. You treat animals right and they'll treat you right."

"So true." Ann smiled warmly at him.

"If you don't need me anymore, I'm out of here," Nathan said as he gathered his equipment.

"As usual, thanks for the help," Wildcat Jack said. "We're done here today."

Storm glanced up, saw Kemp, and beckoned him closer.

He eased into the stall, stroked Daisy Sue down her long nose, and turned to Ann. "Good advice for folks."

"I do my best."

"So you're not really concerned about her pregnancy now?"

"You know me. I'm always concerned about an animal in my care. But so far so good."

"I understand." Kemp didn't add anything more, but they both knew that a cow with a hernia might birth a calf and still not survive afterwards. Still, as she said, so far so good. He would hold on to that thought.

As Nathan moved out of the stall with his equipment, he stopped and stared at Violet. "Lonely hearts club, right?"

"Yes," Violet said. "Actually, it's Cowboy Heart-to-Heart Corral."

"I want in on it." Nathan grinned. "I'm so busy working at the store and for the station that I don't have time to meet and greet."

"You want to join my dating site?"

"What dating site?" Wildcat Jack walked out of the stall, looking as if he'd struck gold.

"She's lonely hearts club," Nathan said.

"Be still my heart. I'm Wildcat Jack, at your service."

"Violet Ashwood. Good to meet you."

Wildcat Jack put a hand over his heart and leaned toward her. "Whatever you want, you've got. I've been squiring ladies around this county for nigh on…let's just say long enough to have a little experience."

Kemp muscled up beside Jack. If there was another Lester in the world, it was Jack. Women loved him, and he loved women.

Wildcat Jack glanced over at him and raised an eyebrow.

"She's staying on my ranch and working with me." Kemp gave Jack a no-nonsense look. He was putting up with no shenanigans from this cowboy.

"Are you saying she's off-limits?" Wildcat Jack appeared ready and able to take on any competition.

"He's not saying anything about me," Violet said. "I'm saying that he's the face of Cowboy Heart-to-Heart Corral. We're doing a photo shoot."

"So that's the way the wind blows." Wildcat Jack gave Kemp a knowing wink. "When your luck turns good, it's pure dynamite."

"If you'd like to join my dating site, let me know," Violet said.

"You bet." Wildcat Jack leaned closer to her. "And if you need another face and body, for your lonely hearts club, just give me a call at the station."

"Thanks." Violet smiled, obviously enjoying the encounter. "Would you care to be the third understudy? Lester's first. Oscar's second."

Wildcat Jack jerked his head toward Oscar, who gave him a smug smile. "I'm not normally out of the loop, but I've got to say I missed this big time. It could be that pretty lady over in Denison has driven me to distraction."

"We don't need a third understudy," Oscar said. "Two is plenty."

"You never know," Wildcat Jack said. "I'd be happy to be on another beautiful woman's list."

"You got it." Violet chuckled. "You're my third understudy."

"I feel as if I just got put on an endangered list." Kemp grinned, shaking his head.

"Accidents happen." Wildcat Jack grinned, too.

"More often than you'd think." Oscar patted Tater's head.

"Violet, whatever you've got going for you," Sydney said, smiling, "I need some of it. I have to chase these cowboys down to star in my calendar. All you have to do is crook your little finger, and you've got four ready and willing to pose for you."

"It's the lonely-hearts-club angle," Violet said. "Maybe you ought to try that next time."

"I'll definitely give it some thought."

"When are you going to have the site up and running?" Ann asked as she walked out of the stall with her vet bag.

"Soon," Violet said. "We've already started marketing, so I need to finish up my part of the plans soon."

"Let us know when you want something from us," Ann said. "There's way too much grass growing under my feet."

"Me, too." Oscar adjusted the bandanna around Tater's neck. "Not that I don't have the best company in the world, but sometimes a man just hankers for a woman in his life."

"Don't I know it," Wildcat Jack said.

Sydney laughed. "When has there ever not been a woman in your life?"

Wildcat Jack cocked his head to one side, as if considering the question. "There's always a first time for everything."

Everyone laughed and he grinned around the group, shrugging his broad shoulders.

Storm stepped out of the stall and put her hands on her hips. "You know, we're not throwing a party here. Daisy Sue needs her rest."

"Sorry," Sydney said. "I guess we're getting a little loud at the idea of so much upcoming fun."

"I appreciate all of you turning out to support Daisy Sue and Fernando," Storm said. "I really do. But maybe y'all had better head on out."

"You're right." Kemp looked back at Daisy Sue. "I'm glad she's stable now."

"I'm ready for that calf any day. Fernando, too. Daisy Sue most of all." Storm gave a big sigh.

"She'll get there. I'm keeping a close eye on her," Ann said. "For now, I need to get back to my practice. I'm sure everybody has someplace they need to be, too."

"I'll check on Fernando." Oscar and Tater headed out.

Violet glanced around at everyone. "And I really do appreciate all the support. I'll let you know as my site progresses."

"We appreciate all the fun you're bringing to our county," Sydney said. "We'll be in touch about the fund-raiser."

"Let me know if you need me." Kemp gestured with his head toward Daisy Sue.

"Will do," Storm said. "Thanks for being here."

"We'll see y'all later." Kemp put a hand on Violet's back, sending a message to everyone present about his relationship with her.

He grinned to himself as he walked with her down the aisle. Lester and Jack could just eat their hearts out. Sometimes the turtle won, no matter how fast the rabbit.

Chapter 26

"I DIDN'T EXPECT SO MUCH EXCITEMENT AT THE RANCH. DID you?" Violet glanced at Kemp as he drove toward Hallelujah.

"You never know what Storm is going to think up next."

"I was impressed with her interview. She sounded so professional."

"She is definitely that when it comes to Fernando and Daisy Sue. And it comes straight from her big heart."

"You can tell she's sincere, and that goes a long way."

"Sure does."

"I'm so relieved Daisy Sue is all right."

"Ann is taking good care of her."

"Everyone is so supportive of each other here...even of me and my ideas. I'm really growing fond of this county."

"I hope that's not all you're becoming fond of."

"You're right. Destiny Chocolatier comes to mind." She couldn't keep from teasing him.

"Chocolate comes to my mind, too."

"Is this on your mind?" She chuckled as she picked up her box of chocolates from the floorboard.

"Oh yeah. Round raspberry in there?"

"You know it."

"Let's get home. It's been a long day. I'm ready to unwind."

"With chocolate?"

He glanced over at her and grinned. "With you."

"I'm ready when you are." She gave him a sultry look, opened the box, selected a piece of candy, and took a small bite.

"If I go any faster, I'll be well over the speed limit."

"It's not that far."

"For the way I feel right now, it's way too far."

"How do you feel?" She nibbled on the candy, knowing she was being provocative and liking it.

"One box isn't enough. We should have bought two."

"We can always make a return trip."

"Not tonight." He glanced at her again. "Once I get you into the cabin, we're not leaving until—"

"Every last piece of candy is gone?"

"Right."

She popped the chocolate into her mouth and enjoyed the explosion of raspberry and chocolate taste. It just didn't get any better, candy-wise, than Destiny Chocolatier.

"Are you going to eat that entire box before we get home?"

"Worried I won't save you any?"

"No." He cast another quick look at her. "I want to share it all with you."

She smiled as she raised the box close to her face and looked at the different shapes and colors, trying to decide which piece to torment him with next. She imagined getting back to their home and leaving a trail of clothes as they rushed up to their big, red, round bed. Yeah, *their* home. She didn't think *separate* anymore. She thought *together*. And now she couldn't imagine it any other way.

As she looked down at her choices, Kemp abruptly hit the brakes hard, tires squealing while his pickup careened back and forth across on the road as he adjusted by skillfully steering into the skids to keep them from sliding off the road and into the deep drainage ditch.

She slammed forward against her seat belt, felt the hit to her sternum, gasped for breath, and lost control of the box. Chocolates flew into the air, cascaded across the cabin, and landed in splats on her, him, the dash, the floor, the console...absolutely everything.

He got the truck under control and stopped on the side of the road. He hit the top of the steering wheel with the palms of his hands.

"What happened?" She felt a little in shock as she rubbed her chest. She'd probably have a bruise tomorrow.

"Are you okay?" He turned in his seat and looked her over.

"Yes. But—"

"I know. The chocolates are a mess, again." He plucked a piece off his lap and popped it into his mouth. "Still good, though."

She wondered how long it would take to pick up the candy. If the chocolate heated up in the sun and melted, the cab would need professional cleaning. The seats were leather, but they might stain. She looked around for the box's top and bottom, so she could start picking up pieces before they did more damage.

"Did you see it?"

"What?"

He pointed down the road. "They're gone. Tore out of my pasture like a bat out of hell. Right in front of me. That's why I had to throw on the brakes. I don't think they even saw me because they were in such a hurry."

"Who?"

"You really didn't see them, did you?"

"No. I was looking at the candy."

"Does a one-ton truck hauling a backhoe on a trailer remind you of anybody?"

"Oh no! The trespassers?"

He nodded. "I could try to run them down, but I've got a bigger issue now."

"What?" She realized the spilled box was only a minor part of their problem.

"I'll show you." He made a U-turn and headed back the way they'd come.

She could see black skid marks on the asphalt road where he'd slammed on the brakes to avoid a collision. She was glad he'd been behind the wheel, because she doubted her experience driving in the city had prepared her to handle country surprises.

"That's Hallelujah property." He pulled off on the right side of the road and pointed across it.

"Oh no." She saw a big gap in the line of silver fence that stretched across the pasture just beyond the edge of the road.

"Oh yeah. They struck again."

"You'll have to fix that fence."

"And the hole I know is back there somewhere."

"I'm so sorry."

"This is getting really old."

"And it's also expensive since you have to rent a backhoe every time."

"Time and trouble and effort, too."

"If you could just find out who was doing it, the sheriff could stop them."

"Right. So far we don't have enough to go on, so I'll just have to suck it up and fix it."

"Maybe chocolate would help." She pointed at a piece stuck to his shirt that looked misshapen and on the melted side.

He glanced down, shook his head, picked up the candy, and popped it into his mouth. "Raspberry."

"And I had such high hopes for this box."

"Me, too."

"What are we going to do?"

"I need to repair that fence right now."

"Do you have stuff to do it?"

"I always keep supplies in my truck."

"Good." She picked up a piece that was melting on her jeans and put it into her mouth. "Blackberry."

"Okay. We need a plan."

"How can I help?"

"If you'll pick up the candy, I'll fix the fence."

"Are you sure you don't need help?"

"Best help you can do for me right now is clean up this mess." He glanced at her with a smile. "At least it's not my mess this time."

"You did throw on the brakes."

"But you were holding the box."

"True." She looked at candy all over the truck's interior, and then she started to laugh.

He joined her laughter.

"It's getting pretty ridiculous, isn't it?" She held out her hand to him, belatedly seeing that her fingers were smeared with goo.

"We might as well laugh." He lifted her hand to his lips and sucked off the chocolate.

"At least you're putting the candy to good use." She shivered at his touch, wishing they were home with an entire box to play with in bed.

"It's the best I can do for now, but I promise to do better with the next box from the chocolatier."

"The next? Do you think it's safe?"

"Somehow or other, we're going to turn our bad-luck chocolates into good-luck chocolates."

"Okay. I'll depend on you to make it happen." She cradled his cheek with her palm for a moment and gave him a warm smile.

"You can always depend on me."

"I'm quickly learning that fact."

He returned her warm smile. "For now, I'd better get to work on that fence."

"And I'd better pick up the candy."

He made another U-turn and parked on the side of the road in front of the section of cut fence.

She unsnapped her seat belt so she could move around more easily. She found the box's top and bottom on the floorboard.

"If you need me, I've got my phone in my pocket. There's cell coverage on this stretch of road."

"Okay." She suddenly felt a little apprehensive about being left alone in so much empty countryside with night falling fast. She'd need to learn to deal with that part of being in the country, but packing a pistol ought to solve that problem.

"I'll call the sheriff and make a report. I doubt it'll do much good, but he needs to know."

"Good idea."

Kemp opened his door, dusted candy off the front of his shirt, and then glanced back at her. "After I'm gone, lock your doors. If anything happened to you…"

"Be careful. If anything happened to you…"

"It won't." He didn't move.

"Good." She didn't move.

Finally, he tore his gaze away and shut the door. He opened the back door, grabbed a dark-green nylon equipment bag, and closed that door, too. He gave a quick wave, and set off for the fence.

She watched him a moment as he tromped into the pasture, then she clicked the locks shut. Could she salvage any of the candy?

She set the top and bottom of the box on the driver's seat. She'd use one container for throwaways and the other for possible keepers. Chocolates on the floorboard were a definite no. Above the floor were possible keepers. Anything stuck to her would be eaten.

She set about her task while he set about his. She found a few good pieces to eat first. She particularly liked the peanut butter crunch, although she even liked the mystery one with a sweet but indefinable taste. Unfortunately, most of the candy was on the floor. She put those in the throwaway box. There were a few brown smudges on the rubber floor mat. She plucked a few pieces off the dashboard and deposited them in the keeper box. She considered those a little on the iffy side. He hadn't dusted the dash recently, or it acquired dust quickly driving with open windows in the country. She found a few smashed pieces on his floor mat, where he'd stepped on them getting out of the truck. She picked those up as best she could and put them in the toss box. Both floor mats would need to be cleaned, but for now they'd do just fine.

All in all, the mess wasn't as bad as it would have been if she'd filled that really big box she'd eyed with a certain amount of lust. And she'd managed to get the cleanup done.

She picked up the boxes from the driver seat, took a look at the contents, and plopped the lid down on top of the bottom, mixing good and bad together. Why had she ever thought she could salvage any of it? Wishful thinking, she supposed. At least she'd managed a few good bites.

That's when she realized she couldn't see Kemp anymore. She could already see bright stars in the darkening sky, but he would have stood out as a darker shape against the deepening gray of the evening twilight. She could see he had fixed the fence, but he hadn't returned to her. What if he'd run into trouble?

She lowered her window, so she could see better, and heard the high-pitched yips of hunting coyotes. No telling what other dangerous, wild animals were out there ready to spring on the unwary. Did rattlesnakes hunt at night like coyotes? Was a rattlesnake about to sink fangs into Kemp's leg?

What if the trespassers were actually deranged killers? What if they'd left someone behind to prey on Kemp when he found the hole they'd dug? What if the holes were simply a diversion, so they could kidnap Kemp for ransom or burn down the ranch or rustle his cattle or steal the silver or...

And then she saw him walk up to the fence using the flashlight on his cell phone to illuminate his way. She breathed a sigh of relief as she watched him pry apart two barbwire strands with his hands, ease himself between them, and head for the pickup.

When he got closer, she unlocked the doors and tried to slow the fast beating of her heart. He was safe. She was safe. Even Daisy

Sue was safe. She blamed her sudden worry on her wild imagination, as well as the really dark night.

He opened the door and sat down beside her.

She could smell the wild outdoors on him. He'd put himself in danger. He hadn't given a second thought to his personal safety or how it would affect her if something bad happened to him. She went from worry to anger in a heartbeat, but she tried to control the emotion.

"Candy all cleaned up?"

"Yes."

"I fixed the fence."

"Good."

"Were you able to save any of the candy?"

"Yes. And I ate it."

"Okay." He started the engine and turned on the headlights. "You ready to go?"

"Yes."

"Violet, did I miss something while I was gone?"

"No."

"Are you mad at me about the mess? I'm sorry, but I had to stop fast or there'd have been a collision. I'll buy you another bigger box."

"Fine. If you want…" She unclenched her fists. She couldn't let this fester or it'd hurt both of them.

"If I want?"

"Kemp, I…I worried about you."

He turned and looked at her.

She took a deep breath.

"What is it?"

"You scared me. It's really dark out there. I heard coyotes. I bet there are other dangerous animals out there, too. Snakes."

"So?"

"And the trespassers could be much worse than just gold hunters. How would I know?"

"Right. City. You're not used to it out here." He reached for her, pulled her to his side, and put an arm around her shoulders.

She felt his warmth and strength like a balm to her spirits.

"I'm fine. I didn't go far. But I shouldn't have been out of your sight. Would that have made it better?"

"Yes. Much better."

"I'll remember that in the future." He squeezed her shoulder. "Once you're used to the country, you'll realize it's usually safer here than in the city. Human predators are much more dangerous than animal predators."

"I don't want you in any kind of danger. Ever."

"I feel the same about you." He tugged her closer and pressed a soft kiss to her lips. "Let's keep each other safe."

"Always."

Chapter 27

A FEW DAYS LATER, VIOLET LOOKED IN KEMP'S LARGE CLOSET upstairs. Clothes hangers hung askew on the long rod. Discarded shirts lay across the dresser. Kemp stood in the light coming through double windows. She cocked her head to one side as she considered how she wanted to present him on Cowboy Heart-to-Heart Corral.

He looked good, of course. He couldn't help but appear hot, no matter what he was wearing at any given moment. She'd let him dress himself for their photo shoot. He'd chosen his good stuff. He looked neat and clean, more like a rancher than a cowboy. He was both in real life, but she needed fantasy more than reality. She wanted him to appear rough and rugged, as if he'd just come off the range and was ready, willing, and able to ride straight into a woman's heart.

And yet, even though she wanted him hot, needed him hot, she'd found more of late that she didn't want to share his hotness with the world. She almost wished she'd taken Lester up on his offer to pose for her lonely hearts club. And yet, Mr. July was her dream come true and the inspiration for her dating site. How could she back down from her longtime goal? She couldn't. She wouldn't. She'd continue to plunge forward with her dream. And that meant revealing Kemp as every woman's dream come true.

"I'm wearing my best Western clothes," he said, "but I can tell by the look on your face that you don't approve. If these won't work, I don't know what will. Do we need to buy other stuff?"

"No. We don't need new. We need real."

"Real?" He looked down at his dark-blue rancher suit with string tie and blue plaid shirt. "This is real."

"I want another kind of real."

He appeared puzzled, then rubbed his jaw. "Are you sure you don't want me clean-shaven?"

"I'm not getting through to you how I want you to appear on my dating site."

He shrugged and shook his head, puzzled.

She looked him over again. Everything was fine except the clothes. She'd requested a five-o'clock shadow to emphasize the strong bone structure of his face. He had a slight curl to his dark hair that he wore a little long, so that it brushed the collar of his shirt. And his hooded, green eyes needed absolutely no enhancement at all. Perfection.

He narrowed his gaze as he looked from her to his hanging clothes and back again. "Work stuff?"

"Yes." She smiled at the breakthrough. "Let me look through everything."

"Some of it's kind of rough."

"Excellent."

She selected a pair of Wranglers that had seen better days. The jean fabric had been washed to softness, faded to pale blue, ripped at the knees, and was ragged around the pockets and hems. She tossed them on the chair beside the dresser.

"I was going to throw those jeans away." He grabbed them, held them up, looked them over, and threw them back on the chair.

"Don't you dare."

"Are you trying to make me look like a down-on-his-luck cowboy?"

"No. I want you to appear exactly as you are…a hardworking cowboy."

She flipped through his shirts and decided on a denim one with white pearl snaps. It looked in about the same condition as the jeans because it had ripped elbows and a missing pocket. She tossed it on top of the Wranglers.

"I was going to use that as an old rag." He grabbed up the shirt and looked it over before he dropped it back.

She checked his belts. She found a wide, natural leather one with a huge, scratched rodeo buckle. She tossed that on the chair, too.

"Okay," he said. "At least that works for me."

Next she focused on his shoes. He had some fine boots, obviously for boot-scooting. Regular cowboy boots. Ropers. Lace-up work boots. Knee-high rubber boots. Athletic shoes. Then she found just what she was searching for and pulled the pair forward. She rubbed dust off a pair of black, pointy-toe cowboy boots with scuffed, scratched, dull finish and worn-down soles and heels. They looked in need of a trip to Gene's Boot Hospital. She set them beside the chair.

"I thought I got rid of those or left them at Gene's for repair."

"Glad you didn't. I like them."

He just shook his head.

She looked through his hats on the top rack. Felt for fall and winter. Straw for spring and summer. It was spring, so she went with straw. She looked through them until she found a natural straw with a dark sweat stain around the rattlesnake band. It was a little on the battered side and misshapen, too. She positioned it on top of the boots.

"That hat? I've got some great ones, and you pick that old work hat?"

"It goes with the clothes."

"Sure does."

"Glad you kept all of this."

"I might've put on some muscle since I wore those jeans and that shirt," he said as he stared at the clothes she'd selected for him.

"Really?" She felt a spurt of excitement that what she'd picked out could be a little on the tight side.

"Yeah. Might be too small."

"Might be just right is more like it." She rolled up the belt and tucked it into a boot, then she picked up the clothes, boots, and hat. "Let's go into your bedroom where there's more room."

"Room for what?"

"Change clothes. I want to see how you look in what I selected for you."

"Are you sure what I'm wearing won't work?"

"Trust me. It won't."

"Okay. It's your show."

"Show, huh?"

"Yep."

She led the way into his bedroom, sat down in the comfy chair beside the bookcase, set the boots and hats on the floor, and held the shirt and jeans in her lap. Soft light from the windows cast a golden glow over the large room with its old oak floors.

He walked over to the windows, glanced out, and turned back, as if not quite sure what to do next or reluctant to do what came next.

"Showtime," she said. "Strip for me, cowboy."

"Strip, huh?" He chuckled, shaking his head as he walked over to her.

"Right."

He stopped in front of her, looking mischievous. "How about for every piece of clothing I take off, you take off a piece, too?"

"But you're the one we're dressing for the photo shoot."

"Don't you need me in the right mood?"

"Well…yes."

"How do you think you're going to get me there? I'm not an actor."

She hadn't thought of that possible glitch in her plans. She needed him to not only look hot but to project hot.

He shrugged off his jacket and tossed it on the bed. "Your turn."

"Is this like strip poker without the poker?"

"Do you want to play for stakes?"

"What stakes?" she asked.

"I wear what *you* want me to wear for the photo shoot. You wear what *I* want you to wear for the photo shoot."

"But I'll be behind the camera."

"Remember, I'm not an actor. I need inspiration."

"I'm not sure about your idea," she said.

"Why should you have all the fun?"

She realized that he had a point, although she wasn't quite sure how they had reached this point in preparation for the photo shoot. Somehow or other, she frequently lost control around him.

He undid his string tie and tossed it on the bed. He waited, appearing relaxed with his hands at his sides while giving her a hot look.

"Maybe you're right."

"You know I'm right. Come on, you know you want to do it."

She smiled at his antics. He was playing with her, and she liked it. She was usually the mischievous one, but he'd just turned the tables and given her a taste of what she'd been giving him. And she wanted more of it. He was teaching her that perhaps she'd been too serious about her lonely hearts club. Lightheartedness and humor could be a definite turn-on.

She wished she were wearing more clothes to draw this out because he'd just turned her on to fun and she wanted it to last. She kicked one flip-flop toward him. He caught it in the air, looking smug and self-satisfied with her action.

"Are you just warming up to the real show?" He set her sandal on the floor beside the bed.

"I thought you'd like a better look at my peach toenail polish."

"I've been looking at it. Pretty…but not as pretty as you."

"Thanks." She smiled at him, feeling kind of soft and squishy at his praise. He so knew how to warm her heart.

He sat down on the edge of the bed, pulled off one of his shiny black python boots, and set it beside her flip-flop.

She chuckled at the sight, because the shoes looked so incongruous together. And yet they also looked kind of right.

"We aren't getting very far very fast," he said.

"Are you in a hurry?"

"With you, never."

She smiled as she removed her other sandal and tossed it to him.

He caught it with a smile and set it beside her other flip-flop. He tugged off his boot and set it next to his other one.

She liked the sight of his-and-hers sets of shoes nestled on the floor beside the bed, as if they represented a longtime couple who went to bed together and rose together to start a new day.

"What've you got for me next?" he asked.

"What do you have for me?"

"It's your turn."

"You're wearing more than me, so you need to catch up."

He pulled off one sock, draped it over the top of his boot and looked at her with a question in his eyes.

She pointed at the other sock.

He grinned as he slipped it off and topped his other boot with it.

She'd stalled as long as she could, making him wait, upping the tension, the suspense for them both. She slipped her T-shirt up and over her head before she tossed it to the floor. She watched his green eyes darken as he feasted on the crimson bra she wore that accented more than it concealed.

She waited for him, but he continued to stare at her. She realized he'd either forgotten all about their game, or he'd raced ahead to the outcome and had already arrived at where he wanted to go.

"Your turn," she said. "Are you making me wait until I become so impatient I leap on you and rip off your shirt?"

"I wouldn't complain." He grinned, eyes lighting up like green fire.

"Lazy?"

"Distracted."

"Can't imagine why." She lowered one of her bra straps so that it dangled down one shoulder.

"You're not playing fair."

"Neither are you."

He smiled as he pulled his shirttail out of his pants, and then, ever-so-slowly, snapped open one pearl button after another until he revealed dark chest hair. He stopped, watching her watching him.

"Do go on."

He snapped open each of his cuffs, waited a moment, and then eased his shirt off his shoulders. He paused again before he slowly shrugged out of his shirt and tossed it on the bed.

Like he'd done with her body, she feasted her eyes on his smooth, tanned skin and the line of dark hair that ran down his chest to disappear under the belt at his waist. Powerful, broad shoulders led into sinewy muscles that roped down his arms to his wrists, honed thick and strong from wrangling thousand-pound-plus beasts. She caught her breath at the picture-perfect sight of him. She'd never share this much of him with her lonely hearts club.

She walked over and sat down on the bed beside him, feeling excited by their game, and by him.

He scooted over, so he could completely watch her, and leaned back with both hands behind him.

She looked down at herself. "I don't have much left to take off."

"Good."

She unbuttoned her jeans, lowered the zipper, and glanced at him.

He smiled and nodded for her to continue.

She stood up, hooked her thumbs in the waistband, and slowly lowered her jeans past her hips to reveal the red thong that matched her bra. When she heard his sharp intake of breath, she continued, lower and lower, until the jeans pooled around her ankles. She sat down, kicked them away, and leaned back in the bed to watch him.

"Beautiful," he said. "You are simply so beautiful."

"So are you."

"No. I'm a man."

"Handsome, yes, but beautiful, too."

He smiled. "Whatever you say. I won't argue with you over words."

"Good. I'm right, anyway."

"Yes. You're exactly right."

She returned his smile, feeling warm inside just by being in his presence with his focus on her.

He put his hand on the big, shiny buckle on the leather belt around his waist, then hesitated as if to build suspense.

"Please, don't make me wait."

He undid the buckle and the button of his jeans in almost one movement, leaving his zipper as the last impediment.

"Please, don't stop now."

But he did stop. "It's your turn now."

"Please?" she prodded.

"Please...the bra."

She slowly put her hands behind her back, watching for his response as she even more slowly unhooked it and let the silky red fabric slide down her arms to her wrists.

He reached out, snagged the bra, and lifted it to his face. He sniffed the fabric as he gazed into her eyes. "Smells like you. Sweet and tart."

"Lavender."

"Perfect."

She glanced down at his zipper. "Please."

He stood up, unzipped, and let his jeans fall to the floor. Now he wore nothing except navy blue briefs that were distended toward her. He kicked aside his jeans and sat down close enough that they were flesh to flesh and heat to heat.

She looked into his blazing green eyes. "I'll need to wear more than a thong when I photograph you."

"Why?"

She chuckled, drawing a line with her fingertip from his collarbone to his navel. "Best not shock the horses and cattle."

"If that's what you wear, I believe you'll get the look you want from me for your lonely hearts club."

"Now I'm not sure I want to share it."

"After all this, you're going to back out?" He tilted her chin up with one fingertip as he looked deeply into her eyes.

She shook her head. "I can't, but I want to."

He smiled, leaned down, and placed a soft kiss on her lips.

She placed her palms on either side of his face and kissed him back, hungrier than she'd ever been for him.

After their long kiss, he raised his face. "I don't want to play anymore." He trailed his hand downward and hooked his fingers in the stretchy fabric of her thong.

"Did you win?"

"No."

"Did I win?"

"No."

She raised an eyebrow in question.

"We both won." And he tugged her red thong free and dropped it over the side of the bed, leaving her completely nude.

"Now you," she said. "I don't want anything between us."

He gave her a slow smile as he removed his briefs and tossed them on top of her thong.

She smiled in satisfaction as he tilted her back on the bed and covered her with his body. He was big, strong, powerful…and all hers. She thrust her fingers into his thick hair as he kissed her face, pressing hot lips over her forehead, eyes, nose, chin, and teasing her ears. She moaned as he moved to her breasts, exciting her with his lips, tongue, hands until her nipples grew hard and sensitive. She dug her fingertips into the hard muscles of his shoulders, hanging on to him as her only reality in a kaleidoscope world of sensation.

Finally, he raised his head. "I can't wait."

"Please."

He jerked open his nightstand, took out a condom, opened the wrapper, and slipped on the rubber.

When he turned back to her, she held out her arms, spread her legs, and drew him down so she could feel his heat and weight as he entered her. She moaned at the pleasure of being joined with him once more. Nothing was better…and nothing else mattered in this time and place. As he stroked deeper, harder, hotter, she met him thrust for thrust, feeling them spiral higher and higher, reaching for their ultimate connection and finding it as they soared over the edge into ecstasy together.

He sighed—a deep, satisfied sound—as he lay back on the bed and pulled her close.

As she cuddled against the heat and breadth of his chest, she could hear the strong beat of his heart sync with her own. She placed her palm gently against his chest, wanting to hold them there always.

After a long moment, he tugged her closer. "Guess we'd better get a shower before the photo shoot."

"Together."

"Is there any other way?"

Chapter 28

A FEW HOURS LATER, VIOLET HAD KEMP IN HER SIGHTS AS she used her 35mm digital SLR camera to skillfully snap stills and capture videos of Mr. July...not Kemp Lander. That was how she had decided to separate them in her mind. Mr. July was for the public, her dating site and app. Kemp was for her alone. Otherwise, she wasn't sure she could bring herself to use him on Cowboy Heart-to-Heart Corral.

He'd been exactly right about inspiration. After coming together in bed, sharing a steamy shower, and changing clothes, they were both well and truly ready for the photo shoot. He looked like the authentic cowboy he was in real life in the outfit she had chosen for him. She'd never complain about the extra muscle that strained against his shirt and jeans every time he moved to a new position. He appeared ripped and ready for action...precisely what she'd had in mind from the beginning.

At the moment, he leaned back against a rough wooden corral rail, its wood weathered gray. He had both elbows positioned over the top rail, and he'd hooked a cowboy boot by its high heel over the bottom slat.

He appeared relaxed and confident, perfect lonely hearts club material.

Blaze grazed on three square bales of hay in the center of the corral. The sorrel wore his best leather saddle and bridle with silver trim and turquoise saddle pad. He'd been groomed to perfection. His sleek coat, dark mane, and long tail shone in the sunlight.

In the pasture beyond the corral, Hereford cattle grazed on

spring-green grass or drank from the blue water of a small pond. Wildflowers waved their colorful heads in a slight breeze, and white clouds drifted lazily across an azure-blue sky.

She couldn't have asked for a more perfect setting, and she was taking full advantage of it by snapping one shot after another. She checked the small screen again to make sure she was getting it all, but she didn't stop often, to avoid interrupting the flow of the photo shoot. She'd look at details later.

She'd had Kemp pose one way and then another. He'd been a little stiff at first, but now he was bored and didn't much care how he looked or acted on camera. All to the good, as far as she was concerned, since he made her job easy.

"Would you get on Blaze and ride him around the corral?" she asked.

"Sure. But anybody who knows anything will realize I'm doing nothing important."

"That's okay. You'll look good doing it."

He chuckled as he came off the railing, put both hands on top, and vaulted over it.

She didn't say one word as she got his athletic prowess on video because that little natural move on his part was probably something most people couldn't even contemplate doing on their best day. And most importantly for her camera, he'd looked totally hot doing it.

She walked over to the corral and kept shooting as he easily mounted Blaze. He rode around the corral, giving her a mischievous smile now and then to let her know what he thought about it all. If they weren't careful, she was going to toss down her camera, grab him, and head for bed. This time, there'd be no clothes involved for either of them.

"That's great," she said. "Would you pick up the bales of hay and move them around or do something else with them?"

"I could restack them. Would that work?"

"Perfect."

She wanted to capture the play of his muscles in his tight clothing as he hefted the heavy objects around, and the bales of hay ought to do it. She raised her camera to capture his next action.

He dismounted and tied Blaze's reins to a corral post. He picked up one bale, moved it to a different location, set it down, and then repeated the process with the other two bales. Then, as if he'd moved the hay for the horse on purpose, he untied Blaze and led him over to the hay so he could eat.

As she captured the scene that perfectly evoked an older, romantic era converging with the modern day, she heard thunder rumble in the distance. Surprised, she looked southwest, where storms usually formed in Texas. She felt a sinking sensation in the pit of her stomach. A line of black clouds with lightning flashing in brilliant-white streaks was moving in their direction fast. She glanced upward. Clouds were thickening overhead as they rolled above the ranch. The sun was now in a peekaboo mode. Not good, not good at all for a photo shoot.

"Better finish up." Kemp pointed at the sky as he walked over to her. "I don't like the looks of that storm."

"I'd planned to take some shots out by the pond with the wildflowers and the cattle."

"Not today." He put a hand to his jeans pocket, then shook his head. "Left my phone in the barn."

"No room in your pockets?" She smiled as she looked at his tight jeans, so perfect for the camera but not practical for carrying anything.

"I need to check the radar and see that storm's trajectory, size, and speed."

"Okay."

He glanced around the corral, at the barn, and back at her, as if calculating what needed to be done before the storm hit.

"What do we need to do? How can I help? Are the horses and cattle okay in their pastures?"

"They should be fine. Hopefully this storm is fast moving, so it'll roll right over us and keep going with no problems or damage to the ranch."

"That's good."

"It's not just the ranch that I need to think about."

"No?"

"I'm a first responder. I'm on call for the entire county."

"That means storms in addition to fires?"

"Yes."

"Big responsibility," she said.

"I'm not alone."

"But it's a huge county."

"We can handle it."

"I'm sure you can, but I want to be of help, too."

He glanced up at the sky. "It's headed right at us."

She looked up, too. He was right. And it was coming fast.

"If you'll take Blaze into the barn, I'll move these bales of hay in there so they don't get wet."

"Okay."

"As soon as I'm in there, I'll check the radar."

"I'll just put my camera in the barn and come right back."

"Hurry."

She packed her camera into its hard case, glanced up at the sky again, and rushed over to the barn. She opened the double doors wide, so she could easily lead Blaze into the building, and walked inside. She set her camera case beside Kemp's phone on a table near the front door that was strewn with several well-worn horseshoes, a broken bridle, and a curry comb.

She quickly returned to the corral. He'd already opened the gate. She walked over to him where he stood beside Blaze.

He handed her the reins. "I'll be right behind you."

"Okay."

She'd ridden Blaze enough that he was comfortable with her,

so she easily led him into the barn. Several closed stall doors were on one side. She caught the now-familiar scents of hay, feed, and manure. She stopped in the center of the long aisle and turned around to watch for Kemp.

He came in right behind her, set a bale of hay down near the table, and rushed back out.

While she waited for him to finish, she held on to Blaze's reins and stroked down his long nose as thunder rumbled closer. She hoped they had time to make it back to the house before the storm hit.

Kemp rushed back into the barn with another bale, gave her a quick nod of approval, and jogged back outside.

She opened a stall door, led Blaze inside, and then quickly and efficiently removed his saddle, blanket, and bridle. She carried those back out and set them in the tack room. She turned on a hose and filled the empty water bucket in his stall before she stepped out and clicked the door shut. He put his head over the top and nickered to her. She rubbed his wide jaw before quickly walking back to the barn doors.

"That's it." Kemp carried the last bale of hay into the barn. "Storm's still coming right at us."

"I can hear it."

"How are y'all doing?"

"Blaze is all set in his stall."

"You're turning into one fine cowgirl."

"Thanks."

"Let's go." He grabbed his cell phone off the table and checked the weather radar app.

She grabbed her camera case.

"Radar doesn't show good news. Let's get out of here."

She hurried outside and glanced up at the sky. It was dark and foreboding. The air felt thick and smelled of rain. Lightning flashed and the rumble of thunder followed almost immediately.

Kemp rushed from the barn right on her heels and slammed

the barn door behind him. He glanced around the area as he held out his hand to her.

She grasped his fingers, glad for his strength and warmth, just as the first drops of rain hit her.

"Come on!" He tugged her forward as he hit a ground-eating stride.

She kept up with him, still hoping to make the house as the storm closed in on them. She could tell it was going to be a doozy. Strong winds drove a cold, biting rain as lightning split the sky in jagged slashes with thunder pounding the air.

They hit the patio running as the storm lashed their backs. Rose blooms scattered across the concrete as the bushes whipped back and forth in the gusting wind.

He grabbed the handle of the kitchen door, jerked it open, and stepped back for her. She ran in, skidded on her wet shoe soles, and slipped on the tile floor, finally coming to a stop when she clutched the countertop with her free hand at the far end while holding her camera case with the other. She set the case on the countertop and looked back.

Kemp fought wind and rain before he finally slammed the door shut and won the battle. He locked it and leaned back, breathing hard as he looked at her. Water dripped from the brim of his hat down the front of his shirt. "Think it will rain?"

She just rolled her eyes as she heard the wind howl around the house and rain batter the windows.

"Good thing you had me wear my old clothes," he said with a mischievous smile.

She smiled back. "Guess storms are one of the ways your hat acquired its current condition."

"Cow stepped on it one time, too." He chuckled as he brushed water off the front of his shirt. It fell in plops to the floor.

She glanced down at her own soggy T-shirt and jeans. She wasn't any better off than him. At least they were inside, where they were safe from dangerous weather.

He set his phone on the countertop, pulled several paper towels off the roll, and dried it off.

"Still work?" she asked.

"Let me check." He scrolled around, then gave an affirmative nod.

"Good." She began to see humor in their situation, now that they were safe and sound. "I'd hate to be blamed for a dead phone all because I had you wear tight jeans."

He laughed as he set down his phone. "If that had happened, it'd be one more thing I wouldn't want getting out about me."

She joined his laughter. "What a way to end my much-anticipated photo shoot."

He turned serious. "Did you get enough pictures?"

"I think so. I had more ideas, but they can wait."

"Those pictures had better be enough, because I don't know if I can go through another photo shoot with you."

"Why not?"

"My Wranglers were tight enough, but add you to the mix and they were flat-out uncomfortable."

"Oh my." She laughed harder.

"You'd better check those pictures for a lot of reasons."

"Are you saying you might not be presentable?"

"Depends on what type of site you're selling."

"Now I really want to check the details of what I captured with my camera."

"Be my guest." He pointed at her camera case. "I'm just warning you to check everything twice before you post anything."

"Mr. July is," she said as she stalked toward him, "all wet and wild again. And this time I'm on the scene."

"Come here and I'll show you wet and wild."

"I'm on my way." She slowed down to increase the suspense as he watched her with green eyes gone dark.

"Faster." As he reached out, his phone made an ominous buzzing sound. He stopped in midmotion, face gone serious.

"What is it?"

"Fire station alert." He grabbed his cell and hit speakerphone. "Kemp."

"We need you," Hedy said in her calm, professional voice. "Lightning struck south of here. Split cedar and pine trees and set fires. You know how fast and furious resin burns."

"Yeah. Storm left there now?"

"Rigs are on their way."

"Good."

"Saw boss needed. You're our only expert."

"Let me grab my equipment."

"I'll send GPS coordinates to your phone."

"Thanks."

"And, Kemp, even with everything wet, it's still a dangerous mess."

"I know."

"You take care."

"I always do."

And Hedy was gone.

He looked at Violet. "I've got to go."

"I'm going with you."

"Not safe."

She walked over and grabbed her camera case. "I want shots for my site. And I don't want to be separated from you."

"You won't be near me."

"What do you mean?"

"Saw boss. Do you know the term?"

"No."

"I'm the firefighter who climbs a tree and cuts out the fire in the top with a chainsaw."

She put her hand to her lips, as if that motion alone could stop him from taking such a terrible risk.

Chapter 29

KEMP HEADED SOUTH DOWN WILDCAT ROAD WITH VIOLET riding shotgun. He wished she were safely at home, but he understood her desire to capture cowboy firefighters performing their vital jobs. He bet Sydney would love the dramatic photographs. She might even use some in the next Wildcat Bluff Fire-Rescue calendar. He'd like that a lot better than those pictures from the dunking booth. He'd just have to make sure Violet stayed safely behind the fire line.

He turned west on Highway 82. No storm left here. By now it would have made its way past Wildcat Bluff to the Red River as it headed northeast into Oklahoma and Arkansas. Everything was wet, but there was little runoff in the ditch beside the road because the rain had been quickly absorbed by the dry ground.

He glanced at Violet. Was she tense about going so near danger? Maybe he ought to distract her. He felt adrenaline pumping through his system as it readied him for action. Firefighters might not show it, but they were under a lot of pressure every time they went out on a call.

"We're headed toward Sure-Shot. Did you ever hear of that small Western town?" he asked.

"Yes. But I don't know anything about it."

"Back in the day, cowboys on cattle drives stopped there. It was named for Annie Oakley, the famous sharpshooter and exhibition shooter. She was called 'Little Miss Sure-Shot' on the Wild West show circuit."

"Did she ever live there?"

"Far as I know, she didn't. She was a celebrity, so everybody knew about her."

"I'd like to see the town."

"We can go another time. Today we'll turn off before we get there."

"I'll look forward to seeing Sure-Shot."

He watched the countryside, keeping an eye out for signs of the fire, as they moved from cattle country into horse country. White round pipe or four-slat wood fences stretched along both sides of the road. Nobody would use barbwire to enclose horses because, unlike cattle, it wasn't safe for them.

One ranch after another flashed by, announcing their names—from whimsical to practical—in black-sheet-metal cut-outs or burned into wood arches that towered over entryways. Thoroughbred horses with rich coats in a variety of shades grazed in some pastures, while in others, brown-and-white-painted ponies sheltered under the spreading, green-leafed limbs of live oak trees. Crimson barns and metal corrals, along with houses that ranged from redbrick, single-story fifties ranch style to cream-colored stone, two-story contemporaries, had been built well back from the road for privacy and convenience.

Finally, he saw smoke up ahead. These ranches were in grave danger if the blaze spread. Wet surfaces slowed conflagrations, but tall grass and dry, downed timber could still be set ablaze. He knew local ranchers must be moving horses away from the fire and closer to their houses and barns. They'd also be using hoses to wet down the buildings they could reach just in case firefighters were unable to contain the fire.

Up ahead, he saw Deputy Bill Winston of the sheriff's department. He wore his usual beige uniform, tan cowboy hat, and black boots. He stood beside his cruiser parked on the side of the highway while he kept traffic moving when folks slowed their vehicles to try and see the fire that would by now be the talk of the county.

Kemp turned down the muddy dirt road beside the deputy, stopped his truck, and lowered his window.

Deputy Winston walked over and leaned down. "We're depending on you to fight that fire. It's spread from the trees where lightning struck. It's a brushfire now, too."

"I'll do it. And I'm depending on you to keep folks out of danger."

"Nobody unauthorized is getting past me."

"Thanks."

"Take care now."

"Will do."

Kemp drove on down the road that led toward a copse of evergreens. Smoke was thicker here. He caught the acrid scent as it swirled into the cab's interior. Violet sneezed beside him. He raised the window.

"We're almost there. You may want to stay in the truck," he said.

"I won't be able to get good pictures from inside."

"I just want you safe."

"I'll be careful."

"If anything happened to you…"

"I don't want anything to happen to you, either." She reached over and lightly squeezed his arm.

"I always think through every move before I make it."

"Still, I'll worry."

"I'll worry about you, too." He realized this was a new experience. He'd been in danger before, but he'd never had someone waiting to welcome him back with open arms and maybe a kiss. It felt good.

"We'll be okay." She opened her camera case and pulled out her camera. She selected a large lens and screwed it into place.

He slowed down when he saw the apparatus. He was always impressed by the big, red engine that had two-thousand-gallons-per-minute pump capacity, one thousand gallons of water, and thirty gallons of class A foam. Two red boosters were parked nearby. Each truck had a three-hundred-GPM pump capacity and a 250-gallon water tank.

Firefighters stood ready. They wore full turnout gear or protective firefighter helmets and high-visibility orange-and-yellow parkas with leather gloves. He'd already changed into modified turnout gear that allowed him to climb a tree and maneuver once he was up there. He'd outfitted Violet with a helmet and parka that she wore with jeans and boots.

He parked behind the rigs. He quickly sized up the situation. The firefighters were gathered together. He was glad to see Cole Murphy, who was his usual partner. Sydney glanced up and motioned for him to join the group. He gave her a thumbs-up sign, then turned to Violet.

"Are you ready?" he asked.

"Yes." She held her camera against her chest.

"Okay. Let's join them and get orders."

He stepped down and closed the door, then led Violet over to the other firefighters.

He glanced around the area to make a quick assessment of the situation. Heat and flames and smoke were compounding by the moment. He saw three blazing treetops. The deputy was right. The fire had spread from the initial lightning strike. He needed to get up in the trees that were blazing with red-orange flames shooting furiously upward, and he needed to do it now. Embers that high in the air could quickly spread near and far. In the meadow around the stand of trees, a brushfire was already expanding fast.

"What's she doing here?" Tall, blond Sydney in full turnout gear shot daggers at him with her ice-blue eyes. "We don't need extra trouble."

"If it's okay, I'd like to shoot stills and video of this fire." Violet held up her camera.

"Maybe we could use her photographs in the next calendar," Kemp said.

"Great idea." Cole gave Kemp a high-five. "Isn't it?"

All the firefighters quickly agreed.

"Y'all would do about anything to keep me from using more of those dunking booth pictures." Sydney shook her head. "It's not a bad idea. But you'll need to stay well back out of danger."

"Absolutely," Violet said.

"It's my rotation as fire captain, so I'm in charge." Sydney looked at the group.

Everyone nodded in agreement.

"The good news is that we're looking at a class A fire size, little to no wind, and we can easily get to the brushfire," Sydney said. "The bad news is we can't get the engine in close enough to use its high-velocity water on those treetops."

"I can get there," Kemp said.

"That's what we're counting on," Sydney said.

"I'm with you." Cole gave him a knowing look with his sharp, brown eyes.

"Thanks." Kemp nodded to his friend.

"We'll use this road as our anchor point for fire suppression activity." Sydney glanced at Violet. "If the smoke gets to you, please go back and get in Kemp's truck. It won't work for us to be distracted from fighting this fire to keep you out of danger. You're here at your own risk."

"I understand."

"If you stay around the rigs, you should be fine." Sydney paced a few steps one direction then another, as if she could hardly contain her energy. "And I want to see some great shots of our firefighters."

"You got it." Violet held up her camera.

"We'll make a direct attack on the ground, wetting and smothering the fire and/or physically separating burning fuel from unburned fuel," Sydney said.

The firefighters nodded in agreement.

"Our objective is to make a fire line around the fire that is to be suppressed. Everything inside that line can, and will, burn." Sydney looked at Violet again. "And if we do our jobs correctly, we'll keep this class A from going to class B."

"We'll do it," Kemp said.

"Right," Cole replied, agreeing.

"As far as an escape route, in case the fire outflanks us, let's use this road," Sydney said. "I doubt we'll have a problem with containment, but let's make this road our safety zone, too."

Kemp nodded in agreement again, as did all the firefighters.

"Hedy will keep us updated over the apparatus radios." Sydney glanced at the radio she wore on her shoulder.

"Violet, we want you safe," Kemp said. "I'll be in the trees, so I can't watch out for you."

"I'll stay well back from danger."

"Firefighters, plans are in place." Sydney glanced around the group. "You'll take the boosters and get out ahead of the fire."

Kemp gave Violet an encouraging look, knowing she'd be on her own pretty quick and knowing she could handle it.

"Okay," Sydney said. "Firefighters, pump and roll. We need some large hose lays from the engine. Some of you can help with that or get out the shovels and picks if you think ditches are needed for containment."

"Try water first," Kemp said. "It's too easy for fire to jump a ditch and waste hard work."

"Suits me." Sydney pointed toward the equipment. "Remember, we've got breathing apparatus in the engine if anybody needs it. Now, let's stay in touch. Radio or vocal communication."

"Visual, too," Cole said.

"Right." Sydney turned to Kemp. "Need anything?"

"Gear's in the truck. I'll get it and be right back."

"I'll wait for you," Cole said.

"Any questions? Any suggestions?" Sydney asked.

All the firefighters glanced around at each other and then squared their shoulders as they refocused on her.

"I'll be here at the apparatus and in touch with Hedy for updates." Sydney gave a sharp nod. "Okay, firefighters, let's engage."

Two firefighters spooled out the engine's large-diameter hose that would expel high-velocity water. It'd take the two of them to keep the line stable, so that it didn't twist, turn, and buck like a wild rodeo bull. Another two firefighters leaped into one booster, while two more tore off in the other rig.

Kemp hurried Violet over to the engine, gave her a quick kiss, and jogged toward his truck. He felt the familiar adrenaline dump revving him up, making him sharper, stronger, and quicker than usual. He needed it to get the job done.

He jerked open the back door of his pickup, snagged a bottle of water, popped open the top, and downed it. He needed the extra moisture, because he'd soon be sweating it out in the heat. He snagged his black nylon gear bag, pulled it toward him, and zipped it open. He lifted out vital gear. He put on padded earmuffs before he tugged on his hard hat with the clear plastic face shield. Smoke would be the biggest problem. After years of fires, the whites of many firefighters' eyes turned yellow. He hadn't gone there yet, but he was a volunteer, not a professional, so he figured that made the difference. He zipped his bag shut and slung it over a shoulder before he slipped off the cover of his chainsaw blade. He'd use the twenty inch. Nothing could compete with the 661 Magnum with its thirty-six-inch bar for large diameter work, but it was too heavy and bulky to carry up a tree.

He slammed his pickup door shut, then jogged toward the engine. The smoke was thicker, the fire more intense, and the trees burned even brighter overhead. He had to get this job done right, not only for his own safety but for all the ranchers, as well as the horses and other critters that made their home in the area. He had no doubt birds had flown to safety. He hoped rabbits, squirrels, snakes, and all the local wildlife had been able to get safely away.

Cole waited for him at the engine with a fire extinguisher slung over each shoulder. Sydney was inside the cab on the radio. He held up his chainsaw for her to see he was on his way. She gave him a thumbs-up.

"Let's do it." He headed for the tree line.

"One thing." Cole jogged by Kemp's side. "This can't be as bad as that time your harness broke and you almost squashed me flat."

"Don't even go there. It never happened." Kemp chuckled, well aware that Cole was doing what first responders frequently did when they headed into danger. They made a joke to ease the tension.

"Right." Cole laughed, then coughed on the smoke.

Kemp felt the heat through his nonflammable pants and jacket. He was thankful for the thick gloves that protected his hands and the heavy work boots. He could hear the crackling of flaming treetops as slender, burning branches crashed to the ground and started small fires. He tromped across those blazes, leaving them for the ground crew or to burn out on their own.

When he came to the lightning-struck tree, he stopped in awe at the deadly destruction that took only a brief moment to achieve. The huge cedar's trunk had been split high up, leaving a jagged, blackened, flaming center post that reached nakedly upward, while the oil-laden green limbs around it burned crimson-orange and black smoke rose high into the sky. Red-hot embers were being blown here and there. They were the worst part of the fire to contain and the most dangerous.

"Let's start with this one." Kemp kicked burning debris aside to make a clear place and set down his gear bag and chainsaw.

"Okay." Cole unslung a can. He sprayed chemical around Kemp's bag and the base of the burning tree.

"Thanks."

Kemp unzipped his gear bag to get to his equipment. First, he put on climbing spikes and spurs, so he could climb straight up the tree as he pulled himself upward by the power of his arms and shoulders.

Next, he removed the bulky harness, not his favorite piece of equipment but a vital one. He shook it out, stepped into the saddle, pulled the wide bands tight so they fit snugly around his upper thighs, and buckled the belt around his waist so he had easy access to its metal rings. He snapped the buck strap, with its hand-spliced eye, onto the harness and attached a pulley and throw line to the other metal rings. If he fell, the rope he would tie to the tree that was attached to the harness would save him, so discomfort when the harness got hot and sweaty was a small price to pay.

He threw the weighted end of the rope over a lower branch of the burning tree and tugged it tight through the pulley. He used a metal zigzag to run the line through because it would automatically tighten if he needed it.

"Ready whenever you are," he said.

"Stay safe." Cole handed him the chainsaw.

"Always." He clipped the chainsaw to one of the rings on his harness belt and let it dangle at his side.

Cole moved a safe distance away from the tree.

Kemp put one foot on the tree and, using the rope, started pulling his way upward…one foot after another on the side of the rough bark of the cedar. Smoke and heat swirled around him, thicker and hotter the higher he climbed. He felt sweat run down his face under his helmet, down his arms, over his chest. He blinked it out of his eyes so he could see, although the smoke almost blinded and smothered him. He'd lose several inches in his waist before this was all said and done, but the belt could be notched tighter to compensate.

When he reached a thick, solid branch, he stepped onto it and looped his throw line around the trunk. He tied it with a firefighter knot that could be instantly undone with one tug and yet was completely secure. He made sure he was completely balanced on the branch before he lifted the chainsaw. He pulled the cord and it roared to life. He held the chainsaw with one hand as he leaned into a major cut of a thick branch.

As the flaming section fell past Kemp, he felt the scorching heat, caught the stench of burning cedar resin, and choked on the thick smoke. And then it was gone, falling far away where it would do no more harm. He moved upward, using his climbing spikes, pulling his buck strap, wielding his chainsaw as he cut and cut and cut. Finally, he had one last branch that he had to get. It was dangerous, but he couldn't let that stop him. He raised his arm high, feeling the chainsaw's weight, hearing its buzz, feeling its vibration, and swung outward, hovered for a millisecond in midair, sawed through the burning branch, and quickly swung out of the way so he didn't get taken down as it fell to the forest floor.

He quickly cut smaller blazing branches, sending them tumbling downward. He worked quickly, efficiently, wielding the chainsaw like a sharp sword, until he'd cut the burning pieces from the tree. All done, he turned off his chainsaw and let it drop to his side.

Cole stepped forward and waved the nozzle of his canister like a wand as he extinguished the burning debris. When he was done, he glanced upward.

Kemp gave him a thumbs-up before he started his climb downward. When he hit the ground, he rolled up his ropes.

"Good work." Cole pointed high in the tree. "You could've trimmed a little neater on that one limb. Wanna go back up?"

"Hah!" Kemp laughed at the firefighter humor. "Come on. Let's finish this up, so we can wet our whistles at Wildcat Hall."

"Sarsaparilla or beer?" Cole asked.

"Do you even need to ask?"

Chapter 30

A WEEK LATER, VIOLET RODE BLAZE BESIDE KEMP ON HIS buckskin. She liked being a cowgirl. She was stronger than she'd ever been in San Antonio. She liked the self-confidence that came with strength. And if the need should arise, muscle gave her the ability to help others. No matter what, she intended to keep going in her new direction.

Soon she would have been in Wildcat Bluff County a month, and yet so much had happened that it seemed much longer. She'd come here as a way to ease lonely hearts, and she'd ended up helping herself first.

She'd set out with Kemp after lunch to check the fence line. He didn't say, didn't have to say, because he knew she knew they were also checking to see if the gold hunters had been back at it. No more holes, as far as they knew, but with a ranch this size, they might have missed them. Sheriff Calhoun hadn't made any progress in finding the trespassers either.

Cowboy Heart-to-Heart Corral was worth every moment she was spending on it. The photographs and videos she'd taken of Kemp were just as wonderful as she'd thought they would be way back in San Antonio. She was also writing a blog about her experiences in the county, because she had so much to share. She wanted her lonely hearts club to exude down-home warmth and togetherness.

The photos and videos she'd taken of the lightning strike fire were spectacular. She'd emailed the best to Sydney, who'd been delighted and planned to build a calendar around them.

She was almost ready to launch the website and app. And yet

she felt as if she needed a bigger hook to persuade people to give her site a chance. Mr. July would be a great draw. She'd been right about that. She couldn't imagine a better look. Still, she felt as if she were missing something important. Maybe she felt that way because of the Buick Brigade and Jake. They'd made Hallelujah Ranch sound mysteriously romantic. She wished the silver spoon would give up its secrets to add to the ranch's story, but she doubted that could ever happen.

She should feel satisfied that she'd put together an intriguing, appealing dating site. And she did feel that way for the most part. She just wished she could set aside the feeling that Hallelujah had more to offer and that she should wait to launch Cowboy Heart-to-Heart Corral until she found it.

She couldn't do anything about that now. Anyway, it was just a feeling. For the moment, all she needed to do was enjoy the beautiful afternoon in early spring. A handsome, loving cowboy rode by her side. And she was about to realize her dream and share her lonely hearts club with the world.

"Penny for your thoughts," Kemp said.

"I guess I'm just getting cold feet about the launch. I feel as if I'm missing something important for it."

"What?"

"I'm not sure."

"Aren't my photos good enough?"

"They're wonderful."

"You don't have to use them."

"Mr. July is a winner." She smiled to let him know she appreciated his contribution to her website.

"You won't keep those pictures up forever, will you?"

"No. They're part of the big launch."

"Good."

"I just wish I had another hook...not that you aren't great."

"Thanks." He gave her a warm look. "What kind of hook?"

"I don't know."

"You've just got prelaunch jitters." He reached over and cupped her hand on the saddle horn. "Once you're up and running, you'll be fine. You'll also be too busy to have any doubts."

"I'm sure you're right."

"I am." He squeezed her hand, then let go.

"Thanks for the pep talk."

"Anytime."

She took a deep breath as she gazed out over the pasture and let the nagging feeling drift away. Cows grazed in the distance. Birds sang in treetops. White clouds scudded across the blue sky. Wildflowers nodded colorful heads in a slight breeze. Kemp was right. Everything was fine. And she would enjoy her day with him without any more disturbing thoughts.

They passed the copse of trees where Kemp had filled in the first deep hole. She'd found the silver spoon there. She was glad to see green grass had already started to grow back and cover up the scar on the landscape.

"I don't think you've been up to Big Rock, have you?"

"Big Rock?"

"That's what I call it. Guess I ought to come up with a better name. Something that fits Hallelujah Ranch."

"Might be fun."

"Let's do it after you see Big Rock." He turned north toward Destiny as he paralleled the barbwire fence.

"Fence looks good." She glanced ahead, hoping against hope they wouldn't find another cut section.

"Yeah. But it's been too quiet. Makes me uneasy."

"Maybe they gave up and are gone for good."

"I wish."

"Let's don't look for trouble." She rode closer to him. "More than anything, I just want some time away from work."

"And worry?"

"Yes."

"You got it." He gave her a warm smile.

She smiled in return as she placed her hand over her heart, wanting to hold their tender emotion forever. He did something to her that she'd never expected to feel with another person. She treasured him and the feelings he evoked in her. Yes, she was right to create a lonely hearts club where others could build their own precious memories together. And right now that was exactly what she was doing with Kemp.

"Big Rock is up ahead. See?" He pointed at a large beige rock.

"What kind of rock is it?"

"Sandstone. That's pretty soft. Means it's got more water in it than other rocks. You can carve into it. Yet it's still strong enough to withstand the elements."

"It looks odd jutting up from the flat prairie."

"Guess it's just one of those oddities of nature. Who knows what originally caused the upheaval that sent it from inside the ground to the outside? Or what huge flood moved it from somewhere else to here?"

"It looks pretty."

As they rode closer, she noticed the grass had been flattened in two rows like a heavily-laden truck had driven through the area from the direction of Big Rock. She felt her heart pick up speed. Had the gold hunters been through here? Had they found another place to dig? Cut more fence?

"I see it," Kemp said in a resigned voice. "I may have to start staking out the place at night."

"Isn't the ranch too big? They could be anywhere on it."

"Maybe Lester was right."

"About what?"

"Maybe I should buy a metal detector and search the place myself. That way I might figure out where they are going to dig in the future."

"You don't have that kind of time right now. Do you?"

"No. Once I get Hallelujah on its feet, then I'll focus on the trespassers. In the meantime, I'll just keep filling the holes."

"Wish I could do more to help."

"Just being here with me is a big help."

She caught his eye and saw that tenderness for her again. She felt the same thing in her own gaze. She hoped he realized that she was here for him, no matter the problem.

"These tracks lead to Big Rock."

"Do you suppose they dug up near there?"

"I'd guess so." He lifted his cowboy hat, ran a hand through his hair, and set the hat back in place. "I'm tired of dealing with their messes."

"I know. Let's go see what they left for you to fix."

She rode on beside him, following the pressed grass trail. She hoped it wasn't too deep a hole. More than that, she just wished the trespassers would go away and leave Kemp in peace. They both had enough on their minds without more trouble.

"That's odd." He pointed ahead. "That looks like a gap in the rock wall."

"Is that normal?"

"No. It sure isn't." He stopped the buckskin and glanced over at her.

"What?"

"I want you to stay here while I go take a look."

"Please don't go into danger alone. I'll go with you."

"Don't worry. I'm armed." He reached down into his boot and pulled out a concealed carry.

"That's good, but—"

"Please, Violet, stay here where I know you're safe."

"Okay." She looked at the top of the rock, then all around because she no longer felt particularly safe. She wanted her own firepower more than ever.

He dismounted, rummaged around in his saddlebag, and came up with a flashlight. He walked across the grass and up to the rock. He hesitated a moment, bent down, and disappeared inside.

She remembered the night he'd hunted the trespassers. She wasn't about to wait and worry again. Besides, he might need her. She dismounted, ground-tied Blaze, and followed him. At the rock that towered over her head, she saw what looked like a blasted-out area, mostly round with jagged, blackened edges. It hadn't been created with shovels or a backhoe. This looked more like dynamite or some other, newer kind of explosive. It must have been a controlled blast by somebody who knew what they were doing, or they'd have brought down the entire rock.

She glanced behind to make sure someone wasn't following to sneak up on them. She didn't see anybody, so she stepped into the dark interior of the rock that she realized now must be the entrance to a cave.

"Kemp?"

"Violet, stay there. I'll come get you."

She moved forward, taking baby steps so she didn't trip on something. Instead, she bumped into a wall. She felt brick under her fingertips. She smelled a dusty, musty odor. She couldn't even begin to imagine what they'd stumbled into on the ranch. And from one side of the wall, she saw light…and then Kemp emerged, pointing the beam of his flashlight on the ground. Even the meager light showed her that he had a big grin on his face.

"What is it?" she asked.

"You're not going to believe it."

"Tell me."

"No. You've got to see for yourself."

"Everything's okay, isn't it?"

"Oh yeah."

"Were the gold hunters here?"

"You bet." He turned away.

"Did they leave a big new hole?"

"Follow me. I'll show you." He turned, stepped to the left, and disappeared to one side of the brick wall.

"Kemp?"

"Come on."

She ran her hand across the wall and realized that it didn't extend far, only enough to conceal what was behind it. She followed him. And she was abruptly transported back in time.

"Lady Mauve's domain, surely," he said as he swept the beam of the flashlight left and right.

"Hallelujah Ranch's speakeasy?"

"Got to be." He cast a beam of light more slowly around the room, then handed the flashlight to her. "Who'd have ever guessed it still existed right here, right now?"

"Frozen in time."

She used his flashlight to capture bits of the room like a mosaic that she slowly put together into one complete picture. It was beautiful, no doubt about it, even with dust and cobwebs. It had been sealed so well that no rodents or other animals had gotten inside to destroy the furnishings.

The single room was a large rectangle with a pressed-tin ceiling and a dull oak floor. A horseshoe bar made of walnut with a white marble top was the centerpiece at the far end of the room. Round, walnut stools with red leather seats surrounded the outside of the bar. Behind the bar were floor-to-ceiling shelves filled with bottles of booze. Above the bar was an Art Deco design chandelier with candleholders on four sides.

A row of plush, scarlet sofas with small, round tables in front of them stretched the length of one side of the speakeasy. Individual round tables with crimson-upholstered chairs were grouped across from the sofas. A grand piano on a dais had been tucked into one corner.

She saw a narrow rope or something like it on top of the closed piano. She went over and shone the light on the object. She was astonished to recognize a long strand of white pearls like she'd seen stylish flappers wear in photographs of that era. She didn't touch them, although she wanted to shake off the dust so she could see them better. For now, she didn't want to disturb anything here.

"What do you think?" Kemp walked over to stand beside her.

"It's amazing. I can hardly believe it's still so intact."

"Not completely. Come over here."

She followed him to the back of the bar.

He pointed at the bottom shelf of liquor bottles. Several were broken and liquid had been spilled across unwrapped rolls of suede leather with untied red ribbon bows.

"I bet Lady Mauve's silverware set belongs in those bags. Don't you think?" he asked.

"Yes. But where is it?"

"They didn't find gold. They found silver." He pointed at several large suede bags. "I'd guess there were trays and bowls, too."

"Valuable. But not like gold." She glanced up at the hundred-year-old bottles that were still full of liquid.

"If those seals are unbroken, that liquor is probably more valuable than the silver," he said.

"Why didn't they take it?"

"They probably didn't have a way to safely transport it all." He pointed at two empty places on the shelves. "I'd guess they took a couple of sample bottles to get an estimate of their value."

"That means they plan to come back."

"Yeah," he said. "And Sheriff Calhoun could catch them in the act."

"Finally."

"He'd need a deputy to stake out the place, but I'm sure he'd do it. He wants these guys caught as much as I do."

"I'm relieved."

"I am, too." He looked around the speakeasy. "Did you know these were also called 'blind tigers'?"

"No. I wonder why."

"Don't know. It'd need a little research."

"But that's for later," she said.

"My concern is the place is open to the elements now, and that includes animals. I'd like to get a tarp installed over the entry. It wouldn't show from the outside, but it'd protect the interior."

"What about the thieves?"

"I'll contact the sheriff. If he can get a deputy out here right away, the thieves could be caught before they ever saw the tarp."

"Sounds good." She shone the light around the room again. "It's romantic here. The colors. The warmth. The beauty. I wish... well, I just wish it could still be used for folks to meet and mingle like in the old days."

"I know what you mean, but it just wouldn't work anymore. It's isolated here on the ranch. And besides, there are all kinds of liquor laws, business codes, and who knows what all."

"At least Lady Mauve's lair...maybe that's why they were called blind tigers."

"Why?" he asked.

"Blind tigers were secret lairs."

"Yeah." He smiled. "Come on. I want to get that tarp up and call the sheriff."

She shone her light back on the long strand of pearls. "Lady Mauve, you're not forgotten."

Chapter 31

BY THAT EVENING, KEMP WAS ON STAKEOUT IN BIG ROCK'S speakeasy on Hallelujah Ranch. He was hidden behind the bar.

It was dark inside. No electricity. It was quiet inside for the same reason. He felt almost as if he'd been transported back in time and space, where at sundown, only kerosene lanterns, oil lamps, or candles would have provided light and the only sound would have come from animated voices, clinking glasses, and the soft, rhythmic strains of early jazz being played on the piano by an elegant flapper...maybe Lady Mauve herself.

Sheriff Calhoun sat beside Kemp on one of the two plush, crimson chairs they had moved from the table area. It might be a long wait, so they'd made themselves comfortable, but not too comfortable. They couldn't afford to fall asleep. And they didn't talk or move for concern of making a sound that could alert the criminals to the trap.

When the sheriff learned of the speakeasy from Kemp, he agreed that the thieves would be back soon for the liquor and other valuables. They wouldn't want to take a chance on Kemp or somebody else discovering the treasure trove before they finished looting it.

Deputy Bill Winston and Deputy Della Calhoun, the sheriff's daughter, were outside, hidden by Big Rock. They had positioned the two four-wheel vehicles that had brought the four of them there out of sight and obliterated the tracks as best they could. Darkness away from lights would hide any traces of their arrival that they might have missed. And now, the two deputies were ready. If the thieves escaped the trap inside set by Kemp and the sheriff, they would be caught when they emerged back outside.

Violet was safely at home behind the locked door of her cabin. She had wanted to be with them, but Sheriff Calhoun was reluctant even to allow Kemp. He decided to bow to Kemp's demand to be there because he owned the land, but Violet had been persuaded that she might not only endanger herself but possibly everyone else if she were on the scene.

Kemp tried to relax in his chair, but it wasn't easy. He was on high alert. He adjusted the leather holster on his hip that held his big Sig, the P320 that much of law enforcement used nowadays. They'd done all they could do to prepare for danger, but they were also prepared for surprises. If they ended up in a shoot-out and someone was hit, his EMT training would be vital out there so far from other medical help. Besides, he'd been deputized, so his presence was official on the stakeout.

Fortunately, he could see into the large room when he leaned slightly to the side and peered around the edge of the bar. The sheriff could do the same thing. They'd just have to be careful not to be seen or heard by the thieves, but as dark as it was, he didn't think they were in much danger of discovery before they sprung the trap.

He had expected it to be cold in there at night. And it was. He wore a padded jean jacket with his Wranglers and boots. The sheriff had pulled a fleece-lined parka over his tan uniform. They didn't wear gloves. They wanted no impediment if they had to quickly draw. All in all, they were as ready as they could be. Now they simply needed the thieves to show up.

He pulled back his coat and shirtsleeve to consult his digital watch that was dark except when he hit a button to illuminate the face. He did that now. Just after one in the morning. If past actions were any indication of future activity, and they usually were, the thieves ought to get here about two or three. They would figure that was the time most people were deep asleep, so the dead of night was the perfect hour to strike. That meant he probably had an hour or two more of waiting to do.

And so, his mind wandered, as it usually did anymore, to Violet Ashwood and her lonely hearts club and her tender smile and her hot body and her loving ways and...

A grating sound outside kicked him into alert mode. He felt the sheriff stiffen beside him. Early. The thieves couldn't wait. And they probably thought that out here on the ranch, nobody would be aware of their presence. He hadn't heard their big truck, so they'd used something smaller and quieter.

He wanted to catch them in the act, so there would be no legal issues that they could try and use to go free. He wanted them behind bars, at least for a stretch, so they couldn't be a danger to others.

He didn't want any bloodshed, hoped they wouldn't be armed with anything more than, maybe, knives or knuckle busters. He wanted an easy, clean capture. But he didn't know what kind of men they were dealing with. What kind of men would drag a backhoe around behind a truck on a flatbed, digging hole after hole, as they searched for probably nonexistent gold? Were they that desperate for money or simply that cocky? They'd even managed to burn down a farmhouse in the process. They most likely were hardened criminals who thought they could get away with anything. And thieves with a police record that, compounded with this new theft, could get them sent away for a good long while, and that could make them even more dangerous. Any which way he looked at it, they were all now in a bad position.

Abruptly, light filled the speakeasy.

Kemp eased slightly to the right so he could tell if it was the same two guys he'd seen from a distance on his ranch a few weeks ago. Hard to say. There were two, but they'd decided to go all ninja. Black spandex from head to toe. They even wore ski masks pulled down over their faces.

He wondered if they expected to be seen by bystanders way out there at Big Rock. Or were they anticipating the law? Maybe something had given the stakeout away. He hoped not.

Both men were tall and muscular. Neither appeared to be wearing a sidearm, but Kemp noticed that one carried what was obviously a ridiculously huge Rambo-style survival weapon, more machete than knife with a long, dangerous sawtooth blade that gleamed in the light. The other man carried something Kemp thought might be a heavy, everyday-carry folding knife, but the EDC's blade had not yet been deployed.

One thief set an ultra-bright, probably LED, lantern on a table. The other set a similar light on a small table in front of the row of crimson sofas.

"Looks like nobody's been here, Jock," the thief with the Rambo knife said.

"Good thing, Jesse. I'm not losing that bootlegger gold to nobody."

"It's got to be here."

"Nowhere else. We combed every foot of this dad-blamed ranch."

"Sick to death of it."

"Can't wait to get back to Hot Springs."

"And get there rich."

"High times then, Jesse. High times!"

"For sure higher than this dead zone of a county."

"Texas. Ugh."

"Give me Arkansas any day," Jesse said.

"You know it."

"Gold'll fix whatever ails us."

"Hard cash might even get that hottie of a librarian who helped us to look our way."

"She's never looking your way. But I bet she'd take a second look at me," Jesse said, chuckling.

"With enough gold, she'll look at us both."

"She's smart. We just had family stories of lost bootlegger gold. She found the Hallelujah Ranch legend for us. You gotta give her that."

"Happy to give her more than that," Jock said.

"Yeah."

"Bootleggers. That had to be the life."

"Wish we were living it."

"We'd be peddling hooch to this here speakeasy," Jock said.

"We'd be driving fast cars."

"We'd be outrunning revenuers."

"We'd be welcomed in every dive in Hot Springs," Jesse said.

"No. We'd be like the fat cats from Chicago and all over that came to our town to take their leisure in the fancy places."

"Yeah. We'd hobnob with the big-time guys."

"Best we can do now is get their gold." Jock gave a loud sigh.

"I'm grabbing those pearls first. They ought to be worth plenty." Jesse pointed at the piano.

Jock opened his switchblade knife with a *snick*.

"Seems a shame to cut up the place," Jesse said, hefting his huge machete.

"It'd be a bigger shame not to get the gold."

"We got the silver."

"Just whet our appetites for the real deal."

"Yeah."

"If we've got to break apart the furniture and cut up the cushions, we'll do it. We've got till dawn."

"Could be under the floorboards," Jesse said.

"If it comes to it, we'll pry those up."

"All this work makes me thirsty."

"Fine bootlegger you'd make. You'd drink up all the hooch," Jock said.

"Not all of it. Just enough to ease the pain of work."

"You got a point. Work. Ugh."

"Ugh is right."

"Wish we had some of those frisky flappers to dance with us," Jock said.

"When did you ever dance?"

"I could learn."

"Too much like work to me."

"You got a point."

Jesse looked around the room. "Guess we better get started. Jawing won't get it done."

"Puts off work."

"Yeah. I'm starting with the pearls."

"You always did like easy."

"Easy gals." Jesse chuckled as he took a few steps toward the piano.

"This job was supposed to be easy."

"No two ways about it, we're talking way too much work so far."

"Gold is the payoff." Jock headed toward the line of crimson sofas.

Jesse reached the piano, grabbed the string of pearls, whirled around, and held them high in one hand, his Rambo knife high in the other. "I got the pearls! We ought to be taking selfies! Now you get the hooch. That's enough work for one night."

Jock pivoted, his knife shining in the lamplight. "Did your brains just run out of your ears and head for Hot Springs?"

"No, I—"

"You're both under arrest!" Sheriff Calhoun leaped up with gun drawn and aimed at Jock. "Drop those knives and put your hands behind your heads."

Kemp was on his feet in an instant and pointed his Sig at Jesse.

The thieves froze and then burst into action.

"You're not taking us alive," Jock hollered, brandishing his switchblade.

"Dirty revenuers!" Jesse cried out, stuffing the pearls into a pocket. "Your tommy guns won't stop us." He waved his machete knife back and forth.

Kemp retained his position, but he wasn't about to shoot at two guys who seemed to have wandered—at least in their own minds—into their own Valentine's Day Massacre episode of *The Untouchables*, the old TV series that he'd checked out after buying Hallelujah Ranch. Maybe regular life was just too dull for them, so they'd come on a quest that, perhaps, was as much about excitement as gold. Or maybe they'd smoked one joint too many. Hard to say.

"Drop your knives," Sheriff Calhoun repeated in his deep, calm, no-nonsense voice. "No one wants to get hurt here."

"Scaredy-cat, are you?" Jock brandished his knife in the air again.

"I'm the one holding the Sig," Sheriff Calhoun said. "Please obey my order and no one will get hurt."

Jesse focused on Kemp. "Hey, you're the ranch owner with the pretty lady, aren't you? I'll trade you the pearls for her."

Kemp took a deep breath, fighting his impulse to be done with these two, particularly now that this one had insulted Violet. "Obey the sheriff's orders and no one will get hurt." He raised his Sig and held it steady as a rock. "Just remember what they say, don't take a knife to a gunfight."

"Drop your knives and put your hands behind your heads!" Sheriff Calhoun barked the orders this time. "Then kick the knives away and lay flat on the floor, facedown, with your hands behind your head! Do it! Now!"

"Do you suppose that sheriff's for real?" Jock glanced at Jesse. "I mean, that's the rancher. What's he doing throwing down on us?"

"You got a point. Maybe that guy is playing dress-up to help out his friend to get us out of his hair."

"Yeah," Jock said. "That's got to be it. No law is going to go to this much trouble for a few holes and some hooch. They want our gold!"

"Okay, rancher. Here's the deal. You keep the hooch and the pearls." Jesse tossed the string of pearls at Kemp.

Kemp let them fall at his feet, not about to take his eyes off Jesse and that huge knife. It could be lethal if the guy knew how to throw it. He was beginning to think they might be smarter than they acted, because they might be buying time for backup to arrive or something. Why else would they act goofy and unconcerned with two pistols pointed at them, whether they believed one was a real lawman or not?

"Yeah, you two take the hooch and pearls. We'll keep the gold," Jock said as he flourished his blade.

"Fair is fair. We went to a lot of work to find this speakeasy for you." Jesse gestured around the room with his sawtooth blade.

"We expect a little appreciation. Right, Jesse? And recompense."

"Right. We want the gold," Jesse said. "It's been a lot of hard work."

"It's been a lot of hard work filling in those holes, too." Kemp couldn't keep quiet any longer. "And fixing those cut fences. And putting out that house fire."

"Sorry about all that," Jock said. "Who knew there were so many dump sites on this ranch? I mean, didn't you all ever hear of trash pickup trucks?"

Kemp started to explain that there were no trash pickups a hundred years ago out there in the country, but he kept his mouth shut. He'd let Sheriff Calhoun handle this confrontation from here on out. He just didn't have the right experience for it. For sure, he couldn't twist his mind around it.

"Bottom line, have we got a deal?" Jock asked. "We can cut your sheriff impersonator there in for a percentage, if that's what it takes to iron out our differences."

"Put your knives on the floor and kick them away. Lie facedown on the floor. Put your hands behind your heads." Sheriff Calhoun's voice was now tight with growing impatience.

"He's good. Don't you think?" Jesse glanced at Jock. "He could be an actor all the way from Dallas or even Oklahoma City."

"Yeah. He's almost good enough to be from Hot Springs."

"That's the truth of the matter," Jesse replied, agreeing. "Ten percent to him."

"First we've got to find the gold," Jock said.

"Right." Jesse looked from Kemp to Sheriff Calhoun. "It'd be quicker and easier if you two put down your fake guns and helped us."

"Good idea," Jock said. "It's gonna be a lot of work tearing this place apart."

"We're not allergic to work." Jesse cocked his head to one side. "We just prefer somebody else does it."

"So, we've got real knives. You've got fake guns. And we've offered you a good deal for a little work," Jock said.

"Yeah." Jesse flipped his huge knife end over end in his hand. "I know my way around a good knife."

"And I know my way around a Sig." A woman holding a pistol in both hands stepped into the speakeasy. She wore a tan uniform, black boots, and a weighted-down utility belt around her small waist. "Gentlemen, Deputy Della Calhoun at your service."

Jesse and Jock whirled around to look at her.

"Glory be, the revenuers are hiring women now," Jock said.

"And comely ones at that," Jesse said. "She's a G-woman for sure."

Jock dropped his knife and held out both hands toward her. "Handcuff me, please."

"Me, too." Jesse dropped his knife and hurried over to stand beside Jock. He held out his hands.

Kemp gave Sheriff Calhoun a questioning look.

The sheriff just shrugged.

"On your knees," Deputy Calhoun ordered.

"Oh yes." Jock dropped to his knees.

"Me, too." Jesse fell to his knees.

"Put your hands behind your heads," Deputy Calhoun commanded.

Jock hurried to do exactly as ordered.

Jesse did the same thing.

"Tell me you're going to search me now," Jock begged. "I might have more weapons hidden on me."

"Search me first, please?" Jesse puffed out his chest.

Deputy Calhoun shook her head. "In those outfits, I doubt you could hide anything."

"I'd never hide anything from you," Jesse said.

"Not unless you wanted me to," Jock said.

"Lie facedown on the floor," Deputy Calhoun ordered.

Jock and Jesse complied, instantly and enthusiastically.

Jesse turned his head and looked at Jock. "I think I like her better than the librarian. She's stern."

"I like stern," Jock said. "Serious is good, too."

"Yeah. Librarian serious. Revenuer stern. Can't make up my mind."

"We don't have to make a choice," Jock said. "We can like both."

"True," Jesse replied. "I'll take both."

"Me, too."

Jesse looked up. "If you're not going to search us, Revenuer Stern, at least handcuff us."

"Put your hands behind your backs," Deputy Calhoun ordered as she holstered her Sig.

Jock and Jesse did exactly that.

Deputy Calhoun held out a hand to Sheriff Calhoun. He slipped his handcuffs off his utility belt and tossed them to her. She caught them in midair, knelt, and handcuffed Jesse. She pulled her own set of handcuffs off her belt and quickly cuffed Jock.

She stepped back, then looked from the thieves to Sheriff Calhoun. A smile twitched her lips. "Need any more help, or can you take it from here?"

Sheriff Calhoun's lips twitched, too. "Thank you, Deputy Calhoun. I believe we can manage, now that you've subdued the thieves."

Deputy Calhoun glanced down at Jock and Jesse, who strained their necks to look up at her. "Gentlemen, that's why you don't mess with revenuers...or Texas. I'll get Deputy Winston and be right back." She turned and left.

"I like her style," Kemp said.

"Just hired out of Fort Worth."

"Wildcat Bluff County can always use another good officer."

Sheriff Calhoun smiled. "Appreciate your help. We can deal with it now."

"Thank you," Kemp said. "You do a great service for our county."

"It's a great county. I'm honored to serve here." He nodded toward the exit. "Why don't you go on back and reassure Violet that all is well here? I'm sure she's worried about you."

"Worried about us all."

Sheriff Calhoun smiled again. "We'll put the tarp back in place. We'll recover your silver. That's what I'll book them on. Best you keep the pearls in a safe place. I doubt you'll get the booze back."

"Okay," Kemp said.

"We'll haul these jokers to jail. If I don't miss my guess, Hot Springs PD might know a little bit about them."

Kemp grinned. "Police maybe, but it could just as well be the town's actor guild."

Sheriff Calhoun chuckled. "I'll let you know which it turns out to be."

"Thanks." Kemp looked at Jesse and Jock. He sighed. "Who'd have thought these two could've caused me so much work?"

"You can put us on a chain gang," Jock hollered.

"But you're getting no work out of us," Jesse said, "unless Revenuer Stern is in charge. Where'd she go, anyway?"

"When's she coming back?" Jock asked.

Kemp just shook his head as he put the pearls in his pocket, walked around the two would-be gold thieves, and left the speakeasy.

Chapter 32

VIOLET WAITED FOR KEMP. SHE DIDN'T LIKE BEING LEFT OUT of the action when he might need her. Still, she understood it was a police matter, so she curbed her impatience. She stood outside on her porch under the overhead yellow light, where bugs buzzed softly around the glow. In case he might call, she'd placed her cell phone on the small table.

She hoped they caught the criminals tonight, so all was safe on the ranch again. She wanted to revisit the speakeasy so she could explore it. She still could hardly believe the once-illegal tavern had been so perfectly preserved for about a hundred years. Beautiful. Romantic. Intriguing.

She'd read that when the Eighteenth Amendment to the United States Constitution passed, all the saloons in towns had gone underground in basements, attics, or upper floors or were disguised as other businesses, such as cafés and soda shops. Anybody who wanted liquor was not giving it up. She wondered if the Hallelujah speakeasy had used a password, particular handshake, or secret knock, as was a requirement at other illegal saloons before a patron could cross the threshold.

It was a fun idea. Maybe she could use something like that on her dating website. She smiled. That's exactly what would happen when users created their own passwords. A hundred years later, and passwords were still needed to access private domains. She liked the continuity across time.

What would Kemp do with the speakeasy? Maybe he'd turn it into a museum on the ranch, or maybe some museum in Texas would carefully remove everything and put it back together elsewhere in a special historic display. She didn't much like the idea of the blind tiger being taken away to a city, but that might be necessary. She couldn't imagine what other options Kemp might have for such a treasure. Above all, it must be preserved for posterity.

As she stood there in the quiet night, she couldn't help but wonder what Lady Mauve would want for her speakeasy now that it had been found. She had created a beautiful, safe space where lonely hearts could meet, mingle, and find love. At the very least, Violet would return the silver spoon to its rightful place, even though she treasured it as her very own. When Sheriff Calhoun recovered the silverware, it could be reunited with the spoon and all would go home to Lady Mauve's secret lair.

Violet sat down in the chair, still watching the night around her. It was so dark and quiet in the country compared to the light and noise of the city. And yet it was just as vitally alive. She glanced up where stars twinkled like diamonds flung across the deep-blue sky and the moon sent silver beams down to caress the earth. She heard the songs of frogs, crickets, and cicadas. An owl hooted in the distance. And coyotes howled in chorus across the pasture.

She had come to treasure the nocturnal sounds of nature while she had lived on the ranch. She no longer missed the bright lights of San Antonio. She wasn't sure when she'd changed from city to country. Maybe it had been gradual, or it had built up until it had burst upon her all at once. Now, three months seemed way too short a time to be there. She wanted to extend her stay so she could drink her fill of Wildcat Bluff County…and a cowboy named Kemp.

As she looked out over the ranch, all shadow and mystery deep in the night, she could imagine how it must have been when moonshiners drove their load of shine under the cover of darkness. She'd done a little research online to understand the era better, so she knew they'd have driven popular Model T Fords to outrun the revenuers, investigators from the Internal Revenue Service, and blend into the cities when they delivered their loads to speakeasies.

She felt a connection to the ranch's romantic past, as if tonight it were coming alive again. She could almost hear the tinkling of a piano, the clinking of glasses, the murmur of voices, and the soothing sound of a nurturing voice that could only belong to the former Lady of Hallelujah.

Perhaps she was being fanciful while she waited and worried about the love of her life. If Lady Mauve were here right now, she would understand. She would serve comforting food, perhaps mashed potatoes, cream corn, and baked chicken, on violet-patterned china with her beautiful silverware. She would whisper comforting words. She would vow that love conquers all.

And Violet could only hope that, in the end, love had conquered all for Lady Mauve before the curtain closed on her speakeasy forever.

As she sat there listening to the night and thinking her thoughts, Violet heard an engine, faint at first, then louder as it came closer. She stood up, heart beating fast in excitement. If she weren't mistaken, that was Kemp's ATV. He was on his way home. He would be with her soon.

She wanted to run to him. She'd been worried about him. She needed to hold him in her arms to make sure he was really and truly all right. She jumped to her feet and clutched the railing with both hands as she leaned in the direction of the sound coming closer and closer.

And then he was there, headlights piercing the dark of night. He leaned forward on his ATV, as if by willpower alone he could make the vehicle go faster. Moonlight bathed him in silver, causing him to appear almost like a knight of old in full metal armor, riding his trusty steed, returning to his lady fair after slaying the dragon.

She could wait no longer. She rushed down the stairs.

He stopped in a cloud of dust and leaped off his ATV.

She ran forward with arms outstretched.

He caught her, hugged her, and spun her around in a circle before he let her feet settle back on the ground.

"Are you okay?" she asked, catching her breath.

"Yes. And you?"

"Yes."

"We caught them."

"Wonderful! Is everyone safe?"

"Absolutely." He chuckled, setting her back as he looked at her face. "There was no danger…except we came close to dying from laughter."

"Laughter?"

"Jesse and Jock."

"They're the thieves?"

"More like a comedy routine."

"I don't follow."

"Don't blame you." He grinned as he pushed a strand of hair back from her face. "I'll tell all, but first let's go inside."

"Hungry?"

"Famished." He traced her cheekbone with his fingertip. "Missed you."

"Missed you, too. And I worried."

"No need, as it turned out." He put an arm around her waist and turned her toward the cabin. "Come on."

She hurried toward the stairs. Now that Kemp was here, she wanted nothing more than to be inside. She felt so relieved that he had safely returned to her. She no longer felt complete without him. Love. It made you vulnerable, but it also made you strong. Lady Mauve would have understood the feelings, because she had provided a place where lonely hearts could be safe while vulnerable in their quest for love.

Inside, Kemp shut the door behind them. He took her in his arms once more. He murmured her name.

She breathed in the scent of him, fragrant outdoors, musty speakeasy, and tangy citrus. She felt the strong, hard muscles of his shoulders. She heard his soft breath as he pressed a kiss to her forehead.

"I've had one thing on my mind all the way back from the speakeasy. Do you know what it is?"

"What?"

He chuckled. "We've never tried out that big, red bed together, have we?"

"No." She grinned, knowing exactly where he was going. "I've never been able to figure out which is the top."

"There's not one. There's only a center." He looked thoughtful. "That's where we meet…in the center of our lives."

"If we hold the center together, we will—"

"Always be all right."

"Yes."

And she gazed into his green eyes, seeing that tenderness darken them, feeling that same tenderness in her own eyes. They were coming closer with each connection in their lives. They were telling each other without words that they were building that center together.

He cleared his throat, glancing away. "I'm hungry. Thirsty."

"I can fix something."

"Would you?"

"Yes, of course."

"I could get a shower while you do it."

"I could take the food upstairs on a tray."

"Would you wait for me in bed?"

"Yes." She smiled. "Would you come naked to me?"

"Yes." He grinned. "Would you wait naked for me?"

"Yes."

"I'll hurry." He whirled around and disappeared into the bathroom.

She smiled a secret little smile of anticipation, and then she walked into the kitchen. Finger food would be perfect. In fact, she'd learned that finger food had been created when illegal taverns went underground, because folks often had to eat on the run or grab their food and booze when revenuers knocked down the front door and revelers had to escape out the back. There'd be no need to worry about interruptions on the ranch this night. They'd enjoy every little thing at their leisure, including each other.

She found a crimson tray and set it on the counter. She selected several red plates and positioned them on the tray. She pulled longhorn cheese and a red apple out of the refrigerator and then sliced them. A box of wheat crackers was just what she needed, so she shook squares from it onto a plate. She arranged the cheese and apple slices in an attractive design on two plates. Red napkins were a colorful touch to go with the plates. Finally, she opened a bottle of wine, chose two wineglasses, and set it all on the tray.

She picked up the tray to go upstairs, but she set it back down. In their hurry to get inside the cabin, she'd left important stuff outside. She quickly opened the front door, stepped out, and picked up her phone. She glanced around, taking a deep breath. All looked peaceful…almost as peaceful as the way she felt now that Kemp was home. Well, peaceful except for the building excitement of being with him again. In bed.

She went back inside, set her phone on the coffee table, and picked up the tray again. She could hear Kemp in the shower, water running. She thought about joining him, even wanted to, but he'd asked her to wait for him in the big, round bed. And she wanted to be there.

She walked upstairs. The nightstand lamp she'd left on cast a soft, warm glow over the entire bedroom. She leaned over and set the tray in the exact center of the bed. Yes, they were constructing a center together. And she was ready to build it even bigger and stronger.

She'd had a shower earlier and put on clean clothes, just jeans and a sweater, but she didn't need them anymore. She heard the shower go off. He would be with her soon. She needed to hurry. She quickly took off her shoes, set them under the chair, slipped out of her clothes, and put them on top of the chair. When she wore nothing more than red underwear, she hesitated until she heard him coming up the stairs. She quickly stripped those two small pieces off and tossed them on top of her other clothes.

She hurried over, pulled back the crimson cover, got into bed, and tucked the sheet under her chin just as he hit the landing. As he stalked over to her, just as naked as she had requested, she could only marvel at the perfection of his body, all long, lean, hard muscles. He was obviously ready to do the bed justice. He carried something in his hand, but she couldn't tell just what.

"I brought you something from the speakeasy." He sat down beside her, holding his hand behind his back.

"Really?" She couldn't imagine what it could be, since he wasn't holding a big bottle of liquor in his hand.

"Close your eyes. I want to surprise you."

She closed her eyes, not sure if this was a good idea or not. Surprises could be tricky. She felt him lower the sheet so her torso was bare to him, and then she felt him drape something over her head until it hung down between her breasts, cold as cold could be. She shivered but kept her eyes shut.

"Can you guess?"

"No."

"Remember the piano and—"

"Pearl necklace!" She clutched the string of pearls. She looked down. They were dusty but still managed to gleam a rosy hue in the lamplight.

"Do you like the pearls?"

"Like them? I love this necklace!" She ran her fingers up and down the long strand, feeling each pearl slowly warm in her hand.

"I know they're dirty, but you can clean them."

She looked up at him, seeing the pleasure she felt at his gift mirrored in his green eyes. "I can't accept the pearls. They may be worth a small fortune. And they're probably museum-worthy."

He smiled, eyes lighting up. "They're Violet-worthy."

"But—"

"No buts. You've brought luck and love to Hallelujah Ranch. You deserve something for that, if nothing else. Besides, I want you to have them."

She ran her fingers up and down the strand again, feeling the pearls grow warmer with each touch. "Pearls are supposed to be worn to maintain their luster. It's been a long time. I don't know if—"

"You'll bring them back to life just like everything else you touch."

"Thank you." She felt a growing attachment to the beautiful necklace. "Maybe I could just borrow the pearls for a while."

"Way I see it, Lady Mauve would want you to have them."

"I suppose they used to belong to her. Why do you think she left them when she disappeared from the speakeasy?"

"Don't know. Maybe she didn't have a choice."

"She left the silver, too."

"Yeah. No way to ever know why."

"Guess not."

"At the moment, I really don't care. These pearls look perfect on you…as if they were made for you." He trailed a fingertip down the row of pearls that ended at her belly button and back up the other side.

She shivered, forgetting about everything except him. "I fixed a tray for us."

"I see." But he didn't look at it. Instead, he left the pearls to stroke her breasts, teasing the tips into hard nubs.

She shivered again. "You aren't hungry?"

"I'm starved. We can eat later." He picked up the tray and set it on the nightstand.

"Are you sure you don't want—"

"I want you." And he took hold of the necklace and used it to pull her slowly—ever so slowly—toward him until they met breasts to chest. And then he kissed her.

She felt as if she'd been waiting a lifetime for this kiss, this man, this moment. She clasped his shoulders with both hands, feeling his strength, not only of body but of mind and soul as well. She returned his kiss, deep with passion and commitment, as their tongues entwined, drawing them ever closer together.

He lifted his head, looked down at her with a self-satisfied smile, and released the pearls.

She felt them warm against her skin, as if they had been waiting a lifetime to come alive, just like her. And that was the way she felt, as if she were coming alive in his hands and his life.

"Center." He pushed the crimson cover to the floor. "I want us exactly in the center of the bed."

"Yes." One word was all she could get past her swollen lips, hot and puffy from his heated kisses.

She eased into the center, letting the pearls slide to the side and pool like a warm current beside her face. She didn't want to wait a moment longer for him…for them. She spread her legs, and then pointed at the nightstand where she'd had the foresight to purchase something for them.

He opened the drawer, pulled out a condom, shucked the wrapper, and slipped on the rubber. He knelt between her thighs, gently placed her legs over his shoulders, and stopped all movement. He looked at her for a long moment, intimately connecting them on that level first. He smiled, green fire lit his eyes, and he gently pushed inside her.

She felt rocked to her core. She clutched his shoulders as he thrust deeply, repeatedly, heatedly while taking her with him on a wild ride into ever more desire-filled territory. She dug her fingers into his thick hair, twining herself around him, urging him to fill her completely. She moaned. He groaned. And he took them both over the edge on the center of the bed that became the center of their universe as they reached the peak of passion together.

He lay back on the bed and nestled her head on his shoulder.

She snuggled against him, feeling complete.

"You mentioned a new hook for Cowboy Heart-to-Heart Corral."

"Yes…but I gave it up." She didn't much care about her lonely hearts club at the moment. It was enough, more than enough, to feel the pearls warm against her skin and listen to the beat of his heart.

"I had an idea."

"What?" She barely got the word out because she felt so relaxed and sleepy.

"You could launch your lonely hearts club from the Hallelujah speakeasy."

"What!" She sat up, instantly awake.

"I bet Lady Mauve, if she were around, would approve."

"Kemp, it's brilliant!"

"Glad you like it," he said.

"The speakeasy is so beautiful, so romantic, so visual."

"You want to do it?"

"Oh, yes!" She clutched the pearls to her chest. "But I'd need to pay you rent."

"How about you do a little extra work as a cowgirl?"

She leaned down and placed a soft, warm kiss on his lips. "I'm not sure there's any way you could get me off this ranch."

Chapter 33

A WEEK LATER, VIOLET SAT ON A BARSTOOL AT THE APEX OF the horseshoe-shaped bar in the Hallelujah speakeasy. She was alone as she gathered her thoughts and prepared to make a major change in her life.

Change. She held the violet-pattern serving spoon. Had her life changed when she'd found the silver spoon, or had it already changed the moment she'd seen Mr. July's photograph in the cowboy firefighter calendar and it had simply accelerated after she'd found the spoon? She didn't know. And she wasn't sure it mattered anymore. Change had come to her. And she welcomed it.

April 30. It was a good day to launch Cowboy Heart-to-Heart Corral. It was a good day to begin her new life as the proprietor of her lonely hearts club. It was a good day to reach out to the world…where in some places it would already be the first of May.

She sat with her back to the floor-to-ceiling shelves filled with the original, sealed bottles of moonshine that retained their hundred years of accumulated dust and grime. She had cleaned the rest of the blind tiger, paying particular attention to anything that needed to be repaired, such as broken chair legs or ripped upholstery. She'd found none of that marred the place's perfection. The bar, chairs, and piano now gleamed with furniture wax. She'd polished the oak floor. She'd vacuumed the sofas and chair seats. She'd lavished particular attention on the Art Deco–design chandelier overhead until it shone again. After Sheriff Calhoun had returned the silver set, she'd polished the pieces until they gleamed like new.

She looked at the serving spoon she held in her hands. Change.

While some things changed, others remained the same…and that was as it should be. She stood up. She turned. She walked the few steps to the white marble countertop beneath the liquor shelves. Lady Mauve's silver set shone in the light where the pieces were now displayed in their full glory.

Violet held the spoon against her heart for a moment, and then she set it down in its rightful place as a companion piece to the silver set. From trash to treasure, Lady Mauve's legacy had finally been reunited in her speakeasy.

Kemp had worked a miracle in hiring a contractor who had managed to install electricity in record time. Central air-conditioning and heating were a huge boon. She also had a regular entry door that locked and kept the speakeasy safe. She even had recessed lighting in the pressed-tin tile ceiling, spotlights over the liquor shelves, and the chandelier had been converted from candles and lamp oil to electric. Lady Mauve's blind tiger had been updated, but it didn't need to be upgraded.

She sat back down at the bar and looked out over her new domain. A row of plush, scarlet sofas accented with small, walnut tables stretched the length of one side. Individual round tables with crimson-upholstered chairs were grouped across from the sofas. A grand piano rose majestically on its personal dais in one corner. Instead of a pianist tickling the ivories, 1920s jazz softly filled the speakeasy from a prerecorded thumb drive inserted into a small music player with attached speakers.

All in all, the scene was set. And that included herself. She glanced down at the vintage flapper dress and ankle-strap heels on loan from the Buick Brigade. They had been thrilled at the news of the speakeasy's discovery. Once they had learned that she would debut her lonely hearts club at the blind tiger, they had insisted she must look the part. She also wore the beautiful pink pearls that hung in one long strand to her waist. She'd even had her blond hair pinned up to complete the 1920s look.

She was prepared. She was excited. She was determined. With the support of Wildcat Bluff County, Cowboy Heart-to-Heart Corral couldn't help but be a big hit. And it was about time to get her show on the road.

She looked down at her setup. She had converted the low shelf that extended around the interior of the bar. Where once it had been used to mix drinks, it now held computer, monitor, camera, and other equipment. All the plug-ins and wires were neatly hidden inside the bar, so that from the outside, it looked the same as it had a hundred years ago.

She adjusted the video camera and mic to their best advantage. She would soon be live on social media at the same time that she launched her website.

A pattern of special knocks came on the front oak door.

She smiled at the fact that the speakeasy now had its own entry code that only a few people knew...just like in its bootlegger days.

When the door opened, the Buick Brigade entered in alphabetical order. Ada. Blondel. Doris. Louise. They were dressed, like Violet, in the best of vintage flapper clothes from their attics in soft shades of blue, rose, mauve, and green, with long, sparkling necklaces. They wore their hair in short bobs with headbands that had single upright feathers.

"Oh..." Ada glanced around the speakeasy.

"Ah..." Blondel echoed as she walked over to the piano, sat down on the bench, and folded her hands in her lap.

"My word..." Doris sat on the edge of a sofa, crossed her legs, and clasped her hands over her knees like a trained beauty queen.

"Lordy..." Louise moved over to the group of tables, sat down on a crimson cushion, crossed her ankles, and tucked her feet back.

"So this is what it would have looked like back in the day." Ada walked over to the bar, stopped, and glanced at the chandelier.

"How do you like it?" Violet stood up. "I didn't change anything except we now have electric lights, heat, and AC."

"It's beautiful." Ada gave Violet a warm smile. "Thank you so much."

"Yes, indeed, thank you," the others chorused.

"I can only take credit for cleaning it," Violet said.

"You found the spoon." Blondel cupped her chin as she leaned forward.

"You brought the love." Doris set her hand on a table as she leaned forward.

"You raised the speakeasy." Louise uncrossed her ankles as she leaned forward.

"And now you heal lonely hearts." Ada tapped the bar top with the tip of a pink-tinted fingernail.

"Thank you all for the clothes and the support," Violet said.

"We were children…" Blondel said.

"So we were never allowed to come here…" Doris said.

"Although it was our deepest desire," Louise said.

"They came to Destiny from the bigger towns," Ada said. "The pretty flappers and their fancy men, all gussied up and out for fun."

"Why Destiny?" Violet asked.

"Hallelujah speakeasy had quite the reputation as the best blind tiger in several counties," Ada said. "Music, liquor, dance."

"But Hallelujah isn't in Destiny," Violet said.

"That was Lady Mauve all over again," Blondel said.

"She was just so smart," Louise said.

"I don't understand." Violet looked around the group, hoping for a better explanation.

"Destiny is where partygoers lost their tails, if there were any," Ada said. "They lunched or had ice cream or whatever in town, where they received the current password and directions to Hallelujah Ranch."

"Pigeons were faster than Model T Fords. They were used between Destiny and Hallelujah to alert the speakeasy if revenuers were on their way," Doris said.

"Those were all Lady Mauve's ideas," Blondel said. "She was so clever that her blind tiger was never raided and her moonshiners never caught."

"That says a lot." Violet was more impressed than ever with the elusive Lady of Hallelujah. "What happened to her?"

"A mystery." Ada stepped back from the bar.

"Do you mean that at the end of Prohibition, Lady Mauve simply closed up shop, made the speakeasy look like it had never been here from the outside, and drove away for parts unknown?"

"Not unknown to her," Ada said.

"Why would she leave her pearls and her silver?" Violet asked.

"Only she knew," Blondel said.

"Maybe she planned to come back, but something happened and she couldn't make it," Violet said.

"Love," Doris said.

"Certainly," Louise said.

"Love?" Violet asked.

"Why else would a woman pull up roots and disappear?" Ada said.

"She fell in love and went with him?" Violet asked.

"Or he left and she had no more reason to stay," Blondel said.

"That's sad, if it's true," Violet said.

"Love is the greatest gift of all...even if it does not last forever," Doris said.

"That is why your lonely hearts club is a great gift," Blondel said.

Ada gestured around the blind tiger. "Violet, you returned the spoon. You wear the pearls. You reopened the speakeasy. Now it is time for you to receive the greatest gift. Love."

"Thank you."

"And it is time to open Hallelujah to the world." Blondel rose from the piano bench and sat down in a chair at the table with Louise.

"And we are here for the big event." Doris stood up, left the sofa, and joined Blondel and Louise.

"If you should need us…anything at all about love, we will be right here near you." Ada walked over to the other ladies and sat down.

"I appreciate your support." Violet sat back on her bench and checked her electronic setup, making sure all was still in order as she listened to the soft, upbeat sound of jazz.

She kept one thought to herself. Lady Mauve had been smart. She liked to outwit the revenuers. She had been an entertainer. Most likely, she had simply set the scene as if she'd be returning any day. She'd hidden the entry to the speakeasy, too. She'd have done it all to confuse the revenuers in case they were still after her. Violet doubted love had anything to do with Lady Mauve's going away. She had probably simply moved to Dallas or another city and set up a legitimate bar…and no one, certainly not the law, would ever have been the wiser. Violet liked that practical idea.

For now, it was almost time to launch Cowboy Heart-to-Heart Corral. She just needed all the performers to gather in Lady Maude's entertainment venue.

As if on cue, the special speakeasy knock came on the door.

"Enter," Violet called, believing that was the proper response as she moved deeper into blind tiger resurrection day.

"Hey there," Kemp said as he opened the door wide.

"Hey there yourself, handsome." She thought that was how Lady Mauve would've responded to a good-looking cowboy, arriving all spiffy in a green-plaid shirt, pressed Wranglers, cowboy boots, and Stetson.

He grinned at her. "Delivery service. Second batch all present and accounted for."

"Send them in." She was glad he'd had the good idea to bring folks in his pickup to this remote location, particularly since no one else knew where the speakeasy was located on Hallelujah Ranch.

"Ladies, I hope you're enjoying your visit here." Kemp smiled at the Buick Brigade, took off his hat, and bowed his head.

"Yes, indeed," Ada said. "Thank you again for bringing us here."

"My pleasure."

"Trust me, the pleasure is all ours." Blondel gave him a coy smile as she picked up her long strand of beads and gave it a little whirl.

He winked at her, put his hat on his head, and disappeared out the door.

Violet was delighted at the Buick Brigade's response to Kemp and the blind tiger. They were getting into their flapper roles… ones they'd never had a chance to enjoy because they'd been too young during the Roaring Twenties.

"We're here! Now we can get this shindig on the road!" Wildcat Jack cried out as he burst through the open doorway and threw wide his arms. He wore his trademark fringed leather jacket over shirt and jeans with his long, silver hair dangling down his shoulders in two plaits.

"Welcome." Violet was glad to see the DJ from their local radio station, the Wildcat Den, arrive. KWCB was going to livestream the launch of her lonely hearts club.

"Oh, Jack, you dear man." Doris held out her arms. "Come here and make our day complete."

"Lovely ladies, I'm at your complete disposal." He hurried across the room and began to give kisses to powdered cheeks.

DJ Eden Rafferty entered next. She wore Western, too, but she'd selected a long, full, turquoise skirt with a matching blouse to go with her rose-colored cowgirl boots. The outfit complemented her dark-blond hair and blue eyes.

Behind her came the tech guys, carrying equipment and looking around in big-eyed wonder. They wore T-shirts, jeans, and sneakers. Their shirts promoted Wild West Days.

"Welcome. I'm so glad you could make it," Violet said.

"Wow." Eden turned a full circle as she looked around the

speakeasy. "Who'd have ever dreamed this fabulous place was here. And to think, against all odds, you found it."

"We had a little help." Violet didn't mention Jesse and Jock. She'd heard enough about their antics from Kemp to figure they were probably joking their way through the system. She supposed not much would happen to them, but at least they were out of Kemp's hair.

"What a find!" Wildcat Jack said. "It'll look great on camera."

"I appreciate y'all livestreaming my launch," Violet said.

"Happy to do it." Wildcat Jack walked over and eyed the liquor. "Talk about the real deal. Did you open a bottle?"

"Not yet," Violet said.

"Good idea. Who knows what it's worth?" he said.

"It's a great backdrop." Eden wandered over there, nodding in appreciation.

"Who else is joining us?" Wildcat Jack asked.

As if on cue, the special knock came again.

"Enter," Violet called out.

Kemp opened the door, gave a quick wave, then stepped to one side and gestured for someone to enter.

Storm Steele hurried past Kemp into the speakeasy, wearing her trademark "Fernando the Wonder Bull" T-Shirt, jeans, and boots. Sydney came in behind her, and Slade Steele was right on her heels.

"I can't stay long," Storm said. "Ann says Daisy Sue could calve anytime now. I wouldn't have left her side at all, except for our cross-promotion. And I wanted to support you."

"Thank you," Violet said.

"We followed Kemp in our truck. We may have to leave early." Slade glanced around the area.

"Good idea." Violet gestured around the blind tiger. "How do you like it?"

"It's really red," Storm said. "I prefer pink. But if I had to go red, I guess this is the way I'd go."

"It's fabulous." Sydney walked deeper into the speakeasy, turning her head back and forth as she glanced around.

"Looks good," Slade said. "I'd like a closer look at those bottles."

"Go ahead." Violet gestured behind her. "It's not wine like you make, but it could still be good."

"It's the real deal. Bootlegger hooch." Slade walked over to the bottles and stood there silently looking at them. "You've got to wonder whatever made them pass a crazy law outlawing liquor."

"They're still passing crazy laws." Sydney joined him. "You just never know about folks."

"True," Slade said, shaking his head.

"Oh, this silver set is gorgeous." Sydney looked back at Violet. "This is simply an amazing place."

"It is beautiful," Violet agreed.

Slade walked over to the Buick Brigade. "Good afternoon, ladies. I'm pleased to see you looking so lovely."

"Good to see you, too," Doris said.

"Hey, we ought to get this show on the road," Storm called. "I need to get back to Daisy Sue and Fernando as quick as possible."

"Okay." Violet glanced around the group. "I'm ready when everyone else is ready."

Storm whipped her cell phone out of her pocket.

Wildcat Jack and Eden went to stand in front of the bar as Violet moved behind it, then they positioned themselves for the camera so one was on either side of her.

And Violet went live.

Chapter 34

"Ms. Ashford, is it true that a Wildcat Bluff Fire-Rescue calendar inspired you to feature Mr. July as the face of Cowboy Heart-to-Heart Corral?" Eden Rafferty asked.

"Yes, that's true." Violet smiled at the camera, then up at Kemp, who stood beside her inside the horseshoe shaped bar.

"And that decision brought you to Wildcat Bluff County?" Wildcat Jack asked.

"Yes. I learned that this county has a high percentage of romance that leads to engagements and marriage."

Eden smiled. "I can be counted in that percentage because I also found love here."

"Congratulations. I'm happy for you." Violet felt the interview was going well, particularly because Eden and Jack were making it easy for her.

"Thank you," Eden said. "I'm interested, and I'm sure all our listeners are, too, in what makes Cowboy Heart-to-Heart Corral different from other dating sites and apps."

"Lonely hearts club. That's the way I think of Cowboy Heart-to-Heart Corral. I want to spread love, because I believe it is the most important thing in the world." She glanced up at Kemp.

"I'm happy to support Cowboy Heart-to-Heart Corral. I hope it helps folks find love." Kemp smiled down at her, green eyes lighting up.

"That's good. I'm all for love," Wildcat Jack said.

"When people sign up, they will have the opportunity to get to know each other, to share interests, to become acquainted before they ever meet in person. Friendship comes first." She gestured around the blind tiger. "That is the way love and friendship bloomed in places like this speakeasy back in its heyday."

"If I understand you correctly," Eden said, "you're bringing country values to lonely hearts who want long-term commitments."

"Yes. That's one of the reasons I'm launching in Wildcat Bluff County. And I've received wonderful support from everyone here."

"That includes me." Storm stepped forward, so she could be included in the radio station livestreaming. She held her cell phone in her hand. "Fernando and Daisy Sue met at the fence between Steele Trap Ranch and Lulabelle & You Ranch. They liked each other first…and then they fell in love."

"Everyone is fascinated by the Fernando and Daisy Sue story," Eden said. "I understand Daisy Sue is expecting their first calf. How is she doing?"

Storm smiled at the camera. "She hasn't had an easy pregnancy, as her fans know, but she is doing well now."

"I'm glad to hear it," Eden said. "When do you anticipate the birth of their first calf?"

"Any moment now. I really can't stay long." Storm grinned, eyes wide. "We're so excited. Fernando is beside himself with happiness…and yet worried about the love of his life."

"We're all worried about Daisy Sue," Eden said. "And yet you came here to be with Ms. Ashford for the launch of Cowboy Heart-to-Heart Corral."

"I believe in love, just as Ms. Ashford does. Fernando and Daisy Sue are proof that there is a special someone for all of us. Cowboy Heart-to-Heart Corral is a terrific way to meet that special someone."

"I'm sure Ms. Ashford appreciates your generosity in joining her today," Eden said.

"That's true." Violet smiled at Storm. "Fernando and Daisy Sue are a great love story. And they're an inspiration to everyone."

"Thank you. I think so, too," Storm said. "They would want me to be here."

"You will let us know the moment Daisy Sue gives birth, won't you?" Eden asked.

"Oh yes, I—" Storm was interrupted by a ringtone on her phone. She put it to her ear, listened a moment, appeared alarmed, and stuffed her phone in her pocket. "Excuse me. I must leave."

"Is Daisy Sue about to give birth?" Violet asked.

"Yes." Storm visibly collected herself. "The veterinarian is with her now. I've been asked to return…immediately."

"Thank you so much for being here," Violet said.

"It was my pleasure." Storm turned away.

Wildcat Jack looked into the camera. "You heard it first here. Fernando and Daisy Sue are about to have their first calf. We'll be taking you live to the barn on Steele Trap Ranch."

"In the meantime, we are here at the Hallelujah speakeasy with Ms. Ashford for the launch of Cowboy Heart-to-Heart Corral." Eden turned to Violet. "We're so happy that you chose Wildcat Bluff County as the inspiration for your dating site. And we're also proud that our very own cowboy firefighter Kemp Lander is personally welcoming all new members."

"Thank you for being here." Violet smiled at the camera.

"And now folks," Wildcat Jack said, "we will return you to the Wildcat Den and your favorite country tunes."

Eden signaled the tech guys, and they stopped livestreaming.

Violet noticed that everyone in the room visibly relaxed now that they were no longer broadcasting to the world.

"What do you need us to do?" Kemp asked as he walked out from behind the bar and stopped beside Storm.

"We'll take it from here. Glad I brought my truck." Slade looked at Storm. "Is there bad news?"

"Not sure, but Ann wants us there." Storm looked up at her uncle with tears in her eyes, and she wound her arms around him.

He held her tight for a long moment. "Sooner we get there, the sooner we can find out what's going on and help."

"Let's go." Sydney glanced at Eden. "You're welcome to come on out to the ranch, but Ann is not going to let you anywhere near Daisy Sue, if I don't miss my guess."

"You're all welcome to come out," Slade said. "It's a momentous event in our lives."

"Fernando needs us, too." Storm took several steps toward the door, then looked back. "Violet, I regret I interrupted your launch, but—"

"Please, go ahead. I'm fine. Cowboy Heart-to-Heart Corral is fine. Now you just need to make sure Daisy Sue is fine."

"Will do." Storm reached the door, then looked back again. "Kemp, I hope you'll come to the ranch as soon as you can. You're always a big comfort to Daisy Sue. And, Violet, you come on out when you can get away." She glanced at the Buick Brigade. "Y'all, too. Everybody come!" And then she was out the door, leaving it wide-open behind her.

"We'll see you at the ranch." Sydney followed her daughter with Slade right on her heels.

"We'd better get over there," Wildcat Jack said. "Violet, your news is a big story, but Fernando is a bigger one."

Violet chuckled at his words. "Go. I'm good here."

"I'll run the radio crew back to the house. They can get in their vehicles there and head out," Kemp said. "Then I'll be back for the rest of you."

Violet glanced at the Buick Brigade. "Is that okay with y'all?"

"Kemp, please, go," Blondel said. "We're fine here."

"We're enjoying the speakeasy," Doris said.

"I'll be right back." And Kemp herded the KWCB crew out the door and shut it behind them.

Quiet reigned in the blind tiger.

Violet checked her monitor. Her lonely hearts club was getting action. All the early promotion, plus what they'd done today, was working to everyone's benefit. She glanced over at the Buick Brigade.

"Congratulations," Ada said.

"You did it," Blondel said.

"Against all odds," Doris said.

"You brought love back to Hallelujah," Louise said.

Violet walked from behind the bar, selected a crimson-cushioned chair, and set it down at the Buick Brigade's table. "To tell you the truth, I can hardly believe it all worked out."

"My dear." Blondel reached over and patted her hand. "Didn't we tell you that love conquers all?"

"Yes, you did." Violet glanced at the beauty around her, including the Buick Brigade. "I do appreciate all your help."

"That's what we're here for," Ada said. "We help others."

"And we watch over new life that comes from love," Louise said.

"Fernando and Daisy Sue created new life," Blondel said.

"And we are honored to be here," Doris said.

The Buick Brigade rose to their feet. They appeared regal and knowledgeable, like the wise women they were.

Violet stood, too.

And the front door opened to reveal Kemp. He smiled and gestured outside. "Your carriage awaits, ladies."

The Buick Brigade walked, with perfect poise, out of the speakeasy.

Violet glanced back at her tech equipment, feeling guilty for leaving in the midst of her launch.

"It'll still be here when you get back," Kemp said. "Cowboy Heart-to-Heart Corral is home now. Just like you are."

She walked over and tucked her hand in the crook of his arm. "Let's go attend a very special birth."

Outside, the Buick Brigade were already ensconced in the back seat of the pickup.

Violet quickly got in the passenger seat while Kemp sat down, buckled his seat belt, started the engine, and tore out of the area. She held on to both sides of the seat as he drove as fast as was safely possible, which seemed too fast to her, across the pasture until he pulled up in front of his house beside a big Buick.

"Thank you so much," Doris said.

"We will meet you at the ranch," Blondel said.

And the Buick Brigade was out of the back seat, into their Buick, and headed down the drive before Violet could hardly blink her eyes.

"Fast, aren't they?" Kemp asked.

"Yeah. Lots of energy."

He glanced over at her with a grin. "Do you need anything from the cabin?"

"Different clothes?"

"No time." He chuckled as he took off after the Buick.

She held on to the seat again. What had happened to her carefully planned Cowboy Heart-to-Heart Corral launch? Somehow or other, she always seemed to lose control in Wildcat Bluff County. And somehow or other, it always worked out for the best.

When Kemp turned under the Steele Trap Ranch sign and crossed the cattle guard, he groaned loud and long.

"What is it?"

"Look ahead."

"I see some vehicles."

"It's a circus all over again."

"What do you mean?"

"I'm the one who brought Daisy Sue back. I'm the one who had to negotiate through a line of fans on both sides of the road while hauling a trailer. I'm the one who managed not to hit anybody who was running back and forth across the road."

"I don't see anybody standing beside the road."

"Only because they couldn't time this birth and let folks know to be here for the big event."

"You sound grumpy."

He glanced at her. "I don't want anything to go wrong."

She patted his arm. "You're doing fine. We all are."

She watched as the Buick pulled up beside several pickups, four-wheelers, and a television van. Eden and Wildcat Jack were out of their vehicle and heading for the barn.

All four doors of the Buick popped open at once, and the Buick Brigade got out. They walked over to a tall woman in a dark-blue suit, high heels, blond hair, and a big white smile, standing outside the corral near the barn. She held a mic in one hand while she patted her hair with the other. A camera operator in a T-shirt and jeans got into position in front of her.

"Oh my," Violet said. "I can't believe it. Jennifer Sales of that Dallas TV station. We get her down in San Antone sometimes. She's good."

"I believe she's taken a personal interest in Fernando and Daisy Sue. That on-air piece she did about him replayed constantly one Christmas," Kemp said.

"If I'd known she was in the area, I'd have invited her to the speakeasy."

"Somebody must have alerted her about Daisy Sue."

"Storm probably." He parked beside the Buick.

Violet looked down at her flapper dress that had been so appropriate for the blind tiger, but was now so totally wrong for the barn.

"You look fine."

She knew she didn't, but there was nothing she could do about it now.

"Look." He pointed at the reporter. "She's interviewing the Buick Brigade."

"What do you suppose they're saying? Do you think it's live?"

"No idea. Anyway, as far as your clothes, you're in good company." He opened his door. "Come on. Let's get up to the barn."

When he opened her door, she was glad for the hand down, because otherwise she might have ripped something. He held out his elbow, and she wrapped her hand around it. She wished she were wearing anything except vintage heels that could get ruined if she stepped wrong.

"There she is." Blondel pointed at Violet.

She plastered a smile on her face and walked with Kemp up to Jennifer Sales.

"Ms. Ashford and Mr. Lander." Jennifer Sales held out her mic. "While we wait for news about Daisy Sue, could I take a moment of your time?"

"Certainly," Violet said.

"I'm sure my viewers will love to hear about Cowboy Heart-to-Heart Corral."

"We explained to her why we are wearing vintage Roaring Twenties clothes," Doris said with a crafty smile.

"They're absolutely breathtaking garments," Jennifer said. "And they are so appropriate for the occasion, as I understand it."

"Thank you," Violet said. "We launched Cowboy Heart-to-Heart Corral today from the speakeasy on Hallelujah Ranch."

"That's exciting news." Jennifer gave a big smile. "Mr. Lander, is it true that you accidentally discovered a fully intact 1920s speakeasy?"

"Yes. It had been closed and forgotten for about a hundred years."

"That's so thrilling. I would love to see it. Perhaps we could record a piece about it."

"Anytime you like."

"Thank you." Jennifer held the mic toward Violet again. "I understand from these lovely ladies that you are reaching out from the county of love to connect lonely hearts everywhere. Is that correct?"

"Cowboy Heart-to-Heart Corral is a dating site and app that, hopefully, appeals to people who are looking for companionship, as well as love. And we are bringing our lonely hearts club to people from the Hallelujah speakeasy."

"Wonderful! We can all use love in our lives." Jennifer looked back at the camera. "Wildcat Bluff County is a never-ending delight and just full of surprises."

"That is true," Violet replied.

"Thank you so much for chatting with us today," Jennifer said, smiling at Violet. "And good luck with Cowboy Heart-to-Heart Corral."

"Thank you."

"We'll go on up to the barn and check in on Daisy Sue." Kemp glanced at the Buick Brigade.

"We'll go with you," Ada said.

"Please let us know if there has been any change in her condition." Jennifer lowered her mic. "I agreed to stay out here and wait for news, so as not to disturb Daisy Sue or Fernando."

"We won't disturb her either," Violet said.

"Ladies." Kemp gestured for the Buick Brigade and Violet to precede him to the barn.

Violet stopped beside Eden and Wildcat Jack, who looked as ready as Jennifer Sales to relay the good news, as soon as they received it, to the world.

Eden leaned close to Violet's ear. "Great coverage. Timing couldn't be better."

"Lucky," Violet whispered with a smile.

Eden gave her a wink.

Violet walked on with the group toward the barn. She couldn't help but think what a sight they must make with five of them dressed to the nines in flapper costumes. She repressed a chuckle, because it was just the kind of thing that would happen in Wildcat Bluff County.

When they reached the entry to the barn, Oscar and Tater stepped out to meet them. Tater wore two bandannas, one pink and one blue.

"Glad you could make it," Oscar said.

"How is it going?" Violet asked.

Oscar shook his head. "It's taking too long. Nobody is allowed in Daisy Sue's stall except Ann, Storm, Sydney, and Slade. Fernando is in the stall next door and fit to be tied. If he gets a mind to, he can kick that door off and get into Daisy Sue's stall."

"That wouldn't be good." Kemp stared at the shadowy interior of the barn.

"It won't be long now," Blondel said.

"Glad tidings are almost upon us," Louise said.

"Double blessings, no doubt," Ada said.

"For the good of all," Doris said.

Violet smiled at them, knowing she couldn't top their words. She just hoped all was well in the delivery stall.

They waited together, silent and expectant.

"Tater couldn't make up his mind whether to wear pink or blue today." Oscar broke the silence and tension.

"Good choice," Kemp said. "That way he's right whether it's a girl or a boy."

"My thought, too." Oscar took off his cowboy hat, ran a hand over his bald head, and set his hat back in place. "Tell you what, this is getting to me."

"Me, too," Violet said. "How long can it take?"

"As long as it takes." Kemp gave her an encouraging smile.

"Oscar, could you go check on Daisy Sue's progress?" Violet asked.

"No." Oscar gave her a hard stare. "None of us are going to disturb them. I'm here on guard duty."

"We're not going anywhere," Kemp said.

Violet just nodded as it grew quiet outside the barn again. She glanced back and saw that Jennifer Sales and Eden Rafferty were waiting just as impatiently, and worriedly, as the rest of them.

A scream filled the air inside the barn.

Violet tensed, along with everyone else. Was it good news or bad news?

And then the scream came again, and along with it the sound of running footsteps down the center aisle.

Storm burst out of the barn, tears running down her cheeks. She threw her arms wide as if to embrace the world. And grinned for all she was worth.

"Twins! Little Fernando and Margarita are here."

Chapter 35

Violet could hardly believe it had been a couple of weeks since the launch of Cowboy Heart-to-Heart Corral. Success was building as more and more people signed up and interacted on her dating site. Kemp was a big draw, but the speakeasy was right in there with him because folks were fascinated by it, as well as her blog about life on Hallelujah Ranch in Wildcat Bluff County.

If she'd thought things would settle down after her lonely hearts club debut, as well as the birth of Little Fernando and Margarita, she was wrong. Things had speeded up as everyone raced to get everything in place for the upcoming Wildcat Bluff Fire-Rescue fund-raiser. She'd believed, along with Sydney and most local folks, that it would be a small county event, but it had taken off because of a popular television reporter out of Dallas.

When Jennifer Sales had been at Steele Trap Ranch for the birth of Fernando and Daisy Sue's twin calves, she had learned about Win a Date with Your Favorite Cowboy Firefighter. She'd loved the idea and had thrown her support behind it.

After her on-air piece about it replayed constantly, the fire station had been inundated with phone calls from out-of-towners requesting information. Wildcat Bluff Fire-Rescue had moved the event from the school cafeteria to the rodeo arena due to so much interest. And they had decided to sell tickets from a website, so folks could purchase online. They'd also started selling *Win a Date* T-shirts designed by Belle Tarleton, owner and clothing designer of Lulabelle & You Western Wear.

Violet wore one of the T-shirts in bright red with Wranglers and crimson cowgirl boots that she'd bought at Gene's Boot Hospital. She sat at a table on the grounds of the Wildcat Bluff County rodeo arena to promote Cowboy Heart-to-Heart Corral. She was giving away crimson key chains with an embossed logo and getting lots of interest and sign-ups for her newsletter. She was one of several promoters in a line of tables positioned against the wall in front of the bleachers down from the concession stand run by the Chuckwagon Café.

She glanced to the side and smiled at Hedy Murray, who was handing out fire safety brochures and bumper stickers. Beyond her, folks promoted county events such as Christmas at the Sure-Shot Drive-In, Wild West Days, Christmas in the Country, and Wildcat Hall's Honky-Tonk Christmas. Storm Steele represented Fernando and Daisy Sue at her own table with T-shirts, ball caps, and a newsletter sign-up sheet. She was selling kid's T-shirts that had a photograph of Little Fernando and Margarita. Belle sat beside her, helping with promotion and sales, because they had created a line of children's Western wear at Lulabelle & You.

Violet could hardly believe the turnout. People were filing in, buying food, drinks, and T-shirts, picking up promotional material, and filling the wooden bleachers that extended down one side of the arena. Most of the women held large, bright-yellow cards with black numbers that they would use to indicate their bid.

How had the simple little idea she and Sydney had gotten excited about back at the dump the first day she had arrived in Wildcat Bluff County turned into this major event? She supposed that it had simply caught people's imaginations, along with Jennifer Sales's on-air piece. As a fund-raiser, nothing could be finer. Wildcat Bluff Fire-Rescue would be able to buy much-needed equipment and supplies after they auctioned off their cowboy firefighters for a date that afternoon.

They had set up a low cedar dais with two stairs up one side and down the other. On the front, burned into the wood, was a

Western scene of a cowboy on horseback wearing a firefighter's jacket. Cowboy firefighters would strut their stuff, or at least stand up on the dais that had been placed close to the bleachers. Violet had a good view of the upcoming event because the promotion tables were directly across from the dais.

The Buick Brigade had been given a place of honor in the lower center of the bleachers for the best view. They all wore big straw hats with colorful silk flowers to protect their faces from the sun.

With so many women competing with each other, Sydney had found it necessary to invite cowboy firefighters from other counties such as Montague, Cooke, Grayson, Fannin, and Lamar across North Texas. They'd ended up with about two dozen men, but even that number wasn't enough to satisfy demand. Still, it'd just have to do—although next year, and it was already looking to be a yearly event, they'd have a longer planning time and so an opportunity to invite more cowboy firefighters from other parts of Texas.

When she saw Wildcat Jack bound up the stairs to the top of the dais, she knew it was time for Win a Date with Your Favorite Cowboy Firefighter.

She glanced over at the group of cowboy firefighters gathered on one side of the concession stand waiting for their moment in the sun. They wore traditional clothes such as pearl-snap shirts, Wranglers, boots, and cowboy hats. Kemp stood beside Lester as they talked with Oscar, who held a red leash on Tater.

She noticed Kemp looking at her, so she gave him a little wave. He smiled back. She planned to outbid any other woman for him. They could just eat their hearts out for not getting a date with Mr. July.

"Okay, cowgirls, let's get this show on the road." Wildcat Jack's professional radio voice boomed across the arena. "Win a Date with Your Favorite Cowboy Firefighter is officially open."

Applause rang out from the audience, along with cheers.

"I want to remind everyone to make your bids high, because

every single cent of your donation goes to fund Wildcat Bluff Fire-Rescue that serves this entire county."

More applause followed his words.

Violet doubted many people would stop by her table now that the bidding had begun. Earlier, folks had picked up key chains, used the pens to sign up for her newsletter, and scattered the brochures. She quickly organized it all, so she could easily slip it into her tote bag and be ready to go later. For now, she was ready to focus on the cowboy firefighters.

"Let's see," Wildcat Jack said. "I have a stack of cards here. Each card lists the name of a cowboy firefighter who is ready, willing, and able to go out on a date with the woman of his dreams. Wait a minute, I believe that's the woman who pays the most for that date."

The audience laughed, staying right with him.

"Why don't we start off with one of the best cowboy firefighters in Wildcat Bluff County? Oscar Leathers is ramrod of Steele Trap Ranch. And...wait a minute." Wildcat Jack held up his white card as if he couldn't quite read it. "And Tater, the best cow dog—so it says here—in the county."

A loud round of applause came from the bleachers.

"Oscar, come on up here." Wildcat Jack gestured toward the group of cowboy firefighters.

Oscar walked over to the dais with shoulders back and head held high. Tater trotted by his side with just as much pride. They quickly mounted the two stairs onto the dais and stopped beside Wildcat Jack.

"Now, ladies, here's your first choice. There are plenty more, but whoever gets Oscar gets Tater, too. That's two for one. Now, what are you going to bid for a date with these two fine fellows?"

And Wildcat Jack went into auctioneer jargon, the energy and tempo fast and furious, the words rollicking and rolling.

Women raised their yellow cards over and over again as they upped their bids for Oscar and Tater.

"Come on—come on—come on," Wildcat Jack continued his fast patter. "You can do better than that. Bid up—bid up—bid up!"

And the bids for Oscar went up and up until they finally stopped. Wildcat Jack couldn't get women to go any higher, so he pointed into the audience at the winner.

Violet looked around to see who had won Oscar and Tater.

Ann the vet stood up, smiling. "I like the dog."

And the crowd burst into laughter.

Oscar took off his hat, covered his heart with it, put it back on, and led Tater down the stairs on the opposite side of the stage and then back to the other cowboy firefighters.

Violet remembered that Oscar and Ann had both expressed interest in her dating site. If this first date went well, maybe they wouldn't need Cowboy Heart-to-Heart Corral. That would suit her just fine. She was happy for everyone to find love anywhere and everywhere.

Wildcat Jack continued on with his cards as he introduced one cowboy firefighter after another, stoking the audience with clever patter as the number of cowboys to be auctioned dwindled down to fewer and fewer.

Violet waited for Kemp's name to come up, but she finally decided that Jack was saving him until near the last. She was also watching for Lester to be up on the dais, but Jack was saving him, too.

As the list of cowboys got shorter, the price increased for each one, as all the women wanted a date with her favorite cowboy firefighter. Wildcat Jack revved them up, teased them, taunted them, urged them on to higher and higher bids. The audience loved it all, laughing, joking, and joining in the fun.

Finally, Wildcat Jack called Kemp Lander up to the dais.

She watched her favorite cowboy firefighter stride up to the dais and bound up the stairs. By the time he stood beside Wildcat Jack, women were calling to him from the audience. She saw that she was going to have her work cut out for her to keep him all to herself.

Wildcat Jack started the bidding high and kept raising it. She held up her card as often as necessary to stay in the bidding, but Kemp was getting more expensive by the moment. He kept glancing at her and grinning because he knew she had promised to pay whatever it took to keep him. And she bid more and more until it was finally down to her and another woman. She looked up and saw what could only be someone from Dallas or another city by her dress and demeanor. She wasn't about to let that outsider win.

Wildcat Jack kept stoking the flames between Violet and the other woman, knowing she wouldn't give up. At the rate he was ratcheting up the bids, she might be buying a new booster for the fire department all on her lonesome. Finally, she had enough of the game. She stood up, raised her card, and offered an outrageous sum for Kemp Lander.

Everyone in the audience clapped for her. And the other bidder remained silent. She had won her cowboy firefighter. He gave her a grin to let her know he'd show her how much he appreciated it when they got home.

And then it was time for Lester Lander.

She didn't know what to expect, but she doubted anybody else did either. You just never knew with Kemp's cousin.

Lester sauntered up the dais, stopped beside Wildcat Jack, and took the mic from his hand. Les took off his cowboy hat and tossed it to the floor. He looked out over the audience and gave a slow, suggestive smile.

"My dear ladies," Lester said in his deep Texas drawl. "It's my pleasure to be here today with all of you."

The arena went totally quiet as he drew in the audience.

"It's getting kind of hot in here. Don't you think?" He took off the blue bandanna he'd tied around his neck and tossed it beside the hat.

And the crowd went wild, hooting and hollering for more.

Violet couldn't keep from grinning because this was bigger-than-life Les Lander and women loved him.

He snapped open a few of the pearl snaps on his Western shirt, then stopped and grinned at the audience. "Did I say hot? Can you say hot?"

"Hot. Hot. Hot." Voices filled the arena with that one word.

"Yeah. That's right. That's good. Hot."

"Hot. Hot. Hot." Women called back to him, waving their cards back and forth.

"I said the pleasure was all mine to be here today, didn't I?"

"Yes. Yes. Yes." The audience shouted at him.

"I lied… Well, to tell the truth, I partly lied."

And the women groaned at his words.

"The truth of the matter is…" And he leaned forward, as if confessing a sin in private. "The pleasure is going to be all yours…that is, the lucky lady who wins me today."

Once more, the audience went wild at his words.

He smiled, winked, handed the mic back to Wildcat Jack. He picked up his bandanna, put his cowboy hat back on his head, and walked from one end of the dais to the other, strutting his stuff.

Violet knew the bidding would be astronomical, because what woman in her right mind could resist Lester? Well, she could do it, but that was because no man could compare to Kemp Lander, not even his cousin.

Wildcat Jack kept the bidding going, upping Lester's price higher and higher until finally only one woman remained in the contest. She stood up, a little bit of a thing with fiery-red hair. She looked like she knew her way around a horse…and a cowboy.

Lester gave her a bow, sauntered off the dais, and returned to the other firefighters.

"And that concludes Win a Date with Your Favorite Cowboy Firefighter," Wildcat Jack announced. "Winners, please step right up, pay for your date, and get your man. They're waiting for you right over there." He pointed toward the cluster of firefighters near the concession stand.

Violet wasn't going to delay a moment longer. No chitchat. No niceties. She just wanted Kemp. She tossed her stuff in her bag and jumped to her feet. She got out ahead of the others who had to walk down from the bleachers. She hurried to the table near the foot of the dais's stairs to pay.

Lester quickly left the group of cowboys and intercepted her. "What's the hurry? Want to get my cousin away from all the lovely ladies?"

"Congratulations. You raised more than any other cowboy firefighter."

"Was there ever any doubt?" Lester grinned.

"No." She laughed.

He laughed with her.

"Enjoy your date." She couldn't keep from chuckling at Lester's cockiness because it so suited him.

"You know it." He winked. "I'll see you around the county." And then he sauntered back to the other cowboys.

Wildcat Jack stepped off the dais and stopped beside her.

"You did great," she said.

"Was there ever any doubt?" Wildcat Jack winked and laid his mic on the nearby table where the winners were lining up to pay their auction money.

"No." She laughed.

"Excuse me. I hate to part company so quickly, but I've got a date with one of those lovely ladies."

"Which one?"

"Don't know yet. She doesn't either. We'll work it out." And he sauntered off toward the bleachers.

Violet just shook her head. Lester and Wildcat Jack were two of a kind. Was Wildcat Bluff County big enough for both of them?

She paid her money, then hurried toward the group of cowboy firefighters waiting for their dates.

Kemp stepped out to meet her, grinning big. "Now that you've got me, what are you going to do with me?"

"I'm taking you home."

Chapter 36

Violet glanced over at Kemp as he turned off Wildcat Road and drove under the Hallelujah Ranch sign. Once more, they were together in his pickup. It seemed so normal now, where not long ago it would have seemed unbelievable. Mr. July. He was long gone. He was a fantasy that had turned into the reality of Kemp Lander. And she would never trade the first for the latter.

At the auction, she had told him that she was taking him home. But what did that really mean? A location? A residence? A place to hold your stuff? Was any of that even important when compared to love? She touched her chest. If she was honest with herself, Kemp was already home…in her heart. Love provided the warm, strong hearth where all lonely hearts could lay down their burden and find peace, hope, and togetherness.

She realized now that she had been home the moment she met Kemp Lander. She glanced over at him again. Sunlight coming in through the windows painted him in golden hues. Maybe the legend of bootlegger gold had nothing to do with the cold metal, but everything to do with the warm value of love. She smiled. Lady Mauve's love of beauty, of hope, of community, of people, of a strong man.

If Violet had learned nothing else since coming to Hallelujah Ranch, she had learned that the photographs of cowboy firefighters in the Wildcat Bluff Fire-Rescue calendar were just the tip of the iceberg. Beauty lay much, much deeper in how these men put their lives on the line for their county, friends, and family. And they did it all in the name of love. And that included Kemp Lander.

"Kemp…"

"Yeah?" He looked at her, then back at the road.

"I'm taking you off Cowboy Heart-to-Heart Corral."

"What?" He hit the brakes. "Am I messing up the site?"

"No. You're wonderful for the site."

"Why then?"

"I don't want to share you anymore, and I'm not going to."

"That's just fine with me." He started up the road again. "Back at the auction, I began to get worried I might end up in Dallas for my date." He chuckled. "Good thing you were willing to put out the big bucks for me."

She smiled. "You're expensive, all right."

"I'm willing to give you your money's worth."

"I like that idea."

"I'm yours to command."

"Even better."

"But first…"

"First?"

"I have a little something for you on the patio in the rose arbor."

"Will I like it?"

"I sincerely hope so, although…"

"What?"

"Well, you'll see."

"I'm not sure I like the sound of that."

"It's okay…at least mostly okay."

She shook her head at his words.

He parked in front of the house, turned to her, and clasped her hand. "I really do appreciate you rescuing me today."

"Anytime, cowboy."

He grinned and squeezed her fingers. "Let's get up to the house." He opened his door, and stepped down to the ground.

She picked up her bag of promotional material and stepped down from the tall truck just like any cowgirl worth her salt.

He twined their fingers together and led her under the rose arbor and onto the patio, where the sweet scent of roses filled the air.

She saw a big white box from Destiny Chocolatier on the table. "Oh my, more candy!" She set down her bag and plopped down on the cushions of the glider.

"Yeah." He sat down beside her.

She opened the box and started to laugh because the chocolates were a mess, as in twisted, smashed, and broken. "What happened to these?"

"Well, I had an idea." He sighed. "It was a good one, but it failed in execution. I kept trying to get it right, but…"

"What were you trying to do?"

He pointed at a big, misshapen lump of goo in its little paper cup in the middle of the chocolates. "Try that one."

"It doesn't look too edible."

"Don't eat it!"

She looked over at him, feeling wary. "Kemp, what is going on with this chocolate?"

"I mean, will you just pick up that piece and set the box aside. It's the only chocolate that counts."

She simply continued to look at him, not sure which way to go.

"Please?"

"Okay." She plucked out that piece, noticing that it seemed a little on the heavy side, and set the box back on the table.

"Good."

"Now what?"

"There's something in it."

"I'm not going to break a tooth on it, am I?"

"I told you not to eat it."

"What do you want me to do with it?"

"I don't know how this idea could go so wrong."

"Me, either."

"We're in it now. Will you just please try to get the chocolate off what's inside of it?"

"Okay." She decided to go with it, so she mashed on the piece and it oozed out both sides. Another big mess. And then she realized that she held a ring.

"This was supposed to be romantic," he said.

"Romantic?"

"I need to get a wet paper towel, but I don't want to leave you." Instead, he pulled a bandanna out of his pocket and handed it to her.

She set the ring covered in chocolate on the fabric and wiped off most of the mess. She held up a beautiful Art Deco–style rose gold ring with a single pink pearl in its center.

"I thought you'd like a ring to go with your pearl necklace."

"It's gorgeous. Thank you." She gave him a quick kiss, then looked back at the ring. "Is this to commemorate my dating site launch?"

"No." He took the ring from her and looked at her with intense green eyes. "I love you. Will you marry me?" He hesitated. "Is that romantic enough?"

She chuckled. Maybe he wasn't the most romantic cowboy, but he was definitely the best. "Yes to both questions. And I love you, too."

"Good. You're the best cowgirl of all." And he slid the ring onto the third finger of her left hand, leaving a smear of dark chocolate.

Can't get enough of Kim Redford's
Smokin' Hot Cowboys? Read on for a
sneak peek at the next in the series

Cowboy
HEAT WAVE

Coming soon from Sourcebooks Casablanca

Chapter 1

"I LEFT MY HEART IN WILDCAT BLUFF COUNTY, TEXAS." AUDREY Oakes whispered the words that weren't her words as she drove deep into that county. Lady Mauve, her great-grandmother, had written the line in her 1933 journal…and those were just a few of the heartfelt words that had brought Audrey to Texas so many years later.

She normally loved springtime, but now she had no thought for pleasure. She needed answers and she needed them now.

Lady Mauve's journal described how she left behind bootlegger gold when she went from Hallelujah Ranch speakeasy owner to legitimate bar owner in Hot Springs, Arkansas, after Prohibition. Why did she abandon the gold? Maybe it was too heavy to transport. Maybe she planned to come back for it. Maybe it had something to do with revenuers or other law enforcers. Now there was no way to know since the last pages of the journal had been ripped out.

At most, Audrey had a couple of months to save her grand-mother's life. It was a long shot to find buried gold. Maybe it was an impossible shot. But she had to take it. If she hadn't stumbled across her great-grandmother's journal in a dusty trunk while looking for old photographs, she wouldn't even have this chance. Medical procedures were expensive, and in this case, experimental procedures that weren't covered by insurance were impossible to fund.

She'd set out from Hot Springs early that morning with noth-ing more than general directions for several possible gold loca-tions written in faded lavender ink on yellowed paper to aid in her hunt. She'd counted on things staying much the same in the coun-tryside, but they hadn't.

She certainly hadn't expected to find a county dump in what should have been a meadow. She stopped her SUV in the entry and looked at the site. It appeared to cover about two acres and was surrounded by a chain link fence with two eight-foot entry gates. A faded metal sign stated hours of operation when an atten-dant would be on duty, but that time wasn't now.

In Lady Mauve's journal, she warned not to trust anyone in the county, so Audrey decided to be on the safe side. She drove away from the entrance and parked in a small stand of trees, so her SUV wouldn't be seen from the highway or too near the dump.

An earlier rain had left the ground muddy, but that didn't stop her. She got out of her vehicle, determined—if at all possible—to find any landscape that still matched the journal's description. She slowly moved around the dump outside the fence. Nothing looked remotely like what she was trying to locate.

Finally, she stopped at the back outside the dump's fence, frus-trated, hungry, tired from the long day that had netted her exactly zero. It'd be dark soon. She wanted to get something to eat and find a place to stay in the nearby town of Wildcat Bluff.

As she turned to head back to her SUV, she heard the engine of a big vehicle near the rear of the waste disposal. What was a truck doing there when the dump was closed? Maybe it was none of her business to investigate, then again, however unlikely, maybe it'd help her piece together information that might lead to the gold's location. In any case, she was curious.

She slowly, quietly made her way to the back of the dump, where she saw a ten foot drop from the top that allowed trucks to back up and discard their trash loads into containers below. None there now. Instead, she saw a sixteen-foot cattle trailer backed into the lower area that couldn't be seen from above. She dropped to her knees and crouched down. She didn't know what was going on, but she didn't figure it was on the legal side of the law...not with the dump closed and the operation out of sight of the road.

She didn't want to be caught spying on the operation, so she stayed still, even when she felt dampness creep into her jeans from the wet ground. Movement on her part might catch somebody's eye while staying still stood the better chance of keeping her invisible.

Two muscular guys dressed in jeans, shirts, boots, and caps pulled low over their eyes leaped out of the black one-ton cab. They opened the back doors of the cattle trailer, pulled out mobile, aluminum panels, and quickly fastened them end-to-end to make a long chute that they extended across the back lane to a pasture fence. They opened a barbwire gate in the fence, repositioned the ends of the chute to butt up to the opening, and leaped outside the chute.

Two cowboys on horseback appeared on the other side of the fence. They quickly drove a line of wild horses—maybe thirty or so—out of the pasture, through the chute, and up a ramp into the thirty-eight-foot semi.

Audrey watched in astonishment at the efficient operation. Nothing had been left to chance. It moved fast, like a well-oiled machine. And they meant business because every one of the guys wore a pistol in a holster on his belt. All went as planned until one of the horses veered away and headed toward her. A cowboy rode after the runaway, jerking off his wide-brimmed hat and waving it to steer the horse back toward the trailer.

She held steady, although she wanted to get up and run away like the horse. Who were these guys? Horse thieves? In this day and age? If so, they knew the dump was empty most of the time without an attendant, so it was the perfect spot for a clandestine operation. Thoughts of old revenuer-bootlegger chases and shootouts came to mind.

She and her mom owned the Oakes Rock Shop & Museum on Bathhouse Row. She'd given many tours and sold lots of books on the legendary Roaring Twenties and Prohibition in Hot Springs that had been a major getaway for bootleggers from as far away as Chicago. It had given her an eye for a particular kind of trouble. Illegal trouble. She suspected that was exactly what she was seeing here and now.

Still, it was none of her business. She wasn't going to get involved, even if this was some type of rustler operation. She had her own agenda and her grandmother's life took precedence over everything else.

She glanced over her shoulder where her four-wheel-drive SUV was mostly concealed in the trees. She wished she could run over there and quietly start the engine, but it'd make too much noise and maybe give away her presence. She just needed to sit tight until the horse thieves were gone, then get out of there.

But she ran out of time. The cowboy on horseback glanced up, saw her, looked back, and called to his friends as he drove the runaway up the ramp and into the semi. One of guys slammed the trailer's doors shut on the horses while the other ran to the back of the one-ton and began to uncouple it.

She could hardly believe her bad luck. Once that truck was free of the trailer, they could come after her. She leaped up and sprinted for her SUV. She was thankful she'd left it unlocked with her purse on the passenger seat. She jerked open the door, fell onto the front seat, and locked the door behind her. She pushed the start button, heard the engine turn over, and hit the gas. She bounced over ruts and downed branches, hearing tree limbs scrape the sides of her vehicle as she got out of there as fast as possible. She made the single lane leading out of the dump before she glanced back. Nothing yet. Still, they'd need time to get back up to the main road from the lane below. She hated to think how fast a one-ton with its powerful engine could catch her and cause trouble for her much smaller SUV.

She hit Wildcat Road just as the gray of twilight turned to the black of night. No streetlights anywhere, so only her headlights cut a swath of illumination through a tunnel made by long stretches of barbwire fence on either side of the road. She was alone out there, no cars, no people, no nothing except cattle and horses in pastures. All she needed to do was get to the small town of Wildcat Bluff and find a place to stay for the night. Hopefully, out-of-sight would be out-of-mind.

She lost that hope the moment she saw bright headlights coming up fast behind her. They were high, like on a truck, and above her back bumper. Trouble. She'd known it the moment she'd seen those vehicles, cowboys, and horses arrive at the dump. If only she'd been there earlier and missed them. No way to rewind time now. She must get off the road.

She looked back and forth on either side of the highway, searching desperately for a break in the fence-lines, a dirt turn-off, an entry to a ranch, or anything that would allow her to leave the road and slip away. So far, she saw nothing except the highway stretching out ahead of her.

She glanced in her rearview mirror. Those headlights were getting closer fast. She needed to find an exit. A rise in the road was coming up ahead. That was her chance. The driver behind her wouldn't be able to see her once she was up, over, and down the other side. And he'd be looking for her SUV's lights. She wouldn't give him that satisfaction.

She took the hill as fast as safely possible. At the top, she looked to either side, hoping against hope, for a break in the fence-line. Finally, she saw one. As she went down the other side, she killed her lights...and was immersed in darkness.

She tapped her brakes, jerked her steering wheel to the right, and careened off the main road. She felt her vehicle fish-tail as she held tightly to the steering wheel and aimed as best she could in the dark for the break between the two fence posts. She bounced over a cattle guard, scraped one side of her SUV on a post, and slid to the left on the roadbed with its deep shoulders.

She hit the brakes, felt her harness tighten across her chest, and her SUV came to a stop. But the left front fender listed downward. She was partly in a ditch. No matter, she needed to hurry and get out of there, so she couldn't be seen from the road.

She threw her vehicle into reverse, but she heard the tires spin, spin, spin. She was stuck. She hit the steering wheel with the palm of her hand. She tried reverse again. Spin, spin, spin. She was going nowhere. She took her foot off the gas. She didn't know how deep the ditch was or how thick the mud. She couldn't afford to grind her tire any deeper in an attempt to get free. She didn't dare turn on lights, inside or out, to check her situation.

As she sat there contemplating what to do next, she saw the truck with its bright headlights zoom past her. She breathed a sigh of relief. They hadn't seen her, going too fast, expecting to catch up with her. But she wasn't safe. When they didn't find her, they'd be back. They'd search the sides of the road exactly like she had earlier. No way should she still be here when they retraced their steps.

She gathered her thoughts. Okay, the long day had turned into what was becoming a long, torturous night. She must handle it. Maybe the ghost of Lady Mauve would lead her to safety. Of course, she wouldn't count on it. Roaring Twenties ghosts were part and parcel of Hot Springs, not Wildcat Bluff County. Still, she wouldn't mind a little help.

Worst luck, she couldn't move her SUV. She needed to get away from her vehicle and call for a tow truck. She didn't want to leave anything important behind just in case they saw her SUV and stopped to check on it. She'd placed her laptop in its case and the soft-sided carry-all with her clothes on the floor in front of the passenger seat. It was also a good thing she wore comfortable jeans, sweatshirt, and running shoes in navy, a dark color that blended well with the night.

She eased her door ajar, glad she'd set the inside light so it didn't come on when she opened the door. All was quiet outside except for the sounds of nature like frogs and insects and coyote howls in the distance. She grabbed her purse, computer, and bag. She listened again, but she didn't hear any traffic, so she had a little time to disappear into the darkness.

Fortunately, she was on the opposite side of where her SUV listed into the ditch. She stepped cautiously onto the lane, felt her foot slide in mud, and stopped to get firmer footing. She looped her purse, computer case, and bag by their straps over her shoulders. She shut the door and locked it. She hated to leave her vehicle in such a precarious position, but she hoped it was dark enough that it wouldn't be seen from the highway. She eased her cell phone out of her purse. She wanted to turn on the flashlight, but she didn't dare give away her position.

She glanced around, nothing but dark countryside. She didn't want to wait any longer to call for help. She crouched beside her SUV. She hit a button for the search engine on her phone, but pretty quickly realized she had no service. She tried several more times before accepting the situation. She dropped her phone back in her purse.

She stood up and looked in both directions. No one-ton yet.

Once they passed her going back to the dump, she could hoof it to Wildcat Bluff. It might take all night, but where there was a will there was a way. Still, she didn't want to be out on a country road alone at night, particularly if she was being hunted…not if she had another choice. She supposed she could walk out across a pasture with her bags, sit down under a tree, and wait for dawn. She might stir up a cow or horse, but nothing more dangerous. She thought there must be a ranch house somewhere on this acreage. If she found it, she might get help she could trust there, although that might be miles away, too.

As she contemplated her options, she heard another vehicle engine, but not from Wildcat Road. Bright headlights about the height and size for an ATV washed down the lane and over her. Somebody from the ranch was coming. Friend or foe? This could be the help she needed, but Lady Mauve's journal stressed that nobody could be trusted in Wildcat Bluff County. Did that still hold true all these years later? Time would tell.

She squared her shoulders, adjusted the straps on her shoulders, and walked away from her SUV to the center of the lane.

The ATV stopped several yards in front of her. Somebody got out. A dark silhouette walked toward her in a long-legged stride. Male. Tall. Broad-shouldered. Narrow-hipped. Big man could equal big trouble. What if this ranch was connected, somehow, with the horse thieves since it was so close by, maybe even shared a property line? But what if it wasn't? Big man could also mean big help.

"Stuck?" the stranger called in a deep voice with the unmistakable Texas accent that invoked hot skin sliding across cool sheets on steamy nights.

She felt that one word slip up and down her spine, making her shiver and wonder at her strong reaction to him.

"Rain will do it." He reached her, a shotgun held easily in one hand at his side.

She looked him over, searching for clues that would tell her about him. He had dark hair worn a little long to his shoulders. Brown eyes in a tanned face of sharp planes and angles evaluated her right back, as if he didn't trust her any more than she did him. Thirtyish. He was all muscle, clad in typical cowboy clothes of Wranglers, big rodeo buckle, blue-plaid shirt, and jean jacket.

He was obviously a man who knew his way around a ranch, so he had to know horses like the wild ones at the dump. But he was here, not there, so that could mean he wasn't part of the outfit, although he could be the mastermind and stay out of the action. She stopped her thoughts. She wasn't back in the Roaring Twenties in Hot Springs, where most everyone pursued an angle, just as liable to be illegal as legal.

She heard the sound of a big truck growing closer. Rustlers coming back or just a local rancher? She wasn't about to take a chance. "Douse your lights."

"Trouble?"

"Quick."

He flicked his shotgun up with one hand, so the business end aimed toward the highway instead of the ground.

"They'll see us."

"So? This is my ranch. Nobody's coming here except on my say-so." He glanced at her, then back at the road. "You're a different story."

"I was down at the dump."

He grew still. "Why?"

"I just…just…" She watched as the truck slowed down, lights illuminating her SUV, as well as her and the stranger. The vehicle crept past, as if the occupants were getting a good look while debating whether or not to take action. And then, decision made, the one-ton roared away back toward the dump.

"Friends of yours?"

"I never saw them before tonight." She faced the stranger. "I'm not from around here."

"I can tell by your voice."

"I'm Audrey Oakes. Hot Springs."

He held out his hand.

She shook it…big, warm, strong. She felt as if he'd touched every bit of her, not just her fingers. She experienced a little thrill at the impact he had on her, then she quickly squashed it. She didn't need a good-looking guy on her mind or tempting her body.

"I'm Cole Murphy." He gestured with his head toward the ATV. "Why don't we go up to the house and you can tell me your story."

"Thank you for the offer, but I don't want to be any trouble. If I can get someplace where I have cell coverage, I'll call a tow truck."

"It's no trouble."

"Still, I don't want to put you out."

"You aren't." He looked at her SUV, then back at her. "Not to worry. We'll get you out of the ditch, one way or another."

"Thank you."

"You may be more shook up than you realize. I'll get you something hot to drink up at the house." He smiled, eyes crinkling at the corners.

"I'm okay."

"I'm a volunteer firefighter. We're also EMTs."

She felt reassured by that news, although he still needed to earn her trust.

"You're right to be cautious. When we get within cell range, you can call the fire station and check me out."

"Thanks, but—"

"No buts. That's what you'll do. It's the only safe thing for a woman alone at night in a strange place."

"I appreciate the help."

"Anytime." He hesitated as he gave her a harder look. "Did you see something unusual at the dump? Did somebody in that truck follow you from there?"

"I think so."

"In that case, I really want to hear your story."

Chapter 2

COLE MURPHY STARED AT THE STRANDED WOMAN...AND FELT hungry. He'd known something big was coming because he hadn't been able to settle this particular hunger for days, weeks, months. Nothing satisfied him. He'd put it down to the horse thieves that were always a step ahead of him.

Now hunger had a name. Audrey Oakes. She was about five-six, thirtyish. And she was definitely a feast for hungry eyes. He felt a connection that drew him to her stronger than any rope, fancy nylon or braided leather.

But he was double-damned. He couldn't trust one hair of her head. She might very well be connected to the rustler outfit that was making his life hell. Three months ago, he'd discovered twenty of the endangered wild mustangs entrusted to his care by the federal government stolen off his ranch. At the time, he'd been irritated and determined to catch the thieves. Sixty mustangs later, he was a lot more than irritated. He was haunted by the thought of what might be happening to them.

He'd done his best to protect the mustangs by moving them from one pasture to another, but the rustlers got to them. On a four thousand acre ranch, cattle and horses could go missing without being noticed for some time, even with alert cowboys. He was closing one horse thief avenue to the mustangs after another, but he still had to be suspicious of anything out of the ordinary. And Audrey Oakes was way beyond ordinary.

True or not, he needed to hear her story, but he'd be skeptical of every little bit of it. Bottom line, why had she come from the direction of the dump this time of night when it was closed to the public? Why had she careened onto his ranch's narrow back road? Why were the rustlers chasing her? Maybe because she'd caught them in the act or maybe because they were setting up a situation where she needed help on his ranch and that gave her an entry into his world that they could exploit since he was limiting their ability to rustle his mustangs? On the other hand, she could be legit, meaning he was letting his concerns and frustrations spill onto an innocent woman. Either way, he needed to know more about her.

He took a closer look at her in the bright lights of his ATV. She had eyes the color of lavender. She sported a wild mane of black hair that hung past her shoulders. Pale skin begged to be stroked, caressed, kissed. She was a rare beauty. And he was all in…even if she might be in the enemy camp.

He took a step toward her, couldn't help himself as his hunger ratcheted up a notch. He wanted her…smell, touch, taste. He caught her scent, sweet and tart. Lavender, maybe. What would her bare skin feel like under his work-roughened hands? Smooth as silk, no doubt. He could almost taste her. Hunger rode him harder. He needed, needed…

"Mr. Murphy, is your gun loaded?" Audrey held up a hand, as if to stop him or put distance between them.

"Oh yeah." He stopped his thoughts in their tracks. What was he doing? He was trying to reassure her that he was there to help.

"I'm not used to weapons."

"On ranches, we're always armed for danger."

She smiled, shrugging one shoulder. "About now, I'd like to be considered dangerous, but as you can see, I'm in a precarious position."

He returned her smile. He liked the fact that she made light of her vulnerability. Strange country. Strange man. Strange situation. And still self-assurance blazed out of her mesmerizing eyes. He liked her sass just about as much as he liked her looks. Yeah, he flat-out liked her. Trouble on two legs, no other way around it… not with a hunger riding him that just wouldn't quit. Suspicion ratcheted up to a razor-sharp edge. Was she naturally self-confident or did she know something he didn't know?

She glanced toward the ranch's entry, as if calculating time and distance in case she needed to quickly getaway.

He throttled down his reaction to her, suspicion and all. "Surprised you saw that turnoff. It's narrow. Plus, I didn't weed-eat the tall grass."

"I was looking for any opening that would let me off the road." She glanced down at her SUV. "If I hadn't had my lights off, I could've managed the turn just fine."

"You were driving without headlights?"

"Not all the way." She gestured back up the road. "Once I got over that hill, I killed my lights so I couldn't be seen."

"They slowed down to a crawl, so they saw you anyway."

"Yeah." She nodded with a slight shiver.

"We don't need to jaw out here. Let's get up to the house and get you something warm to drink."

He took a step back, encouraging her to follow him. He definitely needed to hear her story. If she truly was *in* trouble, he wanted to help. If she *was* trouble, he needed to know. For now, safety came first, just in case she'd been targeted. He didn't figure any place on his ranch except the compound fit that bill any longer.

He glanced up at the motion-censor camera he'd installed on a nearby tree, so he could watch this entrance from his computer or phone. He didn't keep the gate closed here. That left it protected by nothing more than a cattle-guard to keep livestock inside. He wanted the horse thieves to think they could easily breach this entry, so they would use it and he could catch them on camera. So far, they were smarter than him. They hadn't come near it. Until now, maybe.

"Did you lock your vehicle?" he asked.

"Yes."

"Good. Let's get out of here." He smiled, trying to appear as friendly and harmless as possible. He figured he could make it with friendly but harmless was a challenge.

"I'll go with you for now, but once we're in cell range I want to make that call."

"You bet."

"I do appreciate your help."

"Anytime." He glanced toward the open entry to his ranch. Just in case, he didn't want to leave her SUV vulnerable. "Wait a minute."

He walked to the cattle-guard, then leaned his shotgun against the fence. He slid a metal gate out from behind the high grass where he kept it hidden from view across the narrow entry, secured it with a length of rusted chain to a fence post, and clamped the Yale lock shut on the chain. Wire cutters could be used on the lock or the chain, but that'd take time and it'd be on camera. For now, he'd done what he could to make entry harder and provide some protection for her vehicle.

He picked up his shotgun and walked back to her.

"Thanks. I feel better with my SUV behind a locked gate."

"So do I." He gestured toward his ATV. "Want me to carry your bag?"

"Thanks but I've got it."

"Just set it in the back of the ATV." He liked her independence just as much as he liked the rest of her.

"Okay."

She turned and headed uphill.

He checked the perimeter again, then followed her. He was all polite cowboy on the outside, but on the inside he was far from polite as he watched the sway of her hips, the length of her stride, and the determined set of her shoulders. She was hot enough to belong on the glossy pages of a magazine, print or online. He wished he could simply enjoy the show. He couldn't. She didn't belong on a ranch in Wildcat Bluff County. Who the hell was she and why was she really here?

Acknowledgments

My dearest Aunt Jackie, bull rider and rancher, gave me the beautiful silver serving spoon featured in *Cowboy Fire*. She found the spoon in a dump site at an abandoned mining camp in Arizona many years ago. Naturally, I couldn't resist using the spoon, as well as the story, in a book. Lots of appreciation and admiration go to her.

Walter Blevins is a hero to me. Not only was he once a fire-fighting saw boss climbing trees and cutting out blazes with his chainsaw across the United States, but he helps care for the trees at Twin Oaks Ranch. Fortunately, Zander Blevins and Gavin Blevins have taken up their father's calling in tree maintenance. I'm grateful to them for the invaluable knowledge about firefighting, chain-sawing, and tree-climbing.

Over a fun lunch, Deputy Sheriff Julie Garriety set me straight about how Della Calhoun, Wildcat Bluff deputy sheriff, would handle the handcuff scene when Della apprehends the thieves. As always, I'm thankful for her valuable expertise.

After delivering a load of Twin Oaks debris to the local county dump, Logan Williams suggested I think about including a dump site in one of my books. He was exactly right. It wasn't the first time he'd come up with an interesting idea, so here's a shout-out to him.

When I needed information about a cow giving birth to twins, I turned to Christina Gee of Gee Cattle Ranch. We sat at the bar in my kitchen at Twin Oaks to discuss problems, solutions, and possibilities. She had the answers, so I'm happy to give her much-deserved credit.

    Thanks to Rod Williams for his insight into types of rock that led to my choice of sandstone for the speakeasy. He also coined the phrase, "We don't work out. We work outdoors." I delightedly snagged it for *Cowboy Fire*.

    Caridad Piñeiro—bestselling and beloved author—sat down with me at a writer's convention to catch up. I told her about Fernando, Daisy Sue, and their twins. Character names were on my mind, and she was generous enough to help out. She suggested Margarita, since it means daisy in Spanish…and so the unnamed twins became Little Fernando and Margarita in honor of their parents.

About the Author

Kim Redford is the bestselling author of Western romance novels. She grew up in Texas with cowboys, cowgirls, horses, cattle, and rodeos. She divides her time between homes in Texas and Oklahoma, where she's a rescue cat wrangler and horseback rider—when she takes a break from her keyboard. Visit her at kimredford.com.